The Lure of the Cut

The Lure
of the
Cut

Four stories on a canal theme

Rupert Ashby

Paper Cut Books

First published in 2014

British Library Cataloguing in Publication Data

A catalogue record for this book is available from the British Library.

ISBN 978 0 9575135 1 8

Paper Cut Books
(part of Half Cut Theatre)
10 Lichfield Avenue
Werrington
Peterborough PE4 6PF
www.halfcuttheatre.com

Edited, designed and produced by

Priory Ash Publishing
2 Denford Ash Cottages
Denford
Kettering
Northants NN14 4EW
www.prioryash.com

Printed and bound in Great Britain

Contents

Acknowledgements

Writing stories is more than the author sitting at a computer for hours, getting the ideas from head to hard disk. It *is* that, but it also involves much more. From inception to final production many other people are involved, and the book of stories you are holding could never have existed without them.

I must acknowledge:

Will Adams and Mick Sanders at Priory Ash for again taking *The Lure of the Cut* from manuscript to finished book.

The Rank Organisation for quotations from *Brief Encounter* (1945) in 'Too Great a Price to Pay'.

Sacrewell Farm & Country Centre, Thornhaugh, Peterborough, for ideas about the farmyard in 'Three Men and a Goat'.

Richard Rodriguez for factual information about the worlds of IT and finance for 'Short Cut'.

Jennifer Wickham for her encouragement and for reading the first drafts.

Mark and Angela Bradshaw, not forgetting Cirrus the border collie, for illustrating one of the stories for the cover photographs.

Jane, my wife, for her continuing support, advice, alterations – and sometimes improvements – from beginning to end.

To all of these – and to any whom I may have inadvertently missed – my heartfelt and sincere thanks.

For me, this has been a labour of love, but it could never have come to fruition without their invaluable help.

Rupert Ashby
Peterborough
April 2014

Preface

Following on from my first book, *'Izzie' – A Child of the Cut*, I felt that, rather than going straight on to writing its sequel (I'm sure that will happen in time!), I wanted to write something a little different. I had a number of ideas for stories tumbling around in my head but I was not sure if any one of them would develop into a complete novel on its own.

The Lure of the Cut is the result – four different stories set on or around a canal.

Those who have read *'Izzie'* will already know about my love of the canals, which developed from an early age with visits to my grandparents' home at Blisworth. How I wish I could find a boatman or woman among my ancestors!

In each story the attraction of the canal – 'The Lure of the Cut' – has a role to play, sometimes in unexpected ways. Within these pages you will find murder and suspense, the supernatural, gentle humour and romance. The book may introduce you to different, perhaps unfamiliar genres and may encourage you to explore them further in the future.

When you have finished reading, you may have a favourite story. Whichever it is, I hope that you will warm to the characters whose stories are played out here and to the canals with which their lives are so closely intertwined.

Too Great a Price to Pay

A story of love

❈

Meeting

Martin took his cap from its hook in the back cabin and put it on. Stepping out onto the back deck, he closed the back doors of his boat and shut the sliding hatch. He locked the padlock and stepped onto the wooden jetty. It was a warm, sunny June day as he took his morning walk the half-mile from his mooring in the marina to The Butty, a wide boat, nearly twice the beam of his seven-feet-wide narrowboat. She was moored on the canal and had been converted into a floating café. He went there most days for his breakfast.

'It beats cooking for yourself!' he reasoned. 'And it's good to have some company while you're drinking your morning coffee.' He whistled softly to himself as he walked along the towpath and climbed down into The Butty's seating area.

'Dzień Dobry, Jadwiga!' he called to the young Polish girl behind the counter.

'Dzień Dobry, Martin,' she replied. 'Your usual?' Her voice had only the slightest trace of an accent.

'Yes, please.'

'Bacon roll on white bread for Martin, please!' Jadwiga called to Stella, her employer – and owner of The Butty – in the kitchen, as she poured Martin a mug of black coffee.

'Lovely day!' he said, as he paid for his breakfast.

'Beautiful!' she agreed. 'What are you going to do today?' she asked him.

'I don't know,' he answered thoughtfully. 'I could do with a bit of shopping. I might pop into town a bit later and go to that new supermarket that's just opened.'

'I went there yesterday after I had finished work. They have lots of offers on.'

'That's what I like to hear,' Martin replied. 'I don't want to spend any more of my pension than I have to.'

'How I envy you retired people!' she said.

'Your time will come,' Martin smiled. 'You have to remember it's not that long ago that I was like you are today – having to work for a living!'

'And a good worker she is too,' said Stella, as she entered and passed Martin his bacon roll.

'It's one reason I like coming here in the mornings,' said Martin.

'What's that?' Jadwiga asked.

'Your smiling face and your cheerful conversation!'

'That's what all my regulars say,' said Stella. Jadwiga looked embarrassed by the compliment, but inside she felt proud. Secretly, Martin was her favourite customer.

'Oh, but that's two reasons!' she laughed.

Martin took his breakfast, sat down and bit into his roll. As usual, there were no other customers. The early worker-breakfasters had long gone and the lunchtime rush of walkers and gongoozlers – those members of the general public who visit the canals, apparently, for the sole purpose of laughing at any unfortunate mishap befalling those on the water – was a few hours away. Martin always tried to time his daily visit for about this time, as he enjoyed having the place to himself. Although he enjoyed meeting Jadwiga and Stella, he was not one for idle chatter. This morning the sun was streaming in through the windows and it felt good to be alive.

As he was draining his coffee mug, he noticed a lady walking along the towpath. He had seen her many times before, both on the towpath and in the village.

'She looks a few years younger than me,' he had thought. She was attractive, tall and slim, with the highlights in her elegantly styled hair catching the sunlight. She always wore what his ex-wife would have described as 'good clothes'. He thought that she must have connections with the church in the village as he had often seen her coming and going from there, not just on Sundays, but on other days of the week as well. During the two years or so that Martin had lived on his boat in the marina they had built up a nodding acquaintance, passing the time of day with each other when they met. She appeared to be very well-spoken, he had noticed, but seemed reserved – never wanting to stop and talk.

A couple of weeks previously he had seen her walking towards him along the towpath with a border collie running at her heels. It was the first time he had ever seen her with a dog. As she approached him, the dog had run up to Martin, who had stroked it and patted its head.

'Isn't it strange,' he had said, striking up his first conversation of any length with her, 'how they know whether you're a dog-lover or not?'

'He obviously thinks you are,' she had replied with a smile. Martin had immediately noticed her deep blue eyes. They seemed to sparkle as she smiled.

'He's right too,' Martin had said. 'I used to have a dog, a golden lab. It's a good place for dog walking along here, isn't it?'

'It is, and Rex seems to like it.'

'Have you only recently acquired him?' Martin had asked.

'Yes. An old family friend has had to go into a nursing home and he asked if I would look after Rex for him. Poor Rex doesn't know whether he's coming or going. He's a rescue dog and my friend had only had him for about three weeks when he had a stroke. Now it doesn't look as if he'll ever get back home again.'

'That's a pity,' Martin had said. 'Dogs do like a bit of familiarity and security.' She had bent down and ruffled Rex's ears, then she and the dog had walked on.

He had seen her most mornings since then as she walked her dog along by the canal. He had enjoyed their conversation. Although it had been brief and to the point, he had detected a warmth in the tone of her voice and thought that he would try to engage her in conversation again in order to get to know her better. It seemed, however, that whatever time he left to go to The Butty, and however slowly he walked there, he was always in the middle of his breakfast when she walked past without looking down into the boat. He found this frustrating – but he was a patient man.

On this particular morning fate decided to take a hand. As she was passing The Butty with Rex walking alongside her, the dog suddenly spotted a rabbit through a hole in the hedge and took off after it. His route, unfortunately, took him straight across in front of his mistress. She lost her balance and fell flat on her face onto the towpath. Martin was up the steps in an instant.

'Are you all right?' he asked.

'I … I think so,' she said, as he helped her back to her feet. 'I don't think I've broken anything – just banged my knee and my hand.' She looked at her right hand and wiped the dirt away with her left. Then she cautiously lifted her left trouser leg. There was a graze on her knee that was starting to bleed.

'Look, come on down here and let me get you a mug of tea or something. Stella's got a first-aid kit so we can get that knee sorted out.' At that moment, the dog reappeared through the hole in the hedge.

'Look what you've made your mum do, Rexy!' she said to him, sternly. The dog sat down in front of her, whined and licked her hand.

'But I can't really be angry with him,' she said, her smile softening her voice as she stroked his head. 'Once he catches sight of a rabbit, he can't help it. He just has to give chase.' She turned to the dog. 'You wait here while your mum goes and gets her knee looked at. Rexy sit!' Rex sat. 'Rexy lie down!' Rex lay down by the door to The Butty.

'Wow! What a well-behaved dog!' Martin exclaimed.

'Most of the time,' she replied. She winced a little as Martin helped her down the steps into The Butty. She sat on the chair nearest to the steps and Martin moved another one across so that she could put her leg up on it.

'Would you like tea or coffee?' Jadwiga called.

'I think I'd like tea, please,' she said. 'Milk and no sugar.' Martin put his hand in his pocket.

'On the house,' said Stella advancing towards them, first-aid kit in hand. 'Now, let's have a look at this knee of yours.' She examined the graze.

Jadwiga brought over a mug of tea.

'I'm so sorry to cause you all so much fuss!' said the lady.

They both laughed as Stella took out a pair of disposable gloves from the first-aid box. 'Have to put these on,' she said. '"Elf and Safety."' She cleaned the wound with an antiseptic wipe.

'I don't think you've got any grit in it, but it's a nasty graze,' she said, taking a large plaster from the box. 'Are you OK with plasters?'

Martin laughed. '"Elf and Safety" again, I suppose.'

'There! That should be OK now – at least, until you get home.' Stella replaced the lid on the first-aid box. 'It looks like you've ruined a perfectly good pair of trousers, though.'

'Don't worry about that,' the lady said. She rubbed her hand and gently patted her knee. 'Thank you … thank you very, very much, all of you! You're very kind.'

'Are you sure you're OK?' Martin asked.

'Yes. I'm all right – just a bit shaken up. That's all.'

'Of course, you are. That was a nasty tumble you took. I'm Martin, by the way – and this is Stella, proprietress of The Butty, and that's Jadwiga.' He pointed to where Jadwiga was standing behind the counter. 'She's from Poland and she cheers me up every morning.'

'I'm Mary – and I'm very grateful to you all.' She suddenly looked at her watch and a worried look spread across her face.

'Goodness! I'll have to be going. The plumber's supposed to be calling in half an hour to fix a leak in my dishwasher.' She finished her tea and stood up.

'Would you like me to walk along with you?' Martin asked.

'No,' said Mary. 'I'll be all right. I wouldn't want to put you to all that trouble.'

'It's no trouble at all,' Martin replied. 'I've nothing pressing – and I'd rather do that and see you get home safely than think about you getting delayed shock or something on your way.'

'Well ... if you're sure you don't mind.'

'I don't mind at all.'

'Well, thank you. I would appreciate it.' She thanked Stella and Jadwiga again. Jadwiga collected their mugs and Martin helped Mary up the steps. Rex was still lying down patiently waiting, but he jumped up when his mistress reappeared.

'Come on, boy!' she said. She limped along the towpath with Martin. Rex, in what he saw as atonement for his earlier misdemeanour, walked quietly to heel.

'Do you live far?' he asked.

'No,' said Mary. 'The Crescent.' Martin knew The Crescent – large, individually designed, expensive houses. 'There's a little path that leads into it not far beyond the next bridge but one,' she continued. 'What about you?'

'Oh me? I live on my boat in the marina.'

'That sounds like an interesting way to live.'

'It suits me.'

'Is it a longboat?'

'It's a narrowboat. Longboats were what the Vikings used to use.'

'Sorry!' She stopped walking. 'Wrong word!'

'Don't worry!' Martin laughed. 'It's a common mistake.'

'What's the name of your boat?'

'She's called *Guinevere*.' They began walking again.

'Why *Guinevere*?'

'That's what she was called when I bought her. The chap who sold her to me was fanatical about King Arthur and the Knights of the Round Table. His house was called "Pendragon" and the boat was *Guinevere*. I shouldn't be surprised if he'd christened his kids Arthur and Lancelot!' Mary laughed.

'Haven't I read somewhere that it's supposed to be bad luck to change the name of a boat?'

'Only when it's in the water. *Guinevere*'s been out of the water to have her hull re-blacked but I quite the like the name so I've never bothered to change it.'

'I'm sure I must have seen you going along the canal from my upstairs window.'

'That's very possible. I take her out every now and again to keep the batteries topped up.'

'Is it a red and green one?' she asked.

'Yes.'

'Then I've definitely seen you.'

'I usually do a longish trip every year,' Martin said. 'I start about the beginning of September – just about when the kids are going back to school. The cut's a bit quieter then.'

'I should imagine it is.'

'And I get back here by the beginning of November.'

'Just in time for Bonfire Night!' Mary chuckled.

'Yes, we usually have a bonfire and a few fireworks at the marina. I like to be back in time for that.'

'Bonfire Night seems to be losing out to Halloween these days, I think,' Mary observed. 'And this awful American "trick or treat" thing! To me, it seems like nothing short of begging.'

'I agree,' said Martin. 'When we were kids we used to go around asking for a penny for the guy – but we had to put the work in to make the guy in the first place.'

They had arrived at the point where the path to The Crescent led off the towpath and their conversation drew to a close.

'I'll be all right from here,' Mary said. 'My house is just up there. Thank you so much for walking with me. I really do appreciate it.'

'It was no problem,' Martin replied.

'Thank the ladies at The Butty for me, too, will you?'

'Why don't you drop in for a cuppa when you take Rex for his walk tomorrow?' Martin suggested. 'You can thank them yourself then.' Mary thought about this for a moment.

'Yes,' she said, at length. 'I might just do that. I've often walked past it, but never thought of going in.' She seemed to be in no hurry to get home until Martin looked at his watch.

'Isn't your plumber due about now?' he asked.

'Goodness! Yes! Thank you. I may see you at The Butty tomorrow. Bye.'

The following morning, Martin was just finishing his bacon roll when he heard Mary instructing Rex to lie down and wait for her. He looked up as she came, a little cautiously, down the steps.

'Morning, Mary!' he welcomed her with a smile.

'Good morning, Martin.' She turned to Jadwiga. 'Good morning.'

'Good morning,' Jadwiga returned the greeting. 'What would you like?'

'I'd like a mug of your excellent tea, please. The one I had yesterday really set me right again after my little accident.'

Stella came through from the kitchen. 'How's your knee?'

'Oh, it's fine now, thanks. Just a bit stiff and bruised. The bleeding's stopped. I put a fresh plaster on it this morning – just in case I knock it. Thank you very much for your first aid yesterday.'

'It was nothing,' Stella said. 'All part of the service here at The Butty!' She laughed, and went back into the kitchen. Mary picked up her tea and started to make her way over to where Martin was sitting. Halfway there she stopped.

'Martin, I wonder if you wouldn't mind if we sat at that table by the door. It'll be easier for me to keep an eye on Rex.'

'No problem at all,' Martin said, picking up his coffee cup and joining her.

'I really don't honestly know why I've never frequented this place before.' She looked around. 'It's really rather nice, isn't it?'

'Well, I think so. Stella doesn't do anything fancy, but what she does is excellent – sandwiches and rolls, toasties and … what are those Italian things called that you heat up, Jadwiga?'

'Paninis.'

'That's it, paninis.'

'I think I might start coming here for breakfast some days too,' said Mary.

✳

Friendship

Over the following days they often breakfasted together at The Butty, then Martin accompanied her to the path that led to The Crescent. Gradually, they found out a little more about each other, Mary growing in confidence with each conversation. He learned that she had been married to Charles for more than thirty years. He commuted to London each day, where he worked for a firm of stockbrokers. They had one son, Gerald, who was married with two children, but had emigrated with his family to Sydney in Australia about five years previously. In return, Martin explained that he had retired from the company where he had worked in the accounts department just over three years earlier. He and his wife had been through a rather messy divorce quite soon afterwards.

'We're a couple of those "Silver Splitters" that they keep writing about in the newspapers,' he said. 'In the end, she kept the house – and I finished up with the boat. I moved it to this marina a couple of years ago.'

'Well, you seem very happy with the arrangement,' she replied.

'I am! I'm as happy as a sand boy. I always fancied living on the boat – at least for part of the year, but Doreen wouldn't hear of it. But now I get to do it all the year round, every year – every day – and I love it!'

'Do you have job at all?' Martin asked at one of their breakfasts a week or so later.

'No. I'm pleased to say I don't need to work. Charles earns enough to keep us both quite comfortably.'

'So what do you do with your time then?' he asked.

'Well,' she said, 'I volunteer for the National Trust at the Old Manor House, usually for a day a month – more if they're short. I enjoy that – meeting the visitors and explaining about the history of the place. Have you ever been?'

'It's one of those things I've always intended to do but never got round to,' Martin apologised.

'You should. It really is a most interesting house with a fascinating history.'

'It's funny, isn't it?' Martin said. 'Although I've visited lots of places further afield, you never seem to get round to going to the ones on your doorstep, do you?'

'I suppose that's true,' Mary said. 'What else do I do? I'm on the parochial church council at St Michael's. I go to the Women's Institute on the first Wednesday of every month. And when I'm at home I enjoy reading and I also do a lot of sewing and embroidery. That's how I've seen you sailing along in your boat. The window of my sewing room looks out over the field and onto the canal.'

'You'll have to come and see inside *Guinevere* one of these days,' Martin offered.

'Yes,' Mary replied. There was a lengthy pause. 'I'd like that. What about you? How do you fill your time in retirement?'

'Like you, I enjoy reading – thrillers, mostly. I meet a couple of mates at 'The George' on a Friday night for a few beers and a natter – putting the world to rights! I like to watch a bit of sport on the TV. Cricket's my favourite. Come the summer, I like to go up to Edgbaston to see a few days' play – especially if there's a test match.'

'Charles used to play a lot of cricket in his younger days. I used to go along and help the other wives with the teas, but I must confess I never really got into the game. I found it ... well ... boring!'

'A lot of people do!' Martin laughed. 'But for those of us who love it, there's no finer way to spend a summer's day than to sit, watching a game – with a pint in your hand!'

'Gerald plays for a team of ex-pat Brits in Sydney.'

'Like father, like son.'

'In that way, yes!'

'What else is there?' Martin thought for a moment. 'Well, there's always a bit of maintenance needing doing on the boat. I sometimes help out at the marina – serving diesel, helping out in the shop – that sort of thing. I do the books for the marina and prepare the annual accounts. That's all in exchange for not paying any mooring fees. A few months ago I had the idea I ought to do something else – an Open University degree, or something. I sent off for all the literature, but I never got round to signing up for anything. Those courses are quite expensive.'

'So I've heard.'

'Don't get me wrong,' Martin continued. 'I'm not pleading poverty or anything. I mean, I'm not exactly affluent, but my pension's enough for me to live on.'

Their breakfast meetings became a regular occurrence. Martin began to realise that, against his better judgment, he was becoming rather fond of Mary. He enjoyed her company very much. She was everything Doreen had not been. Mary was intelligent, well-educated and well-read. She was interested in what was happening around her, both in her immediate vicinity, and also in the world beyond. OK, so she was not fond of cricket, but that was more than made up for by the other common interests they found they shared. They were both keen on history, albeit different periods. Mary loved the grand houses of the Elizabethan era, while for Martin it had to be the Victorians and the Industrial Revolution. Another common interest, strangely, was old black-and-white British films.

They discovered this when, after a few weeks, Mary first set foot on *Guinevere*. Aware that he was not the tidiest of men Martin had set about putting things away and dusting in anticipation of her visit. This had taken him rather longer than he had anticipated and he vowed, when it was complete, that he would never allow his floating home to get into such a state again – ever – until the next time! Now she looked a picture, her woodwork all polished and her brasses gleaming. Everything was put away in its place and all was clean and tidy.

As he led Mary along the jetty he felt more than a little nervous. This was the first time he had welcomed a woman into his home since his divorce. He sensed that she was nervous too. Her normally smiling face looked tense and taut. Warning her to mind her head as she stepped down into the cabin, he stood back.

'Welcome aboard *Guinevere*!' he said proudly as he removed his cap and dropped it on a chair. 'My little house on the water.'

Mary looked around and smiled.

'It's lovely!' she said. Inwardly, Martin breathed a sigh of relief!

'Take a seat,' Martin invited her. She sat down on the steps.

'You don't have to sit there!' he said. 'I think you'll find one of the chairs a bit more comfortable. She moved towards the first chair she came to, the one nearest the door where Martin had dropped his cap. He quickly picked it up and stuffed it in his pocket. Mary sat down.

'Is it OK if Rex comes in?' she asked.

'Yes, of course!' Martin replied. 'It's not wet outside so he won't have muddy paws.' Mary called to Rex, who had made himself comfortable on the back deck. He bounded down the steps and into the cabin. Then he explored the entire boat, sniffing in every nook and cranny. Satisfied, he settled down on the floor – and promptly went to sleep.

'Well, he's made himself at home!' Martin exclaimed.

'That's just the sort of dog he is,' said Mary. Martin offered her a drink.

'Tea? Coffee? Or something stronger?'

'A G and T would be lovely,' she said.

While he was getting them both a gin and tonic she noticed his DVD collection.

'Your taste in films is very similar to mine,' she observed.

'Really?' he said.

'Yes, *Random Harvest*, *Kind Hearts and Coronets*, *Dangerous Moonlight*, *Rebecca* – I've got all of these.'

'Ah!' Martin said handing her her drink. 'I do like the old black-and-white films. They remind me of Sunday afternoons at home when I was a kid. The BBC – or was it ITV? – one of them usually showed an old British film as I recall.' He paused. 'Of course, they might well have been in colour, but we only had a black-and-white television!' They both laughed.

'They certainly don't make films like those any more,' she said.

'That's a fact,' Martin agreed.

An hour flew past until Martin felt that Mary was becoming agitated. She looked at her watch and said she really must be going. As she stood up Rex awoke and together they clambered off the boat. Martin followed, sensing that she breathed some sort of sigh of relief as she stepped onto the jetty.

'Thank you so much for inviting me to your lovely boat, Martin,' she said, smiling. 'It really is beautiful!'

'Perhaps you might like to come for a little ride on her one day?' he ventured.

'Oh, yes!' she said, then paused. 'I shall look forward to that.'

'Goodbye,' said Martin, rather lamely.

'Goodbye,' Mary replied and, with Rex at her heels, she made her way out of the marina. As he went back inside the boat, Martin thought back over her visit.

'She seemed quite relaxed to sit and chat,' he mused, 'until just before she left. Then she seemed to get all tense and nervous. But the nerves disappeared the moment she stepped off the boat! Very odd!'

※

The following week they arranged an afternoon's cruise. Mary arrived on board with Rex. Martin started the engine and untied the mooring ropes. He gently eased *Guinevere* away from her jetty and out through the marina entrance. He turned to the left so that their journey would take them along the stretch of canal visible from Mary's sewing room window. She stood beside him on the rear deck, smiling.

'All the years I've lived here, with the canal practically at the end of my garden, and this is the first time I've ever been on it on a boat!' she said. 'What an absolutely enjoyable experience!'

'I'm glad you're enjoying it!' Martin replied.

'I've often watched boats going up and down here while I've been doing my sewing and wondered what it would be like. But with everything else I do – well – I suppose I've never got round to finding out any more about it.'

'But you're enjoying it now?'

'Oh, yes!'

Rex had gone down into the cabin and made himself at home. They found him later – fast asleep in an armchair.

As they cruised past The Crescent, Martin asked Mary which house was hers.

'It's that one,' she said, pointing. 'The one with the two silver birches in the garden.'

'I see it,' he answered. It was one of the larger houses in The Crescent.

'What time do you need to be back?' he asked, a little later.

'Charles's usual train gets in at seven,' she said. 'So I need to be home about six-thirty to get dinner organised.'

'OK.' Martin consulted his watch. There's a winding hole just round this next bend. I'll wind her there and we should be back at the marina just after six.' He had pronounced 'wind' as it 'win', not 'wine'.

'That'll be fine,' she replied. 'Um ... what's a winding hole?'

'It's a place where the canal's been made especially wide, so that boats can be turned round.'

'So why is it called a "winding hole"?'

'Well, in the old days, when the working boats needed to turn – all seventy feet of them – they used the prevailing wind to help get them round, hence winding hole.'

'Very clever!' she replied. 'I've got a lot to discover.'

The breeze was behind them on the way back, and they were in the marina well before six o'clock. Unlike on her previous visit, Mary seemed to be in no hurry to leave. She appeared to be quite happy, sitting and chatting with Martin on the seats on *Guinevere's* rear deck, sipping a gin and tonic. It was nearly a quarter to seven when she finally took her leave.

'I'll have to do something quick out of the freezer tonight,' she said as she and Rex left.

She walked along the path and through the gate. As she did so, she stopped and waved to Martin, a broad smile spread across her face. Martin stood and raised his empty glass to her in a farewell salute. He went down into the cabin and started to prepare his own meal.

How he had enjoyed the afternoon! 'She seemed genuinely interested in learning all about *Guinevere*,' he thought. Mary had even attempted steering, but had been grateful to return the tiller to Martin when a boat appeared coming towards them. Martin was knowledgeable about the history of the canal and Mary had been keen to hear about it, asking him intelligent questions about the building of it, what it was used for and the boats that had worked on it. 'So different from Doreen!'

Although he presumed she was happily married (and he certainly did not want to become part of a love triangle), Martin could not deny that the more he saw of Mary the fonder of her he was becoming. He could hardly wait to be in her company again.

While they were walking along the towpath towards The Crescent later that week, Mary suddenly turned to him.

'Martin,' she said, 'as you so kindly let me have a ride on your lovely boat the other day, I want to do something to return the compliment.'

'Oh, yes?' Martin was curious.

'Yes. You remember I told you I was a volunteer at the Old Manor House?'

'Yes, you did.'

'Well, I'm on duty there next Tuesday and I thought that if you would like to join me during the afternoon, I could give you a guided tour and then we could have tea in the coffee shop – my treat!'

'That sounds great!' Martin said.

'Are you a member of the Trust?' she asked.

'I was once but I haven't renewed my membership for years. It was one of the expenses I decided to save on after the divorce,' he replied. 'What time should I get there?'

'If you arrive about three then it'll be teatime by the time I've shown you round. There's a wall map of the estate hanging in the study I'd like to show you. I think you might find it interesting.'

Martin duly arrived in the car park at five minutes to three and followed the signs to Visitor Reception, which was located in the entrance hall. Mary was standing by the open door and her face lit up with a broad smile as she saw him approaching. She insisted on paying his entrance fee and, leaving Sue, her fellow volunteer, in sole charge of the reception desk she commenced the tour. As they walked, she told him how Henry Portlingbury, who had owned the land that most of the village was built on, had ingratiated himself with Elizabeth I and been granted a hereditary knighthood. He had then decided to build a grand house for himself to show off his newly exalted status.

They went from room to room and, in each of them, Mary was a mine of information, telling him which parts of the building had been added when and by whom. She told him about the fire that had destroyed the west wing and how it had been rebuilt.

When they went into the study she pointed out a large framed nineteenth-century map of the village that was hanging on the wall. Martin was most interested.

'Two canals?' he peered at map. 'It shows two canals. I've never read anything about that! Was there going to be a branch off to somewhere else that was never started?' Mary explained that when the canal was first proposed, the line recommended by the surveyor passed to the east of the village, quite close to the grounds of the Manor. Sir John Portlingbury had therefore objected to the line and, after a lengthy legal battle, had succeeded in getting the course of the canal moved to the west side of the village, well away from his house and land. The map clearly showed the two lines.

'There!' she said, laughing and tapping his arm, 'I've done a bit more research since that most enjoyable afternoon on *Guinevere*. I know a bit more about the canals than you think!' Martin laughed with her.

'Oh, Mary,' he thought. 'I do like you!'

Later, as they relaxed in the garden partaking of scones with a generous helping of jam and thick cream, Martin told her how much he had enjoyed his visit.

'Oh, good!' she said. 'I thought you would do – at least, I hoped so.'

'Well, I have. You made it all very interesting. You've obviously taken a great interest in the history of the Portlingbury family, their lives – and about the village.'

'I find it all quite fascinating,' she said. 'The more you find out, the more you want to know.'

'I'm a bit like that with the canals,' agreed Martin. 'There's always something new to find out – like that map today.' He paused and looked up at the house.

'I wonder what would have happened if the last one – Sir Nigel Portlingbury, was it? I wonder what would have happened if he had got married and had a son,' he said.

'We, most likely, would not be sitting here in his garden having tea and scones!' Mary chuckled. 'It was only because he died with no legitimate heir that the family line came to an end and the hereditary title with it. It was his nephews and nieces, none of whom wanted to live in a barn of a place like this, who offered it to the Trust.'

Back in Visitor Reception, as Martin was leaving, Mary said, 'I hope you don't mind me asking, but I wonder if you'd think about renewing your Trust membership?'

'Actually, I really ought to,' he replied. 'I often pass their places when I'm out cruising. It would save me some money, wouldn't it?'

'It certainly would!' said Mary, reaching for the membership forms, 'and if you join here, it's a little feather in the cap for this property, too.'

'I'll see you tomorrow?' Martin asked as he picked up his new membership pack.

'I should think so,' Mary smiled. 'I must help Sue tidy up before we close. She's done all the hard work today.' She turned and began straightening a pile of guide books. Martin put out his hand towards her, then dropped it to his side.

'Bye!' was all he could think of to say as he turned to leave.

While he drove back to *Guinevere* Martin was deep in thought. He recalled how her face had lit up with that beaming smile as he had walked towards the door. He reflected on the wonderful tour of the house she had given him and wondered whether she showed that level of enthusiasm and charm to everyone whom she took round – or was that just because it was him? She had obviously been delighted to entertain him to tea, introducing him to her colleagues as 'Martin, a very good friend of mine'.

He had accepted the fact that he was slowly, but surely, falling in love with this quiet, gentle lady with the sparkling eyes. The acrimony and bitterness of the latter years with Doreen had become a distant memory. But he had also reconciled himself to the fact that Mary was married. Any feelings he had for her, therefore, were doomed to be unrequited. That was until recently. Over the past week he thought he had sensed an openness about her that had not been there before. There seemed to be a new tenderness in the way she spoke to him – or was he only imagining it? His mind kept returning to the inescapable fact that she was a married woman! And married to a man who kept her in a style that Martin, even with his state pension and his works pension combined, could only dream about.

Fate

They continued to meet at The Butty throughout the summer and enjoyed many more afternoon cruises aboard *Guinevere*. Martin began walking up to the path every morning to meet Mary as she started her walk with Rex, although he never went as far as her house. They would walk the dog together, then go for breakfast, always sitting at the table nearest the door so that Mary could keep an eye on Rex. Martin thought she was being a little overcautious about this as Rex always lay dutifully outside on the towpath until she reappeared.

Their conversations ranged over every topic under the sun. How Martin enjoyed a good, level-headed discussion! Religion, politics, their shared interest in films, history, music – they chatted about all of them during those summer months. In all their conversations, however, two people were never mentioned. Mary never spoke about Charles and Martin never discussed Doreen. Martin relaxed. He was happier than he had been for years.

One Friday evening towards the end of August Martin was enjoying his usual couple of pints with his two friends at 'The George' when his mobile rang. Seeing it was Mary's number, he excused himself and walked outside to a secluded part of the beer garden.

'Hi Mary, to what do I owe the pleasure?' he asked cheerfully.

'Oh Martin! Charles was taken ill at work this afternoon,' she said. Her voice lacked any emotion. Martin immediately regretted his jocularity.

'Crikey!' he said. 'Where is he now? Are you all right?'

'He's in hospital in London. I'm just leaving to go there to be with him. I wonder? Could I ask you an enormous favour?'

'Of course, you can.'

'Are you at the pub?'

'Yes.'

'If I call in there on my way out and let you have a house key, will you look after Rex while I'm away – just feed him and take him for walks, basically.'

'Of course, I will.'

'Thank you so much, Martin. I really appreciate it. I'll see you in a few minutes.'

'It's no problem. I'll see you outside in the car park.'

A few minutes later they were standing beside Mary's car, its engine running. Mary explained how to operate the intruder alarm at the house and she ran through what food Rex needed and where he slept at night.

'We'll be fine!' said Martin. 'Don't you worry about Rex. He can stay with me. Drive carefully.'

He was putting her keys into his pocket when she suddenly grabbed him by the shoulders. He looked at her and she smiled.

'Thank you, Martin,' she said – and then she kissed him. It was no quick peck on the cheek, but a lingering kiss full on his lips. Martin stepped back. He hadn't seen that coming! He had hardly recovered from the surprise before she was in the car and turning out of the car park and onto the road.

Without a backward glance she sped away. Martin stood and stared at the car park exit. Had that happened? Had that really happened? He felt a warm tingle pass through his body. He brushed his fingers gently across his lips, sighed and returned to his waiting pint.

Over the next three days Martin walked Rex, whom he had collected as promised. He received regular calls and texts about Charles's health. He had, it transpired, had a heart attack at his desk and the prognosis was not good. On the fourth morning she called to tell him that Charles had died the previous night.

'Poor you!' Martin said. 'I'm so sorry. Are you OK?'

'Is Rex all right?'

'He's fine!'

'I'll be home later today,' she said. 'I've got a funeral to arrange.' She rang off.

'What a strange reaction!' Martin thought. 'She must be in some kind of shock. That's why she seems so matter-of-fact.'

Early the following morning he took Rex home. He rang Mary's doorbell. She answered the door and stood back for him to enter. As soon as she had closed the door he pulled her to him and hugged her tightly. 'I'm so sorry,' he said.

'Don't be!' she replied, coldly. Martin was so astonished at her words that he let her go.

'Any love there ever was in our marriage disappeared a long, long time ago,' she continued, her voice flat and cold. 'I think we only stayed together out of ... well ... convenience, I suppose you'd call it.' She bent down and as she ruffled Rex's fur the dog nudged her leg with his nose as if to say 'I understand too.'

'Oh, I see.' Martin now understood her lack of emotion on the phone when she had told him of Charles's death. She led the way through to the kitchen and made coffee for them both. Martin took off his cap and followed her.

She sat at the kitchen table, her hands clasping her mug, facing the open door. Rex flopped down at her feet. Martin studied her face. She wore no make-up. Her eyes lacked their usual sparkle and there was no trace of a smile dancing at the corners of her mouth. Her face was composed and calm, almost mask-like. It betrayed no emotion. She indicated the chair opposite her to Martin, who sat down. She appeared to take a few seconds to gather her thoughts – almost as if she were trying to remember a rehearsed speech.

'Charles was some years older than me,' she began. 'He could have retired years ago, but he wouldn't. He said he didn't want to spend all day every day here with me, you see.'

'But that's terrible!'

'Well, you're a divorced man. You know what happens when a marriage goes wrong.'

'Yes,' Martin agreed, 'but in my case there was a third party involved.'

'It wouldn't surprise me if that was the case with Charles too,' Mary said. 'Quite often, he used to call me in an afternoon to say he was having to work late and he would get a room in a hotel for the night. Well, he may have been working late. I don't know. I don't have a suspicious nature, and frankly, I don't care. But it makes one wonder.'

As they were finishing their coffee, Martin asked, 'So, what are your plans for today?'

'I called Gerald in Australia last night. So today I've got to arrange for the undertaker to collect his body from the hospital mortuary and then see John White, the vicar, about the funeral – in that order. I registered his death in London yesterday. Gerald can't get over until next week so there's plenty of time to arrange things.'

'Would you like me to come with you – for a bit of moral support?' Martin offered.

'It's sweet of you to offer, but no. I think I'd rather do it myself.'

'If you're sure?'

'I am. But thanks, anyway.'

'I know it's what everybody says at times like this,' Martin said, 'but if there is anything – anything at all I can do to help, you know you only have to ask. I mean it.'

'I know you do,' Mary said, touching his hand. 'I'll let you know, I promise.'

'As you're going to be busy would you like me to keep Rex with me for another few days?'

'That would be an enormous help!' Mary replied.

He got up to leave. Rex stood up and stretched.

'Oh Rex!' Mary laughed. 'It hasn't taken you long to change your allegiance. I'm glad that you're happy with Martin. You know you're special, don't you?' She patted the dog.

Martin suddenly remembered that moment in the 'George' car park. It was right then. It must be right now. He drew her gently to him and kissed her. She put her arms round his back and rested her head briefly on his shoulder before pulling away.

'I'll text you later,' she murmured as Martin replaced his cap and left, Rex trotting happily beside him.

As she closed the door behind them and leaned against it, tears spilled down her face.

Although he had never met Charles, Martin decided he would go to his funeral. He felt he owed it to Mary to be there, to show her some support. He wanted to be there. He had missed her so much over the previous few days while she had been busy making the funeral arrangements. Then Gerald had arrived. Mary texted Martin frequently but that was not the same as seeing her, and he found himself having long, one-sided conversations with Rex as they went on their morning walks – and he was sure that the dog understood every word!

Early autumn sunshine dappled the water as Martin made his way to the church for the funeral. He assumed the other people making their way up the path were Mary's friends from church and from the Women's Institute. He recognised Sue, her fellow volunteer from the Manor.

As Mary followed Charles's coffin into St Michael's Church, hand in hand with her son, Martin thought she looked … well … magnificent! She wore a very simple black dress with a cerise pashmina tossed casually, but elegantly, around her shoulders and fastened with a large silver brooch. He could not take his eyes off her! She stood tall and dignified – a picture of composure, her eyes fixed straight in front of her.

The Rev John White welcomed the congregation and everyone rose to sing the first hymn. Gerald moved to the lectern. He bore little resemblance to his mother – a tall, angular man in his mid-thirties, with a shock of dark hair falling across his forehead. He brushed it aside nervously as he began to read the eulogy to his father. He said kind things, praising Charles for the fun times they had shared when he was a child and thanking him for his generous nature.

'I wonder if Gerald knows the depths of his mother's unhappiness?' Martin thought.

John announced that everyone was invited back to The Crescent for refreshments after the service. Martin decided that he would not be joining them. Mary stood and followed the coffin out of the church. She looked neither to right nor left. The little procession made its way to the corner of the churchyard where a fresh grave had been dug. Martin hung back, watching from the church porch as Mary threw a handful of earth into the grave. She remained composed, her eyes fixed on some distant point on the horizon.

Martin turned and, slipping through a side-gate, walked back down the lane. Now they were both free!

Together

They resumed their walks but not their breakfasts together the morning after the funeral. As they walked back along the towpath, Mary asked him why he had not gone back to the house after Charles's funeral.

'I missed you,' she said.

'Well,' he said, 'apart from you, I didn't know anybody and I suppose I didn't want to intrude on your family's grief. Although, from what you've told me, you're not feeling a lot of grief, are you?'

'No, and neither's Gerald,' Mary continued.

'Isn't he?' queried Martin. 'He said some pretty nice things in his eulogy.'

'A good actor!' replied Mary. 'He never got on with his father. Charles wanted him to join his firm and become a stockbroker, like him. But Gerald was far too artistic. He wanted to do something creative – and I encouraged him! He got a job in television, assisting a set designer. He and Charles never spoke for months. It all culminated in an almighty row, the result of which was Gerald taking his wife and children off to Australia.'

'That must have been hard for you!' Martin sympathised as they reached the path to The Crescent and stopped.

'I was heartbroken! I was losing my only child. I was going to miss out on seeing my grandchildren growing up. I suppose it must have been about then, too, that things began to really deteriorate between Charles and me. He refused to visit them and, by what he said and did, he made it impossible for me to go and see them either. Our marriage of convenience turned into a marriage of endurance! Thank goodness for the wonders of Skype!'

'Skype?' Martin queried.

'Have you not heard of it?'

'I've heard of it, but I've never had any reason to use it, so I'm not sure how it works.'

'It's marvellous! It lets us see and talk to each other almost as if we're in the same room – and it's absolutely free!'

'That must be a godsend!'

'It is. You must meet Gerald before he goes back. Would you like to come and have supper with us tonight?' This took Martin completely by surprise.

'Why … yes … thank you,' he blurted out before he realised what he had committed himself to.

'Good!' said Mary. 'We'll expect you about seven.'

That evening Gerald made him most welcome. Obviously, Mary had told him a little of their meetings. The conversation over the meal ranged over many subjects, but Charles's name was never mentioned.

While Mary was loading the dishwasher in the kitchen, Gerald took the opportunity to have a quiet chat with Martin.

'I've been trying to persuade mother to come out to Sydney. I mean, there's nothing to hold her here now, is there? But she won't hear of it. She says she wants to stay here in this enormous house. It was too big when all three of us lived here – and now there's only her!'

'She's a determined lady, your mum!'

'She's that all right – always has been! Look, I suppose what I'm trying to say is … well … I'd feel a lot more comfortable about her staying here on her own if … well… if I knew that there was someone … well … not looking after her as such, but …'

'But keeping an eye on her?' Martin helped him out.

'Exactly that!' Gerald was relieved. 'I'd be far happier if I knew there was someone over here, keeping an eye on her.'

'You've no need to worry, Gerald,' Martin said. 'Your mum and I have become great friends over recent months. It will be an honour for me to "keep an eye on her".'

Gerald thrust out his hand. 'Thank you, Martin. Thank you very much! That's a great load off my mind, I can tell you. I think mum thinks you're pretty special too. I've noticed the way her eyes light up when she sees you.'

At this point, Mary rejoined them.

'And what have you men been discussing while I've been away?' she asked. Gerald looked at Martin, who spoke. 'Gerald was just telling me you've decided to stay here, rather than go and live in Sydney.'

'Yes,' said Mary. 'I thought about it long and hard, but I've decided that it would be better for me to stay here. Everything here's familiar. The house, the Old Manor, the church – well, the whole village, really. It's what I know. And then there are my friends.' She smiled at Martin. 'If I went to Australia, of course, it would be lovely to be so much closer to my family, but with you and Anita both being at work, and the children at school, I'd end up with a lot of time on my hands and nothing to fill it. I know Anita's due to have another baby in a few months and she doesn't want an interfering busybody of a mother-in-law getting in the way, now does she? So, I've decided – I'm going stay here.' And with that, the subject was dropped.

The day after Gerald flew home Mary and Martin were eating breakfast at The Butty.

'I have an appointment this afternoon with the solicitor,' Mary said. 'He's asked me to go into the office to see to Charles's affairs.'

'Did he leave a will?' Martin asked.

'No, he didn't,' she said. 'I made one some years ago, but Charles always said there was no need because everything would come to me anyway.'

'Again, I'll make the offer. Would you like me to come with you?'

'You're so kind,' she smiled at him. 'But no, I need to do these things on my own. Then if anything goes wrong, I only have myself to blame.' They parted company at the path. Martin kissed her, and wished her the best for her meeting with the lawyer.

Over the next few days they only met briefly and he asked her how the meeting at the solicitor's office had gone. She was evasive in her reply, effectively telling him nothing. Rex was still living with him and when he tried to ring she was often out and her texts were also brief and to the point. Martin assumed that she was busy sorting out Charles's affairs. He concluded that, in a case of sudden death where there was no will and a considerable amount of money, there would be a lot to sort out.

'If only she would let me help her!' he thought. He had started to worry about her, so it was a relief when his phone rang.

'Martin, it's Mary.' She sounded strange – different. Her voice conveyed a mixture of sadness and anger.

'What is it?'

'Are you busy?'

'No. Why?'

'Look, I know I haven't had much time to see you over the last little while. There has been so much to do and I hate to impose. But I wonder, could you possibly come up to the house? I really need to see you.' He realised from the tone of her voice that it must be something important.

'I'm on my way.'

'Oh, thank you. Thank you so much.'

With Rex following him he jumped off the boat and locked the door. He walked quickly – almost ran – along the towpath and down the path to The Crescent, Rex trotting beside him. He rang the doorbell. She opened the door almost immediately and invited him in.

'You've forgotten your cap,' she said as she kissed him on the cheek and smiled a weak smile. She had a glass of something in her hand and he could see that she had been crying.

'In too much of a rush,' he replied. 'What's the matter?' She went ahead of him into the lounge. He followed her.

'Help yourself to a drink and sit down, please,' she said quietly, as she sat down on the settee. He poured himself a whisky and sat down next to her. He reached out and took hold of her hand but she gently pulled it away and sat twisting her wedding ring.

'You remember I told you that I had my suspicions that Charles had another woman in London?' she said.

'Yes.'

'Well, he didn't – or, at least, I don't think he did.'

'That's good, then, isn't it?' Martin attempted to lighten the mood.

'It would be, if he hadn't been doing something much, much worse.'

'Worse? What?'

'Gambling!'

'Well,' Martin said, 'a lot of people like a flutter – National Lottery, football pools.'

Mary picked up a sheaf of papers, stapled in one corner, from the coffee table and passed it to him. 'Look at that!' she said.

As he scanned the pages Martin was filled with horror. Each page was a closely typed list of bookmakers and casinos. Against each one was a sum of money. He turned to the last page where he saw the astronomical total.

'My God!' was all he could say.

'That, as far as Mr Baker the solicitor, knows, is the extent of Charles's outstanding gambling debts. They are now my liability.' She paused. 'How could he?' She began to weep. Martin moved towards her and drew her to him. This time she did not pull away. She sank her head against his chest, her body wracked by deep sobs of hurt, anger and despair. When her crying subsided, he asked, 'What are you going to do?'

'I've spent most of the last few days talking to lawyers, accountants and bank managers trying to find ways round it. But in the end I have no alternative. I'm going to have to put this place on the market to pay part of his debts. An inheritance I had from my parents, which I invested, will just about cover the rest. Then I'll have no alternative but to go and live with Gerald and Anita in Australia. Hopefully, in time, I can save up enough to buy a place of my own out there. I'll have just about enough money left to pay my airfare. I've already telephoned Australia House to see what I have to do.'

Martin was dumbstruck. For many minutes neither of them felt able to speak. Martin continued to study the list of debts, the figures dancing on the page like macabre ghosts. Mary looked at nothing in particular.

'And you had no idea?' he said, at last.

'None whatsoever.'

'But what about your household bills and things?'

'They were totally separate. We each had our own accounts for personal things. Charles paid money from his salary into my account by standing order every month so I could pay all the household bills, school fees, etc. I often asked him how well off we were but he always said that he was the money-man and there was no need for me to worry about it.'

'But there obviously was.'

'Yes. He made sure that everyone he owed money to only had his office address so no threatening letters ever came here.' They lapsed into silence again. Martin then put into words what had been at the back of his mind for many weeks.

'There is another way out of all this – aside from going to Australia, I mean,' Martin said.

'There is?'

'Yes. Well, you would still have to sell your house, I suppose, to pay the debts. But then you could come and live on *Guinevere* with me.'

Tears formed in Mary's eyes again. 'Oh, Martin! If only it were that simple.'

'But why isn't it that simple?' he asked, a frown crossing his face. 'It seems that simple to me.'

'It has nothing to do with my feelings for you,' she said. For a few moments, she said nothing and Martin could see that she was trying to think of the best way to answer him. Eventually she said, 'Do you remember that day when I first visited you on your boat?'

'As if it were yesterday!' he answered.

'But what you don't know is how much courage it took for me to actually walk down those steps into *Guinevere*'s cabin.'

'Courage? Why?'

'Ever since I was a small child I've been claustrophobic – badly claustrophobic – I mean seriously claustrophobic.'

'You mean…'

'I mean I can't stand being in enclosed places. The smaller they are, the worse it is. It all started when I was very young – about three years old – I think. The nanny I had then, Nanny Padgett, she was one of the "children should be seen and not heard" school. I hated her! And, consequently, I used to play her up terribly. One day my parents had gone out and I drove her right to the end of her tether. As a punishment she locked me up in the broom cupboard. It was as black as pitch in there! I screamed and screamed for her to let me out but it wasn't until my parents came home – what seemed like a lifetime later – that I was set free. By that time I was a complete wreck, I can tell you. I'd never been so frightened! My mother was furious with her and dismissed her on the spot.'

'How terrible for you!'

'It was. And ever since then I've suffered from panic attacks whenever I've been in small spaces. It's horrible! They start suddenly with no warning. It's as if I suddenly can't breathe and I'm convinced I shall suffocate if I don't get out.'

'That must be so frightening!'

'It is. When we were first married Charles was very patient and supportive about it. With him helping me, I managed to conquer some of my fear. I even got to the point where we were able to take short trips by plane for our holidays. But then things started to change. I suppose, thinking back now I know about it, it was about the same time as he started to slide into debt.'

'How did things change?' Martin asked.

'He started to put pressure on me – he pressured me into doing more than I was able. He started to blame me, to criticise me, to mock me and taunt me. All that confidence I'd built up plummeted – and my self-esteem too. The claustrophobia came back – big time! I was a prisoner in my own home.'

'Arthur, Rex's owner, was an old friend of my parents. He was a great help and support. He helped to rebuild my confidence. It was him who encouraged me to become a volunteer at the Manor. I only do reception, though, so I can stay near the door. It was quite an effort for me to give you that tour. Most of the rooms are large enough not to affect me but going down the narrow basement passages and into the secret little hidey holes was very hard. I was mightily relieved when we got out into the garden for tea, I can tell you! He also suggested I should get involved with the church. That's fine. It's such a big open space. Even so, I always sit near the back, close to the door. Charles's funeral was a nightmare because I had to sit at the front. The older I get, the more these attacks frighten me, so I try not to put myself in situations where I could have one. When you asked me to visit *Guinevere* – well…'

'But …'

'I managed to hold myself together for an hour or so on *Guinevere*, while we had that drink, but then I needed to get out.'

'Yes,' Martin recalled. 'I remember thinking at the time that your decision to leave seemed a bit abrupt. But once you were out on the jetty the urgency … sort of disappeared.'

'Exactly!' Mary said. 'Once I was out in the open again I knew I would be OK. I could breathe again! That's the main reason why I wanted to stay on here. This house is so big I don't feel trapped in it.' Martin's plan crumbled inside his head.

'You probably didn't notice,' she continued, 'but on all the trips we've had along the canal on your boat, I've never once been inside. I either stand on the back with you or sit out at the front.' She paused. 'Although I believe I would very much like living with you, Martin, I'm afraid the confines of *Guinevere* would turn me into a gibbering wreck inside a day.'

'But you seem OK at The Butty,' Martin said.

'It's that much wider, isn't it? It's got so many windows on both sides. And you remember I always insist on sitting at the table nearest the door.'

'You said that was so that you could keep an eye on Rex.'

'That's just an excuse! I need to be close to the world outside. Even then, I can't spend too much time there. I have to get out again as soon as we've finished breakfast.'

Neither said anything for a few moments.

'You're going to be cooped up on an aircraft for almost twenty-four hours to get to Australia. How are you going to cope with that?' Martin asked.

'I know I am. And I'm not looking forward to it, I can tell you! The only way I shall be able to deal with it is to convince myself that it will be, probably, the very last time in my life that I shall ever feel trapped. I'll get some pills from the doctor to knock me out. That'll help. But after I land I'll never have to do it again – ever.'

'But can't you get some sort of treatment – I mean – hypnotherapy, or something?'

'I've tried all sorts of cures – the sensible ones and the crackpot ones. Nothing seems to work for me. As I said, I just try to avoid those situations now. It's something I've had to learn to live with.'

'I never realised...'

'Well, it's not the sort of thing you go around advertising, is it?'

'I suppose not.' They lapsed into silence again, Mary in despair, Martin stunned and bewildered. How easily he had asked her to live with him! How easily he had assumed she would agree!

'Will you be taking Rex to Australia with you?' he asked, eventually.

'I'm not sure. It would mean asking Gerald to pay his fare because I can't afford it now.' She paused. 'If I left him here, would you look after him permanently?'

'I'd love to!' Martin smiled, putting on a braver, more optimistic face than he felt. God! This was hard! 'I love you, Mary, for Christ's sake!' he thought, then out loud, 'We've built up quite a bond over the last few weeks. He's such an intelligent dog – far more so than Ben, my old labrador. We're getting on so well I've started teaching him a few tricks.'

'It'll be good to know that he's got a good home where he's loved.'

'He's certainly that!' Martin confirmed. Mary stood up.

'I need another drink. Would you like another?'

'Please.' She refilled their glasses and put them on the coffee table. Then she sat down next to him and took both of his hands in hers.

'Look, Martin, I know that since that incident with Rex, when I cut my knee, you've become very fond of me.' She spoke haltingly.

'I think it's more than that,' said Martin, looking straight into her eyes. 'I think I've actually fallen in love with you.'

'I know,' she said, 'and I have with you. And I think we could be very, very happy together. This summer has been so special. But … I just can't live on your boat. I'm trapped by this damned claustrophobia!'

'I know we could be happy together!' There were tears in Martin's eyes.

'I'm so sorry!' She was weeping too. Martin drew her towards him, his arm around her shoulders. She put her hands on his chest and rested her head against them. He felt her sobs. Gently he stroked her hair.

'Oh Mary – it's not as if it's your fault, is it?' He tried to comfort her. 'It's not like you can help it.'

'It's just that … since we've met … I think I've discovered for the first time what love really is.'

'But surely…' Martin was unsure.

'I don't think now that Charles and I were ever in love, not really in love. My parents wanted me to marry well. They were quite controlling. I was the only, much-loved and over-protected child. I saw him as a handsome young man with a good job – security for the future – he was quite a catch. He charmed my parents and I was fond of him. He was kind to me – as I said, supportive for our first few years together. I felt he understood my problems. I don't think he did now – not really. But I was independent at last! I could live my own life away from my parents.'

'And what do you think he saw in you?'

'Oh, a pretty girl who dressed well. I was more of an accessory – a trophy wife. I think that's what they call them these days. I was a clothes-horse to show off at his company parties and cook dinners for his important clients, especially to start with. I started to opt out when things went bad between us – and, of course, a breed mare to give him a son!' Her voice sounded angry.

'Isn't that a bit harsh?' Martin asked.

'No. He virtually told me that in not so many words when we were arguing about Gerald's career. I had given him a son who had turned out not to be the heir he wanted – and that it was all my fault! By that time I was too old to have any more children and he referred to the fact that I was getting on and had lost the best of my looks! I was about forty then.' She chuckled.

'I know one shouldn't speak ill of the dead – and I'm sorry if it offends you – but he sounds like a twenty-four carat bastard to me.'

'He was!' she agreed. 'I found out very early on in our marriage that the only thing he really loved was money. Now I know why.' Another few moments of silence.

'I think I was in love with Doreen,' Martin said, at length.

'Were you?'

'Well, yes, at the beginning, anyway.' He paused. 'Yeah, thinking about it, the first few years were fine.'

'What happened?'

'Oh, the firm I worked for, they were going through a bit of a bad patch. It was only a small outfit and I was trying to chase some fairly substantial bad debts. At the same time, trying to keep the bank sweet while looking to see where else we could borrow some money from – just to tide us over.

'Anyway, I started taking work home and that's when it all kicked off. By the time I'd done what I needed to do I was too knackered to do anything else. At first, I thought Doreen understood. But before long it was obvious she was getting fed up. She started on about how I must think more of the firm than I did of her. So many times I tried to explain! If the firm went under, I'd be out of a job – with precious little chance of getting another one. No formal qualifications, you see.

'Well, I couldn't carry on working at home in the evenings in that atmosphere, so I started working longer hours. By the time the firm turned the corner, and I retired, a couple of years later, I found she'd been seeing a bloke she worked with for all that time. And that was it.'

'That must have been a very sad time for you,' Mary said, quietly.

'It was, very sad. But this, this seems different somehow. I suppose it's like the song says, "Love's so much lovelier the second time around".'

'Oh, Martin! I just … I just wish with all my heart that this could have worked out differently!'

'So do I, my love. So do I.'

'If Charles hadn't died, we could have carried on – having breakfast and walking Rex together, taking trips on your boat and whatever else we may have decided to do with our time together. He would never have known – not that I believe he would have been concerned if he ever had found out.'

Martin lifted her head and kissed her again, a long, lingering kiss. When he opened his eyes he could see that her eyes were sparkling, not with tears, but with something else – anticipation? There was an eagerness there he had not seen before She stood up. Again, she held his hands.

'We both know it has to end, this happiness.' She grasped his hands tightly. 'Even though neither of us wants it to. But I want that to be our only regret.'

'What do you mean?' Martin looked at her face. 'What other regrets can there be?' Her eyes were still sparkling as she spoke.

'Regrets that we didn't take our chance to do something that I know – and you know – we are both aching to do. Come with me.' She led him by the hand out of the lounge and up the stairs. She opened a door into a bedroom. The curtains were closed. Standing by the bed, she gazed into his eyes.

'I'm yours!' she whispered.

As Martin walked back to *Guinevere* later that starlit night his mind was in turmoil. She had given herself to him so completely. He had felt tenderness – and an intense wave of emotion. What pleasure they had both enjoyed! He ruffled the fur on Rex's head. Rex turned and gave him a knowing look!

Martin knew beyond any shadow of doubt that he was utterly and completely in love with Mary. His dear, dear Mary. And he knew beyond any shadow of doubt that Mary was in love with him.

In desperation, another plan began to take shape in Martin's head. If he was brutally honest he knew it was doomed to failure even before it had formed but he had to do something. Oblivious to the lateness of the hour, he booted up his laptop as soon as he arrived back on board. He made a rough calculation as to how much *Guinevere* was worth. He added in his meagre savings and his income. Then he went onto the internet and looked at the websites for local estate agents and letting agencies – only to confirm what he had thought all along. The only properties he could afford, even to rent, were small houses, houses with rooms that were nowhere near big enough to ensure that Mary could live in them.

He sat staring at the calculations on the piece of paper in front of him well into the early hours of the morning. Whichever way he looked at them, the bottom line was never going to be enough. Admitting defeat, he finally went to bed. In the darkness he said out loud to himself, 'You're right, Mary. Our only regret now is that this must end.'

However, as he fed Rex the following morning another germ of an idea sprang into this head.

'Come on, boy!' he said, picking up Rex's lead, clapping his cap on his head and jumping off the boat, 'Let's see…'

While he was walking Rex along the towpath the idea took root and grew in his mind. They made their way along the footpath leading to The Crescent. He pressed the doorbell. Mary opened the door.

'Come in!' she said and kissed him, 'and Rexy too!' She stroked the dog's head. 'Coffee?' she asked.

'Thanks.' Martin removed his cap and followed her through to the kitchen and sat down at the table. She switched the kettle on, put coffee into a cafetière and looked at her watch.

'Is it an inconvenient time?' Martin asked.

'No. It's just that I've got the estate agent coming at eleven. This place goes on the market today!' She looked around at the room and sighed.

'Ah,' was all Martin could think of to say.

'Anyway,' Mary brightened, 'to what do I owe the pleasure of this surprise visit?' The kettle boiled and she poured the water into the cafetière.

'I've been thinking,' Martin began. A worried look appeared on her face.

'What? About last night? You don't…'

'No!' he interrupted her. 'Certainly not about last night! Last night was absolutely wonderful! Like you said – no regrets!'

'Oh, thank goodness! I think it was pretty wonderful too.' Her smile returned as she poured out two mugs of coffee and handed one to Martin.

'Thanks. No,' he resumed, putting his mug down on the table and looking directly at her, 'I was thinking about the future – our future.'

'Have we got one? A future together, I mean?'

'Well, we might have if my idea works.'

'And what's your idea?' She sat down opposite him.

'I was just wondering … with your claustrophobia. I mean … the house is not going to sell immediately, is it? And if a buyer comes along tomorrow it'll take at least three months until completion – and until all Charles's affairs get sorted out.' He paused. 'Anyway, I know it's probably a long shot, but I think I may have an idea as to how we could try and beat it together.'

'How?'

'I was wondering, if you were to keep coming over to *Guinevere* on a regular basis, and every time you came you tried to stay in the cabin a little bit longer than the previous time. I just thought that, over a period of time, you might be able to get used to it and not get your panic attacks. If you could stay inside for longer and longer times – one day – well, you never know. You might just… What do you think?' His voice tailed off.

Mary was silent as she gazed into the middle distance, holding her coffee mug in both hands. 'I don't know,' she said, at length.

'It's worth giving it a go, though, isn't it?' Martin persisted.

'Oh, yes,' she replied as she smiled at him. 'It's definitely worth giving it a go.'

'What then?'

Again, she was quiet for a few moments. The smile disappeared. 'What if it doesn't work? Is it worth the disappointment we'd both feel if it failed?' she asked. 'I've told you, I've tried so many things in the past that are supposed to cure it and none of them has worked.'

Now it was Martin who remained silent, staring into his coffee mug. He looked up. 'Well, it won't be any worse than the disappointment we're both feeling at the moment, will it?' he asked.

'No … no, I don't suppose it will.' She smiled again. 'As you say, the house isn't sold yet. Thank goodness Mr Baker is managing to keep the creditors at bay, pending the sale. I think we can use the time until it sells profitably.'

He stood up. 'Great!' he said and kissed her across the table.

A serious look again replaced the smile on her face. 'Just one thing,' she said. 'Don't bank on it being successful.'

'I'm not,' Martin replied. 'I'm prepared to accept defeat if it doesn't work out. But at least we'll have given it a try. There won't be any regrets there, either. But I think the "something special" we have between us will help it work.'

'I'll walk down and see you after the estate agent has gone,' she said as she let Martin and Rex out of the front door. 'We might as well get cracking with that idea of yours straight away!' She kissed him, lightly and tenderly, on his forehead, the gentle smile that Martin loved so much flickering across her face.

Martin returned to *Guinevere* with a renewed spring in his step. Hope was not all lost.

'Me? In love? At my age?' he asked aloud. Rex flicked his ears. 'You're middle-aged – well, old, nearly – retired! You're a bloody fool, Martin Cole! But I don't care!' He twirled Rex's lead in his hand and smiled to himself.

After she had closed the door, Mary leaned against it. 'I love you, Martin,' she whispered. 'Please, God, let it work this time!' She went into the lounge and plumped up the cushions. The doorbell rang.

'Richard Hampton of Hampton Estate Agents.' The young man with a briefcase introduced himself, proffering a business card.

❋

United

The shadows lengthened as summer turned into autumn. They took many enjoyable cruises on *Guinevere*. The canal-side trees were dressed in reds and golds, while the fields had turned from golden to brown. As they cruised happily together on the boat they were able to forget Mary's money worries. Occasionally they had lunch at a canal-side pub (there were excellent ones in both directions from the marina). One day, as they were finishing their meal, Mary asked, 'Shouldn't you have started your long autumn cruise by now?'

'Oh that!' Martin smiled. 'What? And leave you here?'

'Oh, bless you!' she said and grabbed his hand. 'I'm so glad you haven't gone. I don't know what I would have done without you these past weeks. But I might have…' Her voice faltered and she looked away.

'Shh!' said Martin. 'Not yet!'

Martin's plan seemed to be working well at first. When they cruised, Mary stayed on the back deck with him – although Rex always sought the comfort of an armchair! When they tied up by the side of the towpath, or when they were in the marina, Mary tried sitting in the cabin. Martin did his best to distract her by talking to her and trying to keep everything as normal as possible.

Sometimes it worked and Mary and Rex would leave the boat after a couple of hours, relaxed and happy.

At other times, however, she would feel that all too familiar rush of panic rising from the pit of her stomach. She would start trembling and her breathing would become shallow and rapid. The first time it happened Martin was frightened. He tried to comfort her but she pushed him away.

'Please don't trap me!' she protested, her voice reduced to a hoarse whisper. He watched helplessly as she struggled to calm her breathing, her eyes fixed on some unseen spot in the distance. Sometimes she managed it, but more often than not she would rush from the boat and stand, gasping, on the jetty.

'Please don't be angry with me, Martin!' she said, breathlessly, as he followed onto the rear deck on one such occasion.

'I'm not angry with you, love!' he said, placing a comforting arm round her shoulders. 'I'm just disappointed because other times you do so well.'

'I honestly don't know if this ever going to work!'

'I'm happy to carry on with it as long as it takes,' Martin reassured her. 'The question is…' He paused. 'Can you cope with it? I know it puts you through hell every time you do it. It must be very draining for you.'

'It is – at the time, but as soon as I'm out in the open again and take a few deep breaths, I start to feel better. The panic goes as quickly as it comes.'

'You're prepared to carry on then?'

'Yes, of course. I said I would give it a try and I'm damned well going to give it a try! It's no good giving up at the first setback, is it?'

'That's my girl!' said Martin and gave her a kiss.

They frequently visited The Butty for their breakfast, sometimes walking together from The Crescent. Rex, ever adaptable, happily accepted his master's and mistress's sleeping arrangements.

Over breakfast at The Butty one Friday morning Mary said, 'It's our Harvest Festival at St Michael's on Sunday. We're decorating the church tomorrow. Would you like to come along and help?'

'I can't bring anything,' Martin said. 'I haven't got a garden.'

Mary laughed. 'No, there'll be plenty of produce. I just wondered if you'd like to come and help with the displays.'

'Yes,' Martin said. 'I'd be happy to come and help.'

'I might even persuade you to come to the service on Sunday, as well!' Mary smiled.

'Steady! Steady!' Martin chuckled. 'One thing at a time!'

They arrived at the church, after walking Rex, around half past nine and Mary introduced him to the half-dozen people who were there, including the vicar, Rev John, and his wife.

'Why am I doing this?' Martin thought. But then, he reflected, it seemed the most natural thing in the world to be there at Mary's side.

'Martin has offered to come and help with the high-up bits!' Mary said excitedly.

Three hours later the church had become a harvest celebration itself with flowers, vegetables and fruit tastefully displayed on the windowsills and around the lectern and pulpit. Martin was particularly proud of one window-sill that he had decorated on his own – well, with a little help from the vicar's wife! Mary congratulated him.

'That's excellent, considering you've never done anything like it before,' she said. 'Now, how do you feel about coming to the morning service with me tomorrow?'

'Oh, I don't know,' Martin protested. 'I've never been a great one for going to church.'

'You've met some of the congregation this morning. We don't have two heads or anything. In fact, looking at us, you'd think we were normal people! What are you afraid of?' Martin gazed at his window display and said nothing for a few moments. Then he faced her.

'Nothing, I suppose. All right, I'll come with you … but you'll have to tell me what to do.'

'Don't worry. I will,' she said. 'And thank you!'

At ten minutes to ten on Sunday morning they walked hand in hand up the path to the church door.

'Just remember to take your cap off when we go in!'

'I know!' he laughed. 'I remembered yesterday, didn't I?' A few paces further on, he suddenly stopped.

'Aren't you worried about what your friends might think, seeing us holding hands like this – especially so soon after Charles's death?' he asked, concerned.

'Not at all!' Mary replied. 'They can think what they like. I'm proud to be walking along here with your hand in mine. Did they mind yesterday? Did John mind?'

'If that's the case,' he replied, continuing to walk, 'I'm just as proud to be holding your hand!' He squeezed her hand and she flashed a smile at him. They sat towards the back of the church, near the door. Throughout the service she gave him reassuring smiles and squeezed his hand. Martin relaxed and smiled back. He thought he detected a growing confidence in her.

'What do you need to do this week?' he asked as they were walking back to the house after the service.

'I have to go to the bank to get everything signed over to me, and I've got to go to Australia House again – some more papers to sign.'

'But you're getting on so well staying on *Guinevere*!' he bridled. 'Why do you need to go there yet?'

'I know I am,' she said. 'But we've got a long way to go before I could actually live on her. And we have to bear in mind that I might not make it. Let's just say that by getting all the immigration stuff sorted out now, I'm keeping my options open – in case it all goes pear-shaped.' She paused. 'You do understand, don't you?'

'I suppose so.' Martin could not hide the disappointment in his voice. 'It just seems a bit like you're expecting it to fail.'

It was her turn to stop walking. 'Absolutely not!' she exclaimed. 'As I've said before, I've tried all the cures, the mainstream ones and the alternative ones – even some of the real crackpot ones. But none of them has worked. I hope and I pray every night that this will work. It's just that experience has taught me to prepare for the worst.'

'OK,' Martin said, more cheerfully. 'I see. I understand now. So, I know you like to be independent, but would you like me to come with you on these appointments?'

'No. You're right. I do like my independence. I'll go on my own, thank you. But I'll tell you what I would like your help with.'

'What's that?'

'I haven't touched Charles's personal stuff yet. I really would like a hand to go through all that.'

'When?'

'What about after lunch tomorrow?'

'That's fine with me.'

'What are you going to do with everything?' Martin asked as they emptied Charles's wardrobe.

'Gerald took a few things he wanted. I think everything else will have to go to a charity shop – unless there's anything you want? Although, I can't really picture you in Charles's things – and I don't think I'd want to see you wearing them either.'

They worked without talking, folding and packing away Charles's life into plastic bags. Mary made no comment and showed no emotion. Martin appreciated her need for silence. Charles, it appeared, was an ordered and orderly man. His possessions showed little of his personality. His business attire consisted of grey or black suits and white shirts, his casual clothing browns and fawns.

As they emptied the final drawer, Mary said, 'Please would you do me one more favour?'

'Of course.'

'Take my car and take these to one of those charity shops in town. I don't care which one. Just get them out of the way – now!' Martin took the bags downstairs and loaded them into her car. As she heard him drive off Mary sat down on the bed and sobbed.

In no time at all it seemed that it was time to alter the clocks. British Summer Time gave way to Greenwich Mean Time and the nights began to draw in. Mary found she was able to stay on

Guinevere for a whole afternoon or an evening – with the door closed! She was so proud of herself and Martin was proud of her too. He exerted no pressure. He accepted the situation. He began to read the warning signs and would try to divert Mary's attention. Sometimes he was successful and managed to calm her, but at other times he would sit and wait in pained silence while she battled alone with her fears. They would often sit and listen to music or watch a DVD. In his heart Martin was optimistic. 'Please don't let the house be sold yet!' he often prayed – and him not a real churchgoer!

Bonfire Night came and they stood together on *Guinevere*'s front deck, his arm around her shoulders as they watched the marina's annual firework display. She seemed so happy that Martin was tempted to suggest she stay the night on the boat. But remembering what she had told him about Charles pressuring her into doing more than she could, he decided not to mention it.

As the house was still hanging fire, and in response to the estate agent's repeated requests to lower the asking price, Mary was forced to tell him why she needed the money.

'I can only afford to drop a couple of thousand so I need an offer of that least that much,' she told him. After that he only contacted her when someone had shown an interest in her property. Her visits to Martin's boat continued and she was growing in confidence. There were setbacks but she refused to give up and Martin could not help but admire her determination.

It was one evening towards the middle of December, when, after they had eaten supper at The Crescent, she asked, 'What do you normally do for Christmas?'

'Not much,' he replied. 'I usually stay on the boat on my own. I've got a cousin up north. She always asks if I want to go there. I took her up on the invitation one year. Never again!'

'Why?'

'Her husband.'

'Oh?'

'Yes. He seems to think that the sole purpose of Christmas Day is to get as drunk as possible as quickly as possible.'

'Oh, I see. Well, this year, I'm going to cook Christmas lunch for us!'

'That will be lovely!'

'But you have to do something to earn it.'

'Oh, yes? What?'

'Come with me to the Midnight Communion service on Christmas Eve.'

'Done!'

'You agreed to that a lot quicker than when I asked you to come to the Harvest Festival!' she laughed.

'There wasn't the promise of a meal involved then!' he joked. 'Look! If it makes you happy, then it makes me happy too. Of course I'll come with you. I don't think I'll ever be a regular, but now and again I don't mind.'

Before they left for church on Christmas Eve Mary contacted Gerald on Skype so that she could watch her grandchildren open their presents. Martin was introduced to a heavily pregnant Anita for the first time. They seemed so happy together. Gerald chatted with Martin, telling him about his work and the new car he had bought. He even took his laptop on a tour to show Martin all round their house. It was a bright sunny day in Sydney and the swimming pool in the back garden looked most inviting! Gerald said he planned to take the children windsurfing later. As they talked it seemed to Martin as if he had known them for years. He watched as Mary's eyes sparkled every time one of the two children held up a freshly unwrapped present for her to see. He knew how special they were to her.

When the time came to finish the call the screen faded and Mary sighed heavily.

'You really miss them, don't you?' Martin asked.

'Yes, terribly!' Mary replied. 'But I can't be bitter. It's so obvious that they all have a lovely life out there. It's just at times like Christmas – and the little ones' birthdays – I wish they were all here.'

As Martin took her in his arms she wept softly.

Later they walked to church. It seemed to Martin as if the

whole village was squeezed into the tiny building. He met people he knew from the marina whom he had not realised were churchgoers. Inspired by the carol-singing, they walked back to The Crescent hand in hand. Before they went to bed they sat on the sofa by the fire, nightcap in hand, Martin's arm around Mary's shoulder, her hand resting on his knee, relishing the silent intimacy of the moment. Rex lay at their feet.

Martin dropped off to sleep that night knowing that this was going to be the happiest Christmas he had enjoyed for quite some time – if not ever!

'Merry Christmas, darling!' he said, as he rolled over and drew Mary to him the next morning.

By the middle of January, with Martin's gentle and patient encouragement, Mary was able to spend much of the day aboard *Guinevere*. Fortunately, no one seemed interested enough in the house to make an offer within two thousand pounds of the asking price.

'Winter's a bad time for the housing market,' Richard Hampton told Mary. 'Things will pick up in the spring. You wait and see.'

Wrapped up warm against the weather on a bitterly cold morning, they were out walking Rex along the towpath when Martin said, 'It's the village panto next weekend. Do you fancy going?'

'To be honest, I hadn't given it much thought.'

'It's just that Pete Jackson – one of my drinking mates – he's in it. Do you know Pete?'

'The electrician? Yes. He rewired the house a couple of years ago. Nice chap!'

'They do a matinee at three o'clock on Saturday,' Martin continued, 'and I was wondering if we could go and see it. We can sit near the door so you should be all right.'

'That's what I do when I go to WI.'

'And then I thought we could go back to the boat for dinner.'

'You mean you're going to cook dinner for us?' queried Mary, her eyes widening as she looked at him with incredulity.

'I was thinking more along the lines of getting a takeaway from that new Chinese place that's opened on Church Lane!'

'That sounds more like you!' she chuckled. 'Yes. I've got nothing on this Saturday. That would be lovely. What part is Pete playing?'

'He's been telling us about in the pub for weeks. He's one of the Ugly Sisters.'

'That, I've got to see!'

They laughed until their sides ached! Pete Jackson and his fellow Ugly Sister carried the show. As they made their way through the marina to *Guinevere*'s mooring, still laughing about the pantomime, snow began to fall.

'They said this would happen on the forecast,' Martin said.

'It looks like they were right for once,' Mary replied as she stepped down into the warm and welcoming cabin. Martin took out plates and cutlery.

'Haven't got any chopsticks, I'm afraid,' he said.

'Don't worry,' Mary replied. 'I'm not very good with them anyway.' She set the table and unpacked the meal while Martin opened a bottle of wine and filled two glasses.

The evening passed quickly as they recounted particularly funny incidents from the afternoon's show.

'I never realised Pete had such a good singing voice,' Martin said. 'We'll have to get him to give us a couple of numbers down at "The George" one of these Friday nights.'

After the meal they sat drinking coffee. Martin stole a glance at Mary. She was relaxed. It was warm and cosy as they sat together by the wood-burner. There was no trace of panic or anxiety on her face.

'This is happiness!' he thought. Eventually, they cleared the table and it was late by the time they had finished the washing up. It was time for Mary to return home. Martin opened the back doors of the boat and looked out.

'Oh, my God!' he exclaimed. 'Look out here!' Mary clambered up the steps and peered into the darkness. Everything, as far as the eye could see, was covered with a thick carpet of snow – and it was still falling thick and fast.

'We'll never make it to yours along the towpath in this!' he said. 'And the temperature's dropped too. Look down there!' He pointed to the water at the side of the boat where ice had formed. 'It would be like walking on glass,' he said as they returned to the warmth of the cabin. 'We'd have to leave Rex here too. We can't risk him running out onto the frozen canal.'

'I know it's a lot further, but could we go round by the road instead of the towpath?' Mary suggested.

'We could if we could get down the track and out of the marina. It always drifts down by the gate. Looking at this I should say it'll be at least a couple of feet deep down there by now.'

Mary sat down. 'I guess there's only one thing for it then,' she said slowly, her face solemn. 'I'll have to stay here, won't I?'

Martin's mind went into overdrive. Had he heard that right? Was she suggesting she stay on *Guinevere* – all night? Would she be able to? Would she cope?

'Are you sure, love? I mean, I know you're doing fantastically well, coping with your claustrophobia. And it goes without saying, I'd love it if you stayed – but a whole night?'

'Is there any wine left in that bottle?' she asked.

Martin picked it up. 'No, but I can open another one.'

'No, don't do that. Have you got any brandy? I think I might be all right if I can just get to sleep and brandy usually makes me sleepy.'

'I think I've got a drop somewhere.' He opened his drinks cupboard. 'Do you want anything with it?'

'If ever there was an excuse for a large neat brandy, it's this one!' she said. Martin poured her drink and then went to make sure the bedroom was tidy for Mary. When he returned she was halfway through her brandy and staring into space.

'Are you absolutely sure about this?' he asked.

'No!' she said, draining her glass and swilling it out under the tap. 'But to try to get home in this would be madness. Just don't lock the door tonight, please.'

They prepared for bed in silence. Rex made himself

comfortable in his favourite armchair. As they lay next to each other Martin hugged her and they kissed goodnight. He switched off the light and heard Mary heave a long deep sigh. He decided that he would stay awake until he was absolutely certain that she was fast asleep. After what seemed like an age but, according to the illuminated face of his alarm clock, was only just over half an hour, he heard slow regular breathing. Mary had slipped effortlessly into the arms of Morpheus.

'It must have been the brandy!' he thought with a smile. At that moment the clouds parted and a shaft of pale moonlight shone through the thin curtains onto Mary's face. He watched her sleeping peacefully, her face relaxed. It was his turn to breathe a sigh – a sigh of enormous contentment.

'Oh darling!' he thought, 'you've cracked it this time! After all those years of struggling, you've finally cracked it!' He drifted off into dreamless sleep.

He awoke about a quarter past six. She was not in bed, but it was still warm. He called her name.

'I'm here!' she called from the back of the boat. 'Don't bother looking for your slippers – I've stolen them – and your dressing gown too!' He got up. He put his bare feet into his shoes. Slipping his overcoat over his shoulders and putting his cap on, he joined her on the back deck.

'I've pinched your scarf as well. I couldn't find mine.'

'Don't worry,' Martin replied. 'I've got another one somewhere.'

The snow had ceased falling and the sky was clear. The air was still cold and crisp and the moon shone, bathing the boats on the marina in an eerie mixture of shadows. He put his arm round her shoulders and she rested her head against his chest. He looked at her. She had tears running down her face.

'What's the matter, love?' he asked, concern showing in his voice. She looked up at him.

'Nothing, darling! Absolutely nothing!' she said quietly. 'I'm just so, so happy!'

'So am I, darling!' he whispered. 'So am I!'

❋

Love

Dawn broke. The winter sun crept over the trees and Martin cleared the snow from the front deck. They sat, wrapped in their coats and scarves, eating toast and marmalade and drinking steaming mugs of coffee. Their breath hung in the air as they watched smoke curling from the chimneys of the few other inhabited boats in the marina. Rex sat between them, waiting for any tasty morsels that might come his way.

'Bliss!' thought Martin.

After breakfast they set out for The Crescent. It was easier to see where they were going in the daylight. They noticed the curtains were pulled on The Butty and the door remained locked.

'It takes a lot for Stella and Jadwiga not to open up,' said Martin as they walked past, 'but this snow's beaten them!'

The snow was thick along the towpath, but soft enough to walk on without slipping. They met a few other people who were enjoying a walk through the snowy landscape. On the hill behind the marina they could see children playing on sledges and building snowmen. Rex thought it was wonderful as he romped along, rolling and digging in the snow, and chasing snowballs that Martin threw for him. Mary gripped his arm tightly, her laughter ringing out in the clear air.

'She's so happy!' Martin thought.

When they arrived Mary went upstairs to get changed while Martin went to the kitchen and prepared coffee. He collected the whisky bottle from the lounge. As Mary reappeared he was pouring a generous slug into his coffee.

'Additive – as it's cold?' he called cheerfully.

'Yes, please!' she answered. Until then, neither of them had referred to the success of the previous night. Martin raised his mug.

'Well done for last night!' he said.

'Yes!' she said, as she punched the air. 'Who would have thought it? All the so-called cures I've tried over the years – and what worked? A lovely warm narrowboat, a snowstorm – and you!'

'Not forgetting the double brandy!' Martin added, laughing.

'No, indeed!' she said. 'I've conquered claustrophobia only to become an alcoholic!'

In the midst of their laughter they heard the telephone ring. Mary went into the hall, still laughing, to answer it.

'Who can this be at this time on a Sunday morning, I wonder?' she said. She picked up the receiver. 'Hello?'

It was Gerald and, although Martin could only hear one side of the conversation, it was obviously bad news. It was a long call and when Mary finally replaced the receiver he saw her lean back against the hall wall, her face pale. She sat down on a chair next to the hall table.

'What's the matter, love?' he asked, walking quickly into the hall.

'It's the baby!' she said, sadly. 'Anita's had the baby – a little girl! They've called her Suzanne.'

'But that's wonderful news, isn't it?'

'In normal circumstances it would be, but she was premature. She wasn't due until next month and Gerald's just told me her brain was starved of oxygen while she was being born. She'll be badly disabled. The doctors say she may never be able to walk or look after herself properly!' She burst into tears. Martin hugged her tightly.

'I'm so sorry!' he said. 'You feel so powerless to do anything to help with them being so far away.'

'That's just it!' Mary said between sobs. 'They had it all worked out so that they could afford for Anita to be off work until the baby was old enough to go to nursery. They get eighteen weeks maternity leave out there. But then she needs to go back to work or they won't have enough money to live on. And it'll be a job to find a suitable nursery that'll take a child with a disability.'

'Ah! I see,' said Martin. Mary stood up and collected their coffee mugs from the kitchen and took them into the lounge. They sat together on the settee and he passed her her coffee.

They sat in silence for some moments, rendered speechless by this sad turn of events. Mary's mind was in turmoil, her thoughts twelve thousand miles away with her new granddaughter. Martin realised there was little he could say that would help the situation and relieve her worries.

Mary broke the silence. 'If I hadn't got Charles's damned gambling debts to pay I could have helped them out – sent them some money. Blast him!'

Martin said nothing. They lapsed into silence again.

The enormity and the implications of this new situation began to dawn on them both. After an endless pause, she reached across and took both of his hands in hers.

'You know what this means, don't you, Martin?' she said, tears forming in her eyes.

Martin remained silent. He sat staring at their joined hands. Slowly, he looked up and met her eyes. 'It means,' he said quietly. 'It means … that you'll have to go out there after all.'

'Yes, I will. I'll have to go out there. They're going to need me to look after the baby when Anita goes back to work.' She paused. 'I'm so, so sorry, Martin. Especially after last night. I really am.'

There was another endless pause. Mary could not speak. She was willing Martin to say something – anything – to answer her. He was struggling to find the right thing to say – the best thing to say. He knew what he wanted to say, but he knew he could not say it. Eventually, with as much conviction as he could muster, he spoke. 'No!' he said. 'Don't be! I … I understand. Really, I do! It's your family, and I know your family means such an awful lot to you. I understand that. And … you're absolutely right! They're going to need you. They're going to need you far more than I need you – and God knows I need you badly enough! But your place is with them – with them, and with little Suzanne.' Tears were streaming down Martin's face now. He made no attempt to wipe them away.

'God!' he exclaimed. 'I'm going to miss you so much, though!'

'And I'm going to miss you too, my love.'

He kissed her. 'Life can be such a bitch!' he said with some venom.

'And then you marry one,' Mary replied. 'Sorry! That was one of Charles's so-called witticisms!'

The tension eased a little and they both smiled wanly. Rex, sensing the pain of those he loved most, padded in and sat on the floor between them, his wet muzzle gently nudging their hands, his deep brown eyes gazing mournfully up at them.

Martin spoke first. 'I … I really thought,' he stumbled over his words, 'I thought … well, after last night … we could … well, perhaps … make it work … you and me and Rex on *Guinevere*. Oh Mary, I hate the idea of you going so far away. We may never see each other again.'

Mary looked at him – a long searching look, full of tenderness and emotion. 'We should never say "never"!' she said, at last. Martin watched as she stood up and walked to the window where she stood looking out at the snow-covered garden.

'Last night – well, early this morning – when I woke up I felt a sense of peace I've never known before – never in my entire life.' She turned away from the window and faced him. 'And that's thanks to you, my dearest Martin.' She knelt down in front of him and put her hands on his shoulders. He saw again the familiar sparkle in her eyes. 'No one can ever take that away from me – or from us – ever!' He put his arms round her tightly. She bowed her head and sobbed.

They decided that they would enjoy every last moment. Anita had her eighteen weeks of maternity leave – and the house still was not sold.

'The estate agent says things will pick up in the spring,' Mary told Martin.

'In which case,' he replied, 'I don't care of spring never comes!'

'Neither do I.' They spent some of their time at The Crescent and some living on *Guinevere*. They were both so blissfully happy. They lived each day to the full and only mentioned the future if they had to.

It was one morning a few weeks later while they were walking

Rex along the towpath that they came to a seat and Mary suggested they sit for a while and enjoy the early spring sunshine. They sat in silence for a while, then she turned to Martin.

'I've had an offer on the house.' she said, flatly.

'Oh, yes?' he said. 'Your estate agent chappy said there'd be some interest come the spring.'

'Yes. It's only fifteen hundred below the asking price.' She paused. 'I've got to accept it, haven't I, Martin?'

'Of course, you have to accept it, love! It'd be madness to do anything else.'

'But ... but it would be the beginning of the end of all this ... all this ... wonderful time we're having together!' Tears formed in her eyes.

'I know it would, love.' He put a comforting arm round her shoulders. 'But listen. There's a little girl out there in Sydney who needs you, and your love, a whole lot more than I do.' He paused. 'Isn't there?' He gave her a clean handkerchief and she blew her nose and dabbed her eyes.

'Oh, Martin! You're so kind and understanding.'

'Don't be silly! Anyone could see that that's where you need to be.'

'I don't think so! I think a lot of men – Charles certainly – would be a lot more selfish and tell me I should stay here and let Gerald and Anita sort things out for themselves.'

'Perhaps they would – but I'm not a lot of men – or Charles. I'm me. And I don't see it like that. Of course, I would absolutely love it if you could stay here. But you can't. You need to go, and I have to accept that it's the right thing for you to do.' For a moment she said nothing.

'That makes it so much easier for me,' she said at length. 'So much of me wants to stay here with you, but another part says I must go. The fact that you agree and understand makes it easier somehow.'

'Good!' he said, 'Good!' He felt he had to change the subject. He could say no more. He looked round.

'Now, where's that dog gone? Rex! Rex!'

✳

Over the next few weeks things moved quickly – far too quickly for both of them. Contracts were exchanged and the date was set for completion of the sale of Mary's house. Baker, the lawyer, retained the proceeds of the sale to settle Charles's debts. Martin went with her to Australia House in London to finalise the arrangements for her emigration. She spoke to Gerald on Skype and he assured her that everything was ready for her arrival there. She knew they had a large house. He and Anita had prepared a spacious room with a large picture window as a bed-sitting room. Mary arranged for her clothes and a few special possessions to be shipped over. The house in The Crescent was almost empty – and each day there was another turn of the screw of pain in Martin's heart.

All too soon the day of her departure had arrived. They had spent their last night together on *Guinevere*. Martin had put a protective arm around her one last time. He had slept fitfully as he watched her gentle breathing, while sobs wracked his heart.

'Oh Mary!' he had whispered. 'We – you and me – we would have made it! We really would!'

They had risen early. Mary had slipped off *Guinevere* without a backward glance and walked home alone to await the arrival of the removal men who were calling to take the last few pieces of furniture to the sale room.

Martin took Rex to say goodbye. Mary knelt down and sobbed into his thick fur, whispering words that Martin could not hear. With a heavy heart, Martin walked him back to *Guinevere*.

'Be a good boy. I'll be back soon,' he said, as he left Rex with his favourite toys and returned to The Crescent.

Martin drove her to the airport. As he pulled up outside her house, he saw her standing in the open doorway, waiting for him. She locked the door and walked towards the car. Then she stopped and turned round for a last look at the house. There were tears in her eyes as she sat down beside him and closed the car door.

'Just go, please,' she said, quietly. They took a detour to hand the keys in at the solicitor's office. The drive to the airport was uneventful and passed in long periods of silence, only punctuated by one or the other of them making a feeble attempt at light conversation.

They arrived with time to spare. They sat in a coffee shop, each with a coffee in front of them, but neither of them in the mood for drinking it. They looked at each other, each of them trying desperately to imprint the picture – that one last picture – of the other into their memory.

Suddenly it was time for Mary to go airside. They walked, their arms around each other's shoulders, to the barrier. She began crying again.

'You really do believe I'm doing the right thing, don't you, Martin?' she asked, yet again, between sobs. 'What you think – it's very important to me.'

'You know how much I love you. You know I would give anything for you to be able to stay here and live on *Guinevere* with me. And I know you could do it! We both know you could do it! But we both know too that it's just not possible, don't we? And I know that you'd never forgive yourself for what you would see as abandoning your youngest grandchild. It would simply be too great a price to pay for us to be together. So, yes, for us it couldn't be more wrong. But for you? It couldn't be more right.'

'Thank you,' she said, and kissed him. 'I just needed to hear you say it one more time!'

'And you know I've signed up to Skype!' he said, trying to give their parting a lightness neither of them felt. 'Here's my Skype name thingy.' He handed her a piece of paper, and she put it carefully away in her handbag.

'I'll call you as soon as I get settled in.'

'Don't forget about the time difference,' he said, as he pulled her to him one last time and kissed her, a long, lingering kiss, a kiss that would have to last a lifetime. She pulled away and walked towards the barrier.

'You did get those tablets from the doctor, didn't you?' he suddenly remembered. She turned round.

'Yes, I've had one already.' And she was gone. She disappeared through the door and out of his sight. He stood, rooted to the spot, staring at the doorway, oblivious to the crowd jostling around him. He turned and, pulling his cap from his pocket, slowly made his way back down the long concourse.

With a heavy heart, he walked back to his car. He imagined Mary, sitting on the plane, crying. He had tried to be strong for her sake – and now – now he still did not want to give way and weep.

He drove back up the motorway, his mind numbed with pain and grief.

Stepping onto *Guinevere*, Rex bounded up to meet him.

'She's gone, Rexy boy!' he said as he stroked the dog's head. 'She's gone for good!' He sighed deeply as he poured himself a large whisky and sat down. He was very, very tired – emotionally exhausted. He wept in a way he had never wept before – long, uncontrollable sobs. Rex, ever sensitive, sat at his feet and rested his head in Martin's lap.

After a while he gathered his emotions and drew Rex to him.

'It's just you and me now, boy!' he said.

He paced the boat. He could not settle. Everywhere he looked he could see Mary. He sat down and gazed into space. Everywhere he looked he could see her tear-stained face.

'I must do something!' he said aloud. At random, he picked a DVD from the shelf. Without looking at the title, he slid the disc into the machine. The strains of Rachmaninov told him it was *Brief Encounter*. He remembered watching it with Mary. On the screen Trevor Howard and Celia Johnson played out the scenes of their illicit love affair. He picked up the cover. He refilled his glass. He could hear Mary saying, 'I've conquered claustrophobia only to become an alcoholic!' He smiled. He sat, half dozing, half watching the film. He roused as it neared the end. It was a scene in the station buffet. He heard Trevor Howard say something that struck a chord – something he recognised.

'Too great a price to pay for the happiness we have together.'

'Too great a price to pay.' He ran the phrase though his mind. He had used those exact words to Mary at the airport. 'Too great a price to pay. Yes,' he thought, 'that just about sums it up! It was too great a price to pay for them and it's too great a price to pay for us, Mary and me.'

The music surged. The credits rolled. Martin raised his glass. 'Mary,' he said, his voice strong and determined, 'To us!'

The film ended. He removed the disc. Rex got up.

'Come on, boy!' Martin said. 'Let's go for a walk. You've been cooped up in here all day!' He picked up his cap. How Mary had teased him about that!

'You and that blessed cap!' she had said. 'Winter or summer, it's always stuck on your head! I was surprised to find you didn't sleep in it!'

Rex was following him to the back of the boat when he suddenly stopped and began sniffing behind one of the chairs, whining softly.

'What have you got there, boy?' Martin asked. Rex was trying to pull something out from behind the chair with his paw. He turned to face Martin. In his mouth was a scarf Mary had lost that first night she had spent aboard. It had fallen down the back of the chair and neither of them had noticed it. Rex padded over and dropped the scarf at Martin's feet. He picked it up and held it to his nose. He could detect the faint scent of her perfume. He stuffed the scarf into his pocket.

'Come on, Rex!' he said, stifling a fresh rush of tears. They set off along the towpath – in the opposite direction to The Crescent. As they walked Martin came to a decision. He simply could not let her go! He stopped walking and looked upwards.

'I don't know when,' he shouted to the sky. Rex looked round, startled. 'And I don't know how, but sometime, somehow, I'm damned well going to get myself out to Sydney and be with you again, Mary! I'll do the Lottery! I'll get myself a job! I'll move heaven and earth to be with you again!' He paused. 'We'll get married!'

✳

The next morning he opened *Guinevere's* back doors. Rex leapt off and waited for him.

'Come on, boy!' he said.

Martin took his cap from its hook in the engine room and put it on. Stepping out onto the back deck, he closed the back doors of his boat and shut the sliding hatch. He locked the padlock and stepped onto the wooden jetty. It was a warm, sunny June day as he took his morning walk from the marina to The Butty. Only, as he walked that day, he did not whistle. His heart was somewhere else. It was in a plane – a plane heading to the other side of the world.

Short Cut

A story of intrigue

✳

The job

The phone on James's desk warbled. Single warble. Internal call.

'Damn!' James said, under his breath. The phone warbled again. He sighed and picked up the receiver.

'James Wade.' His voice betrayed his frustration at being interrupted yet again.

'Jimmy, it's Ritchie.' The Californian accent told James it was his boss, even before he had identified himself. He hated being called 'Jimmy' but Ritchie was the CEO of the company. He had been shoehorned in when Gamez-Inc, the American giant, had taken over the small British firm two years previously.

'Yes, Ritchie.'

'Do you have a moment?'

'I suppose so!' Another sigh.

'I'll see you in my office. OK?'

'OK.'

James replaced the phone, saved the work he had done and logged out of his computer. He stood up, stretched and walked the short distance to Ritchie's office, a glass-walled section with venetian blinds, situated at the end of the main floor where James and his colleagues worked. He tapped on the door. Ritchie was on the phone. He looked up, saw James and beckoned him in.

'Jimmy! Hi. Take a seat.' James sat. Ritchie ended his call and made some notes on a pad on his desk. Throwing his pen down, he leaned back in his chair, put his hands behind his head and looked at James.

'You know, Jimmy,' he began, 'guys like you are pretty rare in this industry.'

'We are?'

'Sure, you are! See, in this multi-million-dollar business that we're all part of there are, basically, two kinds of people. There are the creatives, the guys who come up with the characters and the story lines, and then there are the techies, the other guys, the ones who convert those characters and those story lines into pieces of software so all the gaming nerds out there can waste hours of their time playing around with them.' He leaned forward and placed his hands on the desk.

'You're pretty well unique, Jimmy – in this company anyhow. And why are you unique?' he drawled.

'Because I do both?'

'Exactly! Now, you're working on *TechnoTec* Version 4, right? I know you've done the creative bit because I've seen it. I've read it and it's great! And now you're working on the techie bit, right?'

'Yes.' James answered a little tentatively, not sure where this conversation was going.

'Look, I'll level with you, Jimmy. We need it all finished and ready to go by the end of the month. If we don't we can't get it all beta tested and hit the deadline for the Christmas market. OK?'

'Well, yes, Ritchie. That would be fine if…'

Ritchie raised a hand and cut him off. 'I know what you're going to say, Jimmy. You could do it – no problem – if you didn't have all the interruptions, right?'

'That's right.'

'So that's why I'm giving you two weeks to work at home. Download all you need onto your laptop, and I don't want to see you for two weeks. I'll make sure all your calls come through me and I'll only call you if it's absolutely necessary. But when I do see you in two weeks, you better have Version 4 complete, or I'll have your ass!'

'Don't worry! It will be! Thanks, Ritchie! That's great!'

'Get going with that download.'

'Thanks again. Bye, Ritchie.'

'Bye, Jimmy.'

James stood up, left his boss's office and walked back to his desk.

'Ritchie's seen a bit of sense, at last!' he said aloud to his colleagues. 'He's told me to work at home for a fortnight to get this finished.'

'About time too!' said Tina, who had the workstation next to James. 'How the hell you can concentrate on writing a new version in here, I don't know.' As if to prove her point the phone on her desk rang. A double warble. External call. She picked it up.

'Good afternoon. Gamez-Inc. Tina speaking. How can I help you?' She smiled into the telephone.

James connected his laptop and downloaded the half-finished program.

'See you in a couple of weeks,' he called as he left the office.

✳

The next day was Friday and, over breakfast, his wife Laura asked, 'Do you need your car today?'

'No,' he replied, chewing a mouthful of toast. 'I'll be sitting here writing up *TechnoTec*'s latest cases.'

'As mine's behind yours in the drive, I'll drop Gemma off at school and then go on to work in yours.'

'OK. Bye, love. Have a good day!'

'You too. Bye.'

'Bye, Daddy.' He kissed Laura and gave Gemma a big bear hug as they left.

'Peace at last!' James said to himself as he loaded the dishwasher before going into the study. He booted up his laptop and opened the files he was working on. *TechnoTec* burst forth onto the screen. *TechnoTec* was James's baby. It was a computer game with a difference. In it, the player assumed the role of

'TechnoTec', a futuristic private detective, who was placed in a series of high-tech crime scenarios. Using the semi-hidden clues that had been carefully built into the program, the player had to work out who the culprit was, then go on to make a citizen's arrest. The previous versions had sold well, making a handsome profit. The gamers, who all loved Version3, were now crying out for the next set of scenarios.

'Here goes!' James thought, as he settled to his day's work.

Two minutes later the doorbell rang.

✳

At about half past four in the afternoon he heard Laura's key in the lock.

'Hello, Daddy!' Gemma ran into the study and wound herself round her father. He hugged her.

'Hello, Pumpkin! Did you have a good day at school?'

'Yes. It was great! We're designing our own sunhats! Mine's the best – well, I think so, anyway. And I was dinner monitor today. And I got all my maths right. And…'

'Did you have a good day, love?' Laura popped her head round the door.

'Not really,' James paused and grimaced. 'Look, love,' he said, 'on Monday, will you take your car?'

'Sure! Why?'

'Well, at least four of your friends saw your car in the drive and thought you'd got the day off. They either called round for a chat or rang to see if you wanted to go for a coffee or whatever.'

'Oh dear!'

'Yes. Add to that calls about mis-sold PPI, debt management and roof and wall insulation, and it's been one interruption after another. No better than being at the office really. I'm only about halfway to where I should be by now.'

'That's not good, is it?'

'It's not. If I don't hit the deadline we'll miss the Christmas market and it'll cost us a fortune in lost sales. And more to the point, Ritchie will not be pleased.'

'Hmm…' Laura went into the kitchen to prepare their supper. She was looking thoughtful.

'I've got an idea!' she said as James came into the kitchen with an empty coffee cup. 'Why don't you go and stay on the boat?'

Their narrowboat, *Aurora*, had been their special bolt-hole. They had bought her with an inheritance from James's great-aunt before Gemma had been born. Back then they often disappeared for long weekends, tying up in the middle of nowhere, chilling out and watching the world go by. They had been on many cruises while Gemma was a baby as she had travelled well in her cot.

Nowadays, however, she was growing up and it was not so easy. For Gemma, canals were no longer 'cool'.

'But Daddy,' she would whine, 'it's the Brownie Picnic on Sunday,' or, 'It's school cross-country on Saturday,' or, 'It's Lindsay's sleepover on Friday night,' or, 'We really ought to go and see Grandma – we haven't seen her for ages!' Their opportunities for getting away on *Aurora* seemed to be getting fewer and further between. They had toyed with the idea of selling her, but had always resisted doing so. She was moored at a marina on the canal about forty miles from where they lived.

'Your laptop works OK with the inverter on. All you've got to do is run the engine a bit each day to keep the batteries topped up.' James smiled. She was really trying to help him. She continued. 'You could tie up along that straight bit where we've often spent the night. If you stop near the bridge, there's that village I can never remember the name of. It's just down the lane, so you'll be able to top up with food and go to the pub if you have time.'

'So typical of my Laura to come up with a solution!' he exclaimed. 'You are brilliant!' He gave his wife a kiss. 'That's a fantastic idea! It'll be nice and quiet on the canal – and no interruptions!'

'You could go to the marina tonight if you want. Give you an early start tomorrow. You could be up to that bridge by ten o'clock in the morning.'

'Yes, I could.' He looked at his watch. 'It's Friday. The

supermarket's open late tonight. I can stop and get some bits on the way. I'll go and pack some clothes.'

He put his hands on her shoulders.

'Are you sure you don't mind? It'll be such a relief to get it finished. There's so much more to it than the previous versions.'

'Off you go,' Laura smiled. 'It'll help our bank balance as well as Gamez-Inc's, when you've finished it.'

James kissed the tip of her nose. 'You're a good girl, Laura Wade!' he said.

❋

The boat

Tied up by the bridge where Laura had suggested, James worked solidly for seven days – twelve, fourteen, sixteen hours a day.

'Some chance of going to the pub!' he thought wryly. By the end of the seventh day the job was finished. He sat back and rubbed his eyes. Then he stood up and went to the rear of the boat and killed the engine.

'Silence! Marvellous! Battery charged and work finished!' he thought. He looked at the time on the screen – just after half past five.

'I shan't have time to get to the village and post this flash drive to Ritchie today,' he thought. He picked up his mobile phone. There was a strong signal here, unlike many places along the canal. He rang Ritchie's direct line. Ritchie picked up after two rings.

'Hi Ritchie. It's James.'

'Jimmy! How's it going?'

'It's all done, but I can't drop it into the post at the moment. The village post office is closed. It's all on a flash drive. I'll put it in the post for you, Special Delivery, tomorrow. Is that OK?'

'That's excellent! Good work, Jimmy – and way ahead of deadline too.'

'Look, I'm halfway up a canal on our boat at the moment.'

'Halfway up where?'

'The canal. I tried working at home but there were nearly as many interruptions as I get in the office. Laura suggested I take the boat out. With the peace and quiet out here – and my mobile turned off – bingo! All complete a whole week ahead of schedule!'

'Smart cookie, your Laura!' Ritchie said.

'As I'm out on the boat, I won't get back home until tomorrow. So I'll be back in the office on Monday.' There was a pause. Then Ritchie spoke.

'I wasn't expecting you back here till Monday week, Jimmy. So why don't you take next week as additional vacation.' James was taken aback by this unexpected offer.

'Really?' he said. 'OK … thanks! Thanks very much, Ritchie.'

'It's OK. Enjoy! You've earned it, fellah!' Ritchie rang off.

'Well, there's a turn up for the books!' James thought as he made his way to the galley, took a bottle of beer from the fridge and removed the top. 'You've damned well earned this too!' he said to himself as he walked back through the saloon and sat down on *Aurora*'s front deck. It was a warm summer evening and he gazed along the canal. The water was motionless with only the occasional plop of a fish to disturb its surface. Birds sang in the woods on the opposite bank. His eye caught two horses grazing in the field next to the towpath. He had not noticed them before. The dappled sunlight caught the aged brick of the bridge that spanned the canal a little way behind *Aurora*, carrying the narrow lane from the village over its humped back.

'Peace, quiet and serenity,' he thought. Sipping his beer, he took in all the sights, the sounds, the smells of the canal. He realised that he and Laura had been right not to put *Aurora* on the market. An idea suddenly occurred to him. He took his mobile from his pocket and punched her number.

'She'll be home with Gemma by now,' he thought. He had been so engrossed with *TechnoTec* that, apart from the occasional text message, he had had no contact with her or Gemma for the past few days.

'Hi darling! How are you both?'

'We're fine. How's the job going?'

'I actually finished it about…' he looked at his watch, 'ten minutes ago.'

'Really? Oh, well done! You must be feeling very relieved.'

'I am.'

'What are you doing now?'

'Sitting on the front deck and having a beer!'

'No! I mean, are you starting back this evening, or leaving it until tomorrow?'

'That's one of the reasons why I'm calling you rather than sending a text.' He paused before continuing. 'Ritchie's given me next week off and I was wondering, do you think you could manage without me for those few days?' There was a pause.

'I'm sure we could.' Another pause. 'Why?'

'I think I'd like to do a bit of single-handing. It'll help me unwind a bit. These last few days have been pretty stressful, one way and another.' He listened. There was no immediate response.

'Darling…?' he said, hopefully.

'Yes, it's OK.' she said. 'I was just checking the calendar. There's nothing on next week that I can't handle on my own and I thought you would be away for a fortnight in any case. Gemma's going to a birthday bash at her friend's on Monday evening, but I can take her and fetch her from that. So, yes. Why not? Go ahead and enjoy yourself.'

'Are you sure?'

'Listen, darling. I know better than anyone how much pressure you've been under over the last few weeks to get this job finished. I've seen how it's affected you. You've been distracted the whole time. Well, now you've finished it so you deserve a few days to unwind. As long as when you come home, I get the husband back who I know and love. Not the distracted, under-pressure software writer I've been living with!'

'I guess I have been a bit difficult. It's taken so much of my time and energy. It's a great relief to get it finished, I can tell you.'

'I'm sure it is. Now you go off and spend a few days on the water and relax.'

'I will. Thanks, love. I really appreciate it.'

'Just be careful – and send me a text occasionally.'

'I'll do that.'

Whether it was the stillness and the tranquillity of his surroundings, or whether it was because he had had precious little sleep for the previous seven days, but the next thing James knew was that he suddenly woke up. The air was damp and clung round him like a chilly coat. The dark sky was punctuated by an array of twinkling stars with a few scudding clouds occasionally obscuring the moon. He flicked on his phone to see the time. A quarter past eleven.

'I've been asleep for hours!' he said to himself. In front of him was a half-full bottle of flat beer.

'What a waste!' he said to himself. He stood up, stretched, then poured the remains of the beer over the side and went back inside to get ready for bed. As he walked through the saloon he picked a crime novel from the bookshelf. He climbed into bed and opened the book, but his eyes were starting to close even before he had finished the first chapter. His whole body relaxed, lulled by the gentle motion of the boat.

As he turned off the light he heard the noise of a car engine approaching from the direction of the village.

'Volkswagen Beetle!' he thought. 'I'd recognise the sound of that engine anywhere.' The car engine note dropped before stopping altogether. It could not have been far away from the bridge. James assumed it was a young couple who, needing some privacy for their own reasons, had decided to drive far enough out of the village to find an empty farm gateway. There was silence.

It was a few moments later, as he was drifting off to sleep, when the stillness of the night was broken by an almighty splash. Leaping out of bed, James hurried to the back of the boat. He flung open the doors. By the light of the moon he could see a growing circle of ripples spreading out towards each bank close to the bridge. Something had landed right in the middle of the canal. He heard the sound of running footsteps as someone hurried away from the bridge. The Beetle's engine burst into life again and, with a screech of tyres, the car was driven away at high speed. James watched in surprise as the tail lights disappeared into the distance along the narrow lane.

'Another chair to avoid in the morning!' he thought. He realised, reluctantly, that there was nothing he could do about it. Dumping rubbish in the canal was a criminal offence, although the only information he could give was that it had been dumped by someone driving a Beetle. He could not say whether the driver was male or female, and the car had been parked too far away for him to see the registration number as it had driven away.

'In any case, the police wouldn't be interested in it,' he thought as he returned to bed and immediately forgot about the incident as sleep overtook him.

He was awoken the following morning by the sound of the outboard engine of a small cabin cruiser passing the boat. He opened his eyes and saw the dappled light of the sun through the curtains. It was broad daylight. The birds were singing. He got out of bed and peeped through the curtains. There was hardly a cloud in the sky and the temperature was beginning to rise.

'I wish Laura was here!' he thought. 'We really must try to get a break on here soon. Pumpkin's old enough to go to her grandparents' if she doesn't want to come. It would do us good. Put a bit of sparkle back into our lives. Laura is so good. She's a saint. She puts up with my long hours and bad moods when I'm stressed. She's always doing things for other people.' He picked up his watch. It was nearly ten o'clock.

'Damn!' he said aloud, as he remembered the flash drive he had to post to Ritchie. 'However, breakfast first!' He opened the fridge to find that he had run out of milk the previous day.

'Oh well, just a coffee, then!' He went to the cupboard and found he was out of that as well!

As he showered he contemplated the day ahead. He would go to the village and post the flash drive to Ritchie, stock up and set off up the cut. He dressed, tidied the boat, locked it up and made his way along the lane into the village. There was only one shop, the post office, where he posted *TechnoTec* Version4 to Ritchie by Special Delivery, as he had promised.

'On your way, old friend!' he said to himself as the postmistress took the package from him. He then turned his attention to the groceries and bought the provisions he needed, plus a few extras that caught his eye. He left the shop and was about to return to the boat when he spotted a sign outside the pub. It was advertising food. James was no chef and he was getting a little tired of the ready meals he had bought from the supermarket on his way to the marina. The thought of a freshly cooked lunch began to make his mouth water – especially as he had missed out on breakfast!

The friend

He entered the pub, ordered a pint of real ale from the barmaid, and asked for the lunch menu.

'I can highly recommend the steak and kidney pie!' said a voice. James turned to see an imposing man, whom he had not noticed as he walked in, sitting at a table behind him.

'Good, is it?' he asked.

'Excellent!' replied the man, pointing to the plate on the table in front of him. James looked at his meal. The pie certainly looked very appetising. Then he looked a little closer at the man himself.

'Just a minute!' he exclaimed. 'I know you! Aren't you Andrew Knight, one-time captain of the Hurst's School first fifteen?'

The man looked surprised. 'Certainly am! And you are…?'

'James Wade. I was your scrum half for a couple of terms.'

'Wade, old man! Course you are!' He stood up and pumped James's hand. 'Do join me, won't you?'

'Is that a steak and kidney, then, sir?' It was the barmaid.

'Oh, yes please.' James paid her, picked up his pint, and sat down with his former team-mate.

'Seem to remember you were a damned good scrum half…'

'Thank you!' said James.

'… for a scholarship boy, that is,' Knight added. For a second James felt a slight surge of anger. But then he saw the smile on Andrew Knight's face.

'Still the expert wind-up merchant, then?' They both laughed. 'Disappointing you only lasted a couple of terms in the firsts.'

'Yes, it was. A sixteen-stone second row from the local grammar landed on my knee when a scrum collapsed. It's never been right since.'

'Ah, yes! Remember that now. Was damned sorry to lose you from the team, damned sorry. Never found another one with your abilities. Anyway, what brings you to this neck of the woods?'

James told him about his work and the necessity to get this job completed on time.

'Thank you,' he broke off and smiled as the barmaid brought him his pie.

'What sort of game is it?' Andrew asked. 'One of these where you're the goodie who has to go and shoot up a load of terrorists? Not sure it's good for kids to get into all that violent stuff!'

'I agree with you there. No, most of that sort of game is produced in the States.' James went on to explain about *TechnoTec*.

'Sounds interesting,' Andrew said, 'and educational in a way, I suppose, getting kids to be observant and notice what's happening around them.'

'And what about you?' James asked between mouthfuls.

'Me? I live here now. Family's owned a lot of land round here for generations. Most of it's let out to tenants, but we still farm about a hundred and fifty acres ourselves. That field along by the canal – where the two nags are? That's ours.'

'But I thought you were intent on joining the Army?'

'I was – and I did. Look, let me get you another pint and I'll tell you the whole sorry story.' He caught the barmaid's eye. 'Jill! Two more please!'

'I'll bring them over, Andrew.'

'Thanks, love. Yes, much to the old man's chagrin, after Sandhurst I joined the Grenadier Guards and finished up as a major. He was absolutely livid because as far as he was concerned I should have stayed at home and run the farm for him. Was damned glad to get away from here, I can tell you. Army's a grand life and I saw the world, as they say. Came home as little as possible, especially after mother died.'

'That accounts for me not seeing you here when we came by on our boat. We cruised this stretch of canal quite often for a number of years and we nearly always stopped off at this pub.'

'As I say, I was rarely here.' Andrew drained his glass. 'But the old sod got his own back on me. Popped his clogs early last year. Left the farm to me, but all the rents go to my sister. I'd signed on for twenty-two years and, ironically, they were up at around the time the old man went. Rather than extending my service, had to resign my commission and come back here. Couldn't afford to put a farm manager in, you see.'

'I see,' said James.

'Old place needs one hell of a lot of money spending on it. He rather let things slide as he got older. There's a little in the farm account that'll cover some of the repairs, but nowhere near enough to do all that needs doing.' The drinks arrived and they thanked Jill.

'Is your sister not willing to let you have any of the rent money?'

'Problem with her – she's so damned difficult to pin down. Works in IT, like you. Lives in London. All I keep getting from her is how expensive she finds it, living up there.'

'Does she get down here often?'

'Hadn't been anywhere near for months and months after the old man died, but now she comes down most weekends, not that I see a lot of her. Usually arrives on Fridays around seven. We have supper together and then she's out again by eight. That's what happened last night. Shan't see her again now until Monday breakfast, after which she'll be heading straight back to London.' He paused. 'To be brutally honest, we're not that close – never have been – never really got on that well.'

'It sounds from what you say as if she might have a boyfriend living locally.'

'Think she very well might have. Often heard her on the phone, talking to someone she calls "Mal".'

'I'd have thought she must be getting a pretty good salary, though.' James said. 'There's money to be made in IT in London.'

'Not exactly true in her case. Fair bit younger than me, you see, and when she came down from university she took a series of jobs on short-term contracts. So happened that one of these short-term jobs had just finished when the old man threw a birthday party for her here, just before he died. She got chatting to Uncle Tom – Tom Rider – not a real uncle – old friend of the old man's.'

'Uncle Tom!' *Rebecca called from the lounge as she looked through the open door to the hall and saw him arrive. She ran into the hall, her high heels click-clacking on the tiles. She threw her arms round the small, rotund man with a shock of white curly hair who was standing there, beaming at her.*

'I'm so pleased you could come!' *she said, releasing him from her hug.* 'It wouldn't be the same celebrating my birthday without you being here! How are you getting on?' *she asked.* 'I haven't seen you since poor Auntie Penelope's funeral.'

'Oh, I'm managing,' *Uncle Tom replied.* 'I had a few disasters in the kitchen early on, but most of what I cook now comes under the heading of "edible". But let's look at you.' *He put his hands on her shoulders and admired her dark bobbed hair, highlights glinting in the late afternoon sun that streamed in through the open front door.*

'Lovely little black dress!' *he exclaimed. She twirled round.*

'Daddy bought it for me, specially for today!' *she said.* 'Let me get you a drink. What would you like?'

'A G and T would go down rather well, I think.' *Rebecca disappeared in the direction of the drinks table as Tom Rider walked into the lounge. There was quite a crowd there, some of whom he knew vaguely. Andrew spotted him and came over.*

'So glad you could come, Uncle Tom. Beccy's always been so fond of you.'

'I can remember bouncing her on my knee when she was a tot. How she laughed!'

'Can I get you a drink?' *At that moment Rebecca reappeared with Tom's gin and tonic.*

'Ah, I see you're already taken care of.'

It was well after eleven o'clock and most of the guests had gone. Tom and Rebecca, both surprisingly sober, were sitting at the table in the dining room.

'So what are you doing with yourself now?' Tom asked.

'Well, nothing at the moment, Uncle Tom. My last contact finished a couple of weeks ago.'

'You've nothing else in the pipeline?'

'Not really. No.'

'Bright girl, like you – you won't be without work for long, I'm sure.'

'I don't know, Uncle Tom. All I've managed to get since I left university are short-term contracts, and even those seem to be drying up.'

'What? Even for a graduate?'

'Yes, well, I was a bit disappointed with my degree.'

'What did you get?'

'Only a two-two, I'm afraid. I really wanted to stay on and do my Master's but I needed a two-one, at least, for that. None of these contract jobs have been really fulfilling, if you know what I mean. They're not the sort of thing I really want to do.'

'And what sort of thing is that?'

'Well, finance, but not in a general way. My thesis was all about various ways of using IT to try to predict what world stock markets were going to do in the future.'

'And there's nothing out there in that line?'

'Doesn't seem to be at the moment.' Tom was silent, looking past Rebecca. She knew from experience that he did this when he was thinking.

'I've got an idea,' he said, at last. 'Just an idea at the moment, you understand, but let me run it past you and see what you think about it. If it works out it could be advantageous for both of us.'

'I'm all ears, Uncle Tom!'

'Well, since Penny died – as I said – I'm managing, but I'm finding I get bored. I need to get involved with something. But that's only part of it. You see, I had some money invested that I intended to use to keep us in fine style during our retirement, but a lot of it went on medical bills and nursing home fees during Penny's illness. I've got a bit left, but I could really do with using it to make a bit more.'

'So where do I come in?' Rebecca asked.

'We'd need to go into it in a bit more detail before we make a final decision, but this is my idea. You and I could go into partnership. I provide some money and you provide the expertise. You can have free rein to work on a computer program in your field that we can then sell. Being a small operation with reduced overheads, I think we might be able to undercut the big boys, don't you?'

'Oh, Uncle Tom!' Rebecca threw her arms round his neck and kissed him. 'It's a wonderful idea! I'm sure it would work.'

'It would mean, of course, that neither you nor I could take any salary until we'd sold the program. Would that be OK with you?'

'Oh yes. I've saved up some money while I've been working. It should be enough for me to live on for a while. But when we go to the market – we'll both be millionaires!'

'That's what I thought! I'll get my accountant to do some work to see how much I can afford to invest and I'll ring you as soon as I get the figures from him. In the meantime, I'll look for some premises to rent. I don't drive much these days, so they would need to be somewhere not too far from where I live in London.'

'That's OK. I'll get a flat.'

'I'll look round for one for you.' Tom raised his half-empty glass.

'Here's to a successful enterprise!' Rebecca did likewise. As their glasses chinked together, Andrew came into the dining room.

'Ah, there you are! And what cunning plans have you two been hatching?'

※

'Not long after that the old man shuffled off this mortal coil. Couple of months later she and Uncle Tom set up their business partnership. Of course, by that time, she'd got the income from the rents to live on, the jammy minx! Plus the new flat in London that Uncle Tom had found for her. Then she went to some conference or other somewhere down south. Hadn't seen hide nor hair of her since the funeral – just the odd text and the occasional phone call – usually when she wanted something sending on. Then after the conference, she suddenly started coming here every weekend.'

'What sort of business is it?' James asked.

'Don't really understand it. All a bit beyond me, this high level IT stuff. Far as I can gather, it's some sort of computer program. Attempts to predict future stock market movements.'

'I'm pretty sure there's some software out there already that will do all that. Of course, they're improving on it all the time. As with everything else, the really good programs are very expensive,' James volunteered.

'That's her point. Says she's come up with a sure-fire method of making a top-drawer program for less than half the going rate! Says once it's completed and tested, they can put it on the market. They'll be instant millionaires. Only then, she says, will she be in a position to help me out with the farm. Till then, I have to manage it on my own.'

'And when does she think all this is likely to happen?'

'That's just it! Doesn't seem to know. Every time I ask she says it'll be another few months. I tell you, James, I'm not at all sure I can wait that long. I'm really not. Already had people on the phone offering to buy up land for housing. There's a few acres close to the village that I'm damned sure I'd get planning permission for.' He paused. 'But that will definitely be the last of all last resorts,' he said. 'Can't just throw away generations of family tradition. Although I hate damned farming, it'd be like betraying the ancestors.'

James could see that Andrew, battle-hardened soldier that he was, was about to get a little emotional. 'Look, why don't we finish these and then you can show me round your farm?'

Andrew brightened a little at this prospect. They downed their pints and left the pub.

As they walked round the farm, James asked, 'Do you live here alone, Andrew? Any wife or significant other to keep you company?'

'Was married,' Andrew replied, 'soon after I joined the regiment. Girl from the next village, as a matter of fact. Did a bit to get me back in the old man's good books – good county stock, you understand. Just the sort of wife he thought a gentleman farmer ought to have.'

'She's not around any more?' James ventured.

'No. Got back from a tour in Northern Ireland to find that she'd been inviting one of my brother officers to share the marital bed on a more or less regular basis while I'd been away.'

'Oh, I see.'

'Yes. When it all came out he was afraid I was going to go after him and knock his block off.'

'And were you?'

'Well, when I first found out – yes! Pretty livid, I can tell you! I was in love with the damned girl! But afterwards, when I'd calmed down a bit, I thought, "Takes two to tango." She was at least as much to blame as him. Obvious, even to me, she was far fonder of him than me. So, gradually came to terms with the situation and decided it'd be better for all concerned if I handled it with a bit of dignity. Finished up, all three of us, having a drink in the officer's mess – gave them my blessing.'

'That was very noble of you.'

'Yes, well, what I haven't told you is … he was the Regimental Middleweight Boxing Champion!'

'Ah!'

'After that, became "married to the Regiment", as they say. Threw myself into the job, and gradually forgot about her. Since I've been back here, been far too concerned with this blasted farm business to even think about looking at a woman, let alone taking one out on a date.'

The body

A s he walked back up the lane to *Aurora*, James could understand why Andrew was so depressed. He was lucky. He had Laura and Gemma. He had a job he loved – well, most of the time – and a comfortable lifestyle. Andrew had none of these. All he seemed to have was a farm where most of the buildings were an utter shambles and nearly all the machinery was old and rusting and appeared to be on its last legs. He had suggested to him the possibility of taking a loan, but Andrew had replied that without the income from the rents he was not sure, even with his Army pension, whether he would be able to service a sufficiently large loan to enable him to carry out what was so obviously necessary to get the farm up to standard. He had not even got a good relationship with his sister, his only remaining family.

James realised that he had spent the whole day talking. His plans to set off for a few days on *Aurora* on his own had got nowhere.

'Ah well! It won't take me long to put these few bits of shopping away,' he reasoned. 'It's going to be a lovely evening. I'll see how far I can get before it gets dark.' He walked along the lane to the canal bridge, enjoying the peace and tranquillity of the sun-drenched afternoon.

As he approached the bridge the silence was shattered by the sound of a boat engine being revved repeatedly. He walked down onto the towpath and saw a hire boat firmly aground on an underwater obstruction on the approach to the bridge. The hapless steerer, his face red and dripping with perspiration, was unsuccessfully trying to reverse his boat off it. The rest of his 'supportive' crew (his wife and their two boys) were gesticulating from various positions on the boat while offering 'helpful' advice.

'It won't budge!' he called out as James approached.

'Hang on!' James called back, and ran to *Aurora*. He returned with the long pole from the roof of his boat. Placing the end of the pole against the prow of the hire boat, he called out to the steerer to try reverse again. With James pushing with all his might, and the engine pulling at maximum power, slowly the boat eased away from the obstruction and the bow dropped down again into deeper water.

'You're never going to get past that – whatever it is – and neither's anybody else,' James called. 'Throw me a rope and I'll pull you into the side. You can tie up and we'll see what's causing the problem. I should think it's what I heard being dropped into the cut last night. The wash from the boats going past must have sucked whatever it is into the middle of the channel.' As he pulled the boat into the bank and tied it up, James went on to recount what had happened the previous night.

'Pass me your boathook,' James said. The man looked somewhat fazed for a moment, then picked up the boathook from the roof of his boat.

'Do you mean this?' he asked.

'That's it,' James replied, taking the hook from him. The woman and their young boys climbed off their boat, eager to watch what was happening. James stood on the bank near to where the obstruction was and began delving about in the water with the boathook. After a few seconds he caught hold of something. Whatever it was, it was too heavy for him to pull out of the water on his own. He managed to haul part of what appeared to be a roll of tarpaulin about two metres long up to the surface and towards the bank. He passed the boathook to the man.

'Can you hold it there?' he asked. 'I'll go and get my boathook and see if we can drag it out between us.' Using both hooks together, they managed to lift enough of the tarpaulin out of the water to grab it with their hands and pull it, dripping, onto the bank.

'What do you reckon it is?' the man asked.

'I thought it was just a piece of rolled-up tarpaulin at first,' James said, 'but by the look and feel of it I think there's something rolled up inside it.' There were two ropes tied round it and whoever had tied them had not intended them to be untied easily. They had been wound round several times and secured with a series of knots that had tightened as the bundle had been pulled onto the towpath.

They set about untying the knots. The other man managed to untie his rope first and began to unwrap his end of the tarpaulin.

'Oh, my God!' he gasped, standing up quickly. Clasping one hand to his stomach and the other over his mouth, he crouched at the edge of the water, retching. His wife made a move towards him. James looked up. He looked again at the unfurled tarpaulin and was aghast at what he saw.

'Get the kids back on the boat!' he yelled. The woman looked confused.

'Just do it!' he shouted as he pushed her towards the children.

She quickly shepherded the unwilling, protesting boys back into the cabin.

'We'll let your dad sort it out,' she said as she closed the doors on the complaining boys. James noticed that she had thoughtfully pulled the curtains as well. The man was still kneeling, shivering in horror, on the bank. Cautiously, James again lifted a corner of the untied end of the tarpaulin – and found himself staring into the lifeless green eyes of a young woman.

Two hours later he and the other man, whose name, it transpired, was Dave, were sitting in the foyer of the nearest police headquarters and waiting for a lift back to their boats in a police car. They had both made statements, James's including details of the incident with the Beetle the previous night. Two policeman came into the foyer.

'Right, gentlemen,' said one of them. 'If you'd like to come with us, we'll get you back to the canal. We've just had a message to say that the scene of crime people have finished their work and the body has been removed.'

They muttered their thanks and followed the officers out to the car park. As they were leaving the building, James noticed an ancient grey Jaguar arriving. It came to a halt, and out of it stepped Andrew.

'Hang on a sec,' James said to the policemen and walked over to him.

'What are you doing here?' he asked. Andrew looked ashen.

'Been a body fished out of the cut. They think it might be Rebecca – my sister. Asked me to come and identify the body.' Andrew stood motionless, staring at James. 'Can't be, can it?' His tone was pathetic, childlike.

'Oh God!' James turned to the policemen. 'Look, take Dave back. He needs to get back to his wife and kids. I'll get a lift later on with my friend, here.' He took hold of Andrew's arm and went back with him into the police station.

James resumed his seat in the foyer while Andrew was taken through to the mortuary. He reappeared about ten minutes later looking even more ashen, if that were possible. He was followed by a policeman.

'Thank you, Major Knight.'

'That's OK. Has to be done, I suppose.'

'Yes, it does, I'm afraid. I am sorry. Er ... you're not planning to be away at all over the next few days, are you, sir?'

'No. Why?'

'Well, we may need to talk to you at some stage ... eliminate you from the enquiry.'

'Oh, I see. No. Be at home at least until the end of next week.'

'Thank you, sir.'

James and Andrew left the building and walked to the Jaguar.

'Are you OK?' James asked. 'It was your sister, wasn't it?'

'Yes. Yes, it was. I'm OK. Just a bit of a shock ... seeing her there...' His voice tailed off.

'I guess it must be,' James agreed.

During the drive back they were both quiet, wrapped in their own thoughts – James of what he had witnessed on the canal bank, Andrew of what he had witnessed in the mortuary. Both men shuddered inside, shocked to the core. When they approached the junction where the lane to the canal left the main road to the village, Andrew finally spoke.

'Don't know about you, old man,' he said, 'but I could do with a stiff scotch! Care to join me? Still don't know what you were doing at the police station.'

'Stop the car a moment,' James said. Andrew obliged and pulled over. James turned in his seat to face him. 'I was there because I heard Rebecca's body being dumped in the cut last night,' he said, quietly. He paused. 'And I helped fish her out this afternoon,' he added. Andrew did not reply, his mind frozen by the events of the last few hours.

It was only later, as they sat in the lounge of the farmhouse, nursing their drinks, that the words began to tumble out.

'Look, James, old man, I've got an awfully big favour to ask you.'

'Ask away.'

'I know we've only just met up again and I know I only knew you a bit while we were at Hurst's. But I feel I can trust you. Like it or not, you're a part of this whole sorry mess.' He paused, trying to think of the right words.

'I wonder … do you think you could possibly do a bit of digging around … a bit of detective-type work? Do you think you could try and find out what happened to poor Rebecca?'

James was taken aback. 'What?'

'I mean, I know she and I never saw eye to eye on anything much, but she didn't deserve this, poor girl.' James opened his mouth to speak, but Andrew continued. 'You see – thing is … I think I may have, inadvertently, managed to point the proverbial finger of suspicion in my direction.'

'How?'

'Happened to mention to that CID chappy that Beccy and I had an almighty, blazing row just before she went out last Friday evening.'

'Oh, I see. What was the row about?'

'Same thing we always row … rowed about – the blasted rent money! Money I need to get this godforsaken place back on its feet!' Andrew stared at his glass and lapsed again into silence.

❋

'Oh, for God's sake, Andy! Can't you ever talk about anything else besides the damned farm?' Andrew and Rebecca were washing up after supper on Friday evening.

'Actually, Beccy, no, I can't. Constantly on my mind. Millstone round my neck!'

'I can't see what you're so bothered about. It looks all right to me.' Rebecca placed the last plate in the rack, emptied the washing up bowl and removed her Marigolds.

'And what would you know about it? You waltz in here on a Friday evening. Have a bite of supper and you're off out again. Don't see you again till you show up for breakfast on Monday, after which you shoot off again, back to London. When did you last go out in the fields?

When did you last walk round the yard, even? Eh? And while we're at it, where do you disappear to every Friday night?'

'That's my business! My private life is nothing to do with you!'

'Off seeing some fancy man, are we? Someone with plenty of cash – not that you haven't got plenty already!'

'Look, Andy. Daddy left the money to me because I was here for him after Mummy died. I did a damned sight more for him than you ever did then when he needed someone.'

'Always his favourite, weren't you? Ever since we were kids.'

'Have you ever stopped to wonder why? I was always around when he needed me. I dropped everything and came down from uni every time Mummy was ill, didn't I? Did you ever come anywhere near? No, you didn't! Not until she died. Then, of course, you swanned in and took over all the funeral arrangements. Poor Daddy and I never got a look in.'

'Only did that because it was something I knew about. Been involved in sorting out funerals for some of my men. Only wanted to save you and him from the worry of it all.'

'But did you stay on after the funeral when Daddy needed you most? No, you didn't! On the day after the funeral you went off playing soldiers somewhere!'

Andrew was incensed. He put down the cup he was drying and glared at her. 'Playing soldiers? Playing soldiers? Only risking my bloody neck patrolling the streets of Belfast. That's all! Playing soldiers, indeed!'

'I didn't mean ...'

Andrew interrupted her. 'Came damned close to having my brains blown out on more than one occasion.'

'I...'

He cut her off again. 'Just think, Beccy. If I'd been killed out there you wouldn't be sitting so pretty now, would you?'

'What do you mean?'

'Wouldn't be able to go off, enjoying the high life in London. You'd be stuck here with this place.'

'Well, I'm not, am I? You survived, so the farm is your problem – as you never tire of telling me!'

'Just as a matter of interest, what would you have done?'

'That's easy! I'd have sold the whole lot to the highest bidder.'

'What? And let all the work of six generations of our family go to someone else?'

'What does that matter to me? It's all history. It's all in the past – the past, where you seem to be determined to live your miserable life!'

Neither of them spoke for a few minutes. Andrew put the last of the dishes away and slammed the cupboard door. Rebecca inspected her freshly varnished nails to ensure they had come to no harm in the rubber gloves. Andrew turned to her.

'Don't suppose you still have any idea when this project of yours is going to come to fruition, have you? When I can get my hands on the pot of gold you've been promising me so I can get this place sorted out?'

'And what will you do with it when you've got it? You'll get this farm working. You'll be just like Daddy was – continually worrying about the weather! Praying that you'll get a decent harvest.'

'Farming's always been weather-dependent.'

'So why not do something different? Something new and exciting – like I'm doing? But no, you won't, of course. You'll carry on doing what – what did you say? What six generations of Knights have always done. You've spent too long in the Army, obeying orders, to have any original ideas of your own!'

'Well, that's just where you're wrong! Lots of new things I want to try.'

'Like what?'

'Something in Lower Field, for instance.'

'Which one's that?'

Andrew frowned, exasperated at her lack of knowledge. 'The one by the canal,' he said, as he would talk to small child. 'Never been any good for growing much and the grazing doesn't support more than a couple of nags.'

'So? What's the big new idea?'

'A marina.'

'A marina? What – for boats?'

'Of course! What else?' He raised his eyes heavenward. 'This canal is a branch – not that that means much to you either,' he continued, his voice loaded with contempt. 'Comes to a dead end after about

twelve miles, so it doesn't get much use. A marina on Lower Field would increase the traffic and benefit the businesses in the village.'
Rebecca was dumbfounded.

'What's the matter?' Andrew asked. 'Cat got your tongue?'

'No... No, I'm just amazed that you've come up with an idea that doesn't involve either agriculture or shooting people!'

'Right. So as I have come up with something – what was your phrase? "New and exciting." Any chance of getting my hands on some funds to make it a reality?'

'I've told you before.' Rebecca walked into the hall. 'It's going to take a few more months yet to finish and test the software.'

'Months? Last weekend you said weeks.' Andrew followed her, a towering presence behind her tiny frame.

'After the software's done, we've got to work out a marketing strategy and then we've got to sell it. So it will be months.'

'Meanwhile, I have to try to manage this place on peanuts! Why can't you let me have just a little of the money he left you.'

'I've told you the answer to that so many times, but you just don't listen, Andrew Knight! You know I can't take any money out of the business yet. I need Daddy's money to pay my rent and to live and to run my car.'

'In the meantime, you just make a convenience of this place. Come down and meet your fancy man at weekends!'

'Oh, for fuck's sake, Andy!' she screamed, picking up her handbag. 'Change the bloody record, will you!' She stormed out, slamming the front door behind her. A few seconds later he heard her car start and set off, with a grinding of gravel, down the drive. He went into the lounge and poured himself a large scotch.

✳

The investigation

' A nd you told the police all this?' James asked.
'Have a way with their questions, don't they? Have a way of wheedling stuff out of you. Stuff you never intended telling them. Asked me when I saw her last and I told him about eight

o'clock, Friday evening. Then he asked me about her state of mind at the time.'

'So you had to tell him about the argument?'

'Yes. You heard what he said. Don't want me to leave here until they've had another chance to talk to me. So I'm stuck here, but you're not. So? Think you could do a bit of private detective work for me?'

'I don't know, Andrew. I'm a games software writer, not a policeman!'

'I know that. But when all's said and done, those games you write – all about a private eye chappy, aren't they? Have to know about the trail, the clues, the murder – or you can't write the stories.'

James said nothing.

'Look here, old man!' Andrew stood up and drained his glass. His face was pale. His hands were shaking. 'I'm bloody desperate! Far as they're concerned I've got the motive and I had the opportunity. Knowing the local force, they probably won't even bother to look any further! Treat it as an open and shut case and charge me with murder! Afraid I'm getting a bit of a reputation round here as a grumpy old bugger with a chip on his shoulder!'

'I'm sure it won't come to that.'

'I am! They'll think that the row we had on Friday night was enough to push me over the edge. Please, old man! Help your old skipper out … if only for old time's sake!'

James thought for a moment. For a few seconds, in his mind, he was back in the changing room at Hurst's School. 'OK, Andrew,' he said. 'I'll do what I can.'

'Good man!' He shook James's hand warmly. 'And thank you!'

'I guess we'd better start by having a look at her room here.'

'Good place to begin,' Andrew agreed, as he led him upstairs.

'This is … was hers.' Andrew opened a door, then put his hands firmly into his pockets. James glanced at him.

'Fingerprints, old man!' he said. 'If they take mine and then look up here? Don't want to give them any more ammunition.'

James was not expecting to find much in her room since she spent so little time at the farm. Neither had he any clear idea of what he was looking for. 'Something out of place, I suppose,' he thought, 'but what?'

The bed cover, the curtains and the seat of the dressing table stool were all pink. Covering his hand with his handkerchief, he looked in the wardrobe and searched the chest of drawers, but found only clothes and a few knick-knacks. Then he turned his attention to the dressing table and sat on the stool. The drawers contained nothing of interest and he was about to get up and leave when a bottle of perfume caught his eye. Having spent many hours loitering at perfume counters with Laura while she tried out numerous scents, James considered himself something of an authority, but this was one he had never seen before. He picked it up with his handkerchief-covered hand. The bottle was heart shaped and in ruby-red-coloured glass. It was called 'L'Esprit de Nancy'.

'Never seen this one before,' he said.

'Ah yes,' Andrew said. 'One of her little foibles. Can't get it in this country. Came across it on a holiday in France a couple of years ago. Once she discovered it, refused to wear anything else. Ordered it specially over the internet.'

Avoiding touching it with his fingers, James unscrewed the top and sniffed. 'Very nice!' he said. 'Very distinctive.' He screwed the cap back on and replaced the bottle. 'Where do you think we should go from here?'

'Guess her place in London might be the best bet, don't you? You can take my car. Might be an idea to go to the office where she was working with Tom Rider, too. I'll write the addresses down for you.'

James looked at his watch as they went downstairs. He was surprised how quickly he had acquiesced to Andrew's suggestion. He enjoyed a good murder as much as anyone – but only in his imagination, as TechnoTec – not the real thing!

'This is all moving a bit too quickly!' he thought. 'Solving murders on a computer is one thing, but it's a bit different in real life!'

'If I get going now I should get to London before midnight,' he found himself saying. Andrew went to his study, reappeared with a notepad and pen and began writing.

'When I get there,' James asked, 'do you want me to break in? Or did she leave any house keys here?'

'Well, actually, yes, she did,' Andrew smiled weakly. 'Although she was brilliant with her computer stuff, she was a bit of a scatterbrain in many other ways. There's a ring of spare keys to her flat and her car in the drawer in the hall table. Insisted on her keeping them there because she was forever misplacing hers.' Andrew took the keys from the drawer and gave them to James along with the note of the addresses. Then he felt in his pocket.

'My car keys.' He passed them over. 'Think it might be useful if you can get there before the police start snooping around.'

'I agree. I doubt they'll be onto it yet, though. They'll have to get a search warrant signed by a magistrate first. I don't need any such formalities!' James stood up and went towards the door. He suddenly stopped and turned to Andrew. 'Oh, incidentally, Andrew, what type of car did Rebecca drive?'

'Volkswagen Beetle – painted yellow.' James felt his heart drop to the pit of his stomach. He left, closing the door on Andrew, who was sitting on the stairs with his head in his hands, exhausted.

James's mind was in a whirl as he set off towards London.

'What the hell would TechnoTec do?' he asked himself. The journey took longer than he thought. Road works and a pile-up on the motorway meant that it was after midnight by the time he reached Tottenham.

He decided that it might arouse suspicion if he went to Rebecca's flat after dark so he drew into a travel hotel and checked in for the night. He rang Andrew, telling him he would search the flat first thing in the morning, then he sent Laura a text message. He lied to her. Realising that she may well see something on the television news about the murder, once the media got hold of the story, he told her that *Aurora* was now part of a crime scene and he could not move her until the police gave him permission. 'So much for my week's cruising!' he concluded his message.

'No point in getting her worried!' he thought.

Reasoning that if he made his visit early in the morning when most of her neighbours would be enjoying a Sunday morning lie in, he left the hotel at half past six and drove to Rebecca's flat. It was not a particularly salubrious street – not in the expensive area she had led her brother to believe. Her address was in a block of small Victorian terraced houses, most of which had been converted into tiny flats. James parked the Jaguar a little further along the street, put on a pair of gloves and walked back to the front door. It had once been painted white, but was now a dirty grey and the paint was peeling. There were three names against three bell pushes. Knight was printed neatly on a small card against number three. Taking Rebecca's keys from his pocket he inserted one in the lock and turned it. The door opened and he let himself in quietly. He stood in the dim, dingy hall and listened. Silence.

'Good!' he murmured. 'Everyone must still be in the Land of Nod.' He looked at the door to his left. It had a white plastic number 1 screwed to it, and on another straight ahead were the remains of a broken number 2.

'Number three must be upstairs,' he thought, as he carefully climbed the bare treads of the staircase. At the top he was faced by two doors. One had a number 3 on it while the other had nothing. He tried the anonymous one first. The door was unlocked and he opened it to reveal a bathroom, which appeared to be shared by all the tenants. It was certainly not sparkling and there was evidence of damage caused by dampness on the walls and ceiling. A quick look revealed nothing personal to Rebecca, so James closed the door and inserted the other key from Rebecca's ring into door number three.

He found himself in a small lounge. The flat had obviously been rented furnished. There were two small leather armchairs facing a wall-mounted gas fire with a low coffee table between them. A small drop-leaf table stood, folded, in the window with two dining chairs in front of it. A mahogany sideboard with a glass fruit bowl on it took up most of one wall and in one corner was a small kitchenette with a sink, a tiny fridge and microwave oven.

'Rather more charity shop than John Lewis!' he thought. She had, however, left everything clean and tidy.

James went through the door into the bedroom. There was a three-quarter width bed – again covered in pink – a wardrobe, an ancient tallboy and an equally ancient dressing table on which stood another bottle of 'L'Esprit de Nancy'. He looked through the drawers of the dressing table, but found nothing of interest. The same was true of the wardrobe. The drawers of the tallboy revealed nothing either, but in the cupboard he found a laptop and, next to it, a small, hand-held recording machine.

'I'll see what's on there later,' he thought as he dropped it into his pocket. He turned his attention to the laptop. He carried it through to the lounge and sat in one of the armchairs. He placed the machine on the coffee table and booted it up.

'Damn!' he whispered as a screen appeared requesting a password. He tried a number of obvious words, all to no avail. He was about to close the laptop and take it away with him when he noticed a small framed photograph on the mantelshelf. It was a picture of a bright yellow Volkswagen Beetle. On the off chance he typed in 'beetle' – still nothing. Then he noticed the registration number. Copying from the photograph, he keyed in 'REK612M'.

'Bingo!'

The screen came to life! He felt a little guilty as he scrolled through her emails, stopping occasionally to read those he thought might be of help. He felt he was prying into the private business of the dead, but there was nothing to assist him in his enquiry. The remainder of her files revealed nothing either. He was about to switch off when he noticed that she had a diary icon on her desktop. He clicked on it. Rebecca's past life unfolded before his eyes. One thing struck him immediately. On most Fridays in recent weeks there was an entry that read, '20.00 Mal'.

'So that's the boyfriend!' he said to himself. He remembered Andrew had said he had heard her on the telephone to someone she called Mal. He paged back over the weeks to see when the relationship had begun. In the week before the first of the Friday evening assignations there was an entry on two consecutive days that read 'Conference. Swindon. "IT and the Future of Futures"'. Taking from his pocket the empty flash drive he had thoughtfully brought with him, he copied all the data he thought would be useful, then switched off the laptop and replaced it in the tallboy. Checking he had left everything as he had found it, he went out of the flat, carefully locking the doors behind him.

'Well,' he thought as he made his way back to the car, 'TechnoTec would be proud of you!'

As he was unlocking the car door a text message came through on his phone. It was Laura, sympathising with his situation.

'Yeah, right, love!' he thought. 'If only you knew!'

Sitting behind the wheel, he tried to analyse exactly what he had achieved and what else he needed to do. He had confirmed that the reason why Rebecca had been visiting the farm every weekend was that she was seeing a man and that the man was known as Mal. From that he deduced that this Mal must live either in or somewhere close to the village. He then remembered Andrew saying that she had begun her visits shortly after attending a conference 'down south somewhere'. That tallied with the information on her computer about the futures conference in Swindon.

'There must be a link of some sort,' he thought. 'I might find out what it is at her office.'

He consulted the piece of paper Andrew had given him and was about to set off for the office address when he noticed a police car in his rear view mirror. It stopped outside Rebecca's flat. Two officers got out and approached the front door.

'Crikey, they moved fast!' he thought. 'I got out of there just in time!' He sighed with relief as he pulled away.

He encountered some difficulty in locating the office, but he eventually parked outside what appeared to be a hardware shop. As it was Sunday he did not expect to be able to get into the office, only to discover its location so that he could drive straight there the following day. However, as he sat in the car he spotted movement in one of the upstairs windows. Getting out of the car, he noticed a door to the side of the shop with a sign showing an arrow pointing upwards. The sign read 'Knight Rider – Specialist Software'.

He locked the car and went in through the door. As he climbed his second flight of bare, well-worn stairs of the day, he was again surprised by the dinginess of the surroundings. The office was not the salubrious suite that Andrew had inferred from what Rebecca had told him. The only door at the top of the stairs stood ajar, the name 'Knight Rider' repeated on a sign on it. James knocked and entered. An elderly man, who was stacking papers into a box, looked up.

'Yes?' he enquired sharply.

'Mr Rider?'

'Yes. Who are you?'

'Oh, hello, Mr Rider. My name's James Wade. I'm a friend of Andrew Knight, Rebecca's brother.'

'Ah! Poor Andrew! Couldn't believe it when he rang me last night. It's terrible! Just terrible! Just Friday morning she was sitting at her desk in the other office, working away on our project. And now … now…' His voice tailed off.

'Yes. I'm afraid I never met Rebecca.'

'Lovely girl! Lovely … and very clever with this IT business. I knew her father too.'

'What will you do? Look for someone else to carry on her work?'

'I don't know – it's early days yet! At the moment I haven't got the heart to continue with it. You see, it was very much our project – Rebecca's and mine. It wouldn't seem right working on it with anyone else. But we'll see. We'll see.' He sat down at his desk with a sigh and indicated to James to take the other empty swivel chair.

'I've known Beccy since she was a little girl – well, all her life, really. I've watched her grow up. Arthur, her father – he and I were great friends. We used to go shooting together. We had some wonderful times! Of course, he spoiled her absolutely rotten, did Arthur. In his eyes, she could do no wrong. Not like poor Andrew! That was a completely different story, there. He never did see eye to eye with his father. You see, he and Arthur, they were too much alike – quick, bombastic and hasty. That just about sums them both up.

'Well, I'd always dabbled in bits of business. I have a private income, so I don't need to work, although, I have to say, my late wife's medical bills and nursing home fees left me a bit short of where I wanted to be.

'Anyway, to cut a long story short, Arthur threw a party for her thirtieth birthday. I was invited and she and I got chatting. I'm no computer buff, but she was telling me about her IT degree and what she wanted to do with it. Well, I needed something to get my teeth into as well. So I rented this office and we got started. We got along really fine. I enjoyed her company and she seemed to me to be a good worker, full of ideas that I couldn't understand! Then I happened to see this ad in the *FT* for a conference – Swindon, I think it was. It was all to do with something about identifying trends in the stock market. When I suggested that I should pay for her to go on it she jumped at the chance. Anyway, it seemed at the time that it was money well spent because when she came back from the conference she said she had an idea. She was so enthusiastic about it! She said she was absolutely certain that we would be able to make our mark in the financial software market and earn ourselves a great deal of money into the bargain. She started work on it in earnest. The only thing that bothered me was that she seemed to be going through the budget rather quickly.

Sitting at his desk, Tom Rider looked at his watch. It was a couple of minutes before two o'clock.

'Beccy will be back from lunch soon,' he thought. She always took a two-hour lunch break on Thursdays, taking the tube into town to go shopping. Right on cue, he heard the clatter of her high heels on the stairs.

'Hi, Uncle Tom! I'm back!' She breezed into his office, with three carrier bags emblazoned with the names of the more expensive clothes stores.

'Hello, Beccy. Been buying more clothes, I see.'

'Yes. Well, I shall need to look my best when I do the marketing pitch, shan't I?'

'You will, I agree. But when is that going to happen? I mean, I know you're working hard on it, but I don't seem to see a lot of progress.'

'Oh, Uncle Tom!' She sat down. 'Look, I've told you before. There's no point in me explaining everything that I'm doing and how far I've got to you, is there? You've said often enough yourself that you don't understand computers and software and things, haven't you? Just trust me.'

'I do, Beccy, I do. It just seems to me that, at the moment, we're spending money like water and I don't seem to be seeing anything for it – other than additions to your wardrobe!'

'I know it must seem like that, but this is the hard part. This is the part where we need to make the investment – my time and your money. But soon – well – a few months, or even weeks, probably, I'll have made the breakthrough. And then we'll have the good part when the money you're spending now will be paid back a hundred-fold. Believe me!'

'Alright, Beccy. Carry on. But you'll let me know when there are any, what you might call, major developments?'

'Of course I will, Uncle Tom! Don't worry.' She stood up, kissed him on the top of his curly white hair and went into her office.

❋

'So I trusted her and let her get on with it.'

'That's a similar line to the one she spun Andrew!' James thought. 'Have the police been in touch with you at all?' he asked.

'Not so far.' James was relieved.

'Look, Mr Rider, Andrew's asked me to do a bit of looking around to find out a bit about what she was up to. Do you mind if I take a look round her office?'

'Help yourself. Whatever you find, it can't hurt anyone now, can it?'

'I guess not. Thank you.' James went through to Rebecca's office. It was sparsely decorated with nothing on the walls except a calendar supplied by the hardware shop downstairs. Rebecca had done little to personalise it. James thought how plain it looked for a young girl. He knew how the girls at Gamez-Inc liked to surround their workstations with photographs and other bits and pieces. He thought back to Rebecca's bedroom with its pink covers and feminine knick-knacks.

'Bit of a contrast,' he thought.

There was a desk with a computer on it and a printer on top of a two-drawer filing cabinet. He went through the desk drawers but found nothing of interest – a shorthand pad with a few doodles on it, a list of telephone numbers, mostly relating to suppliers, some pens, a photograph of an older man, whom James thought must be her father. There was also a half-empty bottle of 'L'Esprit de Nancy'. He took out the pad and closed the drawer. He riffled through the pages – nothing. Well, nothing obvious, anyway. He decided to take it with him, just in case.

He turned his attention to the filing cabinet. It was locked. But he remembered seeing a key in the top drawer of the desk. He tried it and it fitted. The bottom drawer was empty and the top one contained a few files, which he removed. There was also a glossy folder, the front of which bore the legend 'IT and the Future of Futures'. It then gave the dates and the name of a hotel not far from Swindon. He added this to the shorthand pad. Finally, he turned and faced the PC on the desk. It was password protected like her laptop, but he noticed that the same photograph of her car was also sitting on the desk. He typed in the registration number and the computer sprang to life.

'Either she was inordinately fond of her car, or it was the only way she could remember her password,' James mused. 'Come to think of it, Andrew did say something about her being a bit forgetful.'

He looked at some of her recently opened documents. Some were spreadsheets and word documents, but what caught James's eye was another file. It contained a number of pages covered with rows and rows of computer code. He took out his flash drive and copied them across.

'I have absolutely no idea what all that is, but it's certainly not a game!' he mused as he printed them off and put them with the files. Picking up his pile of files and papers, he walked back through to the other room to where Rider was still packing boxes.

'Just keeping busy,' Rider said, looking up.

'It's strange,' James thought. 'Why does he want to pack up the office so quickly? Why would he come in on a Sunday morning? She's only been dead a couple of days.'

'Do you think I could possibly pinch one of those boxes, please?' he asked.

'The empty ones are behind you. Grab one, by all means.'

James put the files and papers into one of the empty boxes and told Rider what he had taken.

'Look, Mr Rider,' he added, 'if the police do come round here asking questions, there's no need to say anything about my visit. OK?'

'Never seen you!' he agreed. 'Anything to help you to find out how poor Beccy died. Give my condolences to poor Andrew, won't you?' James nodded as he shook Tom Rider's hand and made to leave.

'Oh, Mr Wade!' Rider called him back. 'I don't suppose anything's been done about a funeral yet?'

'Not as far as I know, Mr Rider.'

'I thought it was a bit early. It's just that I need to book my train ticket. I don't drive any distance these days.'

James left to drive back to Andrew's house.

The arrest

Having skipped breakfast, he stopped at a service area for lunch on his return journey.

'This detective business is hungry work!' he thought as he tucked into his plate of ham and chips. The ring of his mobile disturbed him. He answered it.

'James Wade.'

'Oh, good afternoon, Mr Wade.' It was a woman's voice. 'My name's Jessica Loftus. I'm Andrew Knight's solicitor.'

'Oh yes.'

'Mr Knight asked me to contact you to let you know that the police took him in for questioning this morning.'

'What? But how … why?' James was incredulous. He dropped his fork, which clattered to the floor.

'They've interviewed him. They're saying that he had the motive – something about rental income to save the farm? He also had the opportunity as Rebecca was there for the weekend. Then, of course, he'd already admitted that they'd had an argument on Friday evening.' James remembered Andrew saying the same things when he had asked for his help.

'But … aren't they going to investigate it any further?' he managed to splutter out.

'It doesn't look that way at the moment, even though the only evidence they have is purely circumstantial,' Jessica said. 'They're holding him overnight for further questioning. I've just got to my office. I need to check out a few details. Do you think you could come straight here?' She gave him the address.

'I'm on my way.'

On the drive back James reconsidered the events of the last twenty-four hours.

'It was strange,' he mused, 'that Andrew should have such a premonition about having his collar felt by the police. Is he more involved in this mess than he's letting on? He was so determined to get me investigating it that I can't think he could have killed his sister, and when he went to identify her body he was really cut up about it. Is he that good an actor? I doubt it.

'Then there's Tom Rider. Why was he so keen to clear out the offices so quickly? Is he getting so short of money he needs to save a month's rent? Rebecca was obviously spending more of his capital than he thought she should be, but could that be enough of a motive for murder? She and Rider had had words about money and he'd said he was concerned about her spending. But would that make him angry enough to want to kill her? Was that the only way he could see to stop her spending any more of his money?' He mulled the idea over. Had Rider bitten off more than he could chew financially?

'But if that were the case, why would her body be dumped in the canal outside the village? It's miles away from London.

'Of course!' he answered his own question. 'To divert suspicion away from him and implicate Andrew! All this stuff about not driving any more could be nothing but a smokescreen. He could easily have followed her from London on Friday evening in his car, and then lain in wait for her until she came out of the farmhouse. Then he could have got into her car with her on some pretext, persuaded her to drive somewhere quiet and stop for some reason, and then killed her. Then he could have driven to the canal, dropped the body over the bridge, gone back for his own car and driven back to London!' The more he thought about it the more plausible it seemed.

'But where is her car now?' He tried to think where Rider could have left it after disposing of her body. 'Come to that, where would Andrew have left it?'

As he drove on, his thoughts crystallised into their main points.

'There are two possible suspects that I know about. Andrew, who had both a motive and the opportunity. But I don't suspect him for a moment. I'm sure he probably killed a number of people during his days in the Army, but not his own sister, not in cold blood.

'Tom Rider, who may have had a motive and may have had the opportunity, but both are open to conjecture. He certainly gave the impression of being very fond of Rebecca, but was that a smokescreen too? I don't know him well enough to judge whether or not he is capable of murder.

'Or there's a third possibility. Someone else – person or persons unknown, as the police say. Maybe the mysterious Mal, whoever he might be! But, at this time, I have no way of knowing whether he had a motive or the opportunity.

'There are two crucial questions to which I need answers. One – something important obviously occurred at that conference in Swindon, so what was it? And two – the whereabouts of her car. God! I feel like a punter playing *TechnoTec* for the very first time!

When I've written it, I know where all the clues are and I know all the red herrings. Now I'm the punter. I've got to sort out the genuine clues from the ones that will lead me up blind alleys!

'Will the information I've copied from her computers tell me anything? Somehow, I doubt it.'

With these thoughts racing through his mind, he parked Andrew's car and walked to the solicitor's office. He rang the bell as he had been instructed and waited. The door was opened by a casually dressed woman in her early thirties.

'I'm Jessica Loftus,' she said, holding out her hand.

'James Wade,' he said, shaking it and smiling at the attractive woman. She led him upstairs to her office and invited him to take a seat.

'I'm sorry there's no coffee. The receptionist locks the kitchen!'

'That's OK,' James chuckled.

'Now,' she said, 'I understand from Mr Knight that you are – how did he put it – "looking around" on his behalf.'

'That's right,' James agreed and proceeded to give her a resumé of what he had found out. As he did so, she made notes of the salient points. He told her everything from the moment her had pulled Rebecca's body out of the canal to his conversation with Tom Rider.

'It seems to me you've been very thorough, Mr Wade.'

'Oh,' he said, 'it's James, please. There's no need for formality. It makes me feel old – Mr Wade's what they call my dad!' She laughed and they agreed to be on first-name terms.

'Here are Andrew's house keys,' she said, taking a bunch of keys from her desk drawer. 'He asked me to tell you you can use the house, his computer – everything – just to get the bottom of this affair. This is his password.' She handed James a folded sheet of paper.

'Right. Thanks.'

'There's nothing more I can do until tomorrow. Then they've got to either release him or charge him. If they charge him he'll be up before the magistrates in the morning. I'll ask for bail, of course. I'll ring you and let you know what happens.' James stood up to leave.

'Just to warn you,' Jessica said. 'When you go back to your boat, all the trappings of the media circus are gathered. There are TV cameras already set up at the farm and on the canal. The hacks are snooping around everywhere, crawling over the place looking for their angle. I guess it's the most excitement that sleepy little place has had in a long time!'

'Thanks for that,' said James, taking her business card and shaking her hand. He walked back to Andrew's car.

He saw the satellite dishes on the roofs of the media vans long before he arrived at the farm. Luckily, when Andrew had showed him round he had noticed a rough track leading to the rear of the house. He decided to make for that rather than go in through the front gate.

'Was that only yesterday?' The thought astounded him. So much had happened. When he passed the vans camped at the front of the farmhouse, he noticed a reporter leaning on the bonnet of one of them. As James drove past he saw him looking closely at the Jaguar, the registration number in particular. In his rear view mirror James saw him run to his car.

'Damn!' he said out loud. 'Must be one of the local boys. He's recognised the car and thinks I'm Andrew,' he thought. He revised his plan and decided to head back towards the village. As he slowed down for the twists and turns of the village streets he could see he was being tailed by the reporter's Clio. Even though he was not familiar with the area he knew he was going to have to drive the country lanes at speed to try to shake off his enthusiastic pursuer. He had two reasons why he did not want to talk to the reporter. First, he would have to convince him that he was not Andrew, and if he succeeded in that he would then have to explain what he was doing driving Andrew's car. Second, if he, or his name, or anything about what he was doing was mentioned on the television news, Laura would be sure to see it and be worried for him. As far as she knew he was confined to quarters aboard *Aurora*. He could not face having to explain everything to her at this stage. It was a risk he could not afford to take.

Once out of the village, he pressed the accelerator to the floor, only lifting off sufficiently to throw the trusty Jag into the sharper bends. The tyres squealed in his attempts to shake off the reporter.

His mind was racing as fast as the powerfully revving engine. He was 'TechnoTec'! He had written a car chase into the program so many times. Was this the buzz the gamesters got as they played it on their consoles? Squealing round bends and flat out on the straight?

Fortunately, the country lanes were not busy and he met few vehicles coming towards him. He checked his mirror. He was still being followed.

'Oh shit!' he muttered as the lapse in concentration caused him to run out of road on a tight bend. His offside wheels bumped along the grass verge. He accelerated onto a straight stretch – only to slam on his brakes again behind a tractor and trailer crawling along ahead of him at a snail's pace. Without checking his mirror he swung out to overtake. With his foot hard to the floor, he suddenly realised that he was heading, far too fast, towards a hump-backed canal bridge. He stamped on the brakes. The car slowed marginally but was still going too fast as it hit the gradient of the bridge with a deafening thump. The car dipped. The front bumper momentarily hit the road raising a shower of sparks. Then the car shot up to the crown of the bridge and continued upwards. All four wheels left the ground. The Jaguar was airborne! As though in slow motion, the car seemed to hang in the air. James braced himself for the inevitable landing. It came! The car landed on the other side of the bridge with a bone-jarring crunch and a further shower of sparks as the undercarriage made contact with the tarmac.

Amazingly, the ancient Jaguar kept going – with, seemingly, no ill effects.

'That didn't do your suspension much good, Andrew,' he thought.

He glanced again in the mirror. Nothing. There was a small

copse on his left. He flung the car round and onto the track that led into it. Once out of sight, he stopped the car and ran back towards the road, keeping in the cover of the trees. He could see the approach clearly without being seen himself, and waited. He did not have to wait long. The tractor trundled by with its load, followed by an agitated reporter, desperate to overtake.

He walked slowly back to the Jag, climbed in and patted the dashboard.

'Well done, old girl!' he said. 'A Clio's no match for an old Jag any day of the week!'

He looked down and noticed his hands were shaking. He was shocked by what he had just done. Why had he driven like a maniac to avoid the reporter? Why had he acted like TechnoTec, his creation? Why had he risked his life – and those of others too? Why did he need to get away? Why was he so scared of being interviewed? Why had he allowed himself to become involved deeper and deeper in this case? All for a man he barely knew! But he was convinced that he must help Andrew. Something in the back of his mind was spurring him on.

He waited a little longer in case the reporter realised he had been tricked – and to give his nerves a chance to calm down. He suddenly realised that he did not have a clue where he was. Luckily, on the back seat was a road atlas. From it he found that there was a road that ran almost parallel to the canal. It went from near the bridge he had just flown over and joined a lane that ran close to Andrew's farm. He turned the car round and made his way back at a rather more sedate pace.

He avoided the front of the Andrew's house and the gathered press pack. Instead, he headed for the track leading to the rear of the farmhouse. It was a circuitous route, but was hidden from the farmhouse by a high stone wall. Mercifully, the press had not realised where the track led. It ran slightly downhill as it approached the farmhouse, so James switched off the Jaguar's engine and let it glide to a halt in the farmyard.

'No point in announcing my arrival!' he thought, getting out of the car quietly. He noticed that all the curtains were still closed. 'They must have come for Andrew very early this morning. But that's a stroke of luck for me. If I keep quiet they won't know there's anyone here.' Picking up the files he had taken from Rebecca's office from the passenger seat, he unlocked the back door and went into the kitchen.

He carried the pile of files into the lounge and dropped them on a chair. He poured himself a drink and sat down in an armchair. Only then did he realise how exhausted he was.

'I guess the old adrenalin tap has just switched itself off!' He finished his drink, put his head back and nodded off.

When he awoke with a start about half an hour later, he could hear the media hacks chatting and joking outside.

'If I don't draw the curtains. They won't know I'm here,' he thought.

He turned his attention to the pile of files and began going through them systematically. Most of them contained nothing more than bills for the office from various suppliers. However, among them were also statements, reminders, final reminders, letters from debt collection agencies and even the odd threat of legal action.

'Was Rider really getting short of cash?' he wondered. 'Was he actually in debt? Or was Rebecca spending so much time on her software work that she neglected the admin side of her job?' He looked quickly through the other files, hoping to find bank statements to prove his theory one way or the other, but there were none.

'I guess Rider must have kept hold of them himself,' he concluded. 'After all, it was his money.' His mind returned to the thought he had had earlier in the day. 'Was she really fleecing him? And when he found out, would it have made him angry enough to kill her?'

Another file contained miscellaneous correspondence. As he flicked through the letters he spotted one with the farmhouse address printed at the top. He pulled it out. Hand-written by Andrew and addressed to Tom Rider at the Knight Rider office address, it was dated just over two weeks previously.

'What the hell's this doing in here?' He could hardly believe his eyes as he read.

'Dear Uncle Tom

I am very sorry to have to write to you about this matter. I certainly would not normally have ever considered doing so, but I am afraid my situation is fast becoming rather desperate.

As you know, under the terms of Father's will, I inherited the farm, but Rebecca receives all the rents. I am sorry to have to tell you that without some considerable amount of investment the farm will soon cease to be viable. I have spoken to my sister about this state of affairs on a number of occasions, but she has always told me that she will be unable to help me until after your product has been launched on the market, and you have made some money from it. She also says that living in London is so expensive and that she needs all the income from the rents to rent her flat, run her car and to live.

I will be brutally honest. The real reason I am writing to you is, basically, to ask you whether she is, in fact, telling me the truth! Is it true that she cannot draw any salary from the business until you have some sales? And is it true that it is so extraordinarily expensive for her to live in London that she needs all the rental income to survive? You know we have never been that close and I would not be at all surprised if what she is telling me is a tissue of lies!

I am sending this letter to your office address as you mentioned that you were selling your old place and moving to somewhere smaller and I don't yet know your new home address.

As I say, things really are getting pretty desperate here. If I cannot get my hands on some serious funds in the next few weeks I am afraid the farm will go under.

Kind regards
Andrew'

'Wow!' thought James. 'Poor Andrew really was desperate! Funny that Tom Rider never mentioned this letter to me when I saw him.' Then it dawned on him. 'He never saw it! I bet Rebecca opened all the post for the office! She would never have let him see this. So why did she file it instead of throwing it away? Perhaps she wanted to keep it in reserve to use against Andrew at some later date. But Andrew hasn't mentioned it either – probably too embarrassed!' he concluded. He dropped the letter back in the file.

'Three suspects,' he thought again, mulling over the facts for the umpteenth time, dropping into TechnoTec mode. 'If I was writing this as a plot for *TechnoTec*, what clues would there be for him to find? What would he make of the three of them? Andrew, who I can discount – I hope. Why would he ask me to dig around if he knew the only evidence I would find would point to him? Tom Rider could have done it but may or may not have had a motive. And carrying a dead body from the car to the bridge, then heaving it over the parapet would be difficult for a man of his age. And then there's this Mal character about whom I know nothing – not even his full name.'

He cast his mind back over what Tom Rider had told him. Andrew had said the same earlier. Rebecca had started seeing this 'Mal' just after the Swindon conference. Then she had started to come to the farm at weekends – and that was also when she had told Rider she was onto a winner with their project. He pondered.

'There's got to be a link!' he said to himself. 'Come on, TechnoTec! Think it through! There's something you're missing here. What the hell is it – and, more to the point – where the hell is it?'

He continued looking through the papers. At the bottom of the pile he came across the conference folder. Thumbing through the pages of information inside, he spotted the list of delegates. He scanned down it. There was only one 'Malcolm' on the list.

'There! Mal – Malcolm! That's got to be him!' He looked at the full entry – 'Malcolm Booth from Trimble Associates.' He had vaguely heard of the company. They were involved in life assurance from what he knew of them. The list gave a short pen profile of each delegate. He read Malcolm Booth's. He was a graduate from Queen's University in Belfast. He had worked for two other life assurance companies before securing a senior position with Trimble.

'I wonder!' James thought. He crossed the hall to Andrew's study, sat down at his desk and switched on his computer. It requested a password.

'Now, where did I put it?' he asked himself. He felt in the back pocket of his trousers and removed the now crumpled page. He copied the password and Googled Trimble Associates.

'That makes sense!' he thought, as the information appeared on the screen. 'This village is about halfway between Trimble's main office and London. Perfect spot for Rebecca and him to meet up at weekends. So that's got to be him! I'll try them in the morning. I can't do any more here.'

He decided to walk back to *Aurora*. Andrew's car would only draw the media's attention again. The walk would do him good. It would help to clear his head. He closed the back door quietly behind him and set off along the track. When he reached the bridge where the boat was moored all traces of the camera crews had disappeared. The media circus had moved elsewhere. Rebecca's body was yesterday's news.

Aurora was moored by herself next to the bridge. The canal had returned to its quiet self. Only the ripples on the water kept the secret of what had been discovered under its surface a few hours previously. He tumbled into bed and, lulled by the gentle motion, was overtaken by a deep and dreamless sleep, oblivious even to Andrew, still languishing in his cell at the police station.

The conference

James awoke early to another bright, sunny morning, the events of the previous days filling his thoughts once more as he drank his coffee sitting on the front deck of the boat. He looked into the silent, still water. There were no ripples, no movement. Only the song of the birds disturbed the silence.

It was hard to comprehend that Rebecca's body had been dragged from that same still water, that someone, as yet unknown, had intended it to be her final resting place. Why? Who?

His thoughts were suddenly interrupted by a shrill tone. He picked up his phone.

'Laura! Hi love! The police have told me I'm no longer part of a crime scene so I'm setting off this morning. I should get to the end of the arm today.'

'I think I saw *Aurora* on the news!' she said, 'but I didn't see you.'

'Er ... no,' he replied. 'I thought it best if I kept a low profile so I stayed inside the boat, out of sight.'

'They think it was her brother who killed her – something about money.'

'So I've heard. How are you and Pumpkin getting on without a man in the house?' he asked, changing the subject.

'We're fine. She did very well in her maths test yesterday.'

'Oh, good for her!' They chatted for a few minutes, then she gave him her usual warning about not drinking too much as she did not want him falling into the canal! He promised he would not and rang off.

It was about nine o'clock when he set off along the lane back towards the farm. A little way along on the left-hand side was a small, wooded area. As James walked by he caught a glimpse of the sun reflecting off something shiny. He walked back and forth along the road to try to get a better view. It was well away from the road along a track leading to the middle of the trees. Shielding his eyes with his hand, he squinted at it. He could not fathom out what it was from the road, so he decided to investigate further. It was then that he noticed the tyre tracks.

'That's funny! I haven't noticed them before. I'm sure they weren't there yesterday afternoon,' he said to himself. 'They might have been there when I walked up here yesterday evening but I suppose I didn't notice them in the semi-darkness.'

Tyre tracks! Was the reflection from a car windscreen? He followed the track a short distance into the woods. When he got closer he could see that it was, indeed, a car. Moreover, it was a yellow Volkswagen Beetle. He knew what the registration number would be before he saw the plate – REK 612M. It was *the* Volkswagen Beetle. Rebecca's Volkswagen Beetle. His heart missed a beat and he felt a sick feeling in the pit of his stomach. He resisted the urge to try the doors – and immediately called Jessica on his mobile.

'I'll tell the police right away,' she said.

'How's Andrew?'

'Bearing up very well, considering. I was about to ring you. They've just charged him with Rebecca's murder. He'll appear at the magistrates court later today.'

'Oh, no!' James exclaimed. 'I guess we should have expected it. But they've so little evidence to go on.' He also mentioned Malcolm Booth of Trimble Associates. 'I'll phone him as soon as I get to Andrew's,' he said.

'Let me know how you get on.'

'I will. Will you let me know when Andrew's due in court?'

'Of course,' she said and ended the call.

He peered through the windows of the car. It appeared to be completely empty, but the ashtray was open and there were a couple of cigarette ends in it. James realised he could do nothing more and started back to the lane. Something was playing on his mind. Something bothered him. He could not put his finger on exactly what it was, but he sensed that it was something important.

He took the long way round along the track to the rear of the house. As he neared the farmhouse he noticed that the remaining media people were packing up.

'Moving on to the magistrates court, I suppose,' he mused. 'Poor Andrew! And now they've charged him. Yes, he certainly had a motive, but...'

He let himself in through the back door and went into Andrew's study. He focussed his attention as he dialled Trimble Associates. His call was picked up on the third ring.

'Good morning. Trimble Associates. Katie speaking. How may I help?'

'Oh, good morning. I wonder if I could possibly speak to Malcolm Booth, please?'

'Who shall I say is calling?'

'My name's James. He won't remember me, but we met at a conference in Swindon some weeks back.'

'Just a moment, please, sir.' Mozart's *Eine Kleine Nachtmusik* came tinnily down the line for about thirty seconds. Another female voice came on the line.

'I'm sorry, sir. Mr Booth works in our Northern Ireland Office in Belfast.'

'Oh, er … has he been transferred there recently?' James asked.

'Mr Booth's always been in the Belfast Office ever since he joined the company three years ago. Would you like the Belfast number so you can call him there, sir?'

'Yes, please, I would,' he said. She gave it to him and he replaced the receiver. He was surprised how easily he assumed another persona, became the private detective, lied convincingly.

'Just like TechnoTec!' he said quietly to himself. 'So he's not the reason she came down here every weekend because he's in Belfast,' he reasoned. 'But that doesn't mean they're not an item.' He picked up the telephone and dialled the number he had just been given.

'Malcolm Booth.' The Ulster accent was particularly noticeable on the telephone.

'Oh, hello there, Mr Booth. My name's James Wade. I believe we were both at a conference together earlier this year – the future of the stock market one at a hotel near Swindon?'

'Oh, yes.'

'Yes. While we were there I was doing a bit of networking.'

'Weren't we all?'

'Quite. I swapped cards with another delegate but I've lost it. I know it's a long shot, but I just wondered whether you'd done the same.'

'What's his name?'

'It's a her, actually. Rebecca Knight from Knight Rider?' There was silence at the other end of the phone. 'Did you by any chance meet her and exchange details?'

✳

It was the morning coffee break on the first day of the conference. The man in front of Rebecca in the coffee queue turned and smiled at her.

'Hi!' *she said, returning his smile.* 'What do you think of it, so far?' *she asked, half expecting him to answer,* 'Rubbish!', *but he did not.*

'Seems well-organised,' *he said.*

'I guess from your accent you're from Northern Ireland.'

'I am. Belfast, actually.'

'Ah, my brother spent some time in Belfast – with the Army.'

'Did he now?' *He looked away. Rebecca touched his arm.*

'I'm sorry! That was a tactless thing to say.'

He turned back. 'No, it's all right. It's just that one of my friends was mistaken for a terrorist and got pretty well roughed up by the soldiers.'

'So which side are you?' *she asked.* 'Catholic or Protestant?'

'Actually, I'm an atheist, but my parents are both Catholics.' *They arrived at the front of the queue and poured their coffee. He looked at her name badge.*

'And are you the Knight in Knight Rider?' *he asked as they walked to a table and sat down.* 'I saw your name on the list of delegates.'

'Yes, I am.'

'Not heard of your company.'

'We're quite new to the stock market software business. I'm here to pick up some information.'

'I'm looking forward to Dr Griffiths's presentation tomorrow.'

'I've heard of him, of course,' *she lied,* 'but I don't know an awful lot about him.'

'He's the leader in the field. Megatech, who he works for – he's their leading software designer – they produce the gold standard program and they're always improving it. We at Trimble's keep a steady eye on what Dr Griffiths and Megatech are doing. It's hard, though. Their security is watertight.'

'You're not talking industrial espionage here, are you?' she asked, her eyes widening in a quizzical look of feigned surprise.

He grinned. 'You might say that. I couldn't possibly comment!' They laughed.

She took a sip of her coffee. 'Do you work in Belfast?'

'Yes – most of the time – I have to visit our London office for a couple of days every month, though.'

'Whereabouts in London is that?

'It's in the City, Queen Victoria Street.'

'I live in London. Perhaps we could meet for a drink when you come over next.'

'Yes, I'd like that. I stay at the Crowne Plaza in New Bridge Street.'

'I know it,' she lied again.

'The food's excellent there. Why don't you come and have dinner next Monday night?'

'That would be lovely!' She looked at him coyly and smiled.

'I'll meet you in the lobby about eight.'

They returned to their seats in the conference hall.

'Yes, I met Rebecca,' he replied cautiously.

'Oh?' queried James.

'Got on very well with her, as a matter of fact. My work brings me to London for a couple of days a month and we used to meet for dinner.'

'You said "used to".'

'Yes.' James listened as Malcolm Booth sighed heavily. 'Look! If you're going to get into contact with her, let me give you a bit of a warning.'

'A warning?'

'I guess I better tell you the whole story.' He took a deep breath. 'The first time we met after the conference she came over to my hotel in London and we had dinner. Well, to say she threw herself at me would be an understatement. I'd hardly finished my coffee before she was talking about us going up to my room!'

'I see.'

'Well, this happened every time I was over in London. I began to realise she was after something else.'

'What?'

'She was quite devious! I knew her company was new at the game – she'd told me that at the conference – but I gradually realised that she was trying to pump me for information about my work!'

'Oh, really!'

'Yes. Well, it all came to a head when she suggested coming over to Belfast so I could show her round my department! I couldn't let her come here.'

'Why not? Because she could try and pinch your methods?'

'Partly that. But – well – you see, I'm a married man. I knew I'd been a fool – sucked in by flashing eyes and a pair of shapely legs! I told her, if word ever got to my wife that I'd … I don't need to explain, do I?'

'No. Quite. I understand.'

The Irishman exhaled deeply before continuing. 'Well, we had a flaming row over the phone and when I came over the next month she never showed up. I was terrified she was going to turn up in Belfast. You know – hell hath no fury, et cetera?'

'And has she?'

'Fortunately, no. Not yet, anyway. I haven't seen or heard from her in over a month now. Look, I've still got her mobile number if you want it?'

'Please.'

He read the number to James. 'Another thing – I'm pretty damned sure she was seeing somebody else as well. I wasn't her only "fish"! Just a feeling I got.'

'Thanks for the heads up,' James said. 'I can see I'll have to tread carefully.'

'If you take my advice you'll give her a wide berth.' He rang off.

'Scheming little minx!' James said to himself as he put the receiver down. He called Jessica to tell her what Booth had said.

'Interesting!' she said.

'But it doesn't explain why she started going to Andrew's place every weekend.'

'No, it doesn't. Look, I've got to go. Andrew's up before the magistrates at eleven,' she said. 'I'll tell him about the car when I see him, but I won't mention this Malcolm Booth business.'

'No need. It would only depress him even further.' James was about to ring off when he had a sudden flash of inspiration. That's what it was! He had put his finger on it! The cigarette butts! They had the distinctive white filter tip of French cigarettes. He used to smoke them in his student days. He had not seen them – or smelled them – recently. But Rebecca had liked French perfume – perhaps she had liked French cigarettes too.

'Jessica. When you see Andrew will you ask him if Rebecca smoked? And if she did, did she smoke Gauloise Disque Bleu or any other sort of French cigarettes? Also, if he knows of any of her friends who do?'

'Why?'

'There are a couple of fag ends in the car ashtray. They look like Gauloise to me, but I didn't see any ashtrays anywhere in her flat and there are none here either.' They ended the call.

'So where the hell do we go from here, TechnoTec?' he asked himself. His call to Malcolm Booth had raised more questions than it had answered.

'If she'd threatened to go over to Belfast would that have been enough to make Booth kill her?' he wondered. 'He wouldn't be the first man to be caught out playing away from home – nor the first to have resorted to murder to save his marriage.

'If it was Booth who killed her he was incredibly cool on the phone. He didn't even appear to know she was dead. But, then again, that could all be an act. He confessed to adultery with her, but was that a ploy to divert my attention away from the fact that I was actually speaking to her murderer?'

He now had another suspect to add to his list. He picked up a blank sheet of paper and wrote down the three names. As he stared at them the question still niggled away at the back of his mind.

'Why did she suddenly start coming home at the weekends? It couldn't have anything to do with Malcolm Booth because she met him in London. And in any case she carried on doing so after they had last seen each other. There has to be another reason and, whatever that reason is, it has to have something to do with that conference because that's when it all started.'

He picked up the conference folder again, and yet again ran his finger down the list of delegates. Malcolm Booth was the only name on the list who could remotely be referred to as 'Mal', so it had to be someone else.

'It's got to be someone here!' he said out loud. He was absolutely certain that someone Rebecca had met during those two days in Swindon had set in motion the tragic chain of events that had culminated in her death. Jessica rang an hour later to say that although she had applied for bail at the magistrates' hearing the police had objected and Andrew had been remanded in custody.

'Why have they done that? Even if they think he did it, he's unlikely to go and murder anyone else, is he?' James asked.

'I think they're afraid he might skip the country. It's not unknown in cases like this.'

'Couldn't they just ask him to surrender his passport? He wouldn't get far without that.'

'Not legally, no, but there have been cases where the accused has managed to get abroad in a friend's private plane, or a yacht.'

'Fat chance of that with Andrew, poor chap! So he's still stuck in a cell, then?'

'I'm afraid so. The Inspector in charge of the case – Cotton – I've come up against him many times before. He always opposes bail and he usually gets away with it. I think he likes them to spend as much time as possible locked up in the hope that they'll confess – whether they're guilty or not!'

'Well, that's not going to work with Andrew, is it?'

'It may be successful with some of the criminal low-life Cotton's more used to dealing with, but you're right. It certainly won't work on Andrew Knight!'

'Well, I've got more papers to go through here. I'll let you know if I find anything.'

He spent the rest of the day going carefully through all the papers from the filing cabinet a second time, stopping only briefly for a trip to the village shop to get a sandwich. It seemed wrong to him to prepare a meal in Andrew's kitchen, especially when he was living on whatever the police provided for people in their cells. In the afternoon he examined the data he had printed out from the computer in Rebecca's office.

'Nothing!' he thought as he sat back at around half past four. 'Well, nothing I can see that helps in any way. That computer code obviously means something but I'm damned if I can understand what!' He stood up, stretched, and poured himself a large measure of Andrew's excellent whisky. Drinking his whisky did not seem as bad as eating his food somehow! Then he went through to the lounge and sat down in a comfortable chair to savour it. It did not, however, provide the anticipated relaxation. His thoughts kept returning to Andrew in custody and his own inability to make sense of the data – to find any real clues in the paperwork that he had taken from Rebecca's office.

'I could do with a Disque Bleu right now!' he mused to himself – although he had not smoked a cigarette in years.

He drained the whisky and went back into Andrew's study to tidy up the papers. As he did so, the conference folder slid from the desk onto the floor. It fell open at the page giving details and photographs of the speakers. Suddenly, one name leapt off the page at him: 'Principal Speaker – Dr Maldwyn Griffiths PhD, FBCS. Senior Software Development Executive. Megatech plc – Finance Division.'

'Maldwyn … Mal! Of course! There are two Mals! And why is that company name so familiar?' he asked himself, angry because he had not spotted it sooner. Then it came to him. He had passed signs to 'Megatech plc' on the road from Jessica's office to the village.

'It's just down the bloody road!' he almost shouted.

Looking at his watch, he thought he might just catch Jessica before she left for home.

'Maldwyn Griffiths?' she said. 'He's one of their top bods! I met him once briefly.'

'Oh, yes?'

'Yes. I was at a pub with a friend who used to work for him at Megatech. He was there and she introduced us.'

'What was he like?'

'Welsh – obviously, with a name like that. I thought he was a bit odd, actually. Maria, my friend, said she had found him difficult to work for.'

'Meaning?'

'Meaning that he's absolutely brilliant at what he does and can bore the pants off anyone who cares to listen to him talking about it. But he's pretty well useless at anything else – certainly lacking on the social graces front. She said she found him quite intimidating at times – never looks you in the eye. And he doesn't appear to have any friends, or a wife or family. That night when I met him, he was sitting at the bar on his own.'

'I see,' James paused. 'What would you suggest would be the best way to get to see him?'

'You could try ringing Megatech. See if you can make an appointment to see him? You could make up some story, I'm sure.'

'I'll ring them first thing tomorrow.'

'Oh, I asked Andrew about Rebecca's smoking habits.'

'And…?'

'She never smoked, but he doesn't know if any of her friends do.'

'Thanks.' James looked again at the photograph of Dr Maldwyn Griffiths. He appeared to be in his late thirties or early forties. A pinched face looked back at him. He was clean-shaven with straight but unruly blonde hair. He wore a pair of heavy-framed spectacles through which dark piercing eyes peered straight ahead, looking into the distance.

'If you didn't do it I'm certain you're mixed up in this somewhere!' he said to the photograph.

The search

Sitting back at Andrew's desk the following morning, he was still thinking of his friend who had spent yet another night in custody. He rang Megatech.

'Megatech. Good morning.'

'Oh, good morning. Would it be possible for me to make an appointment to see Dr Griffiths, please?'

'Putting you through to Dr Griffith's secretary. One moment, please…' There was a pause followed by a few bars of a current pop song.

'Dr Griffiths's secretary. How may I help you?'

'Oh, hello. I'd like to make an appointment to come and see Dr Griffiths, please.'

'Dr Griffiths is a very busy man. What is it you wish to see him about?'

'My name's Malcolm Booth. I was a delegate at the "Futures" conference in Swindon where Dr Griffiths spoke. There are a number of very interesting issues he mentioned in his presentation that I'd like to discuss with him further.'

'I'm sorry, but that won't be possible. If Dr Griffiths made appointments with every conference delegate who wanted to see him, he would have no time left for his work. I'm sorry, Mr Booth. Goodbye.' The connection was broken.

'Damn!' thought James.

He sat for a long time wondering what his next move should be. Eventually, he left the house, climbed into Andrew's Jaguar and drove to the Megatech offices. Parking a little way away, he walked past the building. It was a large, four-storey 1960s-style glass and concrete monolith – the largest building on a small out-of-town industrial estate. At the entrance to the car park there was a barrier with a security guard sitting in a hut next to it.

'No chance of getting in there!' James thought, and walked back to the car. 'If I can't get to him where he works, perhaps I can find out where he lives,' he wondered. He drove back to the farm and began searching for a local telephone directory. He thumbed through to the Gs. There were four listings in the locality under Griffiths but only one with the initial 'M'. Being unfamiliar with the area, the address did not mean much to him so he called at the village post office to enquire as to its whereabouts. The postmistress was happy to give him directions. The address, she said, was one of row of three recently renovated former farm cottages just outside the village on the road to the industrial estate where Megatech's offices were located.

Back in the car, James drove out to the cottages. His route took him over the canal, and when he crested the bridge he recognised the row of cottages immediately. He knew that their tiny back gardens ran down a gentle slope to the canal – he had cruised past them on *Aurora* many times. As when he had visited Rebecca's flat, he parked a short distance away.

'No point in taking any chances with nosy neighbours!' he said to himself, switching off the engine. He approached the cottages. Everything seemed quiet and as far as he could tell there was no one at home in any of them. He checked the numbers on the gates to the small front gardens and found that Griffiths's house was the middle of the three. It was also the one with the most unkempt garden and the dirtiest windows! It seemed to be a very small house for a man with a senior position in such a large company. There were certainly no trappings of wealth on show.

'Must be so obsessed with his work that he's got no time to think about where he lives,' James thought. 'Either that, or he can't be bothered.'

He had his cover story prepared – he was a life assurance salesman. He walked up the garden path to the front door, rang the bell and stood back to see if there was any curtain twitching in the windows of the adjoining cottages. Nothing – and neither was there anyone at home at Griffiths's place. He peered through the front window but he was not able to see much through the dirty glass. He stood back and looked around. Beyond the end of the terrace to his right was a track disappearing round to the rear of the properties. He made for the track. It did, indeed, lead to the canal towpath running along the back of the cottages, which all had a low wall with gates leading to the small gardens. Again, Griffiths's was the most untidy and uncared-for of the three. Beyond the garden, by the back door, each cottage had a tiny paved yard. James guessed that these yards were where the outside toilets and coal store would originally have been. He walked up to the yard at the back of Griffiths's cottage and immediately spotted one of TechnoTec's tried and tested best sources of clues – the wheelie bin!

Carefully checking there was no one around to observe him, he opened the lid of the bin and began to delve among the contents. There was the usual assortment of household refuse – food packaging, remains of ready-cooked meals, empty bottles, etc. Maldwyn was obviously a good customer of the local supermarket, and its ready meals department in particular. He was also not averse to the odd tipple, judging by the empty bottles, and he was a heavy smoker who had recently emptied an ashtray into the bin. Gauloise Disque Bleu cigarette ends – and some empty Gauloise packets!

'That puts you in her car!' James exclaimed triumphantly. Delving a bit deeper into the rubbish, he suddenly noticed a bottle. It was a bottle, the shape and colour of which he had seen before – first in Rebecca's room at the farmhouse and again in the bedroom at her flat. As he removed an empty cereal packet the sun caught the ruby red glass of a half-empty bottle of 'L'Esprit de Nancy'! A smile spread across James's face.

'And that definitely puts her here in your cottage!' he said quietly to himself. He resisted the temptation to pick it up. 'It wouldn't do for my fingerprints to be found on this!' he reasoned. He returned to the car, drove back the village, found a telephone box and made a call.

An hour later he was sitting opposite Jessica in her office.

'How can we get the police to go and look in his dustbin without making it look as if we're trying to frame him?' she asked.

'Already taken care of,' James replied with a smile.

'How?' Jessica looked at him quizzically.

'Oh, I just rang them from a call box. I used an Ulster accent and told them they'd got the wrong man – and that if they looked in a certain wheelie bin they would find a most unusual bottle of perfume.'

'They'll just dismiss that as a call from a crank! I know Cotton of old. If he thinks he's got a case that will stick, he's not interested in guilt. He just wants another conviction – right or wrong,' Jessica replied.

'Not after I told them they would find bottles exactly identical both in her flat in London and in her room at the farmhouse. And then I said that along with the bottle they'd find a load of dog ends matching the ones in the ashtray of her car. I even gave them the reg number. I rang off without leaving a name.'

'That should get them interested!' Jessica's face brightened. 'Well done! I just hope Cotton is not more pig-headed than usual and decides against looking for anyone else while he's got Andrew locked up.'

'So what do we do now?' James asked.

'We wait,' she replied. 'We wait until they've, hopefully, decided to arrange for a search warrant and gone to Griffiths's house and retrieved the perfume, tested it for fingerprints, and again, hopefully, decided to haul him in for questioning. If they do, I want us to be there.'

'Will they let us do that?'

'It's not normal procedure but I get on very well with the sergeant who works with Cotton, Nick Davies. He seems to think he owes me a favour.'

'How so?'

'Oh, some years back in the magistrate's court he made a complete dog's breakfast of giving his evidence. Well, I knew my client was as guilty as hell so I didn't give him too much of a hard time – didn't go in for the kill. Ever since, he's been saying if there's anything he can do for me to let him know.' She looked at her watch. 'Look, it's nearly lunchtime. Why don't you nip down to the deli next door and get us some sandwiches and I'll give him a ring and call in the favour.'

When James returned with the sandwiches Jessica was smiling.

'All set up,' she said. 'I asked Nick if there'd been any further developments in Andrew's case that I ought to know about. He told me they've sent someone to do some searching around at a cottage somewhere!'

'Good!'

'I asked him to let me know if they decide to question anyone else and he agreed. Then I asked the favour and told him I wanted us to be there.'

'What did he say?'

'He thought about it for a bit, saying it was most irregular and so on. Then I suggested we go in on the pretext of wanting to see Andrew again – fortunately, he hasn't been transferred to prison yet. Then Nick suggested asking us to wait in the corridor near the interview room. He'll "accidentally" leave the door ajar.'

'Brilliant!'

Just over half an hour later Jessica's phone rang.

'If this is Nick, they've worked damned fast!' she said, frowning. She picked up the phone.

'Jessica Loftus... Who...? Yes, send him up.' She replaced the phone. 'That's interesting! Tom Rider's downstairs.' A few seconds later there was a knock at the door.

'Come in.'

Tom Rider entered the room. He saw James and smiled. Then he turned to Jessica. 'You must be Miss Loftus.'

'Mr Rider.' Jessica extended her hand and Rider shook it. 'Take a seat.' He sat on the vacant chair next to James.

'How can I help?' Jessica asked.

'Well, actually, I'm hoping I can help you. I heard on the national news that Andrew had been charged with Rebecca's murder. Dreadful business! I saw you being interviewed, Miss Loftus. Then I wondered whether this would be of any help.' He took a piece of paper from the inside pocket of his jacket. 'This was tucked right at the back of a drawer in her filing cabinet,' he explained. 'I don't think she wanted me to find it, but it looks to me like a delivery note from a company called Compute.com for some software for her office computer. I remember her saying she'd put something on it that was supposed to make it run faster. I don't know if it's important or not. Although the delivery address is her flat – fair enough – the billing address is a company from somewhere round here and the name on it is someone called Griffiths? I can't understand why she should want it delivered to her flat – not for something for work. Unless, of course, she really wanted to hide it for some reason.'

'Let me see that!' Jessica almost snatched it from his hand. James stood up and peered over her shoulder.

'Got him!' she said quietly, and smiled. 'Mr Rider, thank you very much for taking the trouble to bring this all the way from London. This piece of paper could be very important in proving that Andrew did not murder his sister – very important.'

'Yes, thanks very much, Mr Rider,' James added.

'Oh good! I was hoping it might help.' He looked at his watch. 'If I go now I can get the fast train back to London.' He put his hand in his inside pocket again and produced a card.

'Look, this is my new address and phone number. Could you ring me and let me know how poor Andrew gets on?'

Jessica took the card. 'Of course, Mr Rider. And thank you again for making a special journey to bring that delivery note.'

'Perfectly all right. I suppose I could have rung you first but I wanted to give it to you personally. And anyway, I quite enjoyed the ride. Penny, my late wife, hated trains so we drove everywhere. And now I don't much like driving. I think I might take myself on some more train excursions!'

James and Jessica shook Tom Rider's hand warmly before he left.

James took the delivery note from Jessica's hand. 'A present for his girlfriend!' he said.

'Yes,' Jessica agreed. 'Megatech must have an account with Compute.com. He probably got it at a discount.'

She called the police station and asked to be put through to Inspector Cotton. 'Yes, hello Inspector Cotton. Now, I know you believe that my client was responsible for the murder of his sister, but I would like to suggest another line of enquiry... Yes, there's someone else who may have been involved, a man Rebecca Knight was seeing... Dr Maldwyn Griffiths.' She read his address off the delivery note. 'I've been given a delivery note for some computer software he bought for her. Yes, I'll fax it over to you...

Oh really…? No … no, I don't know anything about that… Thank you, Inspector… Thank you. Yes, I'll bring the original when I come to visit my client later. Bye.' She replaced the phone. 'Result!' she said. 'Something about an anonymous tip-off? Now where could that have come from, I wonder?'

'I wonder!' They laughed together in satisfaction.

✳

The password

It was later that afternoon when her phone rang again. 'Of course I don't mind,' James had said when Jessica had asked if he minded if she got on with work for her other clients while they waited. 'Time's money!' she had said. James sat quietly in a corner of her office trying to concentrate on the endless games of patience he was playing on his phone.

'Oh, hello Nick… About fifteen minutes… Right! I'll be there with my assistant, Mr Wade. Thanks for this, Nick.' She replaced the telephone.

'I've been a private eye for a couple of days – and now I'm an assistant lawyer?' James laughed.

'Lawyer's assistant! There's a difference,' Jessica laughed as she picked up her briefcase.

Ten minutes later Sergeant Davies met them as they arrived at the police station and led them to some chairs in the corridor outside one of the interview rooms.

They had not been sitting there long when another door opened and they watched as Griffiths, led by Davies, and followed by Cotton, walked past them and into the interview room. None of them appeared to notice James and Jessica, but James noted that Davies made a point of leaving the door slightly ajar, just enough to enable them to see Griffiths sit at Cotton's invitation. The room was sparsely furnished with a table and four chairs. Cotton and Davies sat opposite Griffiths. Davies switched on the recording machine and Cotton spoke.

'Interview commenced at … fifteen thirty-five on Tuesday the eleventh of July, two thousand and six. Present are myself, Inspector Alan Cotton, Sergeant Nicholas Davies and Dr Maldwyn Griffiths.' He paused.

'It has to be recorded!' Jessica whispered to James.

'I know!' James whispered back. The inspector spoke again.

'Dr Griffiths, what was your relationship with the late Rebecca Elizabeth Knight?'

'Who?' Griffiths's face was expressionless, his voice strong and deep. He ignored his interrogators and seemed to be looking somewhere beyond them at a point on the far wall.

'Rebecca Elizabeth Knight.'

'Never heard of her!' Hearing his voice booming through the open door they could not fail to notice his strong Cardiff accent.

'Come now, Dr Griffiths! It's been all over the front page of the local newspaper. The paper's been full of nothing else!'

'Never read the local rag.'

Cotton paused. 'Well then, Dr Griffiths, since you don't read the local press, have you heard any talk about the body of a woman being pulled out of the canal last week?'

'Some of them were on about it at work … yes. But I don't get involved with office gossip. I go to work to work. I wish some of my staff had the same attitude! I never knew that was her name and – like I say – as far as I know I never met her.' He took off his spectacles and polished them on the hem of his shirt. He replaced them and continued to stare straight ahead. He placed his hands on the table, spreading out his fingers as if he was tapping on an imaginary keyboard.

'Do you smoke, Dr Griffiths?'

'Haven't made that a crime now, have they?'

'No, but do you?'

'I could do with one now!'

'Feel free.' Griffiths took a packet of Gauloise Disque Bleu and a lighter from his pocket, extracted a cigarette and lit it. Cotton picked up the packet and looked at it.

'French?' he said. 'Not many people in this country smoke these.'

'What's that got to do with anything? Smoking French fags

isn't a crime either, is it? I happen to like them better than the ones made over here,' Griffiths retorted.

'Have you ever been in a yellow Volkswagen Beetle, registration number ...' Cotton referred to his notes ... 'REK 612M, Dr Griffiths?'

'What would I want with antiquated German crap? I've got a company car, thank you very much – a Ford Mondeo. Why?'

'The car I refer to belonged to Miss Knight and when it was found, abandoned, there were two cigarette stubs in the ashtray – this brand.' He dropped the packet onto the table.

'Must have been hers, then.'

'She didn't smoke.'

'Friend of hers, then. Look, I know they're a bit unusual over here, but I can't be the only person in this country who smokes them, now can I?'

'Quite, Dr Griffiths. Quite.' He paused. 'And you maintain that you have never met Miss Knight?'

'I told you. Not that I know of. No!'

'So, how then, Dr Griffiths, do you explain the presence of this bottle of perfume – for the benefit of the tape, I'm showing Dr Griffiths a half-empty bottle of "L'Esprit de Nancy" perfume – how do you explain the presence of this bottle of perfume, which, incidentally, has Miss Knight's fingerprints on it, in the dustbin at your property?'

'Just a minute!' The trace of a smirk appeared on Griffiths's hitherto expressionless face. 'You haven't had time to look in all the dustbins in the village, have you? What made you decide to go and look in mine, specifically?' His question took the Inspector off guard for a moment.

'Er ... we received ... um ... certain information that...'

'Then it's bloody obvious, isn't it?' Griffiths interrupted him. His tone changed from disinterest to animosity. He was riled. 'Whoever it was gave you that information must have already planted the bottle in my bin, mustn't they? It's a bloody stitch-up! That's what all this is – a bloody stitch-up! I tell you, Inspector, there's somebody out there trying to fit me up for this murder!'

'And why would they want to do that, do you think, Dr Griffiths?'

'What do you think? To save their own neck, of course.'

'You still maintain that you never met Rebecca Knight.'

'Not as far as I know, no!'

'So could you explain, then, why your name and the name and address of your employer is shown on this. For the benefit of the tape, I'm showing Dr Griffiths a delivery note for some software purchased by Dr Griffiths on the account of Megatech plc from a supplier called Compute.com. It also shows Miss Knight's details as the delivery address.'

Griffiths snatched it from him and peered at it. For a split second he looked frightened, but quickly regained his composure. 'It's bloody obvious, isn't it?' he said again, handing the note back to the inspector.

'It is?'

'Of course, it is! It's a bloody forgery! Anyone with a computer, a printer and half a brain could have produced that! It's like I said, somebody's trying very hard to stitch me up for this!'

'And why do you think this mystery person – whoever he or she might be – would attempt to implicate you?'

Griffiths said nothing.

'Any ideas, Dr Griffiths?' Cotton persisted. Griffiths leaned forward and rested his forearms on the table. He still did not make eye contact with either of the others. 'Because I don't fit in!' he said.

'What do you mean? You don't fit in? Fit in where? Fit into what?' Griffiths dropped his eyes and looked at the table.

'Ever since I moved down here,' he said, 'I've never been accepted, see. Never become part of the community – never been allowed to become part of it! Always been seen as an "in-comer", even though I've been here five years, nearly. I've even overheard some of the locals in the pub talking about me. "The Welsh git." That's what they call me!'

'Oh, save us the sob story, Dr Griffiths! Anybody'll tell you it takes a damned sight longer than five years to get properly accepted in any small village.' Griffiths looked at him. Inspector

Cotton continued. 'Are you seriously expecting us to believe that whoever murdered this girl is trying to implicate you merely because you're Welsh?'

Griffiths looked really angry now. 'Look! Before I answer any more of your bloody questions, I want my solicitor here.'

'That is your right, Dr Griffiths. Interview terminated at fifteen fifty-five to allow Dr Griffiths to call his solicitor.' The CID men escorted him from the room.

'Damn, he's good at thinking on his feet, isn't he?' said James, when they had gone.

'If they can't get anything else on him, he'll walk. They'll examine the car, of course. But he probably wore gloves,' Jessica added. 'If only we had some evidence to confront him with that actually proves the two of them had been together.'

'Not much hope of that, I'm afraid,' James said, sadly.

'I don't know what else we can do to help Andrew – barring a miracle!' Jessica sighed.

Beads of sweat were breaking out on James's forehead. 'Is it me, or is it getting a bit warm in here?' he asked as he removed his jacket and hung it over the back of the chair. Something in one of the pockets clattered against the chair back. He frowned. Plunging his hand into the pocket, he pulled out the small recording device he had picked up in Rebecca's flat.

'I wonder...'

'What's that?' Jessica asked.

'Let's go outside for a minute,' James said.

Standing outside the main entrance, James explained, then turned the machine to 'Play'. They listened in stunned silence. When the recording had finished Jessica was beaming.

'I think we've just found Andrew's miracle!' she exclaimed. She took the recorder and rushed back into the police station, the door slamming behind her. James followed. She knocked on the Inspector's door.

'Come in.' They entered his office. Sergeant Davies looked up.

'Inspector,' Jessica approached him. 'We've got something here I think you might be interested in listening to.'

'Oh, yes? What's that?' Jessica put the machine on his desk and switched it on. His face betrayed nothing as he listened. Afterwards he asked, 'Where did you get this?' Jessica looked at James. James's mind went into overdrive. He should have expected the question but in his excitement he had neglected to think up a story.

'It was on the desk at the farmhouse,' he said with a straight face. 'I told Andrew I was thinking of getting one and he said I could take it. Obviously, I had no idea it belonged to Rebecca.' Cotton appeared to accept this false explanation and James, inwardly, breathed a sigh of relief.

'Well,' he said, 'it would seem that I may owe both you and your client an apology, Miss Loftus.'

At that moment there was a knock at the door and a uniformed constable entered. 'Dr Griffiths's solicitor's arrived, sir.'

'Good!' said the Inspector, smiling. 'I'm going to enjoy this!'

'These might be relevant too,' James said, removing sheets of paper from the pile he was carrying. 'This was on the machine in her office at Knight Rider, where she was a partner. It's the data they refer to on the recording.'

'Ah! Right! Thank you, Mr Wade.' He paused and made a couple of notes. Then he looked up. 'I shan't ask how you came by this – yet! Or, indeed, how, as his lawyer's assistant, you appear to know the accused personally!' Jessica gave a rueful smile and James's face turned crimson as they went back into the corridor.

'Don't worry!' Jessica mouthed to him. 'It'll be fine. We've nailed him!'

The interview room looked much as on the previous occasion but with the addition of Griffiths's lawyer, a sombre-looking man in his late fifties. Inspector Cotton made the announcement that the interview was resumed, gave the time and added that Mr Colin Russell, Dr Griffiths's solicitor was now also present.

'Dr Griffiths,' he began, 'for the benefit of Mr Russell, I would like to recap on what we established at our earlier interview.' Russell nodded. 'You stated that, as far as you were aware, you had never met Rebecca Elizabeth Knight. You had never been inside her car and that a bottle of perfume with her fingerprints on it, found in your dustbin, had been planted there by the murderer to implicate you in the murder. You also stated that a delivery note for some software, delivered to Miss Knight's address, showing your name and your employer's address, was a forgery produced by the murderer. The reason for these attempts to implicate you in the crime being because you're a Welshman.'

Russell's eyebrows raised as he looked at his client.

'Not just because I'm Welsh. Because I've never been accepted in the village, see. Always been made to feel like an outsider.'

Russell spoke. 'As you know, Inspector, I only received details of the evidence against my client as I walked in here so I haven't had time to study it properly.' His tone matched his sombre appearance. 'But from what I've read all the evidence you have against my client is purely circumstantial. As far as I can see there's nothing here to link my client to the murdered woman other than a couple of cigarette ends and a perfume bottle – that are obviously plants – and a possibly forged delivery note. I can see nothing here to contradict my client's assertion that he had never met Miss Knight. No trace of my client's fingerprints were found on the bottle, were they?'

Cotton ignored the question. 'More evidence has come to light within the last few minutes. Before we proceed any further I have something here I should like you both to listen to.' He placed Rebecca's recording device on the desk. 'For the benefit of the tape, I am about to play a recording found on a machine, the property of the late Miss Knight.'

He switched it on and pressed 'Play'. They heard sounds and murmurings of satisfaction, which, fairly obviously, had followed successful love-making.

'Oh Mal!' There was the sound of a cigarette being lit and a long exhalation of breath. 'You're wonderful!' an upper-class woman's voice purred. 'So you keep all that top-secret stuff on your laptop over there?' There was another long pause followed by another long exhalation of breath.

'Yes. See, I don't really trust the security systems they've got in the office.' Griffiths's unmistakable accent was loud and strong. 'They say it's foolproof and we can never lose anything, but I'm not convinced. That's why I keep my own copy here. I back it up every night before I leave and bring it home with me. That way, if anything happens there, all my five years of hard work is safe. It also means that if I'm in the middle of something, I can finish it off here when I get home.'

'But what if someone stole your computer?'

'Well, that's not likely to happen, is it? Not with it being here beside my bed?'

'But what if…' the woman's voice wheedled.

'Anyhow, it's well protected!'

'What? With a password?'

'Yes. But they'd never guess it, cariad.'

'I can never remember passwords.' She giggled a simpering, girlie giggle. 'Mine's the number plate on my car and I have to have a photo of the car on my desk to remind me what it is!'

'Nobody here would ever guess mine. It's in Welsh, see.'

'Oh, Mal! You're so clever! It isn't that village, is it – you know the one I mean – the one on Anglesey with the impossibly long name?'

'Good heavens, no. If it was that it'd take me half an hour to log in every time!'

'Is it any of those Welsh words you've taught me?'

As they listened to the conversation emanating from the little machine, all eyes were on Griffiths. His were glued to the machine, his passive expression turning from one of incredulity to one of horror.

'Yes. As a matter of fact, it is.'

'I wonder if I can guess it? Is it "bore da"?'

'No! That would be far too easy!'

'What about "croeso"?'

'No. Look, I'm not going to tell you even if you get it right.'

There were sounds of laughter.

'Oh, go on! It was you who said we shouldn't have any secrets between us, wasn't it? Is it "diolch"?'

'No, it isn't.'

There was a long pause.

'Is it "cariad"?'

Another pause.

'Might be…'

More laughter.

'It is, isn't it? It's "cariad"!'

'I'm not saying.'

More laughter.

Griffiths, by this time, had his head in his hands.

'I think we've heard enough,' Cotton said as he turned off the machine. 'Dr Griffiths, do you deny that that was your voice?'

Griffiths looked up. 'No,' he said, hardly audibly.

Cotton held up the sheets of paper James had given him earlier. 'For the benefit of the tape, I'm showing Dr Griffiths a print-out of computer code found on a computer, the property of Knight Rider, the company in which the late Miss Knight was a partner. Is this the information that Miss Knight was later able to download from your laptop, you having given her your password?'

Griffiths gave the pages a cursory glance. 'Yes!' he shouted. 'The scheming little bitch was going to use it herself!'

'Would you like to tell us about that?'

Griffiths appeared to be trying to gather his thoughts. Russell looked concerned. 'I'm not sure…' he began.

Griffiths ignored him, seemingly resigned to his fate. 'Yes, I knew Rebecca Elizabeth Knight – and I wish to hell I'd never met her!'

✳

The confession

*H*e had finished his session at the conference, had dinner, and was sitting on his own in the bar nursing a double scotch.

'Dr Griffiths, do you mind if I join you?'

He looked up. It was one of the delegates smiling down at him. He remembered her from his presentation because she had asked a question at the end that showed she had not grasped the concept he had talked about at all. He recalled the unsuccessfully stifled giggles of some of the others. But she was a pretty little thing, so he smiled back.

'Of course, have a seat.'

She sat down, her skirt sliding up her thigh as she crossed her legs. 'You must have such an interesting job!' she said.

'I find it very interesting,' he replied. 'As I said in my talk, devising a computer program to spot trends in the market early and then to analyse them and predict their futures? Well, for me, life doesn't get much better than that.'

She introduced herself as Rebecca Knight and told him she was working in a similar field for a small firm in London.

'Not on anything like such a grand scale as your project, though,' she said, still smiling. She asked him more about his work and he was pleased that she showed an interest.

'Usually, when I start talking about my work people glaze over and switch off. They either change the subject or tell me to shut up,' he said without emotion.

'No!' she said. 'I find it all really fascinating.'

'I better not tell you much more, though,' he said. 'I'll be giving away trade secrets if I'm not careful!' Rebecca laughed.

He smiled a faint smile. 'Live in London, do you?' he asked, changing the subject.

'Yes, I rent a flat there.'

'Do you like it? London, I mean.'

'Oh, yes! I love it! There's so much happening, so much to do! There's never a dull moment!'

'Expensive, though?'

'Well, yes, it is a bit. Fortunately, when Daddy died he left me reasonably well off.'

'Lucky you! I hate London. I only ever go there when I have to. Not one for big cities, me. Comes from being born in a village, I suppose.'

'So how do you spend your time when you're not at work? Do you have any hobbies or anything?' She seemed really interested.

'When I was back home I used to sing bass with the local male voice choir, but there isn't one anywhere near where I live now.'

'And whereabouts is that?'

He told her. 'It's not far from where I work.'

'Well, there's a surprise! It can't be far from where my brother lives either!' she exclaimed.

Maldwyn considered this for a few moments. 'Perhaps we could

meet up some time – when you come to see your brother?' he
suggested, hopefully.

'I'd like that,' she replied, and smiled again. She opened her
handbag, took out her diary and flicked through the pages. *'In fact,'*
she said, *'I could come down next weekend.'*

'Won't you have to check with your brother that it's OK?'

*'Oh, no. It's the family home. My room is still as I left it and I have
my own keys. It's as much mine as it is his!'*

Maldwyn felt his heart begin to beat a little faster. Here was a young
woman, a pretty young woman with a great figure – perhaps not very
intelligent, but never mind – who seemed to be wanting to go on a date
with him! This was unknown territory! Whenever he had asked a girl
out before most of them had made some excuse, and on the odd
occasion when they had gone out together it had usually ended in
disaster. But this was different. This attractive young lady was not
only interested in his work, she was interested in him as a man.

'Well then,' he said, trying to sound more relaxed and casual than
he felt, *'if you let me have the address, I'll pick you up about eight.'*

Her smile disappeared. *'No. Don't come for me. It's my brother.
He's older than me and he'll only start quizzing me. My private life's
my own. Let's meet in the pub instead.'*

'That's fine by me. I'll see you in there – same time?'

'Yes, that'll be fine. I'm looking forward to it!'

'I was over the bloody moon! Well, one thing led to another and
before long she was staying at my place every weekend.' He
paused. He looked up at the ceiling and closed his eyes. There was
a catch in his voice as he said, 'I thought she was in love with me!'
They could see he was fighting to keep tears at bay. 'I've never had
much luck attracting women, see? And I thought, "This is it! At
last, I've found a woman who loves me." And I was in love with
her too! I even asked her to marry me! "Not yet, Mal," she said.
"Let me get my company set up first." I soon realised she wasn't
going to succeed with her enterprise and I even started looking to
see if I could get her a job in my department.

'She said she was into computer puzzles and games and stuff, so I used to set her little challenges. She could never do them, of course – not very quick, see? She was nowhere near as bright as me, but I didn't care. "Let me try and guess, Mal," she'd say to me. I suppose I thought when she was trying to guess my password it was like her attempt at one of the games. I'm a bit naive where women are concerned, see. I saw later that she was setting me up.'

Again, he paused. 'But it was all an act! A bloody act!' he said, returning his gaze to his interrogators. 'The little harlot wasn't in love with me! She didn't even want me, see. All she wanted was my work! Not only that – I found out she was two-timing me as well! She was seeing one of the delegates from the conference. Bloke named Malcolm something!

'I tell you, if I'd had any idea she'd got that bloody recorder going I'd never have let her know my password. After, while I was in the shower, the little trollop downloaded everything from my laptop, see – every last bloody detail! She was going to market it as her own program. She'd could have done it for half the cost of ours!

'But there was no way she could do that without using all that data she'd stolen off me, see! She hadn't got the brains or the knowledge to work out a program of her own! There's getting on for five long years of my work in those files! That's why our software is going to be more expensive. She was going to make herself a bloody fortune out of it by taking a short cut, see. A short cut at my expense! I couldn't let her get away with that, could I? What would have happened to our sales? What would have happened to my reputation?' He began to cry.

'And so you killed her.'

'I don't think…' Russell tried to intervene.

'Yes, I did!' Griffiths was not listening. 'And she bloody well deserved it too! I realised what she'd done as soon as I got to work on the Monday morning. See, I knew I hadn't used my laptop over the weekend but there was an entry in the access log for the Sunday night. When I checked it out I could see what she'd done. I was absolutely livid, I can tell you! Devastated, I was!'

Again his solicitor tried to stop him, but Griffiths ignored his warning and ploughed on with his story, appearing to be almost relieved to be unburdening himself.

'So, what did you do about it?' Cotton asked.

'I decided to play it cool. I wouldn't let her know that I knew what she'd done straight away, see. So when she came to my house the next Friday, as usual, I just carried on as if nothing had happened.'

'I really don't think you should say any more, Dr Griffiths.' It was Russell.

'Look, Mr Russell,' Griffiths turned to him. 'I know you're acting in my interests, but it won't take long for them to find all this out for themselves. I know I'm going down for murder, so what harm can it do?'

'Well, Dr Griffiths, I've given you my advice. If you choose to ignore it, that is your decision.'

'So what happened that Friday night?' Cotton returned to the matter in hand.

'We had sex. And then I challenged her, see. I told her I'd found out what she'd done and demanded she let me wipe the hard disk on her computer and destroy the flash drive. She refused and I threatened to hurt her. She didn't believe me, of course. For a start, she denied she'd even done it, till I showed her the proof on the access log on my machine. Then she got real brazen, see. She said she'd downloaded it while I was in the shower. "Never mind, Mal," she said. "You win some, you lose some. I guess you're just a loser! You always have been, and you always will be!" That really made me see red. The little hussy! By then I knew about the other bloke too. I didn't know what I was doing, see. In that moment I saw through her. I saw that all the loving wasn't real. She'd been acting – playing me for a fool all the way along.' He paused again.

'Next thing I knew, I had my hands round her neck.' Unconsciously, he mimicked the action with his hands. 'She struggled. She had some strength for a petite woman. But I could feel her windpipe under my thumbs ... and I just squeezed ... and squeezed ... until I felt it crush!' He paused again, remembering the moment. 'Then I panicked! What was I going to do next? I had this dead body, lying there in my bed, see. I couldn't think straight! Then I remembered an old tarpaulin I had out the back, so I went and got it and wrapped her up in it and tied it round with an old tow rope. Then I put her in her own car and drove. I didn't know where I was going, or what I was going to do with her body. I stopped somewhere in the middle of the countryside and smoked a couple of fags while I tried to figure out what to do. Then I thought of the canal. I drove to that bridge near the village and dropped her in.'

'And what did you do with her car?' Cotton asked.

'I went back home in it. I parked it up the track round the back of my house. But over the weekend I realised if anybody who knew her caught sight of it they could link me to her, see. So on the Sunday night I went and hid it in the woods.'

Cotton turned to Sergeant Davies.

'Sergeant?'

'Sir. Maldwyn Griffiths, I'm arresting you for the murder of Rebecca Elizabeth Knight on the evening of Friday the seventh of July, two thousand and six. You do not have to say anything. But it may harm your defence if you do not mention when questioned something which you later rely on in court.' The Sergeant stood up. 'This way, please, sir.'

A broken man, Griffiths was led away, followed by Russell.

James and Jessica watched them go past. Jessica mouthed a silent 'Thank you' to Sergeant Davies.

❊

The motive

When the corridor was empty James and Jessica stood up and hugged each other.

'I can't wait to tell Andrew!' Jessica said as they made their way out to the foyer.

'I can't help feeling a bit sorry for Dr Griffiths,' James said. 'He's obviously a very lonely man and he must have thought all his birthdays and Christmases had come at once when Rebecca showed an interest in him. No wonder he went off the rails when he found out the truth. I guess it was what the French call a "crime passionel".'

'And under French justice that's a defence,' Jessica added. 'He would probably get away with it over there.'

A while later Inspector Cotton came through the door.

'I just wanted to thank you both very much,' he said in a somewhat condescending tone. 'But for your hard work and persistence,' he gave them both a knowing look, 'there could have been a serious miscarriage of justice here.' He paused.

'Where is my client?' Jessica asked.

'The custody sergeant's just processing his release. I'll go and see if he's finished.' He left, reappearing a few minutes later, followed by Andrew, who was smiling broadly.

'Have you heard the recording?' Jessica asked.

'No, but Inspector Cotton's just been telling me about it,' Andrew replied.

'Come this way,' Cotton said, leading all three of them back into the interview room, where Sergeant Davies was finishing his notes.

'We'll have to keep the recording machine as evidence, of course,' he said, 'but I think you should hear what's on it, Mr Knight.' They sat down. 'Now, you may find it difficult listening to your sister's voice in this situation, Mr Knight. Please tell me if you want me to stop the recording at any time.'

Andrew nodded. 'How his attitude has changed now I'm no longer the accused!' he thought.

Cotton pressed 'Play' and they listened to the damning conversation. Andrew sighed heavily when he heard Rebecca's voice, but let the recording play to he end.

'There's just one thing bothering me slightly,' Cotton said when the recording had finished.

'What's that?' Jessica asked.

'I can't for the life of me see why she would want to make a recording of all … that … in the first place.'

'That's easy!' said Andrew. 'Answer's there – on the recording. She was such a scatterbrain! Never could remember passwords for the life of her. You heard her – couldn't even remember her own, let alone anyone else's! Had to have it recorded so she could remind herself of it when she got to access his computer later.'

'Ah, I see,' Inspector Cotton smiled. He stood up and shook Andrew's hand. 'You're free to go, sir,' he said.

After a celebratory dinner at a nearby hotel, Andrew, James and Jessica were quietly sipping brandy at a table in the bar.

Andrew turned to James. 'Well!' he said. 'Your computer game hero chappy – what was his name?'

'TechnoTec.'

'Yes, him. Looks like he's solved another case!'

'The thing is, with TechnoTec's cases I know who did it in advance and I know where all the clues are hidden – not to mention the red herrings – the false leads. In your case, Andrew, nether TechnoTec nor I had the first clue – literally – when I agreed to help you.'

'Look here, old man,' Andrew said. 'I know I was a bit desperate when I asked you to do the private eye thing for me. But – have to admit it, never thought for a minute you'd take it on. Tell me, was it just the "old school tie" thing made you do it or was there something else? What was your motive?'

James swirled the remains of his brandy in the glass. 'Well, it was, as you say, partly the "old school tie",' he said, 'but it was rather more about something else.'

'What?'

'Well, you probably don't remember it, but that day when you asked for my help I suddenly remembered something from our schooldays as if it was yesterday. It was as if we were back in the changing room at Hurst's, getting ready for a match.' He drained his brandy and gazed at the bottom of his empty glass.

'Where did you get your rugger boots, Wadey? The Oxfam shop?'
Frobisher said. Two of the other boys laughed.

Ross-Parker joined in. 'Did your mama knit your jersey? She must
be a very good knitter, your mama. It looks almost as good as a real

one!' He picked up Wade's jersey and threw it across the changing room. Wade went after it. Frobisher and Ross-Parker barred his way.

'Not bad for a working class yobbo!' Mason Minor added. 'Where did you practise your rugger before you came to Hurst's, Wadey? Kicking an old tin can in the street outside your tiny, little, rented, back-to-back slum?' The others found this last question wildly funny.

His jersey had landed at the feet of Knight, the first team skipper and tight head prop. A big lad, he was a head taller than most of his team and broadly built. He picked up his scrum half's jersey and walked over to where Frobisher, Ross-Parker, Mason Minor and some of the other boys were changing, his face like thunder.

Grabbing the front of Frobisher's rugby jersey with both hands, he lifted him clear of the ground.

'Look here, Frobisher! I've had just about as much as I can take of you and your henchmen ribbing poor Wadey. It wasn't funny the first time you did it and its even less so now. I'm getting just a little tired of hearing it every time we come in here to get changed for a game. Do you understand what I'm saying, Frobisher? Am I making myself clear to you?'

Frobisher had turned bright red, partly from embarrassment, but mostly because Knight's grip on his jersey was constricting his breathing.

'Yes,' he croaked.

'Good!' Knight let him down, roughly. 'Now listen! All of you! Like me, each one of you is here for no better reason than your family's well off enough to pay your school fees. Yes, Wadey's a scholarship boy. But do you know what that means?'

'It means he's too poor to pay,' Mason Minor chimed in. A back-hander from Knight sent him flying.

'It means,' Knight continued, ignoring Mason Minor, 'that he is here through his own efforts! It means that he has had to work damned hard to prove to the powers that be that he's clever enough to benefit from the education here – without having to pay. In my book that makes him a better man than the three of you put together will ever be.'

He gave Wade's jersey back to him. 'Put it on,' he ordered.

Wade obeyed his skipper. The changing room was silent – everyone had stopped what they were doing to witness what was happening.

'Now, you three are each going to shake Wadey by the hand and

you're going to apologise to him. Understand?' They understood.
'And you better damned well mean it! You first, Ross-Parker.'

Ross-Parker shook Wade's hand. 'Sorry, Wadey,' he said.

'Louder!' Knight said.

'Sorry, Wadey!' Ross-Parker shouted. Mason was next, followed by Frobisher.

'And just remember this! If I ever hear any of you – or anyone else for that matter,' he addressed the whole room, 'mouthing off at Wadey ever again, you'll have me to reckon with! Understood?' Everyone understood.

'I never had any more trouble with any of them from that day on until I left to go to university.'

'Remember it!' Andrew said. 'Yes, remember it very clearly now. Also recall I was quaking in my boots the whole damned time, I can tell you!' They all laughed. 'Could have taken any one of them on their own with ease, but if they had all come at me at once – think I may have needed your help!'

'Well, it was my memory of that incident that came flooding back when you asked me that made me agree to help you.'

'You know what they say,' said Jessica. 'One good turn deserves another.'

As they left the hotel Jessica thanked James for all his help. 'I could never have managed it without you – particularly the anonymous phone call – and, of course, the recording machine.' They shook hands.

Andrew took Jessica's hand and kissed her on the cheek. 'Thank you for everything, Jessica. Thank you so much!' he said. 'All I have to do now is wait for your bill!' They laughed.

'Fine girl, that!' Andrew said as he and James walked back to the Jaguar. 'Might give her a call later in the week – ask her out for dinner.' James smiled to himself.

Andrew drove them to where *Aurora* was still moored and James invited him on board. Before getting on Andrew turned and looked at the bridge.

'So that's where you found her, is it?' he said, solemnly.

'Yes,' James replied, unlocking the boat doors.

Andrew looked at the canal below the bridge for some time. Eventually, he spoke. 'Well, I know we fought like cat and dog. Rather lacking in the moral scruples department and obviously tried to pull one hell of a fast one on poor old Griffiths, but … well, she didn't deserve that!'

'No,' James agreed. 'Industrial espionage is a serious crime, but it doesn't normally carry the death penalty.'

'Did in her case, unfortunately.' Andrew followed James on board.

Later, sitting on the front deck, nursing mugs of coffee, James said, 'I guess the only good thing to come out of this is that, as her only living relative, the rental income now reverts to you.'

'Thought about that as I sat in that police cell. At the time, I thought, "Fine lot of good it's going to do you if you're going to be sitting in another cell somewhere as a guest of Her Majesty!" But now, thanks to you and the lovely Jessica – no longer going to happen. Yes, I do have some plans.'

'How long do you think it will be before get the farm pulled round?'

'Oh, years, I'm afraid. But look, see that field over there?'

'The one with the two horses?'

'Yes. Our land. Got an idea for it that may interest you. In fact, your boating knowledge and experience could prove most useful.'

'I'm intrigued.'

'Well,' Andrew continued, 'what do you think about the idea of putting a marina there?'

'A marina?' James smiled. 'I think that's a brilliant idea! It would probably help to get rid of all the on-line moorings a mile or two back that way.' He pointed.

'Way I see it, a marina would be a sound investment, generating a steady income that I could use in addition to the rents to bring the farm up to date.'

'That sounds like an excellent plan, Andrew.'

'How would you feel about being a sort of "consultant" for the project?'

'I don't know. I'd have to think about it.'

'Of course! Of course!' Neither spoke for little while.

Then James emptied the dregs from his cup over the side and turned to Andrew. 'To be honest,' he said, 'I began to realise when I was working on that last lot of stuff for TechnoTec that it was getting a damned sight harder to come up with fresh scenarios each time I wrote a new version. And, of course, each one has got to be better than the last one. Honestly, it sometimes makes me feel a bit like a hamster on a treadmill.'

'Can understand that,' Andrew said quietly.

'I haven't said anything to Laura about it yet, but I've felt for a while now that I really need to get out of the rat race.'

'Confusing your rodents!' They laughed.

'I suppose, what I am trying to say is that TechnoTec has probably had his day. He may well have solved his last case. Would you be interested in me as a business partner in the marina?'

'Business partner, be blowed! If were doing this, we're damned well doing to do it properly, old man! Fellow director of Lower Field Marina plc more like!'

The minutes

LOWER FIELD MARINA plc

Minutes of a Board Meeting of the Directors held at the Marina on Friday 5 September 2008 at 10.00am

Present
Andrew Knight – Chairman and Managing Director
James Wade – Operations Director
Laura Wade – Finance Director
Jessica Knight – Company Secretary

General
Their fellow directors congratulated Mr & Mrs Knight on their recent marriage.

Operations
Mr Wade reported that all berths were now occupied and that a waiting list for vacancies had been commenced.

Finance
Mrs Wade reported that the finances were in a healthy position and that annual accounts to be presented at the AGM in October would show a substantial surplus.

Rose

A story of perseverance

※

Friday 28 July

Damian was nine – well ten, nearly, and it was the last day of the summer term.

'What are you doing in the holidays?' was the only topic of conversation in the playground. Damian and his friends were sitting on the tarmac resting their backs against the classroom wall after a strenuous lunchtime game of football.

'Where are you going?' Most of his friends were going abroad to Spain or France, a couple to Greece and one to America, but Damian – he was going on an adventure! Some weeks before, Brian and Chris, his mum and dad, had told him that they had, indeed, booked for all three of them to go on a boating holiday.

'We're going on a boat,' he told his friends. 'My dad says we're going to spend a whole week cruising along canals!'

'What's a canal?'

Damian shrugged. 'A bit like a river, I think. I've never been on one before.' But inside, he felt he was really special. 'I'm doing something different!' he thought. 'No-one else is going on a canal boat.' Damian was excited by the prospect.

Still vivid in his memory was that evening not long after Christmas when he had been sitting on the floor in the lounge, watching television. He could not remember which programme he had been watching because what had happened next had driven it completely out of his mind! His parents had been sitting together on the sofa looking at their laptop. They often did this when they were buying something new for the house or the garden. Consequently, Damian did not pay any attention to their conversation, but concentrated on the television.

Suddenly his dad had said, 'Hey, Damian. Come and look at this.' His dad often interrupted him while he was watching one of his favourite shows. Damian had sighed.

'Oh Dad!' he had said. 'But it might be something interesting,' he had thought, so he had got up from the floor and sat down on the sofa next to them.

'How would you like to spend a week in the summer on one of these?' Brian had asked him as he turned the screen to face his son. Damian had looked at the laptop. On the screen was a picture of a boat on some water. It was brightly painted in blue and white and looked very long and narrow. In the background there was a quaint-looking brick-built bridge over the water. Damian had been completely mesmerised by the picture. His grandparents lived near a river and he had seen boats – some of them very like this one – cruising along it and had always wondered what it would be like to go on one.

'Oh, yes!' he had exclaimed. 'That would be brilliant!' Brian and Chris had smiled at each other. 'Are you going to buy that boat, then?' Damian had asked.

'Good heavens, no!' Chris had laughed. 'They're ever so expensive. But there are lots of places on the canals where you can hire them. That's what we're going to do.'

'Watch this,' Brian had then said as he moved the cursor over an arrow on the picture. It showed a video of a family on a boat exactly like the one they were going to have!

'Here!' said Brian, as he had passed the laptop to his son. 'Have a look for yourself.'

Damian had taken the laptop and read the description. It sounded great! It was described as a '4 Berth Luxury Narrowboat'. It was called *Saturn* and the little ground plan showing the saloon, the galley, the bunk beds and the tiny bathroom was intriguing. There was another four-berth boat called *Venus* but that was booked for the week they wanted, his dad had said. Damian had clicked on the 'back' arrow and two other blue and white boats had appeared on the screen. These were smaller – only two-berth – and were called *Mercury* and *Mars*. When he had clicked on the forward arrow twice a very long boat had appeared. It, too, was painted blue and white. It was a six-berth and was called *Jupiter*.

'That's a really long boat!' he had said to his dad.

'Yes,' Brian had replied, 'it's a seventy-footer! Far too long for me to handle.'

'What's that in metres?'

'Um … about twenty-one, I should think – probably twenty-two.'

'That *is* long!' Damian had said. He had gone back to the picture of *Saturn* and stared at it for some minutes, trying to imagine what it would be like living on it for a whole week.

Damian had sat next to his parents while his mother completed the on-line booking form. His father pulled out his credit card and paid the deposit.

'That's sorted then,' Brain had said. '*Saturn* is booked from the 29th of July for one week!'

Damian returned to watching television. He felt a tingle of excitement in his stomach. This was going to be a great holiday!

In other years he had spent many holidays playing on beaches or staying at holiday centres, where he and the other children had been kept amused in the 'Kids Klub' by 'Mr Happy' et al who had made them perform silly dances in front of their parents at the evening's entertainment. But if he was really honest, these holidays bored him. But this year's holiday – this year's holiday was going to be different – a new place to stop every night, and so many new things to see and do. He could not wait to get on board.

Now, at last, after what seemed like a lifetime, the end of term had finally arrived. Tomorrow they would be setting off on their great adventure!

When Chris collected him from school that afternoon, she could see the eager anticipation written all over his face.

'Are we all packed up and ready to go yet, Mum?' he asked as soon as he got into the car.

'Nearly,' said his mum. 'Just a few more bits and bobs to put in the bags. Ah! Look!' she added as she turned into their road, pointing to a British Telecom van that was parked by the side of the green box that served the area. One man was working there and another was climbing a nearby telegraph pole.

'That explains why the phone's not been working all day.' Damian was not the least bit interested in the BT van. It did not affect him – or his holiday!

When it came to bedtime, he made none of his usual excuses. There was no pleading to be allowed to stay up for 'just another five minutes'. Once tucked up in bed, he lay there thinking about all the great things he was going to be doing in the coming days – steering the boat, working the locks, even going through a tunnel perhaps!

✳

Saturday 29 July

The whole family was up, washed, dressed and ready to go bright and early. After breakfast they packed the suitcases and food containers into the car, and clambered in. As Brian was reversing the car out onto the road the British Telecom van pulled away from the green box. The BT men must have made an early start to restore the connection. Brian changed from reverse to first gear and they were on their way! The great adventure had begun! At that precise moment, inside the empty house where no one could hear it, the telephone rang.

Damian thought that the journey to the boatyard was never going to end! Although the weather was dull and overcast, as it was the first weekend of the school summer holidays, the motorways were clogged with traffic and their progress was slow. Many times he was tempted to ask, 'Are we nearly there yet?' but he managed to stop himself. He knew from previous experience how much this exasperated his parents. Thank goodness he had remembered to bring his Nintendo with him!

Chris had the road atlas open on her lap. Neither Brian nor Damian could understand why she preferred to use the map. Didn't the car have a built-in satnav?

Eventually, however, they turned off the busy motorway and onto an A road where the traffic was a lot lighter. Looking out of the car window, Damian noticed that they crossed over a canal – not once, but twice! The second time they went over a bridge he caught sight of some locks, all smartly painted in black and white, and a boat was going into one of them.

'Look!' he called out. 'Some locks! Will we be going through those locks, Dad?' he asked.

'I'm not sure,' Brain replied. 'It depends which way we go.'

After another few miles they turned off the main road and onto a narrow country lane.

'It should be only about two miles along here on the right,' Chris said. Damian could hardly contain his excitement. They rounded a bend and there before them was the village where the boatyard was situated. They crossed over the canal again and Damian looked out of the window onto a wide expanse of water where many boats, all brightly painted in a rainbow of colours and of different lengths, were moored up to jetties. Soon after the bridge Chris spotted the entrance to the boatyard. Brian followed the signs directing them to the car park and parked the car. Damian leapt out eagerly, and ran towards the moored boats. He had seen the boatyard on the internet and now he was experiencing it in real life. He was so excited he felt he would burst!

'I think we need to go this way first,' his dad called after him, smiling. Damian turned and followed as Brian led them towards a wooden building, sporting a sign that read 'Water Holidays Boat Hire' and, below that, 'Reception'.

'Good morning!' The man behind the counter greeted them with a smile. 'Welcome to Water Holidays Boat Hire. How can I help?'

'Morning. The name's Briggs. We've a booking for a boat called…' Brian referred to a piece of paper in his hand. '*Saturn.*'

'Ah, Mr Briggs.' The smile disappeared from the man's face.

'We've had a bit of a problem with *Saturn*. We've been trying to get hold of you on the phone, but we couldn't get through.'

'Our phone was down most of yesterday,' said Chris.

'We kept getting the engaged tone and, unfortunately, we didn't have a mobile number. You see, it was the people who had *Saturn* last week. Somehow they managed to blow the engine up yesterday morning. I'm afraid it's going to be quite a few days before she can be used again.'

'Oh dear!' said Brian. 'Surely there's another boat we can have instead?'

'I'm afraid not. Every single one our boats is booked out this week.' Damian's face dropped. His heart sank. His great adventure was over before it had even started.

'As I say, we tried phoning you all yesterday afternoon to tell you and to offer you another week later in the season. I'm so very sorry to disappoint you, I really am ... very sorry. We hate letting our customers down. I've even tried all the other boatyards on this bit of canal to see if they can help, but with it being the first week of the school holidays, they're all booked out too. It looks as if you've had a wasted journey.'

At that moment, a lady came through from the office behind the reception desk. 'Are these the people for *Saturn*?'

'Yes.'

'Oh!' she said. 'We really are so very sorry. You've come all this way for nothing. I did manage to get the ringing tone on your phone this morning. It would have been...' She looked at her watch. '...about eight o'clock.'

'That's just about when we were leaving,' said Brian sadly. 'Oh, well,' he continued, 'I guess these things happen. There's nothing you can do about it. If only we'd given you a mobile number when we booked.' His voice barely concealed his disappointment.

'Let's see what other weeks we've got available for you, Mr Briggs,' said the man. 'Would you be able to rearrange your time off work? We'll make an adjustment to the hire fee, of course, for the inconvenience.'

'It won't be easy for me to rearrange my holiday for this

summer,' said Brian. 'In our office we've all got young children and the school holidays are carved up months in advance. You know what it's like. Would we be able to hold our booking over till next year?'

The lady looked at Damian's crestfallen face. He was devastated. Tears were forming in his eyes. He had been so looking forward to this holiday adventure so much for so long.

'Just a minute!' she said. 'Ray!' She beckoned the man towards the rear office, leaving them to ponder their misfortune. Chris was muttering at Brian. Brian was flicking through his diary. Damien bit his lip as his eyes filled with tears. He clenched his fists and stared out of the window at the jetties with all the brightly painted boats tied against them.

'All these boats…,' he was thinking when, what seemed to him like an age later, the man and woman came back, both with smiles on their faces.

'Rita's just come up with a brilliant idea that solves the problem. I suppose it takes a woman to sort these things out!' He looked at Chris and laughed nervously. 'She's suggested that you take *Heron* – she's our own boat. Obviously, we can't take her out during the season because we're too busy here so it will be good to give her an outing. I'll go and tell Harry to get her ready.' He left the office.

'Are you sure that's all right?' Chris asked anxiously. 'I mean, we're not very experienced with boats.'

'I'm sure you'll be absolutely fine,' said Rita. 'We hadn't realised that your booking included a young person.' She winked conspiratorially at Damien. 'I know you'll look after her. We might not have been so keen to lend *Heron* out to a party of all adults.' She turned to Brian. 'I couldn't bear to see the look of disappointment on your little boy's face. Now I just need a few details.'

About half an hour later, when the paperwork had all been completed, Ray put his head round the door of the office.

'Would you like to come this way – the boat's ready for you now.' After thanking Rita again for sorting things out, Brian, Chris and Damien followed him to the wharf.

✳

'This is *Heron*.' Ray was standing with his hand resting on the roof of a beautifully painted narrowboat. 'She's a conversion from an old working boat, although you've only got sixty feet to worry about rather than the original seventy!' He laughed as he saw the look of surprise mixed with anxiety on Brian's face. He proceeded to show them over the main cabin that housed the saloon, the galley, a bedroom with a double berth, and the bathroom. Damian's eyes darted round in amazement. He did not know where to look first.

'I don't know where you're going to sleep, lad,' said Brian, 'unless you curl up on the sofa there.'

'No need for that,' said Ray. 'Come and see this.' He led them back onto the wharf, then back towards *Heron*'s stern.

'Being an old working boat she's still got her original boatman's cabin at the back,' he said, opening the back doors and pushing open the sliding hatch in the roof. 'I should think you'll be very snug in here, young man,' he said to Damian. He led them down the steps into the tiny cabin. There was a seat along the right-hand side opposite a black-leaded cooking range. Next to the range was a cupboard. Ray demonstrated how the cupboard door hinged downwards to form a table. Chris looked at the seat along the side of the cabin.

'That doesn't look as comfortable as the sofa in the main part,' she said.

'Never fear!' said Ray, stepping further into the cabin. As they looked through they saw what they thought was an open space with a cupboard to the left-hand side. Ray turned to open the cupboard but it turned out not to be a cupboard at all, but a let-down double bed.

'Now that's going to be better than a crummy old sofa, isn't it?' he asked. They all smiled in agreement.

'Was this the whole of the living area – you know – in the old days?' Chris asked.

'This was it!' said the man. 'Everything happened in here – whole families lived in this tiny little space.'

'Amazing!' said Brian. 'And there's no way through to the main cabin area from here?'

'No, because that's where the engine is.' He patted the bulkhead on the far side of the bed. 'And beyond that would have been all cargo – that's where you are. Now, I'd better show you all the technical bits – the engine, and so on.' Damian was left in the boatman's cabin on his own. He loved it! It was his own little room – his own space for the next six days and nights.

'This is better than all the rest of the boat!' he thought. He opened all the cupboard doors and peered inside and pulled open all the drawers. There were so many little hidey holes. Even the step down into the cabin had a lid with space inside to put more things. On one side of the cabin there was a row of plates with pictures on them. They had holes all round their edges and each one had a coloured ribbon woven through the holes. On the porthole-shaped windows were little lace curtains and the inside of the cabin doors were painted with pictures of roses and fantastic imaginary castles.

'This is amazing!' he thought. 'I can't wait to tell my friends at school.'

Brian brought the car over to the side of the wharf and, after they had unpacked their luggage, he returned it to the car park. Having been shown by Ray how to start the boat's engine, Brian turned it on while Damian and Chris untied the mooring ropes and stepped on board.

Before long, having been carefully manoeuvred out of the boatyard by Ray, *Heron* was cruising along the canal with Brian at the tiller while Ray stood beside him, giving him a lesson in steering.

'We all watched the instructional DVD you sent,' said Brian. 'It was very good, but you can't beat a practical lesson from an expert!' His confidence grew and Ray congratulated him on the way he was handling the boat. Chris and Damian were sitting at the front. Damian's eyes darted in all directions.

'We're off, Mum!' he exclaimed. 'I'm so excited! This is going to be great!' He thought he was getting a bit big for hugs but nevertheless he gave his mum a big bear hug. 'Thanks, Mum,' he whispered and kissed her on the cheek.

At the first lock they tied up and Ray showed Brian where the windlasses were kept. With practised ease, he quickly made the lock ready for *Heron* to enter. With the boat in the lock, he showed them how to operate the gates and paddles. As Brian steered *Heron* out of the lock, Ray closed the gate behind them.

'You'll be fine!' he called. 'Have a good week! Have longer, if you like!'

'I've got to be back at work next Monday,' Brian answered.

'Well, you needn't come back till Sunday, then. Enjoy!' And with that Ray was gone and they were on their own – responsible for sixty feet of someone else's boat! Having got over his initial feeling of apprehension, Brian was surprised to find how easy the boat was to steer. The sun even came out to make things absolutely perfect. While Chris was busy unpacking and putting their things away, Damian, resplendent in his high-vis lifejacket, sat on the roof next to his dad, thoroughly enjoying his canal experience.

'It's good, isn't it, Dad?' he said.

Brian smiled at his son's happiness. 'What do you think it is about it that makes it feel so good?' he asked.

Damian thought for a few moments. 'I think it's two things,' he said at length. 'One is that you keep wanting to see what's round the next bend and what's through the other side of the next bridge.'

'Yes, that is fascinating, isn't it?' his dad agreed. 'What's the other thing?'

'It's knowing that people have been going along here in boats for years, and years, and years,' Damian said.

'Where you're sleeping,' Brian added, 'because this is such an old boat, people have been living and sleeping there for years, and years, and years too.'

After a while, Chris's head appeared above the roof at the front of the boat.

'Lunch!' she called. This was something new for Brian. Keeping the boat cruising along down the middle of the canal was one thing. Steering into the side to tie up was something else entirely. He slowed the engine, moved the tiller over so that the boat was heading towards the towpath, and cautiously approached the bank.

'Can you grab the end of that rope and step off with it when we get near enough?' he called, a slight sound of panic in his voice. Chris duly obliged. As the rear of the boat neared the bank, Brian handed a rope to Damian.

'You step off with this and keep us in tight to the bank,' his dad instructed him without taking his eyes off the front of the boat. They came to a halt hard against the towpath.

'That wasn't too bad!' said Brian, sounding relieved, as he took the two mooring pins and the hammer from the locker where Ray had showed him and joined the others on the towpath. He hammered the pins into the earth and tied the boat up at both ends. It all seemed a bit fiddly at first.

'I'm sure I'll get better at it with a bit of practice,' Brian thought. 'At least we're on our way. It could all have been such a total disaster!'

'Are those knots tight enough?' Chris asked.

'They're fine!' Brian answered, putting the hammer back in the locker. They all climbed back on board and down into the cabin.

After they had eaten their meal, Brian was looking at a guide to the canal he had found in the bookcase.

'We've got a couple more locks to do this afternoon,' he said, 'and I think we'll spend the night here.' He pointed to a spot on the map. 'It says there's a pub there that does food and welcomes children.'

Damian was looking forward to working the locks. He had watched carefully everything that Ray had done when he was showing them what to do at the first lock near the boatyard.

'Are the locks going up or down?' he asked. Brian looked at the guide again.

'Up,' he said. 'The same as the last one.' Damian nodded.

Not long after they had started cruising again, the first lock came into sight.

'These are the locks we saw from the car!' Damian shouted.

He and Chris were going to work the locks while Brian stayed on the boat. There was a bridge just before the first lock where the canal narrowed sufficiently for them to step off onto the towpath and walk on ahead to get the lock ready. Fortunately for Damian and Chris, there was a boat just about to leave the lock, so the gates could be left open for *Heron*. Unfortunately for Brian, this meant that he had steer to the right to allow the other boat to pass, so he was no longer on a straight course to enter the lock.

Damian and Chris waited on opposite sides of the lock, windlasses in hand, ready to close the gates. Damian wanted to get the boat through the lock perfectly, exactly as Ray had done. Brian tried to ease *Heron* into the narrow space, but banged the lock side quite hard as he did so. All three of them winced. Damian covered his eyes in embarrassment.

'Oh, Dad!' he exclaimed. Brian looked a little sheepish. Then Damian leaned back onto the gate and put all his weight against the balance beam, as he had watched Ray do. At first, the heavy gate refused to budge but suddenly he felt it give slightly, then it closed quickly as he walked backwards, leaning against the beam. The gate on Chris's side was already closed and his gate closed against it with a satisfying 'clunk'.

'Wow!' he said. 'I did that!' They walked to the far end of the lock and Chris began winding up the paddle on her side to let the water in. Damian tried to do the same, but the paddle on his side was too stiff for him. Try as he might, it would not turn.

'I'll give you a hand,' said his mum and crossed over the gate to help him. Damian was disappointed. He had wanted to work the first lock by himself without any help. Soon the boat was rising in the lock. However, he managed to lower the paddle on his own and, by pushing with all his might, to open and close the top gate. At the next lock Damian was pleased to find that he could work the paddles on his own. It was only the stiffer ones that defeated him!

They arrived close to the pub with plenty of daylight to spare. So when they had tied up Damian watched the water for signs of fish while Brian tried his luck with his fishing rod. Chris took a chair onto the bank and read one of the magazines she had bought especially for her holiday. Later they walked along the towpath to the pub for their meal. As it was a warm evening they decided to eat in the beer garden. There was a swing and a climbing frame in one corner and, after they had eaten, Damian joined a group of children for half an hour while Brian and Chris sat, glasses in hand, watching the sunset. As it began to get dark they walked back to the boat – their boat. Damien had butterflies in his tummy. Their first night aboard and he was sleeping in his own special private cabin! He climbed on board, full of excitement and, if he was honest, a little apprehension – but he was certainly not going to show that! Chris followed him into his cabin and made sure he was tucked in and settled for the night. Just before she left she handed him a torch.

'It'll seem dark in here,' she said, 'so you'll probably need this to find your way around.' Damian did not think he would, but he thanked her and took it anyway. 'And if you get frightened, just bang on the wall there. I'm sure we'll hear you.'

'I won't be frightened,' he said.

'Well, just in case you are…'

Later, safely tucked up in the let-down bed in the boatman's cabin, Damian thought back over his day. What a day it had been – his first day on a boat! From his impatience in the car, to his anticipation and excitement as they drove into the boatyard, to his depth of depression when they were told the boat they had booked was not available, to his elation when they were told that they could have this boat. And if that was not enough, his spirits had risen even higher when he was told that he could have this lovely little cabin at the back as his own for a whole week! The emotional roller-coaster of the day had made him tired. As he yawned and closed his eyes with the gentle movement of the boat in the water lulling him to sleep, he realised that he had not touched his Nintendo since getting out of the car!

As he lay there in the darkness Damian thought, 'I was right. I don't feel frightened at all.' From time to time he felt the boat rock gently as his parents moved about in the main cabin.

He was drifting off to sleep when he suddenly sensed

something. He was not sure what it was, but his mind told him that something in the little cabin was somehow different from what it had been a few seconds ago. It was not the same as when he had closed his eyes, of that he was sure. It felt as if there was someone else there, someone standing by his bed, watching him. But there could not be. He would have heard if the back doors or the sliding hatch in the roof had been opened. Slowly, a little nervously but unafraid, he opened his eyes. What he saw made him blink in surprise and alarm. Standing beside his bed in the gloom was what he first thought was a girl, a little older than him perhaps. Only … it wasn't a girl – well, not exactly. She looked like a young girl – sort of – but she was wearing an old-fashioned dress with a high neck and pleated skirt. It was all in white. But it was her skin that looked so strange. It was almost as pale as her dress. It seemed to Damian that both her skin and her clothes were so white and clear as to be almost transparent. He looked at her and she stood, motionless, staring back at him.

'Are you a g … ghost?' he whispered. His mouth was so dry he struggled to get the words out.

'I s'pose I am,' she answered. Her voice had a strange, eerie, echoey quality. 'Now!' she continued. An authoritative tone crept into her voice. 'You ain't gonna go silly on me, an' start screamin' an' callin' out for your Mam an' Dad, are you?'

'No,' he said, rather more firmly than he felt, remembering how he had told his mother he would not be scared. 'I'm not.' He sat up and hugged his knees to his chest.

'Good!' said the ghost.

'What … what are you doing here?' he asked, his confidence growing a little.

'I used to live on 'ere,' she said.

'What? On this boat?'

'Yeah! Me an' me Mam an' me Dad – well, this 'un an' the butty.'

'Don't be daft! A butty's a sandwich!' Damian said. 'You can't live on a sandwich!'

'What're you on about? What's sandwiches got do wi' it? A butty's a boat. Everybody knows that! Everybody 'cept you it seems like. It's a boat a bit like this 'un, only wi'out no engine. This 'un used to tow it be'ind, see? Our'n were called *Romford*.'

'You what?' spluttered Damian. 'You lived on here? In here? In this little space?' He tried to visualise the girl and her mother and father living in the tiny cabin.

'But it's smaller than my bedroom at home,' he said. The girl ignored him.

'Me Mam an' Dad slept 'ere on the cross bed,' she said as she pointed to where Damian was sitting. 'An' I slept over there on the side bed.'

Damian's eyes followed her pointing finger to the seat opposite the range. 'You slept there?' he asked.

'Yeah! Why?' Her echoing voice sounded as if she was a little insulted.

'Oh, nothing. It's just that I thought that was a seat. It seems a bit small for a bed.'

'So it were – a seat in the daytime, an' a bed at night.' There was silence for a few seconds. 'Me Mam done the cookin' on the range there – well, not that'd 'exactly cos that's a new 'un – but one jus' like it. We kept the coal for it in there.' She pointed to the step.

'That's clever!' said Damian.

'When we was eatin' me Dad used to pull that cupboard door down for a table.'

'Yes, the man at the boatyard showed us that,' said Damian.

''Course, this 'ere boat were a lot different back then,' the ghost continued.

'Different? How was it different?'

'Well, it were ten foot longer for a start,' she told him, 'an' all that bit where your Mam an' Dad are, that were all space for the load.' Damian could not believe he was sitting up in bed, calmly having a conversation with a ghost!

'Load? What load?' he asked.

'Back in them days there weren't no 'oliday boats on the cut like this 'un is now.'

'What's "the cut"?' It seemed to Damian that everything she said was in some strange foreign language.

'You don't know much, do you?' she said. 'The cut's what we're on – the water as the boat floats on!'

'Oh, you mean the canal!'

'You mean the canal!' she said in a posh voice, trying to mimic him. 'That's what the toffs used to call it. To us as lived on it, it were allus the cut. Any road, like I said, there weren't no 'oliday boats then. They was all workin' boats, like this 'un used to be. Me Dad'd git 'is orders from th' office an' we'd 'ave to go to a place somewhere an' pick up the load. It could be anythin' – coal, sand, wood, food or drink – anythin'.'

'And then you had to take it somewhere else?' he volunteered.

'You're gittin' it!' she said, the slight trace of a smile on her lips. 'We'd take it to wherever it'd gotta go, an' then unload it.' There was another pause while Damian tried to imagine again what her life must have been like. Suddenly, the ghost spoke again.

'What's your name?'

'Damian Briggs. What's yours?'

'Tilly,' she said. 'Well, Matilda, really, but everybody allus called me "Tilly".'

A thought occurred to Damian. 'If you spent all your life travelling around from one place to another on the "cut"...' He made sure he used the right word. '...how did you manage to go to school?'

'Never went to no school.'

'You mean you never learned to read and write, and do maths and PE and Art and DT and...?' He reeled off a list of subjects he learned at school.

'Me Mam learned me about numbers an' countin' money – so's I could go to the shops for 'er, but there weren't no call for readin' an' writin' on the cut. Dunno nothin' 'bout the rest as you're on about. PE? DT? RE? What's all them letters mean?' Damian tried to explain but Tilly began to look bored. 'What a load o' ol' rubbish!' she said. 'You learn a lot better things on the cut – useful things! I'll tell you summat else. You git plen'y o' exercise an' all. You ain't got no need to go around jumping off boxes and things in a 'all!'

Damian had to agree – some of the lessons were – well –

boring. He thought at first that Tilly's life would have been great. Cruising along the canal every day and never having to go to school! But then another thought struck him. He could not imagine how anyone could go through their whole life without ever being able to read. He loved reading. It was the best thing about school.

'Any road,' she said, 'you'll be needin' your beauty sleep. You'd best try an' git some shut-eye.' She looked at him again with that same enigmatic half-smile on her face.

'Will you … will you come and see me again?' he asked. 'We're on here till next Saturday – or even Sunday, perhaps.'

'I might jus' do that,' she said. 'I reckon as I'm gittin' to like you a bit, Damian Briggs.'

'And I like you too, Tilly,' he said. But even as he said it, he realised he was talking to thin air. Tilly had disappeared.

※

Sunday 30 July

When he woke up Damian could not decide whether his nocturnal visitor had been real or whether the excitement of the day, the large plate of burger and chips at the pub – plus a couple of small swigs of bitter from his father's glass – had made him dream. He looked around the cabin. It looked exactly the same as it had the previous evening. Was he imagining things or was the air really tinged with the presence of Tilly, his mysterious visitor? This little cabin, though all new to him, he realised, would have been very familiar to her. It was hard for him to imagine Tilly and her family living and working in it, travelling from one place to another to pick up a load here, and take it there. It was a life so alien to his own. He looked over at the side bed and in his mind's eye saw her getting up in the morning and getting ready for her day's work. He could still see her quite clearly in his mind in her high-necked dress with its pleated skirt. Her strange words and echoing voice still rang in his ears.

As he lay there, he wondered whether he should mention Tilly to his parents, but he decided against it. They would say either that he had definitely been dreaming, or that he was making the whole thing up and he certainly did not want them to stop him sleeping in the boatman's cabin! He stayed in bed until the movement of the boat told him that his parents were up and about. Then he got up.

'Did you sleep well?' his dad asked as he stepped down into the main cabin.

'I was worried that you'd be scared at the back there, all by yourself,' his mum added.

'No, I was fine!' said Damian. 'I didn't feel at all alone. It was great fun.'

As they ate breakfast the sun came out and soon after the meal was finished they were under way. Brian and Chris shared the steering between them and – under Brian's supervision – Damian had a few turns at it too. Steering was great – especially when he had learned how to go through bridges! He enjoyed helping with the locks, of which there were a number that day.

'It's good fun on the cut, isn't it Mum?' he said, as they stood on the lock side, waiting for it to empty.

'The cut?' Chris repeated. 'Where did you get that word from?' He bit his lip. Why had he said that? It was a Tilly word!

'It means the canal. I … er … I think Ray from the boatyard said it – or I might have read it in the brochure.' His mother made no further comment and he breathed a sigh of relief.

Much as he was enjoying the day, he found his mind kept returning to Tilly. In his own mind he was certain that she had not been part of a dream, and neither had she been a product of his imagination. The more he thought about her, the more convinced he became that she was real – well, as real as any ghost could be!

That night they had dinner on the boat. Damian laid the table without being asked. His parents exchanged glances. Why did he never do that at home? Chris had prepared a number of meals the week before the holiday and frozen them, and they were stored in the fridge in the galley. All the fresh air had made them hungry and they soon demolished a chicken casserole and a treacle tart. After they had washed up, they settled down to watch the tiny television. Brian had to waggle the aerial about a bit to get the best picture, but soon it was almost perfect. Damian watched with one eye on the clock. He felt himself getting butterflies in his tummy as bedtime approached.

When Damian was – for the second night running – quite happy to go to bed the first time they asked him, his parents put it down to his having spent so much time in the fresh air. It must have tired him out. They were blissfully unaware that he had a date – a date with a ghost!

'There's no need for you to come and tuck me in tonight, Mum,' he said, feeling very grown-up as he kissed each of them before running along the towpath and clambering up onto the back deck. He pulled the doors closed behind him and quickly put on his pyjamas. Then he crawled into bed and waited. It seemed that he had waited an awfully long time. In fact, he had almost reached the conclusion that she was not going to appear that night – when that was exactly what she did – appear! One minute there was nothing but the empty cabin and the next, materialising out of thin air, there she was!

'It's just like the way the Tardis materialises in *Doctor Who*!' Damian thought.

'Hello, Damian Briggs!' she said in that same echoing, other-worldly voice.

'Hello, Tilly,' he said, sitting up in the bed.

'D'you like it on the cut?' she asked.

'Yes, I do!' he replied. 'It's being the best holiday, ever!' He proceeded to tell her all that he had done that day – how he had steered the boat and worked the locks. 'There's so much to see and so much to do!'

'Ah, there is that,' she said. 'Mind, we never 'ad much time for stoppin' an' lookin' at places – sightseein', as you might say. We 'ad to git the load delivered on time, see? Only time we ever 'ad a chance o' lookin' round was when th' engine broke down, or summat, an' we 'ad to wait for the mechanic bloke to come out an' mend it.'

'But you could see all the trees and the fields and everything as you went along – like we're doing.'

'Oh, yeah, we could do all that all right.'

'And I love working the locks!' he added. 'There's lots of them and they're such fun!'

'You wanna try workin' 'em on a cold winter's day when it's pourin' o' rain! They ain't much fun then, I can tell you!'

She lapsed into silence. After a few seconds, Damian plucked up the courage to ask her something that had been on his mind all day.

'If you're really a ghost … that means you're … well … dead, doesn't it?'

'Oh, yeah!' she answered in a matter-of-fact tone. 'I been dead for years.'

'Well, when you're dead, aren't you supposed to go to heaven, or somewhere?' he asked.

'Summat like that,' Tilly replied, then fell silent again.

Damian again plucked up his courage. 'So … why are you still here? Why haven't you gone to heaven … or somewhere?'

The expression on her pale face changed to one that was even sadder than before. She sighed. 'It's a long ol' story, that is,' she said, 'an' it's a story as I ain't sure as you'd understand.' She fell silent again and Damian yet again plucked up all the courage of a nine – well, nearly ten-year-old – to ask another question that he had been burning to ask even though he was not sure whether he should ask it.

'How did you die?' he enquired quietly. The half-smile returned to her face.

'I were wonderin' 'ow long it'd be afore you asked me that,' she said. 'I 'ad a disease – summat as they called "consumption".'

'I've never heard of that,' Damian said sympathetically. 'Is it anything like chickenpox? I had the chickenpox last year.'

'No,' she said, 'it ain't nuthin' like the chickenpox. The chickenpox ain't nuthin' compared to consumption. When you gits consumption you're really bad. You 'as a real bad pain 'ere, in your chest.' She pointed. 'An' it make you cough. An' sometimes you coughs up a bit o' blood an' all. An' all the time you're gittin' thinner an' thinner – sort o' wastin' away.' She paused, as if she was recalling the pain. 'It's a 'orrible disease.'

Damian was relieved that she had not been upset by his question and decided to ask another.

'So, when did you die?'

'Sixteenth o' February, nineteen thirty-two,' she said, 'right there – in that there bed.' She pointed to the side bed. 'I were ten.'

Damian was intrigued by her candour and encouraged by her directness.

'What happened then … after you'd died, I mean?'

'Oh, they took me body off the boat an' put it in a coffin. Last I seen on it, it were bein' took away in a big black car.' Damian stared at her, open-mouthed, trying to take in what this ghostly young girl with her echoey voice was telling him so calmly. It made him feel cold inside. No one had ever talked to him about people dying, apart from the silly games you played in the school playground where, when you were dead, you got up again when the bell went. Yet here was Tilly telling him, as calmly as if she was talking about a visit to the shops, about dying and about what happened to a dead body afterwards. And it was not just anybody's death she was talking about and anyone's body. It was hers! But he did not feel afraid. There was something … something reassuring in Tilly's voice. He was not frightened. Tilly did not scare him.

'Look,' she said, seeing his expression, 'all this talk o' dyin's gonna put ideas in your 'ead. It'll either keep you awake, an' your Mam an' Dad'll be worried why you're so tired in the mornin', or it'll gi' you nightmares. You'd best go to sleep now.' And with that she was gone.

'Nineteen thirty-two! That's a long time ago,' he thought. 'That was even before granny was born and before the Second World War we learned about at school! No wonder she looks and talks so differently.' He scanned the darkness for her, but there was no trace. He lay awake for a while, mulling over in his mind all the strange things she had told him. There were so many questions he wanted to ask her. He wished she had stayed longer. Eventually he fell into a dreamless sleep.

✳

Monday 31 July

The sky was a little overcast, but fortunately it was not raining when Damian left his secret little world to join his mum and dad.

'We've got the tunnel to go through today,' his father said as they set off after breakfast. 'It says in the guide book it's supposed to be haunted!' he added.

'I'm not scared!' Damian smiled at his father. 'Not all ghosts are bad, you know.' Brian looked at Damian. He was a little puzzled by his son's response but made no comment. Damian continued. 'They're just the souls of people who have died but they can't go to heaven for some reason.'

'Where did you hear that?' Chris asked.

'Oh, no!' thought Damian. 'I've said too much again! I mustn't mention Tilly whatever I do!'

'Oh…' he said, thinking on his feet, 'one of my friends at school told me about them. He'd got a book about ghosts.'

As they approached the tunnel, Damian was in his favourite place on the cabin roof.

'Is it all right if I stay up here, Dad?' he asked. 'I've got my lifejacket on.'

'I think you'd be better off if you sat up the front with Mum.'

'I'll be ever so careful, Dad,' he promised.

'No, I'd rather you weren't on the roof because if you were to fall off I wouldn't be able to see well enough in the dark to rescue you and steer the boat at the same time.'

Reluctantly, Damian joined Chris in the front of the boat.

Brian had never steered through a tunnel before. He was going to need all his concentration. Chris was not too keen on the idea of being underground – but she would not say so, especially to Damian. He was excited and could not wait to get inside into the darkness.

'This is great!' he thought.

The entrance to the tunnel loomed ahead, a brick wall

surrounding a dark, black hole. No one spoke, their gazes fixed firmly ahead. It was a bit scary – with or without ghosts – good ones or bad ones. The boat moved inexorably forwards into the inky blackness. Brian had switched on the tunnel headlight but its beam only probed a mere few metres into the darkness ahead of them. It took some minutes for their eyes to adjust after the daylight outside. Chris had turned on all the lights inside too, but they only seemed to heighten the contrast with the surrounding gloom. They noticed a difference in the noise of the engine too. While they had been cruising along out in the open they could hear the engine but it was not particularly loud. But here, reverberating in the confines of the tunnel, it sounded as if there was a raging beast under the boat. Any conversation between them was virtually impossible unless they shouted at the tops of their voices.

Over the noise of the engine Brian was making what he imagined were ghostly noises and laughing in a scary way. It did not frighten Damian.

'Tilly's not like that at all!' he thought. Chris, however, was unsettled. After a while she stood up and shouted, 'Brian! Will you stop that! Please!' Brian lapsed into silence. Chris and Damian looked at each other and, realising how silly she had been, they both began laughing too.

As their eyes became accustomed to the darkness and their ears to the thud of the engine, Damian and his mum made shapes with their hands in front of the headlight and shadows of flying birds and hopping rabbits appeared on the tunnel walls. They both squealed as, about half way through the tunnel, a stream of freezing cold water cascaded onto them from the tunnel roof.

To Damian's disappointment and Chris's relief they saw no ghosts and it was not long before the far end of the tunnel was looming larger and larger in front of them. As they emerged, blinking, into the daylight, they were pleased to see that the clouds had passed over and the sun was shining.

This was the third day of Damian's boating adventure. The daylight hours were marvellous. 'Really cool!' he told his mum. He was not bored at all. Chris had bought him a canal spotters book and he had already ticked off half-a-dozen things — a lock, a swan, a fisherman, a working boat (well, he was living on one!), a bridge, and now a tunnel. He was collecting the names of all the other boats they passed and writing them down in a notebook. His dad let him steer quite often and he enjoyed running along the towpath, keeping up with the boat. This holiday – this adventure – was certainly everything he had anticipated it would be – and then there was Tilly! Much as he was revelling in the daytime, he was looking forward so much to the nights – the times when he could talk again to the mysterious Tilly.

Again that night he lay awake waiting for her – and, as before, just when he was least expecting her, sure enough, she appeared.

"Ow'd you git on in the tunnel?" she asked him.

'It was a bit scary at first,' he said, 'but I sort of got used to it.' He went on to tell her of his experience. 'Were you scared when you went through a tunnel for the first time?'

She looked at him disdainfully. 'Didn't know much about it,' she said. 'I were only a babby! While I were growin' up tunnels was just part o' the job – part o' me everyday life – like locks. I never got scared in 'em.' She lapsed into silence.

'Tilly.'

'Yeah?'

'Last night you said that the reason you couldn't go to heaven was a long story that I wouldn't understand.'

'Yeah, I did.'

'Well, if you tell me the story, perhaps I could try to understand it.'

Tilly sighed a long, heavy, echoey sigh. Then she was silent for a good minute. Damian waited patiently.

'Awright,' she said at last, 'I'll tell you. But you'll 'ave to let me tell you the 'ole story an' not interrupt me.'

'I won't.'

'An' you won't 'ave to laugh an' say as I were bein' a silly little gel, neither!'

'I won't. I promise.' Damian sat upright on the bed and Tilly stood in front of him, her head slightly to one side and her hands clasped across her chest.

'Right! Well, it all started off when me Gran were took bad. She were real old an' she'd 'ad to give up boatin' when me Grandad died. She were livin' in a cottage on the bank – though she never liked livin' there as much as on the boats. Well any road, me Mam were 'er only daughter so she 'ad to go an live wi' 'er an' look after 'er, like. Well, me Dad couldn't work the boats on 'is own an' I weren't old enough to 'elp 'im proper, like. So it were 'is sister – me Aunt Maud – she come on 'ere wi' us.

'I'd never likcd 'er, an' she 'adn't never liked me neither. She'd never got wed nor 'ad no kids. Good job too! Cos the poor little blighters would've 'ad 'ell of a life if she 'ad! She were so strict! You only 'ad to do the slightest thing as she didn't like an' she were down on you like a ton o' bricks! She even tol' me Dad off once!

'Any'ow, I reckon as I were about your age at the time, p'raps a bit younger. Any road, I 'ad this 'ere doll. She were only a ol' rag doll but she were the only toy I ever 'ad as a kiddy an' I loved 'er. I called 'er Rose an' I loved 'er more 'n anythin' else in the 'ole world.

'Now, I already knew as me Aunt Maud didn't 'old wi' gels o' my age 'avin' dolls. I'd 'eard 'er sayin' to me Mam when she'd been visitin' us afore as she reckoned it were "un'ealthy" cos dolls was only for really young little gels, so I knowed right enough as soon as she come on 'ere as I'd 'ave to do summat about me lovely Rose.'

Damian opened his mouth and was about to ask her what she did. She saw him and placed her finger on her lips. He remembered his assurance that he would not interrupt her and closed his mouth again.

'I tried to keep 'er 'id out the way o' Aunt Maud. But one night she seen me wi' 'er. "Right," says she. "We'll 'ave no more o' this silly little gel stuff!" she says. "An' if I catches sight on it again I'll put that there mucky ol' lump o' rag on the range!" She called my lovely Rose a "mucky ol' lump o' rag!"' Tilly's eyes widened in horror. 'I couldn't bear to 'ave 'er chucked on the range.

'But you can see for yourself as there ain't many places as you could find to 'ide her in 'ere. Well, that night, when me Dad an'

Aunt Maud was gone to the pub, I put Rose in a big ol' empty jam jar as we 'ad, an' I screwed the lid on tight. Then I cut up a bit o' stuff an' made a cover for it an' I tied it on tight wi' a bit o' string. Then I snuck out wi' Rose in 'er jam jar an' we went right round the back o' the pub. See, I needed somewhere where I could 'ide Rose till me Mam come back an' Aunt Maud wen' 'ome again. Then I could go an' rescue 'er.

'Any road, round the back o' the pub there were a railway. It were down a steep ol' bank. I didn't know 'ow long it'd be afore I were gonna be able to rescue Rose agin, so I 'ad to make sure as I knowed where I'd 'id 'er.

'Well, on this 'ere railway there were one o' them signallin' things, I reckon they're called – big white post it were wi' red an' yeller things at the top as flop up an' down. So, right next to that there signal thing I dug 'ole. I dug it wi' me bare 'ands, I did! An' I put Rose in 'er jam jar in the 'ole an then I covered her up again. An' I says to 'er, I says, "Rose," I says, "you'll be awright 'ere till me Mam gits back an' then I'll come back 'ere an' I'll dig you up agin an' rescue you."'

Damian was enthralled by her story but he could not understand why hiding her doll should stop Tilly going to heaven. He was longing to ask but, remembering his promise, he stayed silent.

'Me Gran, she were bad for a long ol' time,' Tilly continued, 'an' by the time as she died I were already bad wi' the consumption. Me Mam come back on 'ere an' Aunt Maud wen' 'ome. But be that time I were too poorly to git out o' bed so I couldn't go an' git poor Rose. It broke me 'eart! Honest! It really did.'

She was quiet for a long time. Damian could contain his curiosity no longer. 'But how does that stop you going to heaven?' he asked softly, his voice gentle and full of emotion.

'You only gits to go to 'eaven if you're free. An' I ain't free, see?'

'How do you mean? You're not free?'

'I made a promise, see? I made a promise to summat as I loved – to Rose. I promised 'er as I'd go an' rescue 'er. Only, I ain't done it! I ain't never been an' dug 'er up, like I promised. I knows as she were only a doll but I loved 'er so much it were almost like she were alive. It were like she 'ad a soul!' She paused. 'Do you reckon as you can ever love summat so much as you can gi' it a soul an' make it come alive, Damian Briggs?' she asked, suddenly.

'I don't know. I don't know much about it. I've never thought about it,' he said, 'but … perhaps…'

'Well, I ain't never been to rescue 'er, see. An' now I won't never be able to go an' rescue 'er neither.'

'Why not?'

''Cos I can't git off this 'ere boat!' she almost shouted as her voice rose in desperation. 'There's like a invisible wall all round it. A wall as I can't git through, no matter 'ow 'ard I tries! An' I can't never go nowhere away from this 'ere boat. Not till I'm kept me promise an' gone back an' got Rose!'

If ghosts could cry then that is what Tilly was doing now. Her unearthly, echoey wailing was a sound Damian had never in his life heard before and he hoped he would never hear again. It was a sound that penetrated to his heart and into his very soul.

'Perhaps … perhaps, I could go and rescue Rose for you,' he heard himself saying. 'I could dig her up and bring her back here for you.' The wailing stopped instantly. For a few moments there was silence. Damian was conscious of his heart beating. Then Tilly spoke.

'Could you?' she said, quietly. 'Would you … would you do that … for me?'

'I can try,' he said. 'Is the pub along this bit of cana … cut?'

'You should be goin' past it tomorra, I reckon. It ain't a pub no more, though. It's a 'ouse now. A big 'ouse, all painted white. I knows as it's still there cos I been past it lots o' times when Ray 'n' Rita's been on 'ere. Would you really go an' git me Rose for me? That'd be a very kind thing to do, that would.' She paused. 'I reckon … I reckon as it'd be the kindest thing as anybody ever done for me!'

'I'll look out for the house,' Damian said. 'If I can get Mum and Dad to stop somewhere near it I'll see if I can get away on my own for a bit.'

There was a pause. 'You dunno what it'd mean to me to git me Rose back,' she said.

'I think I'm beginning to,' Damian said, as Tilly proceeded to explain to him the exact location in relation to the railway signal where Rose was buried.

'It's late,' she concluded. 'You better git to sleep.'

'I'll look out for the house tomorrow,' he said – but she had gone.

Tuesday 1 August

The good weather of the previous day continued into the following morning as Damian and his parents made their usual early start. Damian kept his eyes peeled, looking out for large white houses that may have previously been pubs. He noticed that the railway line, now disused and abandoned, closely followed the route of the canal and they cruised under a couple of old railway bridges. He pointed these out to his father who was steering at the time. As they passed under the remains of one of them, in his imagination he saw a steam locomotive, hauling carriages, thundering overhead.

'All the trains Tilly would have seen going over there were steamers,' he thought.

'I bet it was great to see a steam train going over there,' he said aloud.

His father was impressed by his interest. On previous holidays Damian would have been expressing boredom by Tuesday, he thought, not discussing disused railways. He must be growing up!

It was about mid-morning when they approached a large white house. Damian thought that it might fit the bill but, try as he might, he could not think of a reason why he could suggest that they should stop there. 'And anyway,' he mused as they cruised past, 'I don't think it's close enough to the railway to be the one where Rose is.'

Later that afternoon Chris was steering so that Brian could sit on *Heron's* front deck and enjoy the peace and quiet away from the noise of the engine.

'The best place to sit on a narrowboat!' Ray had told them. Damian, however, was sitting in his favourite place, next to his mother on the cabin roof. The sky became overcast and the wind had risen. As they rounded a bend a large white-painted house came into view on the towpath side of the canal. Looking at the house, Damian was certain he could hear the echoing tones of Tilly's voice in his head. 'This 'ere's the one!' she was saying. 'This 'ere's the one!'

He was brought back to the present by the sound of his father's voice from the front of the boat.

'Look, Chris, there's a decent bit of straight bank along here – just beyond that house. I think we ought to tie up here for the night. It looks as if it might rain.'

'Good idea!' Chris called back. Damian could not believe his good fortune! He looked at the white house, then at the land behind it. Yes! It was just as Tilly had said. The route of the railway line went quite close behind the house and there was a steep bank leading down to it. He could not see the signal yet, but he would have the opportunity to look for that later. There was still plenty of time before their evening meal would be ready – plenty of time for him to go off 'for a walk' – and rescue Rose! He imagined where Rose would be waiting safely buried in her jam jar down at the bottom of that bank next to the signal.

Chris steered the boat towards the towpath and Brian jumped off with a rope. Unlike his father, Damian had been so intent on looking for large white houses that he had failed to notice the enormous black cloud that had been creeping up, inexorably, behind them for the last few miles. As he jumped off the boat to help his father tie up the sky suddenly darkened. There was a flash of lightning. A deafening crack of thunder followed and, almost immediately, he was soaked by a torrential downpour.

'Hurry up and get inside!' his mother called. He and his father fumbled with the slippery ropes with their wet hands. He shuddered as a drop of rain hit his neck and ran down his back. He clambered aboard the boat and stood, shivering. He changed his clothes while his mother rubbed his hair dry with a towel. All the time he was hoping against hope that it would only be a short, sharp shower, as thunder showers often are. He was completely distraught but he dared not show it.

'This was going to be my one chance to rescue Rose,' he thought, 'and the weather has stopped me. There's no way I can suggest I go for a walk now – not in this!' The storm rumbled on right through their meal and it was it still teeming with rain when they had finished. By the time the weather had abated it was almost dark.

Damian was concerned about what Tilly would think of him. Would she understand why he had not been able to go and rescue Rose? Or would she be angry with him for being put off his mission by a drop of rain? In the event, when Tilly appeared that night, he was relieved to find that she was sympathetic.

'It were just your bad luck as that rain started down when it did,' she said, 'but you got another chance afore you git 'em ahead tomorra.'

'What's "git 'em ahead" mean?' he asked.

'That's what we used to call settin' off of a mornin',' she said. 'Gittin' the boats ahead – gittin' goin', like.'

'Dad usually likes to get started pretty early. I don't know if I'll get a chance tomorrow,' he said.

'Oh!' Tilly was downcast.

'But don't worry,' he said, suddenly remembering. 'We've got to come back along this way later in the week.'

Tilly's feelings recovered. ''Ave you?'

'Yes. We've got to have the boat back at the boatyard by Sunday because my Dad's back at work on Monday. He was saying yesterday that wherever we get to by the end of tomorrow, that's where we'll have to turn round and start coming back again.'

'So you'll be comin' back this way again in – what? – couple o' days?'

'Yes, about that, I should think.'

'That's a short ol' run, that is!' she replied. 'Back in the days when this were a workin' boat it sometimes took us more 'n a week to git to where we was pickin' up a load. Then it'd probably take a day or two to load it up – 'specially if it were coal as me Mam an' Dad 'ad to load up wi' shovels.'

'Your Mum had to shovel coal?' Damian was horrified! He tried to imagine his own mother wielding a shovel and loading a 'seventy-footer' with coal.

'Oh, yeah!' Tilly replied. 'All the boatwomen did. It were part o' the job. If there were no one at the coal yard as could 'elp, then there weren't nothin' else for it. They 'ad to 'elp the men. Any road, when the boats was loaded we'd prob'ly 'ave to go for another week or more afore we got to where it were goin'. Like I say, it's a short ol' run, this 'un is!'

There was a pause.

'I been watchin' you workin' them there locks,' Tilly said, abruptly changing the subject.

'Some of the paddle things are a bit stiff for me to turn,' he said.

'Ah!' she said, a knowing look in her eye, 'Not if you knows 'ow to do it right! There's a trick to it!'

'What sort of a trick?'

'If you puts your windlass on wi' the 'andle pointin' down'ards, then they will be stiff cos your pullin' up on it. Now, if you puts it on wi' the 'andle pointin' up'ards, you'll find it goes easier cos you're puttin' your weight on it.'

'But what about when you've done your half turn downwards? You've still got to pull it upwards for the next bit.'

'No, you ain't!' she countered. 'You jus' takes your windlass off an' you puts it on agin wi' the 'andle pointin' up'ards. Simple, really!'

'That's very clever!' Damian said. But as he said it he saw that she was no longer there.

※

While Damian had been talking with Tilly, Brian and Chris had been enjoying a glass of wine in the main cabin.

'I don't know about you,' Brian said, 'but I could really get into this boating thing. I never thought I would enjoy this holiday anywhere near as much as I am doing.'

'I'm really enjoying it too,' Chris replied. 'Especially when I think of the disaster it could have been. Can you imagine what

Damian would have been like if we'd had to turn round and drive straight back home?'

'Unbearable!' Brian replied. 'Totally unbearable – and you couldn't really blame him. He was looking forward to this week so much he'd have been completely devastated. He seems to be really enjoying himself, though, doesn't he?'

'I'll say!' She paused. 'Do you know what he asked me this morning?'

'What?'

'He asked me if I'd had any dolls to play with when I was a little girl.'

'Strange question!'

'That's what I thought – but it gets even stranger. He then asked me if there was one special doll I loved more than all the others.'

'And was there?'

'Oh, yes! Tabitha, I called her. She was my absolute favourite.' She paused again. 'Then he asked the strangest question of the lot.'

'Which was?'

'He wanted to know whether if you loved something – something like a doll, for instance – if you loved it strongly enough could you, in some strange way, give it a soul and make it, somehow – I don't know – make it come alive!'

Brian looked heavenward. 'Where on earth did that come from? It's straight out of left field, that is!'

'Goodness knows where he thought that one up from!'

'What an odd thing to ask! What did you say?'

'I was a bit at a loss for words. I didn't really know what to say. I didn't want to start putting weird ideas into his head so I told him I didn't really know because it wasn't something I'd ever really thought about – but I couldn't see why not.'

'And did that satisfy him?'

'It seemed to. Well, put it this way, he changed the subject after that and we went on to talk about something else.'

'He's getting to be a bit of a deep thinker is our Damian. He said something that surprised me this morning,' Brian said.

'What was that?'

'It wasn't as odd as his conversation with you, but you know how soon he's got bored on holiday in previous years?'

Oh, yes! Tell me about it!'

'It was as we were coming under an old railway bridge – the line's disused now – one of Beeching's casualties probably. Anyway, as we came under it he looked up and said how great it would be to watch a steam-hauled train thundering over the top above our heads!'

'I never knew he was interested in that sort of thing.'

'Neither did I. Perhaps because we're on the canal – which is even older – it's sparked off an interest in past forms of transport.'

'Well, that'll certainly make a refreshing change from that craze he's had just lately on space travel!'

'Who knows?' Brian mused. 'We may have begotten a future industrial archaeologist!'

✳

Wednesday 2 August

A new day dawned and the previous night's thunderclouds had passed. The sun shone in a bright blue sky. As they prepared to cruise along to the furthest point of their journey Damian was busy. He was making plans in his head as to how he was going to go about rescuing Rose. He had been so intent on finding the place where she was buried and trying to think of a way he could get away on his own to rescue her that he had not actually given any thought as to how he was going to do it. That morning, he was standing in the galley, helping Chris by drying up the breakfast things, when an idea suddenly came to him. Brian was sorting out the engine and getting the boat ready to start so, when Chris was looking the other way, Damian finished drying up a tablespoon. Instead of putting it in the cutlery drawer he slipped it, stealthily, into his pocket.

Later that morning, after cruising for a couple of hours, they arrived at a small town with plenty of visitor moorings.

'We need to do some food shopping,' Chris called.

The moorings were quite full of boats but Brian spotted a gap he thought would be just long enough to take *Heron*. He carefully steered into it, then he and Damian tied up the boat.

'Made to measure!' Brian shouted as he saw how the boat fitted snugly into the gap. Damian smiled. All three of them then left *Heron* and went in search of a supermarket to replenish their food stocks.

They had a sandwich and a drink at the coffee shop in the supermarket and, as they were making their way back to the boat, laden down with groceries, Damian noticed a sign that read 'Museum' with an arrow pointing down a side street. He knew his father was very fond of museums, as he was fascinated by the local history of the places they visited. Enthusiastically, Brian would read every word on every interpretation board and examine every exhibit in minute detail. Damian also knew that his mother found museums boring. After about ten minutes she would say to Brian, 'I'll wait for you outside,' and then leave him to it. Damian could take them or leave them, finding some more interesting than others. Brian had not spotted the sign so Damian thought it best to say nothing.

When they had returned to the boat and unpacked the shopping Damian picked up one of the empty plastic carrier bags and, unseen, quickly stuffed it into his pocket. Brian had another look at the canal guide before they started off again.

'There's what they call a "winding hole" a few miles further on,' he said. He pronounced the word as in 'binding'. 'And it's not far past a pub. It does food but it doesn't say whether kids are welcome or not. Ah, hang on! It's got a beer garden. It's going to be a nice night so we can all eat outside.'

'What's a "winding hole", Dad?' Damian asked.

'It's a place where the canal has been dug out especially wide so that you can turn round with a long boat like this one.'

'Why's it called a "winding hole"?'

'I don't know. The book doesn't say.' Brian stood up. 'OK. Let's get going.'

'Let's get 'em ahead!' said Damian without thinking.

His parents looked at him. 'What was that?' asked Chris. Damian panicked. Yet again his loose tongue had let him down! That was one of Tilly's phrases! But he could not tell them that! Again, he had to think quickly on his feet.

'I said, "Let's go on instead." I mean, it's a pity we've got to turn round and go back again, isn't it? Wouldn't it be great if we could just keep going?'

Brian and Chris exchanged knowing glances. This holiday had been a success! They agreed with him. It would have been good if they had been able to continue their cruise for another week, if not even longer.

Considering it was the first time he had ever 'winded' a boat, Brian made a good job of turning *Heron* round in the winding hole and they tied up for the night with the boat facing back the way they had come.

They were about to leave to go to the pub for their meal when they heard a strange noise in the distance. It sounded like an engine – but it was unlike any engine Damian had heard on the canal, or anywhere else – before. Rather than the continuous roar of a car or lorry engine, this was a deep, resonant, booming bass beat.

'What's that noise?' he asked.

'It sounds like one of the old single-cylinder engines they used to put in the old working boats,' Brian replied. 'I think there would have been one like it on this boat once upon a time.' He paused. 'If we hang on here for a bit the boat will be along in a minute.' Sure enough, as they stood watching, round a bend came a traditional working pair. The one with the engine, the 'motor', as Damian had learned to call it from Tilly, was called *Bittern* and the 'butty' was *Scorpio*.

The boats were both beautifully painted in red and green and, as they passed, Damian could see elaborate pictures of flowers and fantastic castles painted on the insides of the open rear doors. The motor was being steered by a young man who was wearing a collarless shirt with a muffler and waistcoat, and a hat with a floppy brim. The smell of the smoke from the exhaust had a completely different smell from the exhaust on *Heron*. The engine sound dropped even deeper and slower as the man dropped the motor's speed when he saw *Heron* moored to the bank. The boats were empty and riding high in the water. Damian watched, transfixed, as they made their stately progress past *Heron*.

'That big empty space is where the load goes,' he thought.

'Hello!' the man called as *Bittern* glided past them. Brian and Chris returned his greeting but Damian stood, open-mouthed, unable to speak. He had never seen anything like this in his life. A young woman was steering the butty and she, too, smiled and shouted a greeting. Dressed in a long dark skirt with a white blouse, she was wearing a sort of bonnet with lots of pleats in it at the back. A dog with a scarf round its neck was sitting on the cabin roof next to her. It stood up and wagged its tail as they passed. Damian watched, transfixed, as the pair of boats disappeared out of sight. It seemed to him as if the whole world had suddenly slipped back in time for that few moments.

'I wonder if Tilly ever steered the motor or the butty,' he thought. 'I bet she did.' They looked as if they would have been returning, empty, back to their base, having delivered their load. When they got back they would get their orders for their next trip, or 'run' as Tilly always referred to the jobs they did.

He was brought out of his reverie and back to the present when his dad asked, 'Do you think you'd like to live on a pair of boats like that? That's what *Heron* was like before she was shortened. And that cabin you're sleeping in? It wasn't just a bedroom for one, you know. It was a bedroom, a living room – and a kitchen – for the whole family!'

'I know,' said Damian. 'Ray told us. Aren't they wonderful, Dad? Where do you think they're going?'

'I don't know,' Brian said.

'There was a poster in the pub advertising a Traditional Boat Gathering next weekend. I should think they're on their way there,' said Chris.

'Little do you know,' Damian thought, 'I know a whole lot more about those boats and about how people lived on them than you think!'

'I wonder what her life was really like?' he tried to imagine. A pair of boats like those was the only home Tilly would ever have known. And day after day, every day, going to collect loads and delivering them, was her entire life. On the one hand, he envied her because she was able to spend all her time on the canal. He had fallen in love with the 'cut' and thought how great it would be to live on a pair of boats. But he did not think he would like to be travelling in all weathers – it was bad enough when it had rained the other day! It was hard enough working locks on a nice day, but when it was raining or snowing it would be even harder. He shuddered at the thought and suddenly felt sorry for Tilly. And apart from everything else, although he often moaned about it, he would really miss going to school and meeting his friends. 'Did Tilly have any friends?' he wondered.

That night, when Tilly appeared, he could hardly contain his excitement as told her about what he had seen.

'Was they all painted up nice?' she asked, 'an' was their brasses all shiny an' their ropes all nice an' white?'

'Yes,' he replied, 'they looked very smart.'

'That's just 'ow they ought to be. That used to be my job, that did – cleanin' the brass an' whitenin' the ropes. Me Dad allus said as the look of a pair told you all as you needed to know about the folk as was on 'em.'

'And you lived all your life on a pair of boats like those?' he asked.

'All on us boatin' folk did. It weren't just a job for the men, see, it were a way o' life for the 'ole family.' Damian had so many questions to ask Tilly. What did they do when there were more children than could be accommodated in the tiny cabin? How did they manage to have a bath or a shower? When did they ever get a chance to go on holiday? Why are there so few working boats left now? And she never tired of answering him, although she did not always know all the answers.

'Why is the place where you turn the boat round called a "winding hole"?' he asked, pronouncing the word the same way as his father had.

'For a start,' Tilly replied, 'it ain't a "windin' 'ole" like you said it. You says it like the wind as blows. It's a windin' 'ole. That's why it's called a windin' 'ole, see, 'cause you use the wind to kind o' blow the front o' the boat round. Do you understand?' she asked.

'Yes,' said Damian, smiling. 'I do enjoy talking to you.' They seemed to have been talking for ages.

Just before she disappeared, Tilly made Damian promise again that he would do everything he could to rescue Rose. And then she was gone.

'I will!' he whispered into the darkness. 'I promise!'

✳

Thursday 3 August

It was a pleasant summer's day, and, as usual, Brian was keen to make an early start. Normally Damian would have protested at having to get up so early – but not on this holiday! He was at the tiller. He had become quite adept at steering under his dad's supervision – although, with all the overconfidence of a nine – well, nearly ten-year-old – he was absolutely certain that he would be perfectly capable of managing it on his own as he knew Tilly had done.

He was, however, becoming concerned because, according to his rough calculations, if they continued cruising at their present rate of progress they would get past the white house and be too far beyond it for him to return to it before they stopped for the night. He tried throttling back on the power but every time he attempted to slow the boat down either the wind would blow her off course so that he found himself heading straight for the bank or his dad would tell him he needed to go a bit faster. Then he had an idea. They were approaching the town where they had stopped for shopping on their outward journey yesterday. He turned to his dad.

'Dad, did you see that sign for the museum when we were on our way back from that supermarket?' he asked.

'No!' Brian replied, sounding interested. 'Was there one?'

'Yes. It was a little way this side of the supermarket, down a side street. Do you think we could stop and go and have a look at it. They might even have something in there about the canals. And we could post the card we bought for Granny and Gramps.'

'You're turning into what you might call a real canaloholic!' laughed his dad, proud of the new word he had just invented to describe his son. 'Look out for the visitor moorings. We'll stop and tell your Mum we're just going to pop down to the museum. I'm sure she won't mind. She might like to go shopping again and we've got plenty of time in hand to get back by Sunday.'

Ten minutes later, Brian and Damian were walking towards the High Street.

'There's the sign,' said Damian, pointing to a side turning.

'How did I miss that?' his father replied.

It was not far along the side street and they soon found the tall Victorian building and went in. Brian paid his entrance fee – children were admitted free, he was pleased to see – and set off towards the first display, while Damian trailed behind. Brian was fascinated, as he always was, by anything old and historic. As usual he read every word on every interpretation board he could find. Damian was getting just the tiniest bit bored – but he could not dream of showing it! He wandered from display cabinet to display cabinet. He was pleased that his plan seemed to be working out for them to arrive at the white house when it would be late enough for them to tie up for the night. He was disappointed that there were no displays specifically about the canal. However, when they arrived at the gift shop on their way out he noticed among the books a small section about canals and canal people. He picked up a book called *Kids on the Cut*, about working boat children in the 1920s and 1930s. He looked through it and saw that there were line drawings of boat people including some of young girls who were dressed exactly like Tilly.

'I think I'm going to buy this one,' he said to his dad.

'Well,' said Brian, 'you haven't had much chance to spend any of your holiday money yet, have you? It'll be a nice memento of your week on the boat, won't it?'

The purchase made, Damian and Brian made their way back to *Heron*. Damian made a point of not hurrying. He took his time, looking in shop windows as they went. Fortunately for him, his dad was not concerned by their slow progress.

As they stepped back on board *Heron*, Damian felt pleased with himself. He looked at his watch and calculated in his head how long he thought it would take them to get to the white house. 'It should all work out perfectly!' he thought, as he smiled to himself.

However, just at that moment disaster struck. Brian started the engine and pushed the lever to drive the boat forward. Nothing happened. He checked it was in gear. It was, so he tried again. Still nothing. He tried reverse and the boat moved. He tried forward again and again, but still nothing happened. *Heron* stayed stubbornly where she was – apart from the fact that she was beginning to drift out, away from the bank, towards the middle of the canal!

'Jump off quickly with a rope before we get too far from away the bank!' he called out.

'Best tie it up again,' he shouted. 'I'll have to phone the boatyard.' He took his mobile phone from his pocket.

Ray answered his call and, having established whereabouts they were by asking Brian the number on the nearest bridge, he said he should be with them in around an hour. Damian became worried again. Would they get to the white house today? And if they did, would they be there in time for him to take himself off for a walk, or would it be too late and starting to get dark?

'Of all the times for the boat to break down!' he thought.

To pass the time – and to take his mind off his problem – he settled down to read his new book. He found it so interesting that he managed to forget worrying about getting Rose. The book put into words everything that Tilly had told him about the hard life of the working boatmen and their families. Now he could appreciate why Tilly had never had the opportunity – or the need – to learn to read and write.

'There was no time for her to go to school. They were never in one place long enough for her to go,' he said to himself. 'And she didn't need to read or write.'

There was a chapter headed 'Entertainment'. It explained how the children had to make their own entertainment when they were on the move. There was little space to store toys and little money to buy them! He began to understand why Rose was so important to Tilly – why she loved her so much.

'Rose was her only doll – the only toy she had of any sort!' he thought. 'And I've got so many toys.' He remembered his toy cupboard back home. 'There are things in there I haven't played with for ages. It must have been hard only to have one toy.'

As well as the line drawings, there were a few old black and white photographs of boat children in the book.

'I wonder if any of these girls in the photos is Tilly?' he pondered as he examined them carefully, looking for her familiar face. 'If I show her these pictures, I wonder if she'll be able to see them – her being a ghost?'

True to his word, Ray arrived about an hour later. Damian watched intently as he skilfully examined the engine and its linkages.

'Throttle cable's broken,' he said as he emerged from the engine compartment. 'I've got a spare one on the van.'

'I do hope it wasn't anything we've done,' said Brian, anxiously.

'Oh, no,' Ray replied. 'It's just one of those things that happens sometimes. Just bad luck it happened while you were on her. How's your holiday, young man?' he enquired, ruffling Damian's hair.

'Oh, it's brilliant, thank you,' replied Damian. 'It's the best holiday I've ever had and *Heron*'s a super boat! Do you know anything about the people who lived on it before you had it?

'I'm sorry, I don't,' Ray answered. 'Rita thinks we ought to find out but it's one of those things we never seem to get round to doing.' Damian smiled and thought of Tilly.

Half an hour later the job was done and Ray departed.

'I hope I don't see you again before Sunday!' he called as he drove away in his van.

'We've lost all that spare time we had because of that,' said Chris.

'I know,' Brian replied. 'I think we'll have to carry on until the light fades tonight.'

Damian was getting very worried now. Would they get as far as the white house before it became too dark to cruise any further? He must get to the white house!

In the event, he had worried unnecessarily.

'Let's tie up here!' called his dad. They had arrived at the straight stretch of canal near the white house just as the sun was disappearing. Damian was more than relieved. It looked as if he would get the opportunity to go and look for Rose!

However, Chris had cooked a meal for them while they were travelling. It was ready to eat as soon as they stopped. Damian's heart sank as he realised his plans had been thwarted yet again. There was no way he could suggest that he would go for a walk when his dinner was on the table.

As they ate their dinner it grew dark outside.

'I know!' said his dad as they were finishing the washing up. 'Let's have a game of Scrabble before you go to bed tonight, Damian. I noticed there was a box in the cupboard and it'll make a change from watching television.'

'Oh no!' thought Damian. 'This is going from bad to worse! I must go and find Rose tonight!' But he dared not say that he did not want to play, or that he felt tired or ill and wanted to go to bed, because if he did his mother would only fuss and fret and make him stay in the main cabin with them all night.

'OK,' he muttered and watched as his dad set up the board. Fortunately, luck was with him. Brian made a number of long words with his selection of letters and soon the game was over. His dad had won by more than a hundred points.

'Better luck next time, son!' he said, patting Damian on the shoulder. 'Now it's time for bed.'

Damian did not mind at all. He kissed his parents, trying not to appear too excited, and dutifully made his way round to the boatman's cabin.

'Night, night. Sweet dreams,' said his mother as he stepped out onto the towpath. She watched as he stepped onto the back of the boat.

He was aware that this was his last and only chance to rescue Rose, his only chance to keep the promise he had made to Tilly.

He stepped down into his cabin and pulled the doors gently together – but he did not fasten them. He did not get ready for bed. Instead, he sat and waited in the darkness. After a while he crept, carefully, onto the back deck and peeped down the side of the boat to see if the lights were still on in the main cabin. At last, when he looked out for the third time, he saw that all the lights were off and the absence of any rocking of the boat indicated that his parents had stopped moving about and gone to bed.

This was his chance! His only chance! He quietly took the tablespoon out of the drawer where he had hidden it and put it in the plastic carrier bag which he still had screwed up in the pocket of his jeans. Then, very quietly and very cautiously, he stepped off the boat onto the towpath. The boat barely rocked under his light footstep. He waited there for a moment to be sure his parents had not noticed any sudden movement. They hadn't. The moon was full and bright, but he had the torch in his pocket, just in case.

'It's come in useful, after all,' he thought. 'Mum would be pleased!' He smiled to himself as he set off into the darkness.

There was a narrow gap in the hedge between the towpath and the field. He squeezed through it and made his way along the outside of the fence that ran down the side of the white house. The moonlight cast eerie shadows all around him but he was not at all frightened. He knew that what he was doing he was doing for Tilly – and that made him feel brave!

At the end of the fence he shone his torch. Yes! There was a cutting ahead of him, a steep bank leading down to the railway track exactly as Tilly had described it. He cautiously approached the edge. He looked down into the cutting – and was filled with dismay. Where the track should have been there was a tarmac path – and of the signal there was no sign.

'They must have taken the signal down when they took the track up,' he thought. His heart sank. With no signal to mark the place he may as well go back to *Heron* now, empty-handed. His search for Rose would be impossible. His mission was doomed before it had even started. But then he heard something. He was certain he could hear Tilly's echoing voice in his head.

'Keep on a-lookin'! Please, keep on a-lookin'!' she seemed to be saying to him.

He shone his torch along the path first one way, then the other. The beam caught something that looked like a pole sticking up out of the ground. In the beam of the torch it appeared to be covered in flaking white paint. He moved carefully along the top of the bank, still looking down into the cutting. As he came closer he could see that the white pole he had spotted was all that remained of the signal! What Tilly had described as 'them red an' yeller things as flop up an' down' had long been removed but the base of the tall wooden post was still there. When he was level with it he started to make his way, carefully, down the steep bank. The ground was uneven and rutted and the grass was still slippery with the recent rain. But fortunately there were some bushes to hang onto as he moved down the slope. He did not want to trip. How would he ever explain a twisted ankle to his mother?

When he arrived at the base of the signal he dropped to his knees. All around it there was grass, weeds, a few bits of rubbish blown by the wind – and some stinging nettles! Much as he did not want to get his hands stung he knew he would have to if he was to get to Rose. Then he had a brilliant idea. He removed the tablespoon from the carrier and put his hand inside the bag – using it as a glove he had pulled the nettles out of the way in no time, leaving a patch of rough grass and weeds. Now he tore at the grass. Some of it came out by the roots and the rest he ripped away. Finally, in front if him there was a patch of bare earth and he began digging. The tablespoon did not have a sharp enough edge to be much use as a spade but using both it and his hands he managed to move some of the earth. For a while, that was all he found – earth!

Having removed the compacted soil on the surface he found that the soil was softer beneath it and he was able to shift more of it using the tablespoon. He dug deeper but he could find nothing apart from more soil and a few stones.

'I'm sure this is where Tilly said,' he thought, as he looked up to make sure. 'She was so precise about it. It has to be here somewhere!' He carried on digging with more urgency – and desperation.

Suddenly the spoon struck something solid. He scraped away more soil and then shone the torch into the hole he had made. It was something made of glass!

'This must be it!' he almost said aloud. He loosened the soil around it. Sure enough, it was an old two-pound jam jar. His heart beat faster as he dug away the rest of the soil around it to loosen it, then gently eased it from its hiding place. He held it up and shone the torch at it. There was still mud caked round the outside of the jar but he could see that there was something inside it. Was it Rose? He could not tell. He put the jar and the spoon in the carrier bag and scrambled back up the bank. His heart was pounding as he made his way back to the boat. He was relieved to see that it was still in darkness.

He crouched down beside the boat and, with trembling hands, examined the jar in the moonlight. There was a length of string tied round its neck, but the material Tilly had used as a cover had practically rotted away. He unscrewed the lid. It was a bit stiff and rusty after all these years but he managed to remove it. He put his hand inside then, very carefully, lifted out what was left of Rose. She had obviously been made of stronger cloth than the jar cover because she was still intact.

He lay her down, gently, on the back deck. He dipped the spoon in the water, rinsed it, and put it in his pocket. Then he took the jam jar and sank it in the canal. He knew that this was wrong, but he could think of no other way of getting rid of it. Then he rinsed the mud off his hands as best as he could in the canal and dried them on his jeans.

Gently picking up Rose, he slipped onto the back deck without causing any movement and stepped down into the cabin, closing the doors silently behind him. He sat on the bed, carefully holding the rescued doll in the palm of his hand.

'You're home again, Rose,' he whispered, looking at her face. She seemed to him to be nothing special. She was a doll made out of some kind of cotton material which, at one time, must have been brightly coloured. But now her face and her dress were so pale it was almost impossible to say what colours they had been originally.

'I suppose they must have faded over the years,' he thought. He looked at Rose's face. Whoever had made her had given her a cheeky grin that was still just visible, smiling back at him.

As he held the tiny doll in his hand he heard a sharp intake of breath. He looked up. Tilly was there, standing in front of him.

'You're got 'er! You're been out an' you're got Rose!'

'Yes,' he whispered. 'I've been out and rescued her just now, while Mum and Dad were asleep.'

'Can I ... can I ... 'old 'er?'

'Of course, you can. Here.' He held the doll out for her. Tentatively, Tilly reached out and with both hands traced the outline of Rose with her fingers. Damian watched as she gazed intently at the doll. He saw tears forming in her pale eyes. It looked to him now as if there were two Roses! Tilly seemed to lift another Rose out of the one in his hands. Then he understood! Because Tilly was a ghost she could not hold the 'real' Rose, but she could pick up the 'ghostly' Rose.

So it was true! You could love something so much that you could give it a soul. That was what Tilly was holding now – Rose's soul! She moved her hands gently as she drew the doll towards her. Her fingers curled and caressed the body of 'her Rose' as she hugged the doll to her breast. She began to weep. But it was not the heart-wrenching wailing he had heard on Monday night. It was the calm sobbing of happiness and joy as Tilly clutched Rose to her.

'I'm got you back!' she sobbed, a radiant smile lighting up her pale features. 'I'm got you back jus' like I promised as I would. An' I'm sorry as it took me so long.' She looked at Damian. 'I ... I dunno...' she faltered. 'I dunno what to say to you.' Damian smiled at her. 'That's got to be the kindest thing as anybody ever done for me, ever!' she said. 'An' it were real brave on you to go out there in the dark wi' your Mam an' Dad asleep just through there. If they'd woke up an' 'eard you – or realised as you weren't in 'ere – you'd 'ave been in a right ol' pile o' trouble. I knows you would.'

'But, they didn't,' he said, still smiling at her happiness. 'It would have been a bit difficult to explain if they had, though.'

'Thank you, Damian Briggs! Thank you ever so, ever so, much! If I weren't dead I'd gi' you the biggest kiss as you're ever 'ad!'

'It's all right, Tilly. I'm just so happy that I was able to get Rose back for you, knowing how much you love her.' Damian was relieved that she was dead! As a nine – nearly ten-year-old – being kissed by girls was definitely not cool! He looked down at the 'real' Rose in his hands.

'You've got your Rose back, but what do I do with this one?' he asked.

'That's one more thing as you're gotta do for me, Damian Briggs.'

'What?'

'You're gotta keep 'er. You're gotta keep 'er safe somewhere. You're gotta love 'er, like I done, an' you're gotta care for 'er – allus. An' you must'n' never leave 'er be'ind, like I done. Will you promise me that, Damian Briggs? Will you? Will you promise me?'

The doll was still lying in his outstretched hands. He was not sure. A doll? A girl's toy! He was a boy! He didn't play with dolls! Then he looked at Tilly and it dawned on him that Rose was no ordinary doll. She was a link with the past, a past that he had never known and had never experienced. A past that he knew he could never know or experience first-hand. However many books he might read about the canals, however many old photographs he might see, he would never learn as much about the life of the boating families as he had from meeting Tilly and her beloved Rose. She had taught him so much. He heard himself saying quietly, 'Yes, Tilly. I promise. Of course I will – for ever and ever.'

'That's all right, then,' said Tilly, reverting to her familiar, matter-of-fact tone of voice. 'You know what this means, don't you?' she continued. 'Now as I'm got me Rose back, an' now as I'm told 'er as I'm sorry as I never went back for 'er, like I promised 'er I would, it means as I ain't a prisoner on this 'ere ol' boat no more! It means as I'm free!'

'Free to go to heaven?' Damian asked.

'Free to go to 'eaven!' she confirmed, her pale eyes blazing with sheer joy. 'Free to rest in peace, or whatever they calls it. Free to go wherever I like! But I'll tell you summat! It won't matter what 'appens to me now. It won't matter where I goes. I won't never forget you, Damian Briggs! I won't never forget you – nor what you're done for me tonight. I won't! Never! That's my promise to you!' As she said this she was looking straight at him, a serious look on her face. He watched as her gaze returned to Rose – and there was that radiant smile again!

'Even if you 'adn't never been an' got me Rose back for me I 'as to say as I'm been 'appy to meet you, Damian Briggs. See, I couldn' talk to no grown-ups about Rose, an' Ray an' Rita's kids was all growed up by the time they bought this 'ere boat. They did 'ave a kiddy on 'ere once – a nephew or summat – but soon as I spoke to 'im he starts screamin' is 'ead off an' callin' for Rita! But you're different, Damian Briggs. You're braver 'n 'e was, an' I'm thankful as you are.' She paused. 'But don't you think you best be gittin' yourself ready for bed now? If not, you'll still be 'alf asleep come the mornin'.'

'Yes, I'd better,' he agreed sadly. She looked straight into his eyes. She looked content and peaceful. Damian met her gaze. He felt proud and somewhat overwhelmed by the night's events. He turned his head for a moment and when he turned back Tilly had gone.

※

Friday 4 August

When Damian awoke the next morning the sky was dark with heavy clouds. He looked around the tiny cabin. Had all that really happened last night? Stealing away after dark? Digging that hole by the signal? Finding Rose? Talking to Tilly? Promising to look after Rose? It must have done because there on the mat were two muddy footprints – and his trainers were muddy too.

'I must clean those up a bit before Mum sees them!' he thought. And there on the side bed, lying where he had laid her last night after Tilly had disappeared, was Rose.

'I've got to put her somewhere safe too,' he said to himself. He had brought a rucksack with him to hold his books, paper and pencils and the pocket games he had thought he might need on his holiday. He tore a couple of pages from his notebook and gently wrapped Rose in them. Then he carefully placed her in the inner pocket of his rucksack and zipped it up.

'You'll be safe in there, at least until we get home,' he murmured to her.

He brushed the dirt off the mat and, rubbing his shoes clean as best as he could on the backs of the legs of his jeans, he went to join his parents for breakfast.

He went into the shower room in the main cabin to wash, paying special attention to his hands. He still had mud under his fingernails, a reminder of his desperate excavations of the previous night. Fortunately, there was a nailbrush in the soap dish by the washbasin. He also found an old cloth in the bathroom cupboard and managed to get rid of the last of the mud from his trainers.

If his parents thought he had spent an unusually long time at his ablutions they said nothing. Over breakfast Brian said, 'It looks as if it's going to start raining before long. Let me see if I can get a photo of us all with *Heron*. It'll look great with that white house in the back ground.'

Damian smiled. 'What a special reminder of an extraordinary night!' he thought. His dad had taken many photographs during the holiday but Damian knew that a print of this one was going to have pride of place on his bedroom wall.

Brian set his camera up on the tripod, pressed the time delay on the shutter, then, while the camera buzzed, he ran across the towpath to join his family who were standing in front of the boat. After a few seconds the camera stopped buzzing and clicked. Brian returned to it and looked at the screen.

'Perfect!' he said. He showed it to them. Damian was pleased to see the white house prominent behind *Heron*.

Just then it began to rain. Brian looked up. 'By the look of that sky I reckon this is going to carry on all day. There's a set of oilskins in the locker at the front. I'll put them on and brave the elements on my own. We've got to keep going or we won't be back to the boatyard by Sunday. There's no locks to do today so there's no point in us all getting wet.' Damian protested that if he wore his cagoule he would not get very wet outside with his dad, but his mum overruled him.

While Brian was putting on the oilskins and checking the engine, Damian dashed back to his little cabin and collected his pencils, crayons and paper, his book about boat children and his 'I Spy' book.

'What are you going to do?' asked Chris as they washed up the breakfast dishes.

'I think I'll do my holiday diary for school,' Damian replied, and when they had tidied everything away he set his writing materials on the table and settled to his work.

While Chris spent the time reading she was surprised at how absorbed Damian was in this project – so different from doing his usual homework. He sat at the table writing and drawing pictures to show what he had seen and done during his week afloat. He was fond of school but he often needed to be encouraged to do his homework and was always ready to stop working for a break and a chat.

About mid-morning, with the rain still lashing down, Chris went to the galley and made coffee for her and Brian. 'Do you want a drink?' she asked Damian.

'No thanks,' was all he said.

'That's odd!' Chris thought. 'At home he would have stopped work and taken his time to get his own drink, then drunk it slowly and not started again until he'd finished it!' She put her cagoule on and walked, carefully, along the side deck to give Brian his coffee.

'Are you OK out here?' she called.

'Fine!' he called back. 'These oilskins really are waterproof – and they keep the wind out too.'

Chris passed him his coffee. 'You'll never guess what our son's doing!' she said.

'What?' Brian asked.

'He's been working on his holiday diary for school ever since we started off first thing this morning!'

'Good heavens!' Brian replied. 'I seem to remember when he did the one for our week at Center Parcs last year it took him all of fifteen minutes!'

'At least it's keeping him quiet and stopping him going on about wanting to be out here!' Chris looked at her watch. 'Lunch'll be about an hour,' she said as she made her way back to the cabin.

Damian was still working on his diary when Chris told him he needed to clear the table so they could have lunch.

'Have you finished it yet?' she asked.

'Nearly,' he said as he packed his things away. 'I'll finish it this afternoon.'

When they had finished eating, Brian retrieved the oilskins from the shower where he had left them to drip.

'Are you sure you're all right out there?' his wife asked, concerned as she looked out of the window. 'It's still chucking it down!'

'Yes,' he replied. 'Like I said, these oilskins keep the wind and rain off. You get used to it after a while. Watch out for when we get to the tunnel. We should be there in about half an hour. Put the lights on before we go in.' He went back out and started the engine.

As soon as they had cleared up from lunch Damian was again working on his diary. After about half an hour he put down his pen and read back over what he had written. Satisfied, he turned to a blank page.

'Finished?' Chris asked.

'Yes,' he said.

'So what are you going to do now?'

'I'm going to write a story.'

'That's good! What's it going to be about?'

'It's going to be about a pair of boats like the ones we saw the other day.'

'What? About them being restored and looked after and going to rallies and things?'

'No. It's going to be about them years ago when they were taking loads from one place to another.'

'That should be very interesting.'

Damian applied himself to his work while his mother kept one eye on her book and the other looking out as they approached the tunnel. As they drew nearer to it she got up and put all the cabin lights on. Suddenly it went dark and the engine noise was magnified. Damian looked out of the window. 'It's the tunnel!' he exclaimed. 'Are you going to sit outside, Mum?'

'Not this time,' she replied. 'It's too wet for ghosts! At least your dad won't get quite as wet in here,' she said as she returned to her reading. Damian continued to look out of the front window for a few minutes but, apart from meeting another boat going in the opposite direction, all he could see was his reflection. He thought of the many times Tilly must have been through this tunnel and others like it. 'She didn't sit outside and make rabbit's ears on the wall, so neither will I,' he thought as he went back to his story.

As the light began to fade the rain eased. Brian brought the boat to the towpath and they tied up for the night. As they sat round the table after dinner, Chris said to Brian, 'Damian spent most of the afternoon writing a story about a pair of working narrowboats.'

'Did you now?' Brian looked at his son. 'Have you read it?' he asked Chris.

'No. He's only just finished it while I was preparing dinner.'

'Are you gong to read it to us, then?' he asked Damian.

'OK,' he said, 'if you'd really like to hear it,' and picked up his notebook.

Chris and Brian sat spellbound as their son read them the story of a father and mother, and their daughter Matilda – who everyone called Tilly – who lived on a narrowboat in the 1930s. When he had finished his story Damian put his notebook down. Neither parent spoke for a few seconds.

'What's the matter?' Damian asked, a worried look on his face. 'Don't you like it?'

'Just the opposite,' his father said, 'it's very, very good! Where did you find out all those details?'

'Oh, there was so much information in the book I bought at the museum,' he lied.

'I think you should give it to Mrs Rowell along with your holiday diary. She'll be impressed with it, I'm sure! Well done!' Chris congratulated her son. 'You've really made the best of a bad day.'

Tilly did not appear on Friday night. Damian sat in bed with his knees drawn up under his chin for a while, listening and looking out for her. He was sad not to see her. There was so much more he wanted to ask her, so much more he wanted to find out about her life on the canal, about her mum and dad. What were they like? Did she have any friends? What did she eat? What did she wear? He even wanted to know a bit more about her Aunt Maud! Finally, he realised, sadly, that she was not coming, so he lay down. As he drifted off to sleep he reasoned that now she was free she had probably gone to heaven.

'I wonder if she would like my story about her?' he thought. 'I don't suppose I'll ever know now.'

He had to be content with the fact that he was happy that he had helped her to be happy, helped her to be free – although he still did not really understand what that meant.

✳

Saturday 5 August

Damian woke up. The rain had passed and the sun was streaming through the porthole into the tiny cabin. It was the last full day of the holiday. He was sad that they were going to have go back to the boatyard tomorrow and hand *Heron* back to Ray and Rita. He had had such a wonderful week! He had enjoyed seeing the countryside from the slowly moving narrowboat. Steering the boat and working the locks had been really cool – and, of course, there was Tilly!

The sunshine lasted all day as they cruised along. No one spoke much. They were all conscious that their very special week's holiday was coming to an end.

Damian was helping his mother to work the locks again. Using the little trick with the windlass that Tilly had taught him he found he could manage the stiffer paddles that had defeated him earlier in the week.

'It looks as if all this fresh air has built up your strength!' his mother laughed as she watched him opening and closing paddles that he had been unable to do by himself on their outward journey. He smiled and showed her how he was using the windlass.

'Ah!' she said. 'I see! And you managed to work that out all by yourself? How clever of you!' He smiled again but said nothing.

In the evening they tied up not far from the boatyard. As they ate their last evening meal aboard they chatted about how much they had enjoyed their week afloat.

'Once I got the hang of it the boat wasn't hard to steer at all,' said Brian.

'Easier than driving a car, in fact,' Chris added.

'I know you've still had cooking and stuff to do but have you enjoyed it?' Brian asked his wife.

'Oh, yes!' she replied. 'I've quite enjoyed cooking in that little galley. It's made a change – and we've had some very nice meals out as well.'

'What about you?' Brian asked Damian. 'Have you enjoyed your week on the canal?'

'Yes, I have!' he said. 'Before we came I thought it was going to be like an adventure. And it has been – a *real* adventure!'

'You've written a lot in your holiday diary. What's been the best bit?' Chris asked him. In his mind he was thinking 'Meeting Tilly', but he could not say so.

'Helping you with the locks and steering the boat,' he replied, rightly thinking that that was what they wanted to hear.

'I'd certainly be happy to do this again next year,' Brian said.

'Me too,' Chris agreed.

After a short pause Damian asked, 'Do you think Ray and Rita would let us have *Heron* again?'

Brian laughed. 'I don't know about that. It's their own boat after all.'

'They've got lots of other boats that they hire out,' Chris added.

'I know,' said Damian, 'but I think there's something special about this one.'

'What makes you say that?' his mum asked.

'I don't know really.' He could not say what he really thought. 'I think it's because *Heron*'s old. It's got a lot more history to it than the hire boats.'

'That's true,' his dad agreed. 'We'll see next year. We can only ask.'

When they had eaten and washed up, Chris said, 'Now, you better go and get packed up before you go to bed. Then we'll be ready to leave when we get back to the boatyard in the morning. Damian went back to his little cabin for one last night. He started to collect his things together as his mother had instructed.

'Make sure you don't leave anything behind,' she had said. As he picked up his Nintendo, he realised that he had not switched it on once since he had got out of the car – over a week ago!

Again that night he waited for Tilly. Again, she did not appear. He was so disappointed that he felt he wanted to cry. He read his story – her story – again, then put his notebook on the floor beside the bed.

'She knew it was going to be my last night on the boat,' he thought. 'I did wonder if she might want to know what I'd done with Rose.' He lay awake in the darkness for what seemed like a long time, but there was no sign of her. With a sigh he turned over and went to sleep.

He was not sure how long he had been asleep when he was suddenly awakened by her familiar echoey voice.

'Hello, Damian Briggs!' He sat bolt upright in bed, immediately wide awake.

'I … I thought you weren't coming. You didn't come last night.' He could see she was still clutching the doll.

'No, I didn't. See, now I ain't a pris'ner on this 'ere boat I can go wherever I want! An' that's all thanks to you, Damian Briggs, cos you went an' got me Rose back for me.'

'This is our last night on *Heron*,' he said sadly. 'We have to go back home tomorrow.'

'Yeah, I know. But you can go home knowin' as you done summat really brave an' kind, can't you?'

'I suppose I can,' he said. 'I … er … I've written a story … about you.'

'A story? 'Bout me?'

'Yes. Would you like me to read it to you?'

'Oh, please!'

'OK.' He picked up his notebook from the floor. Tilly sat down on the side bed and lay Rose in her lap.

'A Day in the Life of a Boat Girl by Damian Briggs. Tilly got up early while it was still dark,' he began. 'Her mum was already up and was busy stoking the fire in the range. Her dad was outside checking the boats and the load of coal they were carrying. They had collected it from a coal mine two days ago and were taking it to a power station.

When her dad came back in her mum put cereals and milk in three bowls for their breakfast.'

Damian stopped reading and looked up. 'Did you have cereals back then?' he asked.

'They was around but we nearly allus 'ad bread an' marmalade for breakfast.'

He picked up his pen and corrected his writing, then continued. 'They had a pair of boats. The motor, the one with an engine, was called *Heron*. This was the one they lived on in the tiny cabin at the back. The butty, the other boat that *Heron* towed, was called Rose.' He looked up and smiled at Tilly.

'Our 'un were called *Romford*, but that's good as you're named it after my doll. I likes that!' She smiled back.

'After they had finished breakfast her dad said, "Let's get 'em ahead." He went out and started up the engine. Tilly and her mum untied the mooring ropes and Tilly got on board *Heron* and her mum got on board *Rose* to steer. Tilly, whose real name was Matilda, but nobody ever called her that…'

Tilly interrupted. 'Me Mam used to when she were cross wi' me – an' Aunt Maud never called me anythin' else!' she chuckled.

'…went in and did the washing up. Next she polished all the brasses on both the boats until they shone brightly. Then she went over the ropes with whitening so they were as white as snow. She had to be careful to get any of the whitening stuff that went on the paintwork off again before it dried.'

'That's right!' Tilly interjected.

'Then they came to some locks and Tilly had to open the gates and work the paddles. Narrow locks only had room for one boat at a time so Tilly had to help her mum pull the butty in by pulling it on the ropes.'

Again, Damian looked up. 'What did you tell me that was called?' he asked.

'Bow 'aulin',' she answered.

Damian wrote down the words. 'When they had to go through a tunnel Tilly had to walk along the side of the motor and light the big oil lamp on the front so her dad could see where they were going in the dark. While they were travelling Tilly would look after the dinner cooking on the range. Her mum had got it all ready before they started off. Sometimes they would have to eat their dinner while they were going along to save time.

'At night her dad let down the cross bed where he and her mum slept. Tilly slept on the little side bed opposite the range. Tilly was very tired because she had been busy all day. And the next day she had to wake up early and do the same things all over again. This was a day in the life of a boat girl.'

He held up the book for Tilly to see. 'Look,' he said, 'I've drawn a picture of the boats with you sitting on the roof holding Rose.'

Tilly looked. He noticed a ghostly tear rolling down her pale cheek. 'That's … lovely!' she said. 'Nobody ain't never writ a story 'bout me afore!'

'Well, I have,' he said, 'and I'm going to show it to my teacher when I get back to school.'

'No!' Tilly exclaimed. 'Who's gonna be interested in readin' 'bout me?'

'You'd be surprised,' Damian replied. 'Lots of people are interested in the history of the canals now. People write whole books about them.'

'Why?'

'I suppose it's because there aren't any people like you and your parents any more. Nobody has a life like you had these days. So people want to know what it was like.'

She was silent for few seconds. 'I never thought,' she said, 'when I were alive as somebody'd ever write a story 'bout me. I never thought as anybody'd want to read about me.'

'Well, they do.'

Again, she was quiet, thinking about what he had told her. At last she stood up and looked at him. 'I won't never forgit you, Damian Briggs,' she said. 'Not ever. Not only did you risk gittin' in trouble wi' your Mam and Dad to go an' git me Rose back for me, but you're gone an' writ a story all 'bout me an' all! But you best be gittin' some sleep now. It's late.' She paused, still looking down at him. 'Goodbye, Damian Briggs,' she said sadly, 'Goodbye ... an' thank you. Thank you from the bottom o' me 'eart!'

'Will I ever see you again, Tilly?' he asked.

'You might,' she said. 'You might – sometime when you least expect it.'

'Goodbye, Tilly. You've been the best thing about this holiday. You've made it my best holiday ever!' He could feel tears welling up in his eyes. Not wanting to be seen crying in front of a girl, he turned away. When he turned back she had gone.

✳

Sunday 6 August

The next morning he could hear his parents moving about even earlier than usual. He got up and carefully checked that he had packed everything – although he knew his mother would also check one last time! He peeped inside the inner pocket of his rucksack. Rose was still safe inside it.

'I don't suppose I'll ever see your Tilly again,' he murmured to her sadly.

They returned to the boatyard, each of them taking a last turn at the tiller on the short journey. Ray and Rita came out to greet them.

'Your boat's still in one piece!' Brian called out, to everyone's amusement.

'Have you enjoyed yourself, young man?' Rita asked Damian.

'It's been brilliant! Thank you!' he replied as he jumped off the boat, beaming from ear to ear. 'The best holiday ever!'

'Good! Good!' Rita said. 'I'm so glad I thought of letting you take *Heron*. When I saw that desperately disappointed look on your face it was almost as if I could hear a little, echoey voice talking in my head. It was saying, "Let them have *Heron*. Let them have *Heron*."' Damian smiled. Rita did not know, but he knew, beyond any shadow of doubt, whose voice that was!

'Perhaps we might see you all again next year?' Ray added.

'You might, at that,' Chris said. 'We've all thoroughly enjoyed our week! Thank you so much.'

Brian went to fetch the car and they transferred their luggage from the boat. They said goodbye to Ray and Rita and drove towards the entrance to the boatyard.

As they drove away, something prompted Damian to turn and look out the car's rear window. Standing there, on *Heron*'s back deck, was Tilly! Clearly, no one else could see her, but to him she was as real as anything. She was cuddling her ghostly Rose with one arm across her chest. With her free hand she was waving him goodbye. He looked at her face. Gone was the sad look. Gone was the wan, half-smile. She was looking directly at him and smiling radiantly, just the way she had done when she first saw Rose again. Her face almost seemed to be glowing, so intense was her smile of happiness. He held up his rucksack and pointed at it. Tilly understood and nodded as she gave him one final wave.

The drive out of the boatyard went round the back of the Reception building, so that he could not see *Heron* for a few seconds. When it reappeared, Tilly had gone.

'Will I ever see you again, Tilly?' he asked again, very quietly.

And he was absolutely certain that a weird, echoey voice in his head replied, 'One day, p'raps, Damian Briggs. One day, p'raps.'

Three Men and a Goat

A story of serendipity

✳

'Getting to Know You'

'You can put that idea right where the sun don't shine, so you can!' Siobhan shouted at him. 'Just look at this place, will you? The washing machine floods the kitchen every time I use it! The dishwasher hasn't worked for months! Two of the rings on the gas cooker won't light! There's wallpaper hanging off the wall in the bedroom where it's got the damp! And what have you gone and done, my darling husband? What have you gone and done? You've only gone and booked for us to fly off to blooming Spain for two weeks? Holy Mary, Mother of God, Michael Murphy! What in hell's name do you think you're playing at?' She paused. 'And for God's sake, will you shut up with that damned singing!' Mick ceased his rendition of 'E Viva Espana'.

He never missed an opportunity to launch into a song to suit the occasion – much to the annoyance and exasperation of those he serenaded. 'Funny how a snippet of conversation can be a cue for a song,' he frequently said. He believed he had a wonderful singing voice. He believed he was the Birmingham Irish community's answer to Pavarotti and that he was blessed with the ability to stay perfectly in tune. He was, however, the only person on the planet who thought that way.

'I just thought…'

'You didn't think! That's your trouble, so it is,' she said, flinging a tea towel into the sink. 'You never do think, you eejit!' The cat, well used to these frequent outbursts, merely curled itself more tightly into a ball and buried its head more deeply between its paws.

'Oh, stuff you, then!'

And with that parting comment, Mick had left the house and gone to the pub. He had found himself doing that a lot towards the end – walking out on her in the middle of a row and going to the pub.

Although born and bred in Birmingham, he was of Irish descent and had met Siobhan while visiting relatives in County Cork. Initially attracted by her striking good looks and her red hair, he had not realised, until after their nuptials were completed, that she also possessed the temper to go with it!

Their marriage had been a roller-coaster affair. They had rubbed along. They had both worked shifts – he at a nearby factory and she at their local supermarket – so the time they had spent in each other's company had been limited, their only regular outing together having been their weekly attendance at mass at St Oswald's. They had lived well – Siobhan was an excellent cook and made full use of the reduced items, the three-for-two offers – and her staff discount – to ensure that. Mick had done a bit of fishing and had watched a lot of sport on television. Anyone who swam, jumped, ran, kicked or threw anything, Mick watched them. Siobhan, on the other hand, seemed to him to have spent all her time cleaning.

'She's always got that duster in her hand,' Mick had often thought.

The only issue of this turbulent relationship, their son Jimmy, had escaped from the permanent state of virtual war that existed in the house by moving in with his girlfriend as soon as they were able to afford a place together.

The trouble had really started when Mick and Siobhan both retired. Being in each other's company twenty-four hours a day, seven days a week had exposed crucial differences in their relative expectations of what retirement would bring. Mick, a free spirit at heart, was all for jetting off around the world as often as their joint pensions would allow. Siobhan, on the other hand, saw it as her husband's opportunity to catch up on all the jobs around their semi-detached two-and-a-half-bedroom semi that had been on hold pending his retirement.

As a result of these widely differing aspirations, three years into retirement neither of them was happy. Siobhan had started to work part-time at the supermarket again while Mick had lost count of the number of lost deposits on cancelled holidays! Far from getting long-standing tasks completed, Siobhan had seen the list lengthen as, one by one, various appliances had developed faults. For his part, Mick refused to get anyone in to make the repairs, insisting that he knew how to do all the necessary work himself. He just never got round to actually doing it.

Eventually the situation had progressed to its logical conclusion.

'You can bloody well move out, so you can!' she had screamed at him one day. 'Go and waste your time somewhere else!'

So he had.

Despite his protestations, in the divorce arrangements he had lost the marital home, the cat and most of his savings. He could not afford to buy anywhere else to live. After renting a bedsit for a few months he had come up with the idea of using what was left of his money to buy a narrowboat and live on that. He had moved his home to its present canal moorings to be nearer to where Jimmy lived. Not surprisingly, the boat needed some work doing on it.

'I can do all that in my spare time,' he thought. But, of course, he never got round to it.

Ron Barton kissed his wife goodbye and walked towards the exit of the hospice, tears of despair filling his eyes. The forced smile he had maintained while he had been in her room had disappeared as soon as he had crossed the threshold.

'Mr Barton!' He looked in the direction of the voice. It was June, one of the nurses. 'Hello, Mr Barton,' she said, her voice heavy with sympathy. 'Dr Reynolds would like a word – if you're not in a hurry, that is?'

'No hurry, June,' he replied, wistfully. 'No hurry at all.' He followed her into the doctor's office.

'Ah, Mr Barton,' Dr Reynolds said, getting up and walking round his desk to shake Ron's hand. 'Take a seat,' he said, pointing to one of two easy chairs arranged round a low table in a corner. Ron sat. Dr Reynolds sat down and was about to speak when Ron cut him off with a raised hand.

'I know what you're going to tell me, Doctor. I've seen it happening myself over the last few days. My lovely Daphne … she hasn't got long left, has she?'

'No, Mr Barton. I'll be perfectly honest with you. I'm afraid she hasn't.'

'Would you like a drink of anything, Mr Barton?' It was June, the nurse.

'No thanks, love,' he said, 'unless you've got a bottle of scotch hidden somewhere.'

'I'll see what I can do,' she smiled as she left the room.

'We've done absolutely everything we can to make Daphne comfortable while she's been in our care.'

'I know you have, Doctor. I know you have. I'm absolutely certain nobody could have done any more for her than you and your lovely people here have done. It's just such a horrible, nasty disease!'

The doctor continued. 'And I'm absolutely certain that the fact that you've been able to come in and see her every day has prolonged her life.'

'I hoped it would. I really did. You know I took early retirement from my job with the council so I could come and see her. They were ever so good about it.'

'Have you any family, Mr Barton?' the doctor enquired.

'No, just me and Daphne. We tried for a baby, but … well, nothing happened. No IVF and all that in those days, Doctor. But we were happy with each other. Soul mates, Doctor, soul mates. Daphne's got a brother, but they've never been that close.'

June reappeared carrying a glass with a small drop of whisky in it.

'They keep a bottle in the kitchens, Mr Barton.'

Ron was surprised. 'I wasn't serious!' he said. 'But thanks very much, all the same.' He sipped the scotch. 'That's an example of what I mean, Doctor. Nothing's too much trouble for you people. You've all been absolutely wonderful!' He paused and took another sip. 'There's just one thing you can't do, isn't there? You can't help my Daphne to live any longer, can you?' He burst into tears. June knelt down beside his chair and held his hands in hers.

'How much longer has she got, Doctor?' Ron asked between sobs.

'I'm afraid we're talking about days rather than weeks.' June squeezed his hands tighter.

It was the day Barry had been looking forward to for months – no, years! Today was his last day at work. Today he was going to retire! He had arrived at the Inland Revenue office where he had worked for the whole of his forty-two-year career at his usual starting time of eight o'clock. He had alighted from his usual bus and had taken the familiar walk to the town-centre office. Arriving at his floor, spot on five minutes to eight – he had only ever been late when the bus was held up – he took off his coat and hung it on the wooden coat-hanger he had brought in from home forty-two years ago. Before sitting down at his desk he plumped up the cushion on his chair. This was not the same cushion he had brought from home forty-two years ago. That one had long ago gone to be scattered on the great sofa in the sky. As had its three successors. This cushion was the fourth of the line. He then followed exactly the same routine as he had followed every working morning for forty-two years. He opened the top drawer of his desk and extracted a yellow duster. This duster was taken home every Friday evening to be washed, ironed and brought back, clean and fresh, on Monday morning. He proceeded to dust the desk top – even though the cleaners did so every evening after he had left for home. He then moved his telephone until he was satisfied as to its precise angle.

'Damned cleaners! Why can't they leave things where I put them?' he thought, as he thought every morning. Neatly folding and replacing the duster in the drawer, he then took from it his pen (Government issue), his propelling pencil (his own) and his eraser (provenance uncertain – it had just appeared on his desk one morning). He arranged these items in precisely calculated positions on his desk. Once he was completely satisfied that everything was in its correct and rightful place, he clapped his hands together once, as if in self-congratulation, then opened the second drawer of his desk and, taking a camomile teabag from the packet there, set off in the direction of the kettle.

However, unlike every other day at the job, since setting out his desk as usual he had not once touched either his telephone, his pen, his pencil, or his eraser. He had not done a stroke of work all day. It had been more difficult setting his desk out that morning because his colleagues had decorated it after he had left the previous evening. He knew they would. It was the custom. He smiled and thanked them for their efforts – without meaning a single word.

As the clock ticked round towards four o'clock he noticed some of his colleagues beginning to gather around his part of the office with smiles on their faces. At four o'clock precisely, the management inspector's office door opened and she made her stately progress towards his desk. Barry stood up and proceeded to listen patiently to all the usual platitudes that he had heard a hundred times before as one by one his older colleagues had also 'worked' their final days. Some of them had even come in to observe his transition to join them in the ranks of the retired.

As his manager spoke, he surveyed the faces of his colleagues as they stood, listening. A confirmed bachelor – 'not the marrying kind' was his usual answer to any questions on the subject – he had had liaisons of varying durations with most of the single, divorced or widowed ladies of a certain age – at least in his own mind! He was going to miss their company.

The management inspector was drawing to a close and presented him with his card, signed by everyone, together with an engraved half-pint silver beer tankard. His nickname in the office was 'Half Pint Barry' as he had never been known to order or drink a whole pint. There was also a book about British wild birds since he had expressed his intention to become a 'twitcher' in his retirement. He solemnly removed his own speech from next to the packet of camomile teabags in the second drawer of his desk, and delivered it. It was short and sweet. He thanked everyone for his gift and for their company over the years.

'I shan't miss the work,' he said. 'But I shall miss all of you – especially the banter that seems to be such an intrinsic part of the life of this office!' They all laughed at that.

When he sat down and the rest of them had returned to their desks, a few came, individually, and wished him well. As soon as the coast was clear, however, he cleared his desk. From the bottom drawer he took out a 'bag for life', picked up his pencil, his duster and his cushion and put them in it. Then he invited everyone to join him at the Skinners Arms, the pub opposite the office. He put on his coat and placed his coat-hanger in the bag with the duster and cushion. He was pleased to note later that many of his colleagues had accepted his invitation.

At eleven thirty that evening he staggered out of a taxi and up the stairs to his second-floor flat, where he half slumped, half fell down, into his armchair.

'Ah well! Barry lad,' he said aloud to himself, slurring his words. 'You've been looking forward to it long enough. Now it's here.'

Inside, though, if he was brutally honest with himself, he was just a little afraid – afraid of loneliness.

It was the following morning that he discovered, together with a king-size hangover, that he no longer had his bag, his propelling pencil, his duster, his cushion or his coat-hanger.

'Oh, bother!' he said – very quietly.

❋

'Yes, that's all taken care of,' Diane said, smiling, as she saw the young couple out of the shop. 'I'm sure you and your guests will have a really lovely time.' They thanked her and left. She closed the door behind them. 'Coffee!' she said aloud to herself, plumping up the cushions on the armchairs as she went past them on her way to the store room at the back of the shop to boil the kettle, her high heels clicking on the tiled floor. As she filled the kettle she glanced in the mirror on the back of the storeroom door to check her make-up, and flicked a stray lock of brunette hair back behind her ear.

Slim, elegant and stylishly dressed in one of the tailored suits she always wore when at work, Diane was in her early forties. She looked after the 'front of house' side of the business. A stickler for presentation, she always ensured that the window display caught the eye. Once inside the shop, the brochures encouraged browsing and, hopefully, concluded in a booking. Everything was immaculate. That went for the books, too. She prided herself on passing them to the accountant without a receipt or an invoice out of place.

She had just poured out her coffee when the telephone on her desk rang. She picked up her mug and walked quickly to her desk, promptly spilling most of its contents all over the papers on it – and picked up the receiver.

'Dream Holidays. Good morning.' She sat down and listened to the caller while trying to mop up the spillage with a tissue.

'Turkey? Yes… Yes, I can get some brochures in the post for you today. What's your address?'
She dropped the tissue, picked up her pen and wrote it down.
'Yes, have a look at them and see what there is. I'm sure there'll be something there you'll like. Fine! I'll look forward to hearing from you again. Thank you. Bye.'

As she replaced the receiver, Philip, her husband, came into the shop.

'Damn!' she shouted.

'Bloody traffic!' Philip exclaimed as he came in. 'It's just taken me…' He looked at his watch. '…three-quarters of an hour to get to the bank and back!'

'And I've just spilt coffee all over this booking form!' She held up the form. 'It's still legible – just.' She turned her attention to her husband.

'It's a pity there isn't a branch in walking distance,' she sympathised. 'Look, I've just done a pot of coffee. Pour yourself one, sit down at your desk and calm down.'

'Thanks. I will.' He disappeared into the back of the shop. She picked up her mug. It was nearly empty. 'And while you're there, will you get me another one, please!' she called.

'OK. Where are the Greek Island sailing brochures?' he called back.

'Usual place.'

'No, they're not! Oh, yes … sorry. They were hiding under the tea towel! Chap in the bank asked me to take some in for him tomorrow.'

'They've been really popular this year.'

Philip reappeared with the brochures and two mugs of coffee. Passing one to her, he sat at his desk. Tall, dark-haired, with flecks of grey appearing at the temples, and a couple of years older than his wife, it had been his idea for them to spend the legacy she had received from her parents to start their own travel agency. He was the salesman of the pair. Anyone who came into the shop who did not book a holiday before they left he regarded as a personal failure. Together, they made a good team. Their attention to detail and their willingness to find something 'a little bit different' meant that their business had expanded beyond their wildest dreams.

'Anything happened while I was out?'

'That couple who came in last week looking for a beach wedding in Jamaica?'

'Oh yes.'

'They've been in and booked.'

'Oh, excellent!'

'Home Cookin''

M ick didn't cook. He never had done.

'That's what you have a wife for,' he told anyone who asked. 'Otherwise, it's a bit like having a dog and barking yourself!'

Siobhan had always cooked beautiful meals. But now, if he was honest, he missed her roasts, her Yorkshire pudding, her meat pie, her lasagne, her gammon and egg…

However, being the resourceful chap that he was, he had come up with a plan. He could put cereals in a bowl for breakfast and toast and jam made a good tea. But he could see no point in going to all the effort of buying food and attempting to cook for himself. Not when there was a perfectly good chip shop just up the road from the canal, together with a pizza place and a curry house, not to mention a Chinese take-away in the town. He visited these in rotation. However, he had adopted the habit of walking the few yards along the towpath to The Navigation pub on a Saturday lunchtime to tuck into his favourite pie and chips.

Barry had always taken a pride in his ability to cook – nothing fancy – just plain straightforward meals. 'More Belling Cook Book than Delia Smith,' was how he described his culinary abilities. He always watched what he ate as he believed he had a delicate stomach – nothing too spicy or seasoned for him! He took the Government's advice – 'I always have my five a day,' he frequently told his colleagues, 'and my fibre. Oh, and not too much fat and sugar.'

While at work, however, he had always subjected himself to the sometimes questionable delights of the office canteen for his midday meal – choosing carefully, of course. Now retired, he found that cooking for himself, far from being the occasional enjoyable occupation it used to be, had become something of a chore now that he was doing it seven days a week.

He also realised that what he had feared, as he had sat in his flat on the night he had retired, was not the result of a surfeit of alcohol. What he had said in his retirement speech about missing the people with whom he had worked was proving to be more true than he had thought. Not to put too fine a point on it, he realised, with a degree of despair, that he was lonely.

He had a good pension from the Civil Service, but it would not run to eating out on a daily basis. As he prepared his meal one Friday lunchtime a thought struck him. He had noticed that his local pub, The Bell, always had a blackboard propped up outside proclaiming its economically priced 'pub grub'.

'I think I might pop along there and sample it tomorrow as a treat,' he decided.

❄

Ron had never cooked a meal in his life. Daphne had cooked such lovely meals! He had helped, of course – laying the table, washing up, even peeling the occasional potato. But Daphne had loved cooking.

When she was first taken ill, before she had to go into the hospice, Ron had tried to cook. Daphne had been there to instruct and advise, but it never seemed to turn out right.

'That's lovely, Ron!' she would say. But he knew it was either burnt or undercooked. Try as he might, he could never get the vegetables cooked at the same time as the meat.

When Daphne had gone into the hospice he had relied on a diet of ready meals from the supermarket. Since she had passed away he had continued to do so. One Saturday morning, however, while he was taking a leisurely walk along the canal towpath a couple of miles from his home, he decided he deserved a change from 'ping food', as he called his microwaved meals. He made his way to The Navigation Inn as he had heard of its excellent reputation for bar meals.

So much did he enjoy his lunch that he decided, there and

then, that this would be his regular Saturday morning routine from now on – a walk by the canal for exercise followed by a meal and a couple of pints at The Navigation for relaxation.

After a few weeks he noticed that there was another man who lunched there most Saturdays. Like him, he sat alone at his table. Like him, he appeared to have a meal and a couple of pints, then leave. They had begun to pass the time of day with each other as they entered the pub.

There was a knock on the cabin roof.

'Hello! Anyone at home?' Philip opened the front doors.

'Hi Sal! Come on in.'

'How are you, Phil?' She kissed him on the cheek.

'Sal! Good to see you!' Diane came through from the galley. 'Dinner's almost ready.'

'Good!' said Sally, greeting her. 'I'm starving!'

'Drink?' Philip asked.

'Thanks. A white wine if there's one going, please.'

'There's always one going aboard this boat!'

After the meal they were sitting and drinking coffee when Sally said, 'It's always so lovely and cosy on your boat – even when it's cold outside! How long have you lived on it? I've known you for what? Eight years? And you've lived here all that time.'

'We've been here ever since we got married,' Diane said.

'Fifteen years,' Philip added. 'When we'd set up the shop we hadn't enough money to buy a house here in London and we knew we couldn't afford the place we were renting while we were getting the business established. We saw an ad for a second-hand boat, at a price we could manage, moored not too far from the shop. We liked it, so we bought it.'

'And very nice it is, too,' Sally said. She placed her empty coffee cup on the saucer. 'Now, when you rang and invited me for supper, Di, I got the distinct impression that it was going to be more than just a social visit. So how may I help you?'

'Am I that transparent?' Diane laughed.

'Well,' Sally said, 'the giveaway was you asking me to bring my laptop with me!'

'Yes! Well, you are our finance guru as well as our friend.' Diane passed her a set of accounts for the business. 'We seem to have a rather a lot of money sloshing around in the business account. I think we ought to invest it somewhere to make it work for us.'

'Well, you've worked for it!' Sally quipped.

'More coffee?' Diane asked.

'Please!' Sally passed her cup. While Diane did refills Sally looked at the balance sheet, took a notepad from her briefcase and asked some questions. Eventually, she suggested a couple of ways of making their money work better for them. They agreed.

'If you'd both like to sign where I've pencilled those crosses,' she said a few minutes later as she passed a sheaf of forms to Philip and Diane who duly appended their signatures.

'Thanks. Right! I'll get these all processed tomorrow.' She put the papers in her briefcase. 'Now, is there anything else I can help you with on the financial front?'

'No,' said Philip. 'I don't think so.' He looked at his wife. 'I don't think there's anything else is, is there, darling?'

'Well,' she said, 'it's a bit of an idle enquiry, really. We're not intending to do it – not yet, anyway. I haven't even mentioned it to Phil yet. But I was just wondering the other day, with the money we've got invested, how soon could we think about retirement?'

Sally's eyes widened. 'Really?' she said.

'Retirement?' Philip exclaimed. 'Hang on, love! We're only in our forties!'

'I know we are. Like I said, we're not even thinking about it yet. But I've no clear idea – and I'm sure you haven't either – about how much we would need behind us before we started to think about it.'

'Yes,' Philip admitted. 'Fair point. Well, you're the expert, Sal. Can you give us some advice?'

'I can. It's an interesting idea.' She turned to a fresh page in her notepad. 'Now you've both got private pensions, haven't you?'

'Yes,' said Philip, 'for what they're worth.'

'Your business premises – I've always presumed you leased them.'

'No, their ours. We were lucky. We bought just before London property prices went sky high,' Philip said.

'And you've owned the shop for fifteen years?'

'I know what you're wondering,' Diane said. 'How could a pair of newly married, twenty-somethings afford high street business premises in a fairly expensive part of London?'

'Well, I did wonder,' Sally smiled.

'It's quite simple, really. As you know, I was adopted. My adoptive parents were both in their late forties when they decided to give a home to an orphan. Mum died in her sixties and Dad passed away a couple of days after my twenty-seventh birthday. Phil and I had both been working in the travel business since we left school – that's how we met – so we decided to spend my inheritance on setting up on our own.'

'What a lovely story! You've never mentioned that before,' said Sally. 'Right, just give me a few moments.' She took her laptop out of her bag. 'Can I plug this in somewhere. I haven't been in the office at all today and the battery's almost out.' Philip took the proffered plug and inserted it into a wall socket.

'It's OK,' he said. 'We're hooked up to the mains here.'

After a few minutes Sally sat back. 'Now, it all depends on the kind of lifestyle you want in retirement. I've had a quick look on the internet at what shops like yours in that area are fetching currently. I've added the proceeds of sale to your existing investment capital, then I've converted some of it to an investment paying a monthly income and added in your pensions. This is approximately what you would get if you sold the shop and retired tomorrow.'

'How much are we looking at?' Philip asked. Sally turned the laptop round so that they could see the screen. Their mouths dropped open.

'That much?' Philip whistled.

✳

'Friends and Neighbours'

As Ron walked along the towpath one Saturday morning he could not fail to notice that there were far more boats tied up there than usual. In the field adjoining the canal a group of marquees had been erected.

'Must be the boat rally thing they've been advertising,' he thought as he continued to The Navigation.

When he arrived, however, he was surprised to see that it was heaving with customers. People were standing three deep at the bar. He waited patiently until he could get served then, with his pint in his hand, looked round for an empty table. They were all taken. He spotted the man to whom he usually nodded a greeting, sitting at a table on his own. He made his way over to him.

'Hello,' he smiled. 'Do you mind if I join you? There doesn't seem to be any room anywhere else.'

The man smiled back. 'Help yourself, mate.'

'Never seen the pub this busy on a Saturday lunchtime before!' He sat down on the vacant chair.

'There's a big boat rally on,' the other man said. 'Daft buggers were too late applying for a licence for the beer tent.'

'Oh! So all the boaters have come in here!'

'Most of them, by the look.'

'I'm Ron, by the way.' He held out his hand. The other man shook it.

'Michael,' he said. 'Michael Murphy. Everybody calls me Mick.'

'Pleased to meet you, Mick.'

'And I, you, Ron.'

Ron picked up the menu and looked at it. 'Now what shall I have today?' he asked.

'I always have the same,' Mick said. 'Best meat pie and chips in town here – and lovely gravy!'

'I fancy fish today,' Ron said, still scouring the menu. 'There!'

he said. 'Plaice, chips and peas. That'll do me.'

'Excuse me. Is anybody sitting here?'

Mick and Ron looked up to see a tall man with a half-pint of beer in his hand.

'No,' Ron said. 'That seat's free.'

'Thank you,' said the man, pulling up a stool.

'This is Ron,' said Mick, extending his hand, 'and I'm Mick.'

'Barry,' said Barry. 'Barry Edwards. Is it always this crowded in here on Saturday lunchtimes?'

Mick explained why all over again.

'I've never been to this pub for lunch before,' Barry said. 'My local's The Bell. I used to go there for lunch every Saturday, but they've got a new chef now.'

'Oh, yes?' Ron said.

'Yes,' Barry continued. 'Far too liberal with the herbs and spices for my taste – not to mention my stomach. So I thought I'd try somewhere else. I've often passed by here, so I thought I'd give it a try.'

'*Sugar and spice, and all things nice. Kisses sweeter than wine.*' Mick started to sing. Ron and Barry looked at each other, surprised by this sudden and unexpected outburst.

'Well, I don't think you'll be disappointed!' Ron spoke quickly to hide his embarrassment. 'I've been coming here for a few weeks now and I'm very happy with the fare.'

'Best pie and chips in town!' Mick added.

Barry picked up the menu. 'Ah!' he said. 'Fish pie! That's me sorted.'

'Look,' said Ron, 'I was just about to go and order mine. Would you like to come with me?'

'Lead on!' said Barry.

'I hope you're not in a hurry, gents,' Mick warned as they got to their feet. 'There's a half-hour wait for food they told me when I ordered mine.'

'I've got all afternoon,' said Ron.

'I've nothing pressing either,' Barry added.

❋

Over lunch, a few days after Sally's visit, Diane suddenly said, 'We could live well on that income.'

'Sorry?' Philip looked up.

'Those figures Sally showed us the other night.'

'Oh yes?'

'Yes. I think we could live very comfortably.'

Philip was not convinced. 'What?' he asked. 'Us? Pack up the business? Retire? In our forties? At our age people may have a career change, but they don't – retire!'

'Why not? Why do you think people work until they're sixty-five? Because they can't afford to pack up without getting their pension, which they can't get until sixty-five. Well, we *can* afford it. We could afford to retire now.'

'Let me see those numbers again.' She passed him the piece of paper. He studied it. 'I suppose we could,' he said slowly. 'It's certainly worth thinking about.' He put the figures down on his desk and looked at his wife.

'Say we did decide to give it all up. What would you want to do when we've retired?'

Diane thought for a moment. 'Well,' she began, 'we've been virtually everywhere overseas that's worth going to. I think I'd like to see a bit more of this country.'

'What do you mean? A caravan? A motorhome?'

'No. By boat.'

'Boat?'

'Yes, our boat. *Cormorant.* I want to cruise the canals. There's some lovely places to visit – just look at the brochures,' she continued. 'We've been living on the damned thing for fifteen years and she's never been off her mooring. Have you ever tried to start the engine?'

'No. Never. Never needed to. She was already moored where we wanted her, so there was no need to move her, was there?'

'Well, I think it sounds like fun! And I'd say that it's something worth retiring for.'

'I'm still not convinced. I need to look at those numbers a bit more closely. I tell you what, though. It be worth seeing about getting that engine going.'

'Doesn't Keith – you know, the chap from two boats along – doesn't he do engines?' Diane asked as they drove home.

'Yes, he does! Good thinking! I'll pop down and have a word with him.'

That evening, Keith spent half an hour delving in the nether regions under the floorboards, investigating the finer parts of *Cormorant*'s engine. As he emerged, Philip was standing on the towpath looking concerned.

'Apart from the fact that all your batteries are so old they're not taking charge any more, your starter motor's jammed, there's precious little lubricating oil and even less coolant – apart from all that she's in perfect working order!' He smiled.

'My God!' Philip exclaimed. 'Is all that … repairable?'

'Oh, yes!' Keith replied. 'I've brought engines back to life that have been a lot nearer death's door than this one!'

'Do you think you could sort it all out for me – get it in working order? I'd pay you, of course.'

'No bother, Phil. I've got a few day's holiday due, and I've got nothing on back end of the week. I'll start it on Wednesday, if that's OK with you?'

'That'll be fine. I'll drop the keys into you Wednesday morning on my way to work.'

✳

'Young And Foolish'

'My wife was in tears for most of the time we were there!' The belligerent customer was in full flow. 'I really don't think that that is the kind of treatment one expects from a hotel in Tuscany – or anywhere else for that matter, do you?' He was middle-aged and, Philip thought, on the fast track to becoming a grumpy old man.

'I'll take your complaint up with the hotel company and let you know, Mr Swann.'

'Let me know? You'll let me know? I don't want you to let me know anything! Well, I do – I want you to let me know when I'll get a refund! That's what I want!'

'Look, Mr Swann!' Philip was beginning to lose patience. 'I can do no more for you at the moment. As I've said – a number of times during this conversation – I will forward your complaint to the hotel company, expressing your extreme dissatisfaction with the treatment you and your family received. They will investigate your complaint and report back to me. They may even get in touch with you direct. Believe me, the minute I hear anything back from them, I'll be in touch with you!'

'Well, I have to say I'm not happy – but if that's the best you can do, I suppose I shall have to go along with it. I look forward to hearing from you!'

'Yes, Mr Swann,' said Philip as the customer retreated towards the door and opened it. Before leaving, he turned.

'Needless to say, that was the last holiday we will ever book with this travel agency!' He left, slamming the door behind him.

'Thank goodness for that!' Philip said.

'That's a good start to the week!' Diane replied. Philip thought for a moment.

'Are the hotels and resorts we use really lowering their standards? I mean, we used to get an occasional complaint, but now they seem to be coming in at the rate of at least one a week – sometimes more than one!'

'I think,' Diane said, 'it's the customers! They're getting more demanding, more picky. I suppose it's part of this "blame culture" thing. You know, there's no such thing as an accident any more. If something goes wrong, then someone must be to blame – and they're the ones you sue.'

'I don't think anybody's threatened to sue us yet, have they?'

'No, but they all want a refund, don't they?'

'Hmm…' Philip was thinking. 'You know?' he said at last. 'I think I'm beginning to come round to your idea.'

'Which particular idea would that be?'

'Early retirement!'

❋

Ron had just made his mid-morning cup of coffee when the doorbell rang. He put his cup down and answered it. It was Daphne's brother, Bob.

'Bob!' he exclaimed.

''Allo, Ron!' he said, smiling broadly. ''Adn't seen you since poor Daphne's fun'ral, so I thought I'd git the bus in and pay you a surprise visit. See 'ow you're gittin' on, like.'

'Well, it's certainly a surprise!' Ron replied. 'Come on in, Bob.' They shook hands and Bob followed Ron to the kitchen.

'I've just made myself some coffee. Would you like one?'

'Jus' the ticket! Thanks.' They took their mugs into the lounge and sat down. 'How've you been doin', then?' Bob asked.

'Oh, I'm not doing too badly, not too badly at all,' Ron said. 'I can look after the house and the garden – keep Daphne's lovely roses happy. It's just the cooking that's a bit of a problem.'

'Cookin'? Nothin' to it!' Bob said. 'When you're always lived on your own, like I 'ave, you 'ave to cook or you starve.'

'I never needed to,' Ron said. 'Daphne, bless her, she loved cooking.'

'Ah,' said Bob, 'our Mam, she learned us both about cookin' when we was little 'uns. Spent a lot o' time at 'ome wi' our Mam, Daphne did.'

'Why was that?' Ron asked.

'It were when she were poorly.'

'Was she poorly often, then?' Ron was suddenly serious. 'I never knew she was ill as a child.'

'More of'en than I were. She were what they called, back in them days, "delicate". But she seemed to grow out of it as she got older.'

'Did she have to stay in bed when she couldn't go to school?' Ron asked.

'Not always. Sometimes she'd just stay at 'ome wi' our Mam an' 'elp 'er wi' the cookin'. An' if she were feelin' a bit better she'd be out 'elpin' our Dad in the garden.'

'She loved gardening,' Ron said.

'Always did,' Bob agreed. 'She were so keen on it, our Dad give 'er a bit o' the garden to look after 'erself when she were only seven or eight. Real picture, it was.'

'And what about you?' Ron asked, finding memories of Daphne painful. 'What are you up to?'

'Oh, still doin' enough to keep me busy. Now I got me pension I just do a bit to 'elp out, like, an' get bit extra.'

'So you're still living in the cottage, then?'

'Oh ah! They'd 'ave a job sellin' it, see. It bein' miles off the road in the middle o' nowhere.'

'I suppose they would.' Ron looked at his watch. 'Look, Bob, it's Saturday. Saturdays, I usually go for a walk along the canal and then meet a couple of friends for a pub lunch. Would you like to join us?'

'Are you sure they won't mind, these mates o' yourn?'

'They won't mind a bit.'

'Well, thank you, then. I will.'

An hour later they arrived at The Navigation and Bob was introduced to Barry and Mick. They had their lunch and afterwards Bob, who, it transpired, was quite a raconteur, began to regale them with stories of the things he (and Daphne) had got up to when they were youngsters.

'Got into some scrapes when we was nippers, I can tell you!' he said. 'We 'ad to be a bit careful, mind! Livin' in a little village, see, everybody knew everybody else's business so if we got caught doin' summat as we shouldn't our Mam an' Dad'd soon git to 'ear all about it.'

'What kind of things did you get up to, then?' Mick asked, egging him on.

'Scrumpin' mostly – amongst other things,' Bob said, 'down Alder's orchard. Nearly got caught once. We seen Fred Alder comin' only we was too late to run off wi'out bein' seen. All as we could do was jump over the wall an' lie low till 'e'd gone – an' 'ope 'e never seen us.'

'And did he?' Barry asked.

'No – lucky for me an' Daphne – 'e never! 'E walked round for a bit, lookin' up at the trees – prob'ly wonderin' where some o' the fruit 'ad gone – an' then 'e went back. Our 'earts was in our mouths all the time 'e were there, I can tell you! As soon as we was sure as 'e'd gone we run off, takin' out ill-gotten gains wi' us! Then we went round sellin' 'em to the neighbours, if I remember rightly.'

Ron smiled. 'I can imagine you and my Daphne doing that,' he said, his eyes misting over. 'I think the most daring thing I ever got up to as a kid was knocking on doors and running away. Me and a couple of other lads had great fun doing that!'

'We had a variation on that when I was a boy,' Barry joined in. 'Near where we lived there was a cul-de-sac, Chapel Lane it was called. There were two rows of terraced cottages, facing each other across the narrow lane. We used to get a big ball of string and tie the end to the knocker on the first door. Then we tied it to the door opposite and so on, all the way down the rows.'

'What happened then?' Ron was all agog.

'We knocked on the first door and then we hid,' Barry continued. 'The woman would come to the door and open it. Seeing nobody there she shut it again. But opening the door pulled on the string and knocked the knocker of the house opposite, so they came to the door and opened it – so the string knocked the next knocker and so on!'

By this point the other three were rocking with laughter.

'I have to point out at this stage,' Barry added, 'that I didn't actually do the tying. I just stood and watched my friends do it and then hid with them to watch the fun.' He paused. 'I think I might have provided the string, though.'

'Did you ever get up to anything like that, Mick?' Bob asked.

'Near where we lived in Brum there was a tunnel on the canal. We used to climb up on the parapet and wait for a pair of boats to come along. There was a lot more traffic on the canals back then. As a pair was coming we used to crouch down behind the wall and just as the second boat was going into the tunnel we'd jump up and drop a lump of turf on the back deck. You should have heard the old boatwomen cursing us as they went in the tunnel! But, of course, they couldn't do anything about it.'

And so the lunchtime passed, with each of them entertaining

the others with their stories of mischievous children's pranks perpetrated on the unsuspecting. By the time they were on their third pint – or in Barry's case, his third half – their stories were becoming more and more fanciful.

❋

On Saturday morning Keith was ensconced in the bowels of the engine compartment merrily whistling away to himself, working on *Cormorant*, as he had been for most of the past three days. Suddenly there was the unmistakeable sound of a marine diesel struggling to start. The starter motor turned the engine a number of times, then there came a sound rather like a cough.

'Come on, my little beauty!' Keith's voice was just audible over the noise. Then, with a splutter, the ancient engine burst into glorious – and noisy – life! Philip and Diane hurried to the back of the boat and, seeing Keith's oil-smudged – and beaming – face, broke into spontaneous applause.

'Congratulations, Keith! Now all we need to do is to learn how to drive her,' said Diane.

'Steer!' corrected Keith.

'Oh dear! We've got a lot to learn,' grimaced Diane.

After a crash course – in more ways than one – in steering and the rudiments of boat handling from Keith, they felt sufficiently confident to venture further than the marina.

During the following week they took short cruises most evenings after dinner. They both became more adept at steering and controlling the boat. At the weekend they decided to take a longer cruise, leaving after they got home from work on Saturday and staying out until Sunday evening. As they were returning to the marina with Diane at the tiller, Philip was gazing ahead and looking thoughtful.

'A penny for them?' his wife asked.

'Just thinking,' he said. 'I've really enjoyed this weekend.'

'Good!' said Diane. 'So have I.'

'But wouldn't it be great to go on even further?'

'How do you mean?' Diane was puzzled.

'Well, I think I've really been bitten by this boating bug. I can't understand why we've never done it before! It's a great way to unwind.' Diane could not believe her ears.

'I mean,' Phillip continued, 'we've only ever looked on the boat as a place to live, and all the time we've had this option of travelling around and taking the comforts of our home with us! I've come round to your way of thinking. I don't think I want to run a travel business any more. I want to cruise the canals. Damn it! Let's retire early and tour the country – by water!'

Diane threw her free arm round her husband's neck and kissed him.

'Watch out!' he shouted. She returned her attention to what *Cormorant* was doing and, with some quick work on the throttle and the tiller, narrowly avoided a collision with a moored boat!

'Thank you, darling!' she said, beaming.

'What for? Preventing the crash?'

'No, silly! For seeing my point about retiring early! My workaholic husband has finally seen sense!'

'And the Mr Swanns of this world can go and damned well complain to somebody else!'

'Didn't we get an enquiry a while back from "Your Travels", asking if we wanted to sell?'

'Yes, we did! I wrote back and said "not on your nelly" – in rather more polite terms, I might add.'

'I wonder if they'd still be interested.'

'I'll ring them first thing in the morning.'

The following day Diane was bringing the first coffees of the day through into the shop. Philip was looking through a filing cabinet.

'Ah!' he pulled out a piece of paper. 'Here it is!'

'Here's what?' Diane asked, putting his coffee on his desk.

'That letter from "Your Travels".' He looked at the letter. 'It was only six months ago. Chances are they're still in the market!' He picked up the phone and dialled the number on the letter.

Ten minutes later he put the phone down.

'They're sending someone round tomorrow afternoon!' he said. 'About three o'clock.'

The next afternoon Philip looked at his watch at five minutes to three. 'The "Your Travels" chap will be here soon.'

'OK.' His wife took the duster she had wielded over the fresh polish on her desk and disappeared into the storeroom. 'Do you think the place looks all right? Do you think he'll be impressed?'

'They'll no doubt want to refit it in their house style. I think he'll be more impressed with the turnover in the last couple of years.'

'Do you think we ought to contact Sally? We might need her financial advice,' she called.

'I guess we should. She'll be keen to know what we're planning. I'll ring her later when we've got an idea of what "Your Travels" are going to do.'

At that moment the shop door opened and a young man in a suit and carrying a briefcase entered.

'Mr Tyler?' he asked.

'Yes,' Philip answered, standing.

'Darren Prentice, Your Travels,' said the man, extending his hand.

'Good afternoon, Mr Prentice,' said Philip, shaking it. 'Coffee?'

✳

Once the directors of 'Your Travels' had decided to buy out the Tylers, things moved very quickly indeed. The 'Your Travels' legal department handled the conveyancing of the property with the minimum of delay and within three weeks, having talked the new branch manager through the existing bookings, Philip and Diane were packing up their personal belongings and preparing to leave the shop for the last time.

'Hard to believe, isn't it?' Diane said as they prepared for home on that Friday afternoon. 'We won't be back here, opening up again on Monday morning.'

'Yes, it is,' Philip agreed. 'But I don't think we'd get in if we did. It'll be closed for a couple of weeks at least while they fit it out in the "Your Travels" house style.'

'Oh, yes!' Diane replied. 'All that ghastly purple and turquoise! Yuck!'

'Instead,' said Philip, 'on Monday morning we'll be somewhere up the Grand Union Canal and opening our bedroom curtains on a completely new view.'

'Yes, I'm really looking forward to that.' She paused. 'But in a funny way I'm a bit sad that we won't be coming back here any more.'

'It's certainly going to be different.' Diane looked around at the shop. 'It's been good to us, this little shop.'

'It has,' Philip agreed. 'It's the money we've made here that means we can go and leave it.'

As they locked the shop door for the last time, he noticed a tear rolling down Diane's cheek.

The following morning, after breakfast, Philip started the engine, Diane undid the mooring ropes and *Cormorant* eased gently away from the jetty.

They stood together on the back deck. As they turned out of the marina Philip turned to his wife.

'Welcome to retirement, Mrs Tyler!' he said, and gave her a kiss.

❊

'Oes Gafr Eto'

Harry Rodgers put his head round the farmhouse kitchen door.

'Has he been in yet?' he barked.

'Not seen him!' his wife barked back. The door closed and Rodgers got into his Landrover and drove out of the farmyard to the tied cottage where his one and only semi-retired farm labourer lived. He had actually retired some years earlier, but still helped out his old boss from time to time, in return for living in the cottage rent-free.

Fifteen minutes later the Landrover was back in the farmyard. Rodgers walked through the kitchen to the hall and picked up the telephone.

'Don't make him no coffee!' he called to his wife as he punched in the number. 'Old bugger's dead!'

'Oh,' said Mrs Rodgers, as she took one of three mugs – the chipped one – off the table and replaced it on its hook.

The first few days of their cruise passed in a euphoric haze. Enjoying the sheer novelty of chugging along the canal, Philip and Diane kept travelling during the daylight hours, rising early and not looking for somewhere to moor for the night until the light was beginning to fade. Everything was a blank page for them to write on with new and exciting experiences. 'Let's see what's round the next bend' and 'I wonder what's through this next bridge' frequently formed part of their conversation. Before they had set off Philip had armed himself with a guide to the canal that showed the pubs, and on some evenings they were able to moor close to a waterside hostelry where they dined outside in the summer evening sunshine.

As the weeks passed they found themselves travelling fewer hours each day and stopping more often to visit places of interest. They started spending two or three days at the same place before moving on.

One day they had tied up near a marina and were sitting on the front deck watching the sun set when Philip noticed that Diane was unusually quiet.

'Penny for them?' he asked.

She sighed and said nothing for a few moments. When she spoke her voice was quiet. 'I know that retiring early and setting off on the boat was my idea. And I know that we haven't been doing it for long.'

'You're not regretting it, are you?' Philip looked concerned. 'It's a bit late now.'

'No! No, I'm not … I love it ! It's just that … I don't know … I just feel…'

'You feel…' Philip paused. 'You feel there's something missing?' he offered.

'Yes! That's how I feel. I mean, I love cruising; I love stopping and visiting new places and tying up somewhere different every night. I love the open spaces, the sky, the lap of the water along the side of the boat. I love it even when it rains – but that's all it is, isn't it? It's just for our own amusement. There's no point to it – other than that – is there?'

'Isn't that what retirement is all about … pleasing yourself?'

'Yes, of course it is. I don't miss "Dream Holidays" one bit, or the customers, or London. But I'm not forty-five yet! Don't you think it would be even better if we were pleasing ourselves by actually doing something? I mean, we've been so lucky with the business doing so well. I wondered whether perhaps we should think about giving something back … I don't know…' Her voice tailed off

'I know what you mean,' Philip said. 'It was fine when we started out – just you and me and no one else and nothing else to worry about. But over the last few days, a bit like you, I've been sort of wondering whether we ought to have some kind of goal in mind.'

'You have? It's not just me, then?'

'No, it isn't. Perhaps we needed to sell "Dream Holidays" to find out what we really wanted to do. While you were gone to the village shop yesterday I was giving it some thought.'

'Were you?'

'Yes, but I wasn't sure how I was going to bring the subject up. But now you have, so that's fine.'

'And what were your thoughts about?' his wife asked.

'Well, you remember that place we stopped and looked round the other afternoon?'

'Yes.'

'I just wondered whether we could set up something like that. It wouldn't be so pressured as running the business,' Diane smiled.

'I'm sure we could!' Her eyes lit up. 'I think I'd really enjoy that.'

'While you were out I popped into the shop at the marina and bought this.' He picked up a copy of a waterways magazine from the table. 'And have a look at this.' He opened the magazine at the page where he had turned down the corner. It was the classified advertisement section. He pointed to an ad he had circled in pen. 'What do you think?' he asked.

'It sounds wonderful!' Diane said as she threw her arms round her husband's neck.

'OK,' said Philip, laughing. 'Come the morning, I'll start making a few phone calls and we'll see where we get to.'

'We're a team,' Diane said, resting her head contentedly on his shoulder. 'We can do anything we want!'

✳

The three friends were sitting at their usual table in The Navigation Inn. Their conversation at these weekly meals ranged over every subject under the sun and each of them was always ready to express an opinion on anything. During a rare lull in the conversation on this particular Saturday, Ron asked, 'Do either of you know anything about goats?' There was a moment's stunned silence.

'Goats?' Mick queried.

'Goats,' Ron repeated.

'Four-legged hairy things with horns. Eat anything!' Barry volunteered, raising his eyebrows. As their acquaintance had grown Mick and Ron had noticed he had the annoying habit of raising his eyebrows whenever he said anything that he thought sounded clever and, since he regarded himself as the brains of the trio, this occurred quite often. They had also learned that he had a tendency occasionally to sneeze – very loudly and very violently. They had christened these sudden and unexpected outbursts 'Barry Specials'.

'My fellow countryman – Val Doonican – he sang a song about a goat, "Paddy McGinty's Goat",' Mick added and immediately broke into song. They had also got used to Mick doing this at the slightest provocation.

'I can quite understand how Siobhan got fed up!' Barry had confided to Ron on one occasion.

They had found the best way to silence him was to interrupt as soon as possible – before he was in full flow.

'*There was Riley pushin' it, shovin' it and shushin' it. Hogan, Logan, everyone in town…*' Mick sang.

'I think you'll find that was an entirely different song that he also sang entitled "Delaney's Donkey",' Barry corrected him.

'You're right! As usual! It was,' agreed Mick, peeved. Seeing he was about to launch into another chorus, Barry cut him off with a question to Ron.

'Why do you ask?'

'Well, it seems my dear departed Daphne's brother has just died.'

'Oh, you mean Bob!' interrupted Mick. 'The chap who came to lunch here with us a while back?'

'The very same,' said Ron. His friends muttered their condolences. Ron continued, 'Although he'd retired from working on the farm, he was still living in his tied cottage. He never married and it seems that, as his brother-in-law, I'm his only living relative. The solicitor's been in touch, asking me to clear the house and take ownership of his pet goat.'

'You're joking!' said Mick.

'He never mentioned anything about owning a goat,' Barry said.

'No, he was too busy reminiscing.'

'It's my considered opinion that you're winding us up!' Barry said to Ron, raising his eyebrows again.

'I'm not! Look, I've got the letter here.' Ron reached into his inside pocket and pulled out an envelope. He passed the letter to them. They both read in silence.

'It says here that the farmer, Mr Rodgers,' Mick read, 'wants the place clearing and the goat removing as soon as possible.'

'Hence, my question,' said Ron. 'Do either of you know anything about goats?'

'I'm afraid not,' said Barry.

'Me neither,' said Mick, handing the letter back.

'Is there likely to be anything in the house that might be worth anything?' Barry asked.

'Doubt it,' Ron replied. 'I don't think Rodgers ever paid him very much – bit of a "hand-to-mouth" existence. I'm pretty sure he'd got no savings either.'

'Billy or nanny?' Barry asked.

'Pardon?' Ron queried.

'Is the goat a billy or a nanny – male or female?' he explained.

'Oh, that – I haven't the faintest idea.'

'Does it have name?' Mick asked.

'If it has, I've no idea what it is.'

'Don't know much about it at all, really, do you?' Barry continued, again raising his eyebrows.

'No, I don't,' Ron paused. 'Look, I'm driving over there this afternoon to start clearing the house. I'll probably know a bit more about the goat when I've seen it. It's in a field next to the cottage, apparently.'

'I look forward to next Saturday's luncheon with interest!' said Barry.

'*I'm riding along on a goat with no name...*' Mick began singing.

'Who recorded that, then, Mick?' Ron interrupted immediately.

'I can't rightly remember,' Mick said.

'It wasn't a goat. The song was entitled "A Horse with No Name", and the band was called America.' Barry's eyebrows went up. Fortunately for all concerned, this put Mick completely off his stroke and he sang no more that lunchtime.

✳

'The Lonely Goat(herd)'

The following Saturday Mick and Barry were at the pub first, impatiently waiting for Ron to arrive to tell them more about his inheritance.

'Where's he got to?' Mick asked.

'I've no idea,' Barry replied. 'He's probably looking for a field to keep the goat in.'

Just then Ron came through the door and walked over to join them.

'My round!' said Mick, standing up. 'I'll get you your usual, but don't say anything about the goat till I get back.'

Ron sat down and he and Barry waited in silence for Mick to return.

'Well?' asked Mick, resuming his seat with a pint of best for Ron, a pint of Guinness for himself, and a half of IPA for Barry.

'What?' Ron looked bemused.

'The goat, man!' said Barry. 'What about the goat?'

'Oh that!' said Ron. 'Not much to tell really. I went over there last Saturday afternoon and started clearing the cottage. Spent all day there – and Sunday – and got the job done. Bob didn't have much in the way of possessions and there was a skip nearby, so I dumped most of his gear in that.'

'And what about the goat?' Barry sounded a little exasperated.

'It was in the field, eating grass.'

'Is that all?' Mick sounded deflated.

'Apart from the fact that I had a phone call from Rodgers's solicitors yesterday, saying he's giving me a week to get it off his property.'

'Did you see this Rodgers chappy while you were over there?' Barry asked.

'No. I think they must have been away for the weekend. I knocked on the farmhouse door both days but there was no reply.'

'How did you get into the cottage with no keys, then?' Mick queried.

'Wasn't locked. Bob never locked the doors. And well, it's miles away from anywhere and, to be honest, there was nothing there worth pinching.'

'What's this Rodgers chap going to do with the goat if you don't remove it within the week?' Barry asked.

'According to his solicitor, he's going to call the vet in and have it put down.'

'Might be the best option,' Barry surmised.

'Before last Saturday I'd have probably agreed with you. But having seen Billy trotting round his field … well … I haven't got the heart.'

'Billy?' said Mick. 'You've given him a name?'

'Well … yes! I've decided I'm going to keep him.'

'Keep him? Where?' Barry asked.

'In my back garden,' Ron replied.

'It'll save you mowing your lawn,' Mick said, helpfully. 'You could hire him out to your neighbours. *Where have you been all the day, Billy Boy, Billy Boy? Where have you been all the day, my Billy Boy?*' he sang.

'The only problem is how am I going to get him home?' Ron cut in.

A silence fell as they pondered the problem. Suddenly, Mick's eyes lit up.

'My Jimmy's got an old Bedford van. He doesn't use it very much at the weekends. Shall I ring him and see if we can borrow it tomorrow to go and fetch your goat?'

Ron thought for a moment. 'Why yes! Thanks Mick. That'll be a great help.'

'I'll ring him now.' Mick pulled his mobile phone from his pocket and keyed in a number. He looked at the phone. 'No damned signal!' he grumbled.

'You never get one in here. You have to go out in the beer garden,' Barry advised, raising his eyebrows.

A few minutes later, Mick reappeared. 'We're on,' he said. 'Jimmy'll have the van in the car park here at ten sharp.'

'Is he going to drive?' Ron asked.

'I'm the named driver on his insurance, so I can drive it.'

'That's great, Mick. I owe you a pint.'

'Isn't it what friends are for?'

'I wonder if I might be allowed to join you gentlemen on this mercy mission tomorrow?' Barry ventured.

'Of course!' Ron replied. 'The more the merrier. And, anyway, we might need all the help we can muster to get Billy into the van.'

'Many hands make light work,' Barry added.

'But too many cooks spoil the broth!' said Mick, smiling.

'I wasn't aware that the manufacture of broth was part of the exercise,' Barry protested, and his eyebrows shot up.

'Till ten tomorrow morning, then.' Ron drained his glass.

❋

'That's it! That's just what we want! We could use that!' Diane stood up in the well deck at the front of the boat. 'Phil! Stop!' she shouted, pointing towards the next bit of bank where there were no moored boats and grabbing the end of a rope.

Philip, at the tiller, was carefully negotiating a route between moored boats on both sides of the canal, while Diane was sitting on the front deck enjoying the sunshine. Out of the corner of her eye she had spotted a roughly painted sign. It said 'For Sale', followed by a mobile telephone number. The sign was propped up on the roof of short narrowboat – about thirty feet long. The first thing Diane noticed was that for most of its length the sides were open to the elements. Then she saw that there neat rolls of what looked like tarpaulin on the edges of the roof. The only furniture aboard appeared to be seating along each side. She realised that it was a 'trip boat' for taking parties on short cruises along the canal.

Thinking his wife had some kind of a problem, or was suddenly feeling ill, Phil throttled back and steered towards the bank at the end of the line of moored boats. As *Cormorant* nudged the bank Diane leapt off with the rope and a mooring chain, pulled the boat into the side and proceeded to tie up.

'Why are we stopping here?' Philip asked, stepping ashore with the other rope.

'Tie that rope up and I'll show you,' she answered enigmatically.

Philip followed her instructions. 'Right!' he said. 'I've done that. What's it all about?' He followed her a little way back along the towpath.

She pointed to the trip boat. 'We could use that, couldn't we? Why don't we take them along the canal?' she asked, excitedly. Philip looked at the boat. It appeared to be in a reasonable condition. He saw the 'For Sale' sign.

'Why not, indeed?' he agreed. 'Let's go and have a look at it.' They walked further along the towpath.

'Looks OK from here,' Diane said as they approached the boat. 'How many do you think it would hold?'

Philip looked at the seating and made a quick calculation. 'About thirty, I'd guess, probably one or two more if they weren't too fat!'

'That's about the ideal size for what we want. Needs a repaint,' Diane said.

'That's nothing we can't handle – and we could get Keith up here to give the engine the once over.'

Philip took his mobile from his pocket and rang the number on the sign.

'Hello. I'm interested in your trip boat…'

❋

'I'll Be There'

True to his word, Mick's son Jimmy was in the car park with his rather ancient van just before ten o'clock on Sunday morning. As he got out of the cab Mick greeted him and introduced the others.

'I've cleared my stuff out the back,' he said.

'What are you going to do now?' his father asked.

'I've brought the paper to read and I can watch a bit of telly on your boat, Dad. How long do you reckon you'll be?' Everyone looked at Ron.

'Don't know, really,' he said. 'Shouldn't be more than a couple of hours … perhaps three to be on the safe side.'

'Pub'll be open by then,' Jimmy smiled. 'I'll pop in for a pint.'

'Let's go, then,' said Mick, climbing into the driving seat. The others clambered in next to him. 'You'll have to give me directions,' he said to Ron.

'Straight out of here and turn left onto the main road,' Ron replied.

The journey passed without incident – although with much rattling, clanking and grinding of gears – and they duly arrived at the farmhouse. Mick's 'Song of the Day' was 'Let's go to San Francisco', with which, to their discomfort, he serenaded them for the whole journey!

There was really no necessity for all of them to go to the farmhouse door. However, the springs in the van seats were so uncomfortable that they all needed to stretch their legs. They clambered out, and as Ron knocked at the door Mick and Barry stood behind him rubbing their numb backsides. After what seemed like an age the door opened a crack.

'Yes?' said a female voice, abruptly.

'Mrs Rodgers?' Ron enquired.

'Yes,' the voice said again.

'My name's Barton. Ronald Barton. I've come for Bob's goat.' The crack in the door widened slightly to reveal a middle-aged woman with a mournful face.

'You want my husband,' she said. 'He's in the top field.' As she said this she pointed vaguely in a direction further along the track they had used to reach the house. Ron looked in the direction of her pointing finger.

'Thank you, Mrs Rodg–' Ron said as he turned back, then realised she had closed the door.

'Chatty soul!' said Barry as they made their way back to the van.

As they continued along the track in the direction she had indicated, the ground began to rise. As they crested the hill they saw a man on a tractor, pulling a machine.

'This must be the top field,' said Barry.

'And that must be him,' Ron said as Mick stopped the van and they tumbled out. They walked into the field and waited for the tractor to reach them. As it did so, Ron walked forward and waved at the driver – who promptly turned the tractor round and drove back down the field. Ron ran a few steps after him, but soon stopped and walked back to the others.

'Well, I'll be…!'

He tried again when the tractor approached them for the second time, but with the same result. Not until he had finished the whole field did the driver stop, switch off the engine and acknowledge their presence.

'Yes?' he said.

'I've come for Bob's goat,' Ron said, remaining calm.

''Bout time too,' replied Rodgers. 'Been dead over three month now.'

'I only heard from your solicitor a fortnight ago,' Ron retorted.

'Bloody lawyers!' came the reply. 'You'd best go and get it then.' Rodgers restarted the tractor's engine.

'Why do you want him out of the way so quickly?' Ron shouted over the engine noise.

'Sold that land.'

'Sold the land?' Ron asked.

'More than I want now. Want the goat out the way, though. You just go and get it. You know where it is.' And with that he drove off.

As they watched the tractor recede into the distance Mick said, 'I guess they're well suited – him and his missus.'

'Both as miserable as each other!' Ron agreed.

'*The world is treating me bad, misery.*' Mick began to sing again.

They all piled back into the van, bounced over a humpbacked canal bridge, and a few moments later arrived at the field next to the cottage. They tumbled out of the van again and leaned on the gate, looking at the goat.

Billy was a stocky creature, bigger than a large dog, but smaller than a donkey. He was covered with black and white hair. However, his head was nearly all black, but with a white stripe that ran from the tip of his nose, up between his eyes and his enormous curved horns, which gave him a rather sinister appearance. Oblivious to their presence, he continued to munch grass.

'Hello Billy!' Ron called, an excited grin breaking out all over his face. Mick and Barry exchanged a knowing smile.

'He looks a bit evil to me,' said Mick. 'It's those slitty eyes!'

'Well, you know Satan's supposed to have a goat's head, don't you?' Barry added, unhelpfully, raising his eyebrows. Billy kept on munching. 'Now, how are we going to set about managing this?' Barry continued.

'Well, I've brought a bag of carrots,' said Ron. 'They're in the van. I thought we could use them to sort of entice him in.'

'Good idea!' said Mick. 'I'll back the van up to the gate while you two get it open.' With a great crunching and grinding of gears, Mick reversed the van into position and opened the back doors. Ron and Barry were still trying, unsuccessfully, to undo the gate.

'What's the problem?' Mick asked.

'The gate's tied up with binder twine and I'm afraid we can't seem to untie it,' Barry said.

'Let me see.' Mick pushed his way in. 'Ah!' he said. He sang, tunelessly to himself while his fingers worked busily at the twine. In seconds, it was undone.

'How did you do that?' Ron asked, amazed. Barry raised his eyebrows.

'You don't live on a narrowboat as long as I have without learning a thing or two about knots,' Mick replied with a look of self-satisfaction on his face.

As the gate opened Billy stopped munching grass – but he did not move. His head remained an inch or two from the ground. Only his eyes moved. His gaze shifted from the tasty herbage to his would-be captors. He surveyed each one of them in turn. For a moment no one moved. Then, taking the carrots from the van, and while the others stood by its open back doors, Ron slowly approached Billy.

'Come on, Billy,' he encouraged. 'Nice juicy carrot?' The goat raised his head and looked at Ron. For a second or two Ron thought that he too saw a look of malevolence in Billy's eyes. But then, noticing the proffered carrot, the goat took a step towards Ron. Nearly taking Ron's hand as well, he took the carrot.

'Good boy!' said Ron, checking he still had all his fingers. He backed towards the open doors of the van and repeated the move with the carrot. Again Billy took the bait. It was working well. After two more carrots the goat had almost arrived at the open van. Ron was inching his way towards the open doors and was about to throw the remainder of the carrots into the back in the hope that Billy would jump in after them, when Barry sneezed! It was not just a plain, ordinary, common or garden sneeze. It was a 'Barry Special'. It had happened a few times in The Navigation and, on one famous occasion, had caused the barman to drop an entire tray full of glasses!

The result of this 'Barry Special' was no less dramatic. The goat, frightened by the explosion, veered away from Ron and, pushing his way through the gap between a temporarily hors de combat Barry and the gatepost, set off at a gallop along the track. Ron and Mick stared unbelievingly at Barry.

'Sorry!' said Barry, raising his hands, palms uppermost, in a sign of despair and embarrassment. 'I can't avoid sneezing, now can I?'

'So what do we do now?' Ron asked.

'We'll have to go after him in the van,' said Mick. They slammed the back doors shut and clambered into the front. Mick revved the ancient engine and they set off in hot pursuit. As they bumped along down the rutted farm track, Barry noticed something sticking out from under the seat. He bent down and picked it up. It was a rope.

'If I can, in some small measure, make amends for allowing – albeit, quite accidentally – the animal to escape, perhaps this item may be useful in effecting his recapture?' he said, holding the coil of rope up in front of him.

'Ah!' said Mick. 'Jimmy's towrope! He always carries it. He says it's in case he comes across someone who needs a tow, but I reckon it's been used a damned sight more for somebody else to tow this heap of tin!'

'I assume it's got an MOT, this van?' Ron queried.

'I ask no questions – and I get told no lies!' Mick replied.

Just then they saw Billy. He was happily munching on a particularly leafy bush at the side of the track. Mick brought the van to a grinding halt and turned off the engine.

'Now, let's think about how we're going to tackle this,' Ron said. They thought in silence for a few moments. 'Any ideas?' he asked.

'There's a gateway just back there – we passed it on the right,' said Barry. 'If Mick uses it to turn round, we can get the back of the van facing the goat. Then with the back doors both open wide, they'll just about cover the whole width of the track.'

'Yes, and if one or all of us goes into the field and walks quietly down so we're the far side of him, we can get back over the fence and chase him towards the van!' Ron added.

'He'll have no option but to jump in!' Mick smiled. 'I love it when a plan comes together!'

With more unhealthy sounds of metal being forcibly scraped against metal, eventually the van was in position with its back doors open. The track was effectively blocked. Billy carried on munching.

'He can't get past it so we'll all go and encourage him to run towards it,' Ron said, picking up Jimmy's towrope. They climbed over the gate, then crept quietly past Billy, who continued to munch on the high-density foliage. Finding a gap in the bushes beyond Billy, one by one they squeezed back through and found Billy standing in the middle of the track, facing them, a wicked glint in his eyes. As they stood there, eyeing each other, Billy calmly bent his head round and scratched his back with the end of his horn.

'That's clever!' said Barry.

'Look! Tie the rope into a noose and try and get it over his head,' said Mick, sounding more positive than he felt. Ron was all fingers and thumbs.

'Give it here!' Mick said. He tied the noose deftly and handed the rope back to Ron. 'There.'

'Thanks,' Ron mumbled, looking warily at Billy. 'It's down to me to lasso him, is it?' Billy continued to stare at them malevolently.

'Your goat!' Mick said, indicating Billy with a wave of his hand. Ron, slowly and cautiously, approached his quarry.

'Come on Billy-boy. We're not going to hurt you,' he cooed.

Suddenly Billy dropped his head and charged. Ron performed a neat sidestep – a trick he had never forgotten from his younger days on the rugby field. Quick as a flash, Mick took off his jacket and threw it with great accuracy over Billy's head.

Then a very strange thing happened. The goat stopped dead. Ron slipped the rope over his head.

'What on earth made you think of doing that?' Barry asked.

'Well,' said Mick, 'they do that with horses that won't go into the stalls for the flat races. They put a hood over their heads to cover their eyes. It calms them down. I hadn't got a hood, so I used my jacket!'

'Well done, you!' said Ron.

'Don't be premature,' Mick warned. 'We haven't got him into the van yet!'

Ron, holding tightly to the rope, proceeded to lead Billy along the track towards the van. Mick followed at Billy's head, firmly gripping one of his horns through his jacket. Barry brought up the rear, keeping a safe distance away from the potential danger inherent in Billy's hind legs.

'If we get him right up close to the back of the van,' Ron suggested, 'so his head is actually sort of inside it, and then we close the doors as far as we can, sort of round him. I'll chuck the rest of the carrots right inside the van, so they'll be the first thing he sees when we take Mick's jacket off his head. He won't be able to see outside the doors.'

'Sounds like a plan to me,' Mick agreed.

It worked. On a count of three, Mick retrieved his jacket. Billy immediately spotted the carrots and jumped up into the back of the van. Ron and Barry slammed the doors shut. A cheer went up and there were handshakes all round.

'Right!' said Ron. 'Back to my place it is!'

Billy, the goat, had entered their lives.

The run back started well. They bounced back over the canal bridge and, with minimal complaining from the gearbox, set off down the road. They drove in silence apart from Mick entertaining them with selections from his vast repertoire. As they entered town, however, while waiting for some traffic lights to change, they heard a different loud, metallic clang – this time from behind them. This was not the gearbox. They all felt as if they had been shunted forward.

'Has someone run into the back of us?' Barry asked.

Mick looked in his wing mirror. 'No. Nothing behind us for miles,' he said. Then it happened again.

'It's Billy!' Ron shouted. 'He's butting the bulkhead.'

'He must have consumed all the carrots and become bored,'

Barry said. Fortunately, Billy was only able to do this while the van was stationary, as he ceased as soon as they started moving again.

Mick, with more grinding of gears, backed the van into Ron's drive. Ron fetched a sturdy stake and a sledgehammer from his garage and they processed round to the back garden. With Mick and Barry holding it steady, Ron drove the stake a good two feet down into the middle of the lawn.

With the van stationary, Billy had resumed his butting tactics.

'One of us has got to get in there and cover his head again,' said Ron.

'Your goat!' said Mick for the second time that day, waving his hand towards the back of the van. 'And you're not using my jacket this time either. It stinks of goat now!'

Ron took the sledgehammer back into the garage and came back with an old blanket. 'I'll use this,' he said.

'Are you ready?' asked Mick.

'Ready as I'll ever be, I suppose,' Ron replied.

Slowly, they opened the doors an inch or two. Billy was just about to charge the bulkhead when he became aware of movement behind him. He turned and walked towards it, blinking at the daylight. Ron noticed that there was a strong smell emanating from the van.

'What the…?' he said.

'That's because he's been cooped up in a confined space,' suggested Barry, raising his eyebrows.

'Bit wider,' Ron said. The others opened the doors a little further.

'Wider,' said Ron again, his eyes never leaving the goat. The gap grew again.

'Now!' Ron shouted. As the doors opened wide, in one swift movement Ron covered Billy's head with the blanket and grabbed the rope, which was still dangling from the goat's neck. Holding it tightly, he proceeded to lead Billy out of the van and towards the garden. As before, Mick followed, gripping one of Billy's horns through the blanket, and Barry brought up the rear. Mick tied the rope to the stake in the lawn.

'I wonder what he'll do when you take the blanket off his head,' said Mick.

'We'll soon find out!' Barry replied. Tentatively, Ron approached the goat from the side. He grabbed a corner of the blanket and, with one tug, removed it, then stepped back quickly out of harm's way. Billy looked up, surprised. He looked around and took in his surroundings – and then began to munch on the grass.

'Well, I'll be…!' said Ron. 'As cool as you like!'

'Like I said, you won't need your lawnmower any more,' said Mick with a grin.

They trouped inside the house.

'I hope you don't mind removing your shoes, gentlemen. Daphne was always particular about her carpets.' Ron poured them all a generous glass of scotch.

'Thanks, lads,' he said, raising his glass. 'I couldn't have done it without your help.'

'We'll be interested to hear how you've got on with him when we meet up next Saturday,' said Barry.

'We will that!' Mick agreed.

✳

'Fings Ain't Wot They Used T'Be'

For Philip and Diane their cruise now took on a different dimension. They left *Cormorant* tied up at some visitor moorings and caught a train back to London to keep appointments with their solicitor and with Sally to arrange for the funds to be made available for their new project. Diane was so anxious that their plans would come to fruition that she refused point blank to give the scheme a name. She only ever referred to it as 'It'.

'Not until we know It's really going to happen!' she said whenever Philip brought up the subject.

As they walked back to the boat from the railway station that evening they both felt a sense of achievement. Things were moving. They had taken the first steps into their new venture.

'You know?' Philip said, as they arrived back at *Cormorant*, 'we've managed to get the best of both worlds.'

'How do you mean?'

'Well, not only have we got our new life on the boat, but we've also got a new project to get our teeth into.'

'I see what you mean. Yes, we have. I just feel so happy and excited about the whole thing!' Diane's smile was radiant.

'So do I, love,' Philip said, pulling her to him and giving her a kiss. 'So do I!'

❊

When Ron joined the others at The Navigation the following week, Mick and Barry noticed that he looked haggard. They placed their usual orders at the bar – plaice and chips for Ron, pie and chips for Mick and fish pie for Barry ('I've got a delicate stomach, you know!') – sat down with their drinks and waited.

'Well?' asked Barry, impatiently. 'And how's Billy?'

'Oh, he's fine!' Ron replied. 'I just wish I could say the same for my garden. Poor Daphne! She'd never forgive me!'

'What's happened?' Mick asked.

Ron took a deep breath. 'Well, Monday morning I was woken up by this pitiful bleating noise. I looked out of the bedroom window and he'd obviously been eating the grass in a sort of circular motion and, as he'd walked round the stake, the rope had got wound round it tighter and tighter. The poor devil was stuck with his head right up against the stake and he hadn't got the sense to go round the opposite way to free himself.'

The others chuckled.

Ron continued. 'As I was walking him round the stake in the opposite direction, I remembered that it was your Jimmy's towrope.'

'He missed that on Wednesday,' Mick interjected.

'Did he?' Ron queried.

'Van broke down again. I had to take him one of my spare ropes off the boat.'

'Well, I've brought his rope with me today. It's in the car. I didn't have time to walk here today,' Ron said. 'Anyway, having realised it was Jimmy's rope, I went down to Alf Watts's chandlery to get a new one. I got it home and tied Billy to the stake with it. I told him, "Go round the stake in both directions," I said to him, "Then you won't strangle yourself!" What I didn't realise until later in the day was that my new rope was a bit longer than Jimmy's.'

'So you got more of your lawn cut?' Barry suggested.

'Oh, yes!' Ron replied. 'I got all my lawn cut – but I got all the rest of the stuff in my garden eaten as well! Daphne's roses, the hedge, lots of things I don't even know the names of – they're either eaten or trampled on!' Mick and Barry tried, unsuccessfully, to stifle their giggles.

'It's not funny!' Ron protested. 'He's eaten virtually everything! It's got to the point now where I'm having to buy food for him, and I've only had him a week!'

'So Billy-boy's costing you money?' Mick asked, then launched into Abba's 'Money, Money, Money'.

'Too right he is!' Ron stopped him. 'I've never known anything with such an appetite. And what goes in has to come out!'

'You mean…' Barry grimaced.

'Yes! The whole place is ankle deep in goat poo!'

'So what are going to do with him?' Mick asked.

'I don't know,' Ron replied. 'I must admit, I'm nearly at the end of my tether.'

'And Billy is at the end of his?' Barry asked, raising his eyebrows.

'Oh, very funny, I'm sure!'

'Well, there's always the other option I mentioned right at the start,' Barry said.

'What? Having him put down, you mean?' Ron asked.

'Solve all your problems!' Mick added.

'Believe you me,' Ron said, 'there have been times this week when I've seriously considered it. The thing is, though, it would cost me a fortune for the vet to come out, so we'd have to borrow Jimmy's van again.'

'Not on, I'm afraid,' Mick interjected.

'Is it completely beyond repair this time, then?' Barry asked.

'Oh no! It's fine – well, no worse than it was before, mechanically.'

'What then?' Ron enquired.

'Remember when we let the goat out at your place?' Mick said.

'Yes.'

'Remember that God-awful smell when we opened the van?'

'Yes.'

'Well, it wasn't because he'd been cooped up in there, as we thought.'

'What was it, then?' Barry asked.

'A bloody great pile of goat shit!' Mick explained. 'He'd dropped a load before he'd even seen your garden.'

'Oh! I'm very, very, sorry!' Ron was mortified. 'Please tell Jimmy if I'd known I'd have made sure it was cleaned up before you left. I'm quite the expert at it now!'

'Well, it's all clean now,' Mick continued. 'But Jimmy still reckons the back of his van reeks of it. So he said, "If your mate wants to move his goat any more, he can ask some bugger else!"'

'So there we are, then!' Ron said, feeling strangely relieved. 'I can't have him put down because we can't move him and I can't afford for the vet to visit.' He paused. 'And anyway…'

'Anyway, what?' Barry asked.

'Well…' Ron faltered. 'Well … in spite of all the problems he's causing me, I'm getting quite fond of Billy – in a funny sort of way.'

'So you're going to keep him, then?' said Mick.

'Well, yes … I think so. But it would be nice if he could go somewhere else, though – even just for a few days – a week perhaps. Just so I could have a few days without worrying about where he is and what he's getting up to. Sort of … respite care.' He paused again. 'I don't suppose either of you could…?'

'I live on a boat, don't I?' Mick explained. 'That harridan I married took my house. I've got no garden to keep a goat in.'

'Barry?' Ron asked, hopefully.

'Sorry, Ron. I live in a second-floor flat. I've got no ground either.'

'Looks like you're stuck with him!' Mick said.

'It looks like I am,' Ron reluctantly agreed. 'The biggest worry is leaving the house – like to come here. I don't know what he's doing while I'm not there.'

As soon as he had finished eating Ron looked at his watch. 'I better go. Billy's been on his own for a couple of hours already. He might have eaten his way through the fence and started on next door's garden now for all I know! I'll see you next week, gents.'

After he had gone Mick said, 'It's a bit of a quandary for poor old Ron, isn't it?'

'It certainly is!' Barry agreed. 'It's obvious that it's getting him down. Did you notice how he kept referring to his watch all through lunch?'

'Yes, I did.' Mick paused. 'I wonder if there's anything we could do to help him.'

'I'll cogitate on that while I'm getting the next round in. Same again?'

'Please.'

While Barry was at the bar, Mick tried to come up with a solution. But apart from them all chipping in to help pay the vet's bill he could think of nothing and, anyway, he knew that Ron was not keen on that solution.

Barry returned with a Guinness and his half of IPA – and Mick noticed he also had a notepad and pen, gripped between his teeth.

'What have you got those for?' Mick asked.

Barry put the beers on the table and took the notepad from his mouth. 'While I was standing at the bar waiting to get served, I caught sight of the pub noticeboard, and wondered if we were to put up an advertisement about the goat, whether anybody would see it who might be interested. What do you think, Mick?'

'I reckon it's worth a try. Nothing ventured, nothing gained – as they say!'

'Right!' said Barry as he opened the pad and clicked the ballpoint. 'I borrowed these from the barman. Now what are we going to say?'

Mick thought for a moment. 'Do you think Ron would want any money for him?'

'Doubt it.'

'Right then: "Free to a good home – male goat – answers to the name of Billy".'

'Good start!' Barry said as he wrote this down. Then he suggested, '"Purchaser to arrange transport". That way Ron won't have to throw himself on your Jimmy's mercy.'

'Jimmy's not the merciful type,' said Mick.

'I didn't somehow think he was,' Barry said. 'Now, do we need to say anything else?'

'Well,' said Mick, 'assuming someone reads the advert and wants the goat, that's all taken care of. But what about the fact that Ron's got fond of him? I mean, if someone goes and takes his goat away, to Ron it'll be the same as if he's been put down, won't it?'

'I see what you're getting at,' Barry said. 'A moment!' He wrote some more, then turned the pad round to show Mick, who read, '"Current owner to retain visiting rights". Yes! That solves it! I'm sure Ron would like that.'

'All we need now is Ron's phone number to go on the bottom and it's complete. Could you go and ask the barman if we can borrow the phone book.'

'Right.' Mick went to the bar, returning a few moments later holding a battered, dog-eared telephone directory. 'You're not going to put that page of the notepad on the noticeboard just like that?' he asked.

'Oh no!' Barry replied. 'I'll take it home and do something with it on my computer – something a bit striking to catch people's attention.'

Mick opened the directory. 'What's Ron's surname?'

'Barton.'

'Ah, yes.' He flicked through the pages, then ran his finger down the column of names.

'Barnett … Barrett … Bartlett … Barton! Barton, Ronald – yes – that's his address.' He pointed to the number and Barry wrote it down. 'Are you going to put the ad up without talking to Ron first?'

'Oh, no! If he started getting phone calls concerning his goat without knowing about the advertisement, he'd only think it was you or me trying to wind him up.'

'And in his present state, I don't think he'd take too kindly to that.'

'Quite. So, now we know what we want the advertisement to say, I'll take it home. I'll phone Ron before I start on it and see what he thinks.'

'If he agrees we can put it on the board next Saturday.'

✳

'With A Little Help From My Friends'

'It doesn't seem possible that we've been out cruising for more than six months, does it?' Diane said.

They had tied up early in a sheltered spot close to a bridge. It was a beautiful afternoon, and the late summer sunshine shone through the overhanging trees, casting a pattern of sunshine and shadows on the surface of the water. There was the chugging of a tractor working in a distant field and a couple of cows mooed as though calling to each other on the opposite bank.

Philip had placed two chairs and a picnic table on the wide towpath. He had made a pot of tea and carried two mugs full to the table. Diane had been baking that morning and she stepped off the boat with a plate of scones in one hand and a sheaf of papers in the other. Philip laughed. 'You and your lists! No, it doesn't seem possible. "Dream Holidays" is a lifetime away.'

'There's so much to think about,' she said, arranging the lists to her satisfaction on the table.

They had changed their planned cruise so that they could approach 'It' by water.

'What a good idea!' Philip had said. 'We didn't really have long enough to see it properly last week, what with the train being delayed and the agent having to dash off to another appointment as soon as he'd dropped us back at the station. If we go there by boat we can spend as much time as we like.'

The sound of Philip's mobile broke the silence.

'Hello?' He spoke for a few moments, then put his phone down. 'Such a nice old chap!' he said. 'Well, you can give "It" a name now!'

✳

Barry arrived first and, taking a couple of drawing pins from the side of the noticeboard, he pinned up the advert for Ron's goat. He stood back and admired his handiwork.

'Although I say it myself, that's not bad,' he murmured to himself. 'Not bad at all.'

While he was waiting at the bar to be served, Mick arrived. 'Well? What did he say?'

Barry pointed at the noticeboard, and Mick went over for a closer look. 'Ah, you've even got a photo of Billy on it!' he exclaimed gleefully, as he returned.

'Yes, I popped round to Ron's house on Wednesday to take a photo. Poor Ron! What a mess he's in! Goat excrement everywhere! I've got his mobile number on there, as well.'

'He was obviously happy with the idea, then?' Mick said.

'He was very grateful that we had thought of a way to, at least, try to get him out of his predicament.'

'Oh, good!'

Ron was late arriving. As he came in he paused and looked at the advertisement on the noticeboard.

'Sorry, I'm late,' he said as he approached the table, pint in hand. 'You've done a lovely job on that advert. Thank you both.' He looked even more haggard than the week before.

'We've ordered for you,' Barry said.

'Your usual,' Mick added.

'Fine,' Ron said, sitting down with his pint and taking a long swig from it. No one spoke for a moment. Neither of them wanted to ask the question but, eventually, Mick could contain his curiosity no longer.

'How's it going with … Billy?' he diffidently enquired.

'Don't ask!' Ron said. 'Still eating me out of house and home! Billy's the reason why I'm so late.'

'Why? What's happened?' Barry asked.

'Well!' Ron began. 'I'd shortened his rope so he couldn't reach the hedge. He's getting very good at wandering round the garden and not getting himself tied up on the stake.' He took another swallow of ale. 'It was so warm this morning, I opened the patio doors to let a bit of air in. Without thinking, I went upstairs and left them open.'

'Oh dear! I think I may know what's coming,' Barry said.

'Next thing I knew, there's this terrible banging and crashing downstairs. I ran down as fast as my old legs would carry me – and there was Billy – in the lounge! I'd forgotten the rope was long enough to reach the house – and inside it!'

'Had he done any damage?' Mick asked.

'Apart from chewing a great hole in the curtains, leaving scratch marks with his hooves on the sideboard where he'd demolished the contents of the fruit bowl, smashing the glass doors of the cocktail cabinet and leaving a pile of poo on the carpet – no, no damage at all! Poor Daphne! What would she think? That cocktail cabinet was her mother's and she used to get cross with me if I ever came into the house with dirt on my shoes. What would she say to a goat?'

'Oh my God!' Mick exclaimed.

'What did you do?' Barry asked.

'I managed to pull him back outside and shut the patio doors. I cleared up his deposit as best as I could. I can see what your Jimmy means about the smell! It's so much worse in an enclosed space. I'll have to have the carpet cleaned. I'll need some new glass for the cabinet doors – and a french-polisher to get rid of the scratches on the sideboard. He's eaten my week's supply of fruit. That goat's costing me a fortune!'

'Don't worry. We'll get it sorted,' said Barry, soothingly.

When the waitress brought their meals they tucked in and, at Mick's instigation, the conversation turned to the weekend's football.

Ron was placing his knife and fork neatly on his plate when his mobile rang. 'Hello? Yes,' he said. They all heard a voice say, 'Hello, I'm ringing about the goat. Your poster says "Free to a good home"?'

Ron was sitting with his back to the pub entrance and to the noticeboard beside it. Mick and Barry sat facing it. Mick noticed a couple studying the advert, the man with a mobile phone to his ear.

'Hang on!' Ron said. 'You're breaking up. I'm in the pub. I'll just go outside. The signal's never very good in here. You're interested in the goat, you say?' He stood up and started for the entrance, but Mick tapped him on the arm and pointed to the couple. Ron smiled and made his way over to where they were standing.

'Very interested!' said the man. 'When can I see you about it?'

'Right now!' said Ron, tapping him on the shoulder.

The man spun round. 'Well, how about that!'

'Come over and join us and we'll talk about it,' said Ron. 'These are two friends of mine – Mick and Barry. They did the advert for me. I'm Ron, as you know.' The couple pulled up two stools and joined them round the table.

'My name's Philip Tyler,' the man said, extending his hand first to Ron, then to Mick and Barry, 'and this is my wife, Diane.'

'So you'd like my Billy, would you?'

'Yes,' said Philip.

'And why would you want such a thing as a goat?' asked Ron. They did not seem the sort of people who would want a goat. City types, he thought, judging by their clothes.

'Diane and I are starting this exciting new venture.'

'And what would that be?' Mick asked sceptically. He, too, was looking at their smart city 'designer country' clothes.

'Well,' Philip began, 'it's a long story.'

'We've got all day,' added Barry, raising his eyebrows.

'We took early retirement. We had a successful travel business in London.'

'Very early by the looks of you!' laughed Mick.

'Yes. After a while, we decided that it was a bit too early. We needed something to get our teeth into. So we bought some land.'

'And what do you propose to do with your land?' enquired Barry.

'We're going to start a farm for children!' Diane continued the story. 'These days there are so many children, especially from the cities, who don't even recognise farm animals let alone know how to care for them.'

'We've both always liked animals. I was brought up in the country before I was lured to the city. We always had dogs and chickens when I was a child. My sister had a pony. So we decided to open a farm to show kids from the towns and cities a bit of the country life,' Philip explained.

'What a great idea!' said Mick. 'So what made you think about setting up a farm for the benefit of "underprivileged kids", as I guess they're called?' he asked.

Philip looked at Diane. 'You tell him, love. It's your story.'

'Well,' Diane began. She spoke quietly and earnestly. 'I wanted to give something back.' She obviously believed deeply in what she was saying. 'I was adopted when I was young. My adoptive parents were lovely. I loved them dearly. They were a bit older than the average parents, but they couldn't have given me a better home nor a better upbringing.

'When we decided to look at another business venture, I suddenly thought about all the others in the children's home where I was before they adopted me. I know for a fact that some of them were there until they'd grown up. Then I thought about the children who are born into families who have to struggle money-wise and I wondered whether there was something we could do to help them – give them new experiences and help them to learn about taking responsibility for something other than themselves. A farm seemed to be the answer.'

There was a pause and a silence almost quiet enough to hear Barry, Mick and Ron let out a collective 'Ah!' Perhaps these young city types had more going for them than they thought.

'It all happened rather quickly, really,' Philip said. 'We obviously needed some land and we came across a few acres not far from here. It's land by the side of the canal. The sale was completed yesterday so we can get started straight away.'

'Having got the land – we needed some animals,' added Diane.

Mick launched into '*Don't fence me in, Oh, give me land, lots of land and the starry skies above. Don't f–*'

Diane and Philip looked startled by the unexpected musical interlude.

'Don't worry about him! He often does that,' said Barry. 'It's best to interrupt him!' he added in a whisper.

'And that's where my Billy comes in,' Ron added, quickly.

'We've had offers of some chickens so far – nothing definite – but a goat would be a great addition!' said Diane.

'Where's the goat at the moment?' Philip sounded interested.

'He's in my back garden,' Ron said. 'At least, that's where I left him.'

'You've got a big garden, have you?' Diane asked.

'Not especially,' said Ron. 'That's why I need to get him somewhere else.'

'So how did you come to get him?' Philip enquired.

'It's another long story,' Ron began.

'We've still got all day!' quipped Barry, raising his eyebrows again.

'He belonged to my brother-in-law,' Ron commenced, 'who lived on a farm a couple of miles up the road from here. But when he died – my brother-in-law, that is, not the goat – the farmer wanted rid of him – the goat, that is, not my brother-in-law.'

'We had some fun moving him, I can tell you!' said Barry.

'Made a right old mess in the back of my Jimmy's van, he did!' added Mick.

'And he's wrecked my garden!' said Ron. 'My poor Daphne's roses! They're all gone! All gone!' He paused. 'How am I going to get Billy to you?'

'Don't worry about that,' Diane said. 'Phil's Dad's got an old horse box we can borrow – and his car. We can come and collect him. His name's Billy, you say?'

'Well, that's what I call him. I don't think Bob ever gave him a name.'

'Then Billy he shall be,' said Philip. 'Now, let's all have a drink to seal the deal. What'll it be, gentlemen?'

As Philip returned with a tray of drinks, Ron asked, 'Will I be able to come and see Billy sometimes?'

'As often as you like!' Diane said.

'I'd be grateful for that,' said Ron.

When Philip and Diane had gone the three of them mulled over what had happened.

'Well, that was stroke of luck!' Ron said.

'The advertisement did the trick,' Barry added.

'All's well that ends well,' said Mick.

'Shakespeare!' said Barry, raising his eyebrows.

'I knew that,' said Mick.

❋

'Goin' Home'

The next day Ron had a call from Philip to say that, as he had someone to keep an eye on the goat for a week or so until he and Diane moved to the property, permanently, they would collect Billy the following Saturday.

'We hope you and your friends are going to follow us so you can see Billy in his new home,' he added.

'Love to – and I'm sure Mick and Barry will too.'

'Only another week – and then I can tidy up what's left of my garden!' he thought as he replaced the receiver.

Philip and Diane duly arrived at Ron's house with the horse box. Philip seemed to have a way with animals and Billy appeared to trust him. He stood patiently while Philip untied the rope from the stake and trotted beside him up the ramp and into the horse box.

'Well, I'll be…!' said Ron.

Just then Mick and Barry arrived and Ron made coffee for them all.

'So what brought you two to The Navigation last week?' Ron asked, as they sat in the kitchen with their coffee. 'Did you think you ought to come and suss out some of the locals?'

'Well, as I mentioned,' Philip said, 'the land is a little way out of town, but when we saw that it was by the canal – well, we live on a boat ourselves – we had the idea of having a trip boat so we could pick the kids up from that place in town. What was it called, again, love?'

'The Old Town Wharf.'

'That's it. The Old Town Wharf.'

'We thought we could pick the children up from there and take them to the farm by boat,' Philip continued. 'The Council seem very interested in the project.'

'We've got a couple of chaps coming next month to build us a landing stage,' Diane added.

'Might stop them treating the cut as a rubbish dump!' Mick added, with feeling. 'I live on a boat as well and I never get through town without something or other fouling my prop!'

'Quite,' Philip agreed.

'I'm sure the children will thoroughly enjoy it,' said Barry.

'We cruised the proposed journey to get a feel for it. We noticed the pub and decided to stop for a spot of lunch, met you guys – and the rest is history!'

'And have you got a feel for it?' Ron asked.

'Oh yes,' Philip replied. 'It's not a bad little trip, actually. Just the right length, and fortunately there are no locks or tunnels where we could lose any of them!'

They drained their mugs and went to their cars. Billy was waiting in the horse box in patient silence. Philip and Diane set off with Billy in tow, en route to his new home, followed by Ron, Mick and Barry in Ron's car.

'I think you're going to miss him,' Barry said as they travelled along.

'*You've grown accustomed to his face...*' Mick started. Fortunately, he couldn't think of any more of the words.

'In a funny sort of way, I am,' Ron agreed. 'But Philip says I can go and visit whenever I like, so it's not like I'm never going to see him again, is it?'

'And you won't miss the worry about what he's getting up to while you're out,' Mick said.

'Or while you're upstairs,' Barry added.

265

'It's certainly going to be a great weight off my mind, that is!' Ron agreed.

The two-vehicle convoy travelled along the road for few miles, then turned onto a farm track.

'This all looks a bit familiar!' said Ron as he bounced along behind the trailer.

'Bloody hell!' shouted Mick. 'This is the same road! It goes to that farm where we collected Billy from.'

'You don't think…?' Barry stopped speaking as the horse box turned onto another track that ran alongside the canal in the direction of the farmhouse owned by the taciturn Mr and Mrs Rodgers!

'Well, I'll be…!' said Ron as he followed the horse box along the track, turning off towards the cottage.

They drew up next to the all-too-familiar site of their struggle with Billy of a few weeks previously. The three of them got out of the car and watched in disbelief as Philip led Billy to the field by the cottage. Billy walked happily through the gate and, when Philip took off the rope, he kicked his heels in the air and charged round the field. After a couple of circuits he settled down and began munching grass.

'Welcome to your new home, Billy!' Philip said. 'You're looking very relaxed – anyone would think you'd always lived here!'

'He has!' chorused Barry, Ron and Mick in unison.

'What?' asked Diane.

'You're not going to believe this,' Ron exclaimed, 'but this is the field where he used to live! That cottage,' Ron pointed, 'is where my brother-in-law lived!'

'Never!' exclaimed Diane. 'That's where we're going to live. It's a lovely little cottage and we've got great plans to do it up.'

As they spoke, an ancient Landrover bounced its way across the field and pulled up at the gate. Mr Rodgers clambered out clutching a large cake tin. He held out his free hand.

'Mr Tyler, Mrs Tyler. Saw you coming up the track. Pleased to meet you again. Mrs Rodgers's been doing some baking. Thought you might be a bit peckish.' He proffered the cake tin.

'Well, I'll be…!' spluttered Ron. Barry stood transfixed. Mick was at a loss for words – and even a song!

'You again is it?' Rodgers glowered. 'Harrumph!' He clambered back into the Landrover and bounced his way back across the field.

'Well, I'll be…!' said Ron again, regaining his composure. 'It's not that long ago that man was threatening to have Billy put down if I didn't take him away!'

'What's the phrase?' Philip asked. '"Circumstances alter cases"?'

'J. M. Barrie,' Barry said, raising his eyebrows.

'Pardon?' Ron asked, bemused.

'That's where the quote comes from,' Barry said. '"Circumstances alter cases" – J. M. Barrie's play, *The Admirable Crichton*.'

'Oh,' Ron replied.

'Have you seen this?' Mick said, pointing to the gate to the field. Ron and Barry walked across to join him. On the gate was a small, laminated notice that read '"Billy" the Goat. Kindly donated by Mr Ronald Barton.'

'Oh!' said Ron. 'Oh, that's nice. That's really, really nice! Thank you, Philip.'

'No,' said Philip. 'Thank you for Billy. The kids will love him, I'm sure. And that sign's only temporary – we'll have proper ones made for all the animals.'

'I wonder,' Ron said. 'When you get the proper one done for Billy, could you possibly add a bit to it?'

'Of course! What would you like?'

'Just put underneath, "In Memory of Daphne, his wife".'

'No problem, Ron,' Philip smiled.

'Come over to the cottage and have a cup of tea,' Diane said.

Over numerous cups of tea and Mrs Rodgers's cake – she proved to be an excellent cook – Philip and Diane explained further their plans for the farm.

'You did say I could come and see Billy any time I want to?' Ron asked.

'Any time at all,' Diane said. 'The gate on the track's never locked so if there's no one here just wander in. All three of you will always be welcome here. As donors of our first animal you chaps will always have a special welcome.'

'Thanks. That'll be great. Billy seems really happy to be back.' Ron looked out of the window at the goat in his field. Billy looked up at Ron, who imagined he could see the faintest trace of a smile on his black, whiskery face.

Back home, Ron surveyed his garden – or what was left of it! It resembled a battlefield. He could not believe that one goat could wreak so much havoc! He spent the next few days tidying it as best as he could, muttering apologies to Daphne as he worked.

'But it was your brother's goat who caused it all!' he said at one point. He straightened up and realised that he missed Billy. That little goat with the evil glint in his eyes, lethal horns and an insatiable appetite had dug a special little hole in his heart.

By Wednesday the garden was as tidy as it could be, so Ron decided to go and see him.

'Well,' he reasoned, as he bounced up the track in his car, 'Diane and Philip said I could visit any time.' He parked his car next to Billy's field and grabbed the bag of carrots he had brought.

He was not sure whether Billy recognised him or if he saw the carrots, but he immediately trotted up to the gate to meet him.

'Hello, Billy,' Ron said and stroked the goat's head. The carrots soon disappeared. 'Still permanently hungry, then?'

Just then he heard a voice behind him.

'Ron!' He turned to see Diane coming towards him. 'I wondered how long it would be before you came to see him.' Ron smiled. 'Come on over to the cottage and have a coffee. We're up here sorting a few things out. We've moored the boat at the bottom of the field for a day or two.'

After a while Philip joined them. They sat on around a picnic table in the kitchen.

'Have you had a chance to look round the place properly yet?' Ron asked.

'Yes,' said Philip. 'I think we've more or less decided where everything is going to go, haven't we, love?'

'Just about, I think,' Diane agreed. 'But there's an awful lot of work to do out there.'

'Can I help?' Ron asked.

'Well, yes you can, actually,' Diane said. 'We're applying to charities for funds but the money they come up with will be for projects. There won't be enough for us to pay any staff. For the most part we're going to have to rely on volunteers...' She paused.

'Then I'd like to be your first volunteer!' Ron volunteered.

'That's exactly what we hoped you'd say,' Philip replied.

'And I'm sure Mick and Barry would want to be the second and third,' Ron continued.

'Oh, that would be wonderful!' Diane exclaimed. 'With the three of you on board we could make a really good start.'

'If they agree to help, I think we all need to get together to sort out priorities and see who can do what,' Philip added.

'I'll be seeing them both on Saturday. I'll put it to them. When were you thinking of having this meeting?'

'As soon as possible. We really need to get started.'

'Well, as you know, we're all retired, so we can come in the daytime.'

'We've got to be in London on Monday, but any other day next week will be fine,' said Diane.

'We'll sort out a day on Saturday and I'll let you know.'

'Excellent!' Philip said.

❋

'*We All Stand Together*'

At ten o'clock the following Tuesday morning the three men climbed out of Ron's car and, having been to see Billy, who appeared genuinely pleased to see Ron again, they made their way up the path to the cottage. Philip welcomed them and, with all five sitting round the picnic table, the meeting was soon under way.

After a couple of hours Philip looked at his watch. 'I think we've covered all we can do at this stage,' he said. 'Let's just summarise where we're up to – and then I suggest we all adjourn to The Navigation for some lunch.'

'I'm starving!' Mick added.

'Good idea!' said Diane, referring to the copious notes she had made during the discussions. 'First, let me say again how grateful Phil and I are that you've all agreed to volunteer to give us your help. There's no way we could contemplate doing a fraction of this without it.'

'I think I speak for my two friends when I say we're looking forward to it,' Barry said.

'Now let's see…' She picked up her pen. 'Ron. You're going to look after the gardening side of things – flowers and vegetables. Things that the children can help with.'

'That's right. I'm going to start by creating a rose garden at the front of the cottage that my Daphne would be proud of.'

'Excellent! Now, Barry, you're happy looking after signs and posters and, with Philip, to be our safety person. You'll go on a Red Cross First Aid course and a Health & Safety course as well, won't you?'

'That's right,' Barry replied. 'Those things are most important and have to be taken seriously.' He raised his eyebrows. 'I think I need to complete those courses before anyone starts work.'

'I don't think I fancy having the kiss of life from you, Barry!' Mick laughed. 'If I collapse, just leave me be, will you?'

'Mick!' Diane said in mock horror. 'You're taking on the trip boat?'

'Yes. I'll have to look at it and have a word with your mate Keith. The engine will need a fair bit of work, I'm sure. I'll give it a complete overhaul – it'll save Keith coming all the way up here – and then I'll paint it up. When's it getting here, by the way?'

'We're towing it up tomorrow. Perhaps you'd like to give us a hand?'

'Thanks! I would. I can get started on it soon, then.'

'What are we going to call the boat?' Barry asked.

'Not given it much thought,' Philip replied.

'What's its name at the moment?' Mick asked.

'*Pixie*,' said Diane. 'Apparently, there was a pair of them called *Pixie* and *Dixie*. Dixie was sold some time ago.' There were a few moments of silence while they all tried to think of obscure or fitting boat names. Then Ron spoke.

'Seeing as the first attraction – at the moment, the only attraction – we've got here is a billy goat, why don't we call it *Billy Boat*?'

'Brilliant!' said Diane. '*Billy Boat* it shall be!'

'That's settled!' said Philip. 'Let's get to the pub. Oh, and by the way, lunch is on us!'

✳

As they drove back the cottage after lunch Philip and Diane discussed their plans.

'Now we've got those three on board we can really start to move forward. Barry starts his course next week, so he'll be practically qualified by next month, and then we can start the work in earnest. I'll get cracking on a schedule of what we need to get done in the first year and then we can get the guys together again next month and share it with them.'

'Another of your lists?' Philip chuckled.

'Well, they've worked for us so far, haven't they?'

'I can't deny that!'

As they approached the track leading to the farm they saw an ambulance turning out onto the road with its sirens wailing and blue lights flashing.

'It must be one of the Rodgers!' Diane exclaimed. They stopped off at the farmhouse, but there was no one there.

Later that afternoon the phone rang. Diane answered it. Tearfully, Mrs Rodgers told her that she had found her husband slumped over the wheel of his tractor. The paramedics had done their best but he had died on the way to hospital.

As a mark of respect, they all went to the funeral. Mrs Rodgers invited everyone back the farmhouse afterwards for tea.

Ron and Mick stood chatting in a corner. 'Have you noticed?' Mick said, a gleam in his eye.

'What?' Ron asked.

'Our Barry's being rather attentive to Mrs Rodgers.'

'Yes,' Ron replied. 'He's hardly left her side since we got back from the church.'

'Mind you, she seems to be enjoying the attention!'

'Yes. She doesn't seem too upset about her husband's death either, does she?'

'Would you be? He was such a miserable old sod.'

'You shouldn't speak ill of the dead.'

'Well, he was!'

One evening a couple of weeks later there was a knock at the cottage door. Philip answered it.

'Mrs Rodgers! Do come in.' When Diane had joined them sitting round their new kitchen table with mugs of coffee, Mrs Rodgers spoke.

'I shan't beat about the bush,' she said. 'I've come to make you a proposition.' She paused. 'Now Rodgers is gone, there's no way I can run the farm on my own.' Diane and Philip agreed. 'So I was wondering whether you'd like to use the rest of my land as well as the bit he sold to you?'

'Are you serious, Mrs Rodgers?' Diane asked.

'I am – and it's Vera – please.'

'What sort of rent would you be looking for?' Philip asked, warily.

'Nothing!' Vera replied. 'Rodgers had got a bit of money invested and there's his life insurance with the NFU – I start getting my widow's pension next month, so I don't need any more. But I would need to carry on living in the farmhouse.'

Philip and Diane were speechless

'I don't know what to say!' Philip finally said after a lengthy pause.

Diane's mind went into overdrive. 'It'll give us so much more scope!' she said excitedly. 'Not only will we have the yard and the fields, but there's that woodland area behind the farmhouse too – and the orchard.'

'Oh, the kids will love that!' Philip agreed. 'We can make dens with them and put nesting boxes up for the birds – all kinds of things.'

Vera smiled as she heard them making these plans.

'It's exceptionally kind of you, Vera,' Philip said.

'Well, I'm very much in favour of what you're trying to do here. City kids ought to learn more about how we go on in the country. And besides, it'll be good to have some youngsters around the place. Cheer it up a bit! Rodgers and me never had any kids, you see.'

'I'll ring the solicitor in the morning and make an appointment for us to go and get the legal side sorted out,' Diane said.

When Mick, Ron and Barry arrived for their next meeting the three friends saw many changes in the cottage. One end of the kitchen had been converted into an office with a desk on which stood Diane's laptop and a telephone. Attached to the wall behind it was a year planner with a lot of writing and arrows on it, and alongside it a notated plan of the farm. The chairs had been moved from around the table and arranged to face the planner. They had been advised to bring diaries with them. Barry had an electronic organiser, and Ron had a small pocket diary, while Mick produced from his pocket a dog-eared notebook with a torn cover.

'Never use a diary,' he said as he noticed the others looking scathingly at his book.

Diane spent an hour explaining what needed doing and where. There were courses to be completed, fences to be erected, enclosures to be made and buildings to be renovated. There was painting to be done and signs to be made. There were hutches and runs to be constructed and erected.

'We're aiming to hold an Open Day in six months time,' she said. 'So there's a lot to do!'

'Phew!' said the men collectively.

'The courses are going well,' Diane continued. 'They'll be

completed before we welcome our first visitors. Phil and I are on a course about animal management and we're starting one on children on the farm.' She had insisted that they all did a basic first aid course. However, Barry was doing the advanced course, as well as health & safety and risk assessment. Mick had passed the Royal Yachting Association steerers' course with flying colours but had made limited progress on *Billy Boat* despite frequent visits to the landing stage. Ron had spent all his spare time researching about the propagation of roses and gardening with children.

The first major project they undertook together was the farmyard. It was going to be an area for small animals – rabbits, guinea pigs, chickens and ducks. Under the heading 'Billy's Farmyard Friends', Diane had drawn a plan showing the yard divided into different sections. They all laughed when they saw that she had given each walkway a name.

The plan showed the roughly rectangular yard bisected by a path leading from just outside the farmhouse to its far end. This was to be 'Animal Avenue'. It was crossed by two other paths that divided the yard into six areas. The furthest from the farmhouse was called 'Guinea Pig Grove' on the left and 'Chicken Close' on the right, the nearer one 'Bunny Boulevard' and 'Duck Drive'. Around the perimeter was another pathway called 'Farmyard Way'. (Diane had not been able to think of anything else alliterative!)

With Diane's plan firmly affixed to the inside of one of the open barn doors for reference, they began the construction work. First they marked out the pathways and pens. Barry and Ron each held an end of a long tape measure while Mick painted white lines to demarcate the boundaries. Philip arrived with an electric jackhammer that Mick had volunteered to use.

'No jobs to do on *Billy Boat*?' Phil had jokingly said.

Small areas of the yard were still the original cobblestones but most of it had been concreted at various times in the past and this needed to be removed before the topsoil and turf could be laid. With all the lines painted, Mick asked, 'Where do we plug the drill in?'

'I'll go and ask Vera,' Barry immediately replied, and set off hotfoot to the farmhouse. Ron was rolling up the tape measure and packing away the paint when Barry returned.

'It's plugged in!' he called, 'and Vera says there's an extension lead in the barn if we need it.'

'Didn't realise it took such a long while to stick a plug in and put a switch down,' Mick muttered. 'Good!' he called. 'We will.' He pulled the ear defenders over his ears, put on the protective glasses (Barry was most insistent about this!) and started on the concrete.

Mick wielded the jackhammer while Ron and Barry loaded the spoil into a wheelbarrow and took it round to the back of the barn where it was piled up for future use as hardcore. It was back-breaking work. Vera appeared with very welcome mugs of coffee and a plate of biscuits.

'Looks a bit different!' she said.

'It'll look even more different when we've completed the enclosures,' Barry replied.

It proved to be a big job. Apart from Mick, none of them had been used to manual labour – and Mick had to admit that it had been a few years since he had wielded a jackhammer. It took a couple of days to clear the concrete and make good the pathways. Philip had ordered some old wooden railway sleepers, which they put down to form edging for the paths. Then they were ready to set to on the enclosures.

When they arrived on the third morning, Mick looked at the plan and, picking up a spade, set off in the direction of the pen earmarked for ducks.

'They'll need a pond in that one,' he said, jabbing a finger at the bottom right-hand corner.

A lorry-load of topsoil arrived and Ron and Barry started to spread it around the other enclosures. Out of Mick's earshot, Ron commented, 'Can't believe the change in Mick!' He nodded in Mick's direction, where he was attacking the site of the duckpond with determination.

'In what way?' Barry asked, sotto voce.

'When we first started up here he was never around when there was any work to be done. He always made excuses – supposedly working on the trip boat, out of sight of anyone. Now, though, he's getting stuck in with the rest of us!'

'Yes. I'd noticed that too – but I'm not complaining!'

'Me neither. He seems happier too.'

With the duckpond dug and the topsoil deposited, there only remained the turf to lay.

'I vote we pack up now and leave the rest till tomorrow,' suggested Ron.

'Fine by me,' said Barry. 'I think we've done pretty well today, though.'

'We have!' Mick agreed.

'Only the turf to lay and the fences to erect, then we're ready for when the hutches and their occupants arrive.'

'Thanks, chaps!' said Philip, shaking each of them by the hand.

One advantage of working so close to the farmhouse was that Vera continued to keep them supplied with coffee and biscuits in the morning and tea and freshly baked scones in the afternoons.

'I shall be the size of a house before this job's finished!' Ron joked. Vera smiled and went back into the house. Barry took it upon himself to return their empty mugs to the farmhouse kitchen.

'Takes him a while to stick three mugs on the table, doesn't it?' Mick said to Ron as they took a break from erecting the fences.

Ron wiped the sweat from his forehead with the back of his hand. 'You noticed it first at the funeral tea. I think him and Vera are getting a bit fond of each other,' he said.

'She's a different woman since her husband died, isn't she?'

'Complete change of personality! Amazing!'

'Do you know what I think? I think she was afraid of him – in a way. And so she thought that because he was a miserable old bugger she ought to be the same – so they could rub along together.'

'You could be right,' Ron agreed, surprised at his friend's insight. 'Barry seems happier too.'

'I never realised Mick thought so deeply about anything!' he thought. As Barry reappeared they returned to their work.

One afternoon the following week the coops and hutches were delivered. Mick opened one of the flatpacks and studied the instructions. He read through them, picking up odd pieces as he did so. Eventually, he turned to the others. 'Either of you any good at putting stuff like this together?'

'My entire flat was furnished courtesy of the late-lamented MFI,' Barry replied. 'Nothing's collapsed yet,' he added.

'Good! Then you can show me and Ron how to do it!'

'No problem,' said Barry with more confidence than he felt. However, he smiled to himself as he realised he would be working a little longer outside the back of Vera's house!

A few days later the animals started to arrive. 'A bit like Noah's Ark!' laughed Ron as first six chickens, then four ducks, followed by a family of guinea pigs and an assortment of fluffy bunnies were shown their new homes in the farmyard.

'But they haven't arrived two by two!' said Barry, raising his eyebrows.

Mick launched into '*Chicks and ducks and geese better scurry, when I take...*'

'*Oklahoma!*' Ron and Barry chorused.

If they thought 'Farmyard Friends' was hard work, a bigger challenge in the first six months was converting – well, rebuilding – one of the outbuildings into a stable for a pony that would be arriving soon. Mick's son Jimmy, who had some bricklaying experience, was recruited to renew the brickwork in the walls, then Philip, Barry and Ron managed to erect the roof and fit out the inside. Unusually these days, Mick was noticeably absent.

'Anybody seen Mick?' Ron asked, as he and Philip, standing on ladders, manoeuvred a roof beam into position.

'He said he'd got a job to do,' Barry replied.

'He's not back on the boat again!' Ron exclaimed. 'That boat's going to be the best-maintained vessel on the cut, the amount of time he spends on it.'

'I don't think it's the boat this time,' said Barry. 'I saw him heading in the direction of the barn behind the farmhouse.'

'What's he up to in there?' Ron asked as he gave the beam a final shove into position.

'Goodness knows!'

'At least we don't have to put up with his singing today!'

Even without Mick's assistance the stable was completed on time and Philip fetched the pony, a black Shetland they christened Jack, who quickly settled in to his new abode.

Any resentment they might have felt at Mick's absence from the working party was dispelled a couple of days later. After their mid-morning coffee break, he stood up.

'Now!' he said. 'I've got something to show you.' Intrigued, they followed him to the barn.

'What is it?' Ron asked as they walked.

'Wait and see,' was Mick's reply.

When they arrived Mick said, 'I heard we were getting a pony, so...' He pushed the barn door open with a flourish. 'Well, I thought he might want something to pull!'

The barn door swung open to reveal a freshly painted cart. The others saw it and burst into a round of spontaneous applause. Mick smiled proudly.

'Take a look,' he invited them, waving an arm in the direction of the cart and stepping back against the wall.

'It's beautiful!' Diane exclaimed as she ran her hand over the gleaming green and red paintwork. 'Well done, Mick!'

'Was it in here all the time?' Barry asked.

'It was over the back there. The paint was all peeling and the wheels were rusty. The tyres were flat, but they've still got some tread on them.'

'Was the timber sound?' Ron asked, taking particular interest in the cart's construction.

'All but one place where it had got damp and rotted. I put a new bit in.'

'How many children do you think it would hold?' Philip asked. Mick looked at the cart.

'I don't know,' he said. 'Half a dozen or so, I should think – more if they're little ones.' They continued to heap compliments on Mick and his handiwork.

'We now have this beautiful conveyance,' said Barry, raiding his eyebrows, 'but does anyone know how to drive it?'

'No, but we can learn,' Diane answered. 'I think it's going be a great asset!'

They headed back to the cottage garden where there were picnic tables to assemble.

'Where's Barry?'

'I saw him wandering over to Vera's when we left the shed,' Mick replied, giving Ron a knowing wink.

'I definitely think there's something going on there with our Barry and Vera.'

'Odds on!' agreed Mick.

❋

'Come On Over To My Place'

At the end of a hot summer's day of working around the farm, all five of them were sitting in the kitchen with cool drinks.

'I hope the kids'll appreciate all this work we're putting in on their behalf,' Mick said.

'I'm sure they will,' Diane replied.

'How are you going to publicise it?' Barry asked.

'We need a name and a logo for the farm – something eye-catching to go on letterheads and all the publicity. The postal address here is Church Farm, but I've noticed that we've all started to refer to the place as "Billy's Farm". I think that has a real child-friendly ring to it and, of course, we already have *Billy Boat*. Do you all agree?'

They all nodded in agreement.

'Billy's Farm at Church Farm, it shall be, then,' Diane said. 'I was hoping that was what you'd say because I'm thinking of this for a logo.' She picked a sheet of paper from the file in front of her and put on the table in front of them. 'Here!'

'What do you think?' she asked.

'It's good!' said Ron. 'I like it!'

'The picture resembles Billy quite closely,' Barry observed, raising his eyebrows, 'except that it hasn't got his slitty eyes.'

'That's a good thing,' said Mick. 'It's those eyes that give him the evil look. We want to attract people – not scare them off!'

'I've been in touch with some printers and got prices for what we'll need,' Diane continued. 'Now the logo's agreed I can tell them to get going. We need to get it done so that we can publicise the Open Day.'

'Can they do a few of those logos on transfers, do you think?' Mick asked.

'Transfers? Why?' Diane asked.

'I could put them on the sides of Jack's cart.'

'Well, if they can't I'm sure we can find a firm that will be able to,' Diane replied. 'That's a good thought. You're looking after that side of things, Phil.'

'I'll ring them later,' Philip agreed.

'Phil and I have made a list of all the local schools,' Diane said. 'We're going to send them an information pack and details of what we can offer the children. It will explain about the animals and the work the children can do on the farm. We'll also invite a member of the staff to the Open Day.'

'The hope is that we can get enough of the kids sufficiently interested to start the kids club on Saturdays,' Philip said.

'You were going to help with that, weren't you, Barry?' Mick asked.

'Yes!' Barry replied.

'Have you thought what we could call the club?' Philip asked.

'Yes. As a matter of fact I have – I thought we might call it the SJA.'

'SJA?' Ron queried.

'The Society of Junior Agriculturalists.'

'Hardly trips off the tongue, does it?' said Mick.

'Well, it's the best I could come up with,' Barry protested. 'But I'm open to suggestions.'

'We can't call it a Young Farmers Club because there's one already.'

There was silence for a few moments while they all tried to think of a better name. Suddenly, Diane spoke. 'I've got it – I think!' She turned to her laptop. 'You know most youngsters these days have got mobile phones and are into textspeak? Well, how about this?' She printed something and held it up for them to see.

'Very good!' said Ron.

'Excellent!' agreed Philip.

'Love it!' said Mick.

They all looked at Barry. Barry stared at the piece of paper for a good ten seconds.

'Well,' he said at last, 'I suppose it's a bit more punchy than mine… Yes, I like it.' There was a collective sigh of relief. 'We could use the logo on badges and sweatshirts for them.'

'Now, what are we going to put on the publicity leaflet?' Diane asked. They all contributed their ideas and Diane wrote them on her flip chart.

'There's the garden,' said Ron.

'And Jack and his cart,' added Mick.

'Don't forget "Farmyard Friends",' said Barry. 'The kids will love "Bunny Boulevard" and the rest!'

'Have you mentioned the wildlife garden?' Ron asked.

'Oh, yes, and the beehives too. The local beekeepers' association are bringing two over this weekend.'

Soon Diane's page was full of suggestions. For the leaflet they put these under three headings, which they called the Three A's.

Active – den-building, woodland trails, gardening.

Animal – looking after their growing menagerie of sheep, chickens, rabbits, guinea pigs, ducks – and, of course, Jack and Billy

Arty-crafty – cooking, sewing, collage, painting in the conservatory.

This last was Diane's suggestion. 'I've got some work to do on this one,' she added, 'but I've got a plan!'

And, of course, there was *Billy Boat*. Mick had suddenly set to with a will. It was now freshly painted, engine serviced, seating revarnished and tied up at the new landing stage, waiting to transport its first complement of passengers. They had a couple of trial runs in it, as Mick was planning to pick up the visitors from the Old Town Wharf on the Open Day. It was agreed that a photograph of the boat, together with one of Billy himself, should go on the front of the leaflet

The months sped by and the date of the Open Day got closer and closer. Diane and Philip recruited other people to become volunteers and help with their project but, Barry, Ron and Mick were their most important, committed and regular supporters. 'The Special Three', Philip called them. It was with them that he and Diane shared their detailed plans over meals at The Navigation or over mugs of tea and coffee in the kitchen after everyone else had gone home. They were sometimes joined by Vera, who came along with a tray of scones or cake or flapjack.

And Billy, who was fast becoming the star attraction, took a great interest in all that was happening. If there was any activity anywhere near his field he would stop whatever he was doing – usually eating – and watch it intently. He was still wary of people, watching them with his 'evil' eyes whenever they went close to him. But with Ron it was different. Ron always made a special fuss of Billy whenever he went to the farm. He always brought a few carrots with him for a treat for the goat with whom he had built up a special bond. Billy would run to the gate when he saw Ron, who was the only person Billy allowed to stroke his head.

A local farmer had promised to donate two sheep to the project and Philip decided that they should go in the enclosure next to Billy's. The day they arrived Billy looked up and watched as the horse box was reversed up to the gate. Philip lowered the ramp and, with a little coaxing, the two ewes walked gingerly down it and into their new pasture. As soon as Billy saw them he ran over to the fence and waited there. Eventually the sheep made their way over to him. Billy bleated a greeting and the sheep responded.

'He's welcoming the new arrivals,' said Ron, who had been watching events unfold.

'I hope he's telling them what a good place this is to live!' Philip joked.

'I'm sure he is!' Ron chuckled and made his way over to the barn.

Mick had noticed that Ron had been spending a lot of time in the barn recently. Curiosity got the better of him and, later, he walked over that way. As he approached he could hear Ron using language he had never heard him use before, nor yet ever imagined he would ever use! Something had driven him beyond the limits of his patience!

Unsure of the welcome he might get, Mick gingerly opened the door. Ron looked up. He was red in the face – and was that the trace of a tear in his eye?

'What's up?' he asked.

'Oh, Mick!' Ron gasped. 'It's this bloody thing! Whatever I do with it, it keeps falling to bits!'

Mick had been right. Ron was almost crying with frustration. At his feet was a set of pram wheels and some pieces of timber together with a saw, and he was holding a hammer in his hand.

'What are you trying to do?' Mick asked.

Ron sighed. 'Well, I saw that lovely cart you'd repaired for Jack and I got to thinking I could make something similar for Billy to carry my garden tools and things in. I'd seen this old pram on a skip outside my neighbour's.' Mick looked at the wheels and the roughly sawn pieces of wood around Ron's feet.

'If you don't mind me saying so,' he began, choosing his words carefully, 'you don't seem to be getting on too well with it.'

'You can say that again!' Ron exclaimed. 'I was no good at woodwork at school. I'm OK if I'm helping somebody else and if they tell me exactly what to do.' He kicked the pram wheels. 'I'd better chuck the bloody lot!' he shouted, angrily. 'I'll forget the whole idea!'

'Hang on a minute!' Mick interjected. 'Don't be hasty! Let's have a look.' Ron sighed again and stood back. Mick sat down on his haunches and examined Ron's work.

'What you can't see on Jack's cart,' he said, 'is the framework underneath that everything else is attached to. You've been trying to make this without a frame. That's why it falls apart – and you need screws, not nails.'

'Oh!' Ron couldn't think of any other comment to make.

'When are you up here again?' Mick asked.

'Day after tomorrow,' Ron answered. 'I've got the dentist tomorrow.'

'Well, I'm here tomorrow,' Mick said. 'I'll get some timber for the frame and see if I can't help you out a bit – if you'd like me to, that is?'

'Oh, Mick!' An enormous look of relief spread across Ron's face. 'Oh, would you? I'd be so grateful. I really would!'

'No problem. Isn't that what mates are for?' Mick put an arm round Ron's shoulders and, as they left the barn, he started singing.

'*If I can help somebody, as I pass along, then my living shall not be in vain…*'

For once, Ron did not feel disposed to stop him.

Ron arrived two days later and made straight for the barn. As he opened the door he saw Mick on his knees with a paint brush in his hand.

'Morning, Ron,' he said, and stood up, smiling. 'What do you reckon?'

Ron looked. There was an almost exact Billy-sized replica of Jack's cart! He gazed open-mouthed. 'Well, I'll be … Mick!' he managed to say. 'It's beautiful!'

'Will be when I've glossed it. This is just the undercoat. Don't touch it. It's still wet.'

'It's beautiful!' Ron said again as he walked round the cart, unable to take his eyes off it.

Mick was smiling. 'I'm glad you like it,' he said.

'Like it? I love it!' Ron replied. 'It's just as I imagined it! You've done it so much better than I ever could. What do I owe you?'

'Nothing.'

'Nothing? But you've bought wood and then there's your time. You must've been working on it all day. I must pay you something.'

'No, you mustn't. It's all for Billy's Farm, isn't it?'

Ron shook Mick's hand warmly, oblivious to the paint smear he picked up on his palm in the process. 'Thanks, Mick. Next time we're at The Navigation, your meat pie – and your Guinness – it's all on me!'

Two days later Mick and Ron wheeled the now resplendently painted cart down to Billy's paddock. Ron had bought the necessary tack to go on Billy's back so that he could pull the cart. As they approached, Billy looked and, seeing Ron, ran over to the gate.

'You'd better do the business with Billy,' Mick said. 'He trusts you.'

Ron opened the gate and showed Billy the harness. Billy looked at it and sniffed it. He was about to try to eat it, but Ron pulled it away.

'No. It's not food,' he said, speaking gently to the goat. 'It goes here.' He laid the harness gently on Billy's back. Billy stood patiently and allowed Ron to fix the strap under his belly and place a halter round his neck.

'Now for the cart,' Ron said. Mick wheeled the cart behind Billy while Ron was stroking his head. Between them they attached the cart to the harness.

'Come on, Billy!' Ron said, giving the halter a gentle tug. Billy responded immediately and trotted along beside Ron, pulling his cart quite happily.

'He seems OK with it, doesn't he?' Mick called.

'I think he's actually enjoying it!' Ron replied as he turned Billy round and returned to Mick.

'You and your cart,' he whispered in the goat's ear. 'You really are the star attraction!' And everyone else thought so too when they saw him pulling his cart around the farm. Ron was convinced he could see a look of pride on Billy's whiskery face.

❋

'Welcome To My World'

The Open Day was a resounding success. Diane, Philip and all the volunteers wore sweatshirts with the Billy's Farm logo emblazoned on the front. Advertised as a 'Come and See Our Work in Progress' event, Mick was in his element, steering *Billy Boat* with its delighted visitors to and from the Old Town Wharf. Then he joined Barry and Ron to show them what had been achieved to date. Diane and Philip were on hand with plenty of publicity material. Billy and Jack, their coats brushed and shining, attracted much attention pulling their respective carts behind them. (Jack had been introduced to his cart, which he appeared to love pulling. And Mick proved to be a natural when it came to driving it. 'We Irish have always been good with horses,' he said.)

Their next planning meeting was held in the large conservatory that had been built at the back of the cottage and was now awaiting its furniture. It was to be used as an assembly area for the children, and a place where they could eat their packed lunches if the weather was inclement.

'I'd like us to discuss my next idea,' Diane said. 'This conservatory – it's such a lovely big space and, as you all know, we eventually want to open to the general public as well as for the groups of children. I thought it would make an ideal tea room for light refreshments.'

'Brilliant idea!' Mick agreed.

'However, the pressing problem is that we need someone to cook with the schoolchildren using produce grown in Ron's garden. You remember that was part of the Arty-crafty section. I'm sure the same person could both cook with the children and run the tea room.'

After a few moments silence Barry said, 'I think I may know someone who could help us out there.'

'Oh yes?' said Diane. 'Who?'

'I'll have to see whether they'd be happy to do it before I tell you that,' he said. 'I'll let you know tomorrow.'

'OK,' Diane agreed and asked no more questions.

The following morning Diane was at her desk compiling a rota of volunteers on the computer when there was a knock at the door.

'Come in,' she called.

Barry entered. 'You remember at yesterday's meeting I said I may know someone who might help out with the children's cooking and run the tea room when it's started?' he said.

'Yes,' Diane replied.

'Well, here she is.' He stood aside and a smiling Mrs Rodgers walked in.

'Vera!' Diane exclaimed, standing up. 'So you'd like to help us with the catering? I didn't know you had done any catering before.'

'I haven't – but I'm willing to learn.'

'Well, we already know what a good cook you are from the cakes that you keep tempting us with. Would you be happy to go on a course to learn the business side of it?'

Vera thought for a moment. 'I should think I'll be the oldest one there, but that doesn't matter. Yes, of course I'll go.'

'Excellent! Let's have a chat about what we could do.' Barry walked out and left the two women talking.

Although the others had their suspicions (none of them were really sure if it was true), Barry had begun a liaison with Vera – and for once it was not only in his imagination! She cooked delicacies for him that suited his weak stomach and he took her out to the theatre or the cinema. They were becoming quite fond of each other.

✳

Some weeks later, Mick, Ron and Barry had left for the day and Diane and Philip were sitting in the kitchen. Diane looked over at her desk.

'Goodness!' she exclaimed. 'I haven't looked at today's post yet. I've been so busy.' She opened the envelopes and read the letters.

'That's two more school parties confirmed!' she said, excitedly. 'They're coming in thick and fast!'

'And the first one arrives when?' Philip asked.

'The middle of March next year.'

'With any luck there'll be a lamb or two around for them to feed by then.'

'Yes, they'll enjoy that.' Diane noted the details of the new bookings on her spreadsheet.

'Let's see,' she said, closing the spreadsheet and opening up another. 'Who have we got coming up tomorrow?'

'All the "Special Three" said "See you tomorrow" when they left tonight.'

'That's right,' Diane confirmed. 'Mick, Barry and Ron are all due. They're such a help. I don't know how we would have managed without them this last couple of years. It was fate that we went to that pub that Saturday.'

'It certainly was! I'm glad they're all here tomorrow. I want to get as much of the outdoor work done as I can before the cold weather arrives so we'll need all the help we can get for the next few weeks.'

'Right!' said Diane, closing the computer down and pushing her chair back. 'What next?'

'Dinner?'

'Yes. It's all ready in the oven. It just needs heating through. You do that while I go and shut the animals up for the night.'

'You better take your mac. It's just started to rain hard. Do you want me to go?'

'No. I shan't dissolve. You do the dinner.' She went out as Philip turned his attention to the cooker.

By the time she returned, the meal was ready to be served. She came into the kitchen looking for all the world like a drowned rat and sat down.

'Are you happy?' Philip asked as she pulled off her mud-caked boots.

'Ecstatic!' she replied. 'And I'm not being ironic. I'm cold and I'm soaked through. My hair's gone all frizzy and I nearly slipped over in the mud at least twice, but I'm just so happy!'

'You don't miss London, then?' Philip asked, serving their meal.

Diane looked at him and smiled. 'Where?' she asked, smiling through the dripping rat's tails of her hair.

❋

The following day Mick and Ron arrived at the usual time, but there was no sign of Barry.

'I hope he's all right,' said Ron, anxiously.

'Could be anything,' Mick reassured him. 'Car wouldn't start, phone call as he was leaving, anything.'

Barry arrived an hour later.

'Sorry I'm late,' he said. 'I had to call at the estate agent. It took a bit longer than I thought it would.'

'Estate agent?' Mick queried.

'Are you moving?' Ron asked. 'I thought you liked your flat.'

'I do,' Barry replied. 'But, yes, I am relocating.'

'Where?' Mick asked.

'I'm moving in with Vera,' he said, trying to speak casually, but not quite succeeding.

'Vera who? Vera Rodgers?' Mick feigned surprise.

'Yes.'

'Well, I'll be…!' Ron spluttered. 'Aren't you the dark horse?'

'Well,' said Barry, 'we've been seeing rather a lot of each other recently so it seemed to be the obvious thing to do. She's all alone in that big old farmhouse.'

'Congratulations!' Ron said, shaking his hand. Mick slapped him on the back. 'I thought you always said you weren't the marrying type?' he asked.

Barry smiled. 'In the words of J. M. Barrie, "Circumstances alter cases".' This time he did not raise his eyebrows.

'I've heard that somewhere before,' said Ron.

✳

The weather was kind during the winter and by early March the first stage of Billy's Farm was complete. Barry's signs were all finished and in place. Ron's vegetable garden was fully planted alongside his rose garden There had been a few hiccups along the way. A fox had crept into the chicken coop when the door blew open one windy night and killed two hens, and some of the equipment had been delivered to another Church Farm miles away. It had taken over a week to locate it. Jack had picked up a virus that led to the vet visiting him a couple of times – another bill they weren't expecting!

Although they had stuck closely to their budget, Diane and Philip found that their savings were disappearing at an alarming rate. They had never intended to make a profit from Billy's Farm, but they needed to make enough to live on and to feed the animals.

But now Billy's Farm was all set to receive its first visitors. After the three friends had left for the night Diane and Philip were walking round the site, re-checking that everything was in its rightful place, and shutting the animals in for the night.

'All the "Special Three" seem genuinely excited about tomorrow, don't they?' Diane said.

'Yes, they do. I guess it's the same for them as it is for us – it's what we've all been working towards these past few years.' He paused. 'I'm excited – and I'm sure you are!'

'Oh, yes! We've come an awful long since "Dream Holidays", haven't we?'

'You can say that again! "Dream Holidays" was just work. This is work – damned hard work at times – but it's fun as well!'

'Isn't it? We've had fun! The chaps have had fun! Let's hope the kids have fun too!'

'I'm sure they will.' They walked on in silence. It was a calm evening and the sun was setting behind the trees. Suddenly, Diane took hold of Philip's hand and stopped walking. He turned to face her.

'Thank you, darling,' she said, quietly.

'What for?'

'This! All this – it was my idea – my dream! And you've come with me – all the way. You've come with me and we've made it a reality. So thank you.' She kissed him. He gazed into her eyes as they glowed in the crimson sunlight.

'Somewhere along the way, you know, it became my dream too.'

✳

'School Days'

Diane and Philip still managed to slip away on *Cormorant* for the occasional weekend. 'Just to get away and recharge the batteries!' Diane said. But today she was standing on the landing stage next to the boat and looking along the canal. The engine noise in the distance heralded an approaching boat.

'This sounds like it,' she thought. A few moments later she saw a resplendent *Billy Boat* chugging round the bend and into view – with a young boy at the tiller under Mick's watchful eye and Philip in the bow chatting animatedly to the children. Mick took over from the lad and skilfully guided *Billy Boat* into the landing stage. Philip jumped off with a rope and held her in while Diane and Mick tied her up. Mick turned off the engine.

'Good morning!' Diane called out, 'and welcome to Billy's Farm!'

'Good morning!' the children chorused in reply.

'Now, be careful getting off the boat. We don't want any of you falling in,' Philip warned.

All the children disembarked and stood on the landing stage.

'I'm Diane,' she informed them. 'Hands up those who have been to a farm before?' Two or three of the children put up their hands.

'Good!' she said. 'You might be able to show the others what you have to do.'

'OK,' said Philip, 'follow me.' He and Diane led the excited gaggle of children from the landing stage to the farm. Mick stayed to tidy the boat.

Their route to the cottage took them past Billy's paddock. Philip asked everyone to stop.

'This is the famous Billy, after whom the farm is named,' he announced. Billy looked up and, seeing so many eyes looking at him, stared, unblinkingly, back. 'Billy was the very first animal we acquired for the farm and he is our star attraction!' Philip continued. 'You may see him again later, trotting round the farm pulling his own, specially made little cart.'

The children moved on to the cottage and were invited to sit down in the conservatory to be introduced to Ron, Barry and Vera.

'Barry is our first-aider, should any of you need him,' Diane said to the group – but looked knowingly at the accompanying teachers.

Sticky labels for their names were issued, written on and affixed, and they were divided into groups ready for their first activities of the day.

Ron's group set off for the unenviable task of mucking out the stable where Jack lived. One or two of the children said 'Urrgh!' But as they got on with the job they realised that actually doing it was nowhere near as bad as thinking about it!

When the stable was clean and fresh straw had been laid, Ron picked up a bucket of manure, gave a spade to a child and told his group to follow him to the garden in front of the cottage where he showed them how to 'manure up' his pride and joy, the roses.

'Now,' he said to them, 'if you come back up here in the summer all these roses will be in bloom. And I guarantee that they'll all look beautiful – all because of this manure. They love it, roses do, and it helps them to grow.' The children found it difficult to understand how something as smelly and yucky as 'horse shit', as they insisted on calling it, could ever help anything to look beautiful.

'You wait till the summer and see,' Ron said. There was some manure left over. 'Spread it on the vegetable plots over there,' Ron advised. 'Then they'll be ready for another group of children to plant the seeds in a few weeks time.'

Barry's group had a much less smelly, but equally challenging job. They were in a pen with two young lambs.

'Nobody knows why,' he told them, 'but sometimes a mother sheep won't feed one of her lambs. It's a bit of a mystery. What would happen to the lamb if it didn't get any milk?' he asked.

'It would die,' one of the children said.

'Sad, but true,' Barry answered. 'If the mother doesn't feed it, it dies. That's where you come in. These two lambs here have been abandoned by their mothers.' He held up two bottles he had been carrying. 'And in these bottles is what we call "formula". It comes as a powder and you mix it with water. It's very clever stuff! It contains all the good things that the lamb should have got from its mother's milk – and the lambs can't get enough of it! I'll show you what to do.'

He unscrewed the top of one of the bottles, put a rubber teat on the end and offered it to the nearest lamb, who immediately took it in its mouth and began sucking greedily at its contents. The other looked on enviously.

'Who wants a go?' Barry asked. Hands shot up to a chorus of 'Me! Me!' Barry picked out two of them.

'Don't keep on too long,' he warned them. 'So everyone can have a turn.'

Vera took a group to the cottage kitchen.

'We're going to make some soup today,' she announced. 'Now, hands up anybody who has never had soup that has not come out of a packet or a tin.' No hands were raised. There followed a discussion about the origins of the ingredients for various different flavours of soup.

'Well,' said Vera, 'we haven't got any tails from any oxen, or any chicken or any mushrooms. But we have got some carrots, some parsnips, some onions and some potatoes. These were all grown in the garden here at the cottage. You'll find out more about that when you go and see Ron in the garden.' Soon they were all busy peeling, chopping and stirring.

In the barn Philip and his group of excited children made nesting boxes from kits that Mick had prepared earlier. 'MFI for birds!' he called it. They then set off to the wood at the far side of the farmhouse and held the ladder while Philip attached them to the trees.

Six children went with Diane to the farmyard.

'Welcome to Billy's Farmyard Friends,' she said. 'First of all I want you all to go off with a friend and find out the names of all the paths and what sorts of animals live there.' The children scampered off enthusiastically.

Then Diane introduced them to the chickens and showed them where they had laid their eggs. Carefully, the children picked up the eggs, put them in a basket and proudly carried them back for Vera to use to make a cake.

As they walked along, a little girl tugged at Diane's sleeve.

'I do like your animals!' she said, a big grin spreading across her face. 'This is the bestest trip I've ever been on. Thank you!' She ran on ahead.

Diane felt a lump in a throat. Now she knew that all the hard work had been worthwhile.

The girl turned round. 'I'd like to take Billy home with me!' she called. A tear rolled down Diane's cheek.

Mick appeared at the cottage with Jack and his cart. Six at a time, he gave the children a ride round the farm.

All too soon it was time for the children to return to school. When this was announced it brought forth a collective 'Oh no!' Before they left they gathered in the conservatory to sample the soup Vera's groups had made and Diane told them about 'Billy's Farm4Kids'. Barry handed out leaflets about the club for the children to take with them.

They trooped back towards the landing stage. At Billy's field they stopped. Billy trotted eagerly to the fence and stood proudly while the children had their photographs taken with him. 'Bye, Billy!' they shouted as they waved him goodbye and traipsed to the landing stage in a long, straggling crocodile.

Back aboard *Billy Boat*, Diane and the others said their farewells and waved them off. Mick started the engine and Philip pushed the boat off and stepped aboard. The children's excited chattering could be heard above the noise of the engine as *Billy Boat* rounded the bend and headed off in the direction of the Old Town Wharf.

'It's a bit like being a sort of part-time Dad to the children Daphne and I couldn't have,' Ron said when the 'Special Three' got together later.

'Takes me back to when our Jimmy was a nipper!' Mick replied.

Barry, who had never had much to do with children, was thrilled to find he seemed to have a natural talent for keeping them interested.

When Philip returned to the cottage he found Diane sitting in the kitchen, still in her overalls, sipping a glass of wine, with a silly smile on her face.

'How do you think it went?' he asked. 'As if I didn't know!'

'If all the school visits go as well as that, it's going to be great – totally knackering – but great!'

The spring and early summer months flew past. The school visits became increasingly popular. There was a waiting list for a place on 'Billy's Farm4Kids'. Every Saturday children arrived sporting t-shirts, sweatshirts and baseball caps, all with the Billy's Farm logo on the front.

Billy's Farm was also open to the public at weekends and became a popular attraction featuring on the local tourism website. The tea room opened for business.

Vera had now become a competent and confident outgoing

catering manager who was always ready to leave her kitchen to chat with her customers and give them copies of her recipes. Whether this change was a result of Mr Rodgers's unfortunate demise, or Barry's influence, no one could decide.

The fact that they were all busy at the farm on Saturdays, however, denied the three friends their favourite lunches at The Navigation. So instead, when all the visitors had left, they, together with Diane and Philip – and Vera – went with the children on *Billy Boat*. Having dropped their charges off at the Old Town Wharf, they stopped on their return journey for dinner at the pub. Over their meal they discussed the week's events and planned for the week ahead. How all their lives had changed!

One evening, after they had eaten, Diane took an envelope from her handbag.

'I thought you might like to read this,' she said casually. Removing a letter from the envelope, she unfolded it and placed in the middle of the table. They all read it – then let out a collective gasp!

'He's coming to the farm … Billy's Farm?' Mick spluttered.

'The Prince of Wales?' Barry said.

'Well, I'll be…!' was all Ron could manage.

'Yes,' Philip said. 'The letter arrived this morning. Apparently, the Lord Lieutenant of the County is a great friend of the local head man at the National Farmers Union. So when he heard that HRH was coming this way he asked him where he should visit.'

'And the NFU bloke suggested Billy's Farm?' Ron queried.

'Yes. We know how highly the local NFU think of what we're doing at the farm. They think it might lead to more youngsters taking up agriculture when they get older. But this is a fantastic opportunity.'

'Think of the publicity we'll get out of it – not to mention the kudos of a visit by a member of the Royal Family!' Diane added.

'When is it again?' Mick picked up the letter.

'He's coming on the 26th of next month.' said Barry.

'That only gives us four weeks!' Ron exclaimed.

'And we've got a lot to do if we're going to be ready on time,' Diane added.

'We'd better get started first thing tomorrow then,' Barry said.

'Does anybody know what he likes to eat?' Vera asked.

'I'm sure we'll be advised about that before he comes,' Diane reassured her.

Mick launched into a rendition of 'Some Day My Prince Will Come'.

Ron looked at his watch. 'Is that the time?' he interrupted.

'Er ... I think we've got time to draw up a plan before we go!' Diane said, pulling out a notepad and pen.

The following day work began in earnest. Mick, who had become something of an expert with a paintbrush, was detailed to smarten up every door and window frame on the site. He also checked every inch of *Billy Boat*. 'In case the Prince'd like a ride,' he said.

Ron was delighted with the timing of the Prince's visit and spent his time tidying up the garden. 'The roses should be looking their best,' he said. 'My Daphne would have been really proud to know the Prince of Wales was going to see my roses.'

Barry re-read every sign and notice, repairing any damaged ones. With his Health & Safety folder in his hand, he checked and rechecked for any tripping hazards, bumping hazards, slipping hazards – and any other kind of hazards that did not appear on his list.

Philip went round every square inch of the farm, trimming, raking, nailing and mowing until everything looked immaculate.

Vera, when she heard that their Royal visitor would be staying for a cup of tea, practised her favourite biscuit recipes over and over again until the others were tired of sampling them! In secret, she rehearsed her curtsy.

Diane? Diane made lists!

Over the weeks everyone worked tirelessly to ensure that Billy's Farm would be perfect when the big day arrived. The evening before the visit, after the 'Special Three' had gone home, Philip and Diane were walking round the farm, checking once more.

'The only job I didn't get round to doing was fixing the lock on the gate to Billy's paddock. It doesn't always catch,' Philip admitted.

'I don't think he'd go far if he escaped. He only ever leaves his paddock when Ron's with him.'

They returned to the cottage and Philip poured two glasses of wine. He raised his glass.

'To us!' he said.

'To Ron and Barry and Mick and Vera as well,' Diane added.

'OK!' Philip raised his hands in submission. 'I'll rephrase it. To all of us!'

'I'll drink to that!' Diane laughed.

'I'll tell you one thing, though, love,' Philip said after a sip of his wine.

'What?'

'We'd have waited a hell of a long time for a member of the Royal Family to visit "Dream Holidays".'

'Indeed, we would.'

✳

'A Wonderful Day Like Today'

I t was a warm, bright and sunny morning when Ron picked Mick up and drove to the farm. At the entrance to the track they saw a police car parked and two policemen examining the bushes on either side.

'I wonder what they're up to,' Ron said. When they arrived at the farmhouse Barry was waiting for them. He climbed into the back seat.

'What's with the coppers?' Mick asked.

'Security,' Barry said. 'There are those two and some more of them further up. They arrived about half past seven.'

All three had forsaken their overalls for their smartest outfits. Today they were all wearing suits and ties.

'You two scrub up well!' Barry commented, looking his friends up and down. 'Well, Ron has, but that's more than can be said for you, Mick!' Mick appeared to have been poured into his suit.

'He's done his best!' Ron came to Mick's defence.

'It's the only suit I've got,' Mick explained. 'It's the one I was married in.'

'You've put on a bit of weight since then,' Barry observed.

'Tell me about it!' Mick answered. 'I can't get the waistcoat on at all – not that I need it today, thank God! The jacket won't do up and it feels like the trousers are cutting off the circulation to my legs!'

'Well,' said Ron, 'like I said, you've done your best.'

'I'm glad the Prince isn't going on *Billy Boat*. I've never steered a boat wearing a tie. It wouldn't feel right somehow,' Mick remarked.

'I think he might take a peek inside,' said Ron. Mick broke forth with 'It's A Lovely Day Today', and neither Barry nor Ron complained or attempted to engage him in conversation to stop him.

The 'staff' car park was already full of police vehicles when they arrived.

'I'll park up by Billy's paddock,' Ron said.

❋

About an hour and a half later Diane, dressed in a smart new suit she had bought especially for the occasion, looked at her watch.

'Where are the "Special Three"?' she asked. 'They were supposed to be getting here early today.'

'I don't know,' Philip replied, as he tied his tie and put on his suit jacket. 'Perhaps the police have stopped them to search them – and the car.'

'That wouldn't take this long. Vera!' she called. 'Do you know where Barry and the others are?'

'No,' Vera replied from the conservatory. 'I left the house before him this morning.'

Just then there came a knock at the door.

'It's probably one of the Prince's security chaps wanting to check over the cottage,' Philip said as Diane went to answer it. When she opened the door she stared, open-mouthed, at what she saw before her. She did not know whether to laugh or cry. Standing there were Barry and Mick. Behind them stood Ron holding Billy by a halter round his neck – and every one of them was dripping wet!

'Oh my God!' Diane found her voice. She looked at her watch. 'The Prince is due in just over an hour – and look at you all!'

Barry opened his mouth.

'No time to explain now!' she said. 'Come in and get out of those wet clothes!' She opened the door of the washing machine. 'We'll get your trousers and underwear washed and tumble-dried. It won't do your jackets much good though. Philip, find three of the extra-large size kids t-shirts, will you? And when you've done that, put some overalls on over your suit and sort Billy out!'

Vera came through from the conservatory and gasped when she saw Barry and the others.

'Oh Barry! What happened to you?'

'I'll tell you in a minute. It's a long story,' Barry said as he undressed.

'When you've got your clothes off go up to the bathroom,' Diane instructed. 'You'll find spare towels in the cupboard. Then come down and tell me what in heaven's name has been happening!'

Philip quickly put on his overalls and went out to dry and groom Billy.

Half an hour later there were three men sitting in the kitchen, naked except for towels round their waists. Philip returned having taken Billy, who now looked more presentable, back to his paddock.

'Billy's gate was wide open,' he said as he took off his overalls.

'I know the catch is a bit dodgy,' Diane said. 'But I made doubly sure it was locked last night!'

'It must have been one of the security chaps. He couldn't have shut it properly when he'd gone into the paddock,' he sighed. 'Oh well! What's happened has happened!' He turned to the trio. 'Now what exactly *has* happened?'

'Well,' Ron began, 'when we parked up I noticed Billy's gate was open and he'd gone. So we went looking for him.'

'I hadn't seen him down by the farmhouse, so we knew he must still be up this end somewhere,' Barry added.

'We looked around here,' Ron continued. 'But we couldn't see him, so we thought he must have gone in the direction of the canal. Sure enough, there he was on the bank, biting lumps out of the bushes. Fortunately, I'd had the presence of mind to take his halter with me. I talked to him quietly and managed to get the halter round his neck. So far, so good.'

'Then the fun started!' Mick chipped in.

'I was leading him back along the bank with these two following on behind and...'

'I sneezed!' said Barry.

'Not a "Barry Special"?' Diane asked.

'Oh yes!' said Mick. 'A "Barry Special" – and then some!'

'Oh, Barry!' said Vera. 'How could you?'

'I couldn't help it!' Barry protested. 'It's the pollen. They said on the news it's a high pollen count today!'

'You'd better carry on with the next bit,' said Ron.

'As I said,' Barry took up the tale, 'I sneezed and, I'm sorry to say, it knocked me a bit off balance. I realised I was falling towards the water and I just grabbed at anything I could to save myself.'

'You did!' said Mick. 'Me! As you fell into the cut you pulled me in with you!'

'I heard all this going on behind me,' Ron took up the tale again, 'and turned round, taking my eye off Billy. The noise of the sneeze and the splash spooked him and he tried to run off. But I was still hanging on to the halter so instead of running off down the bank he sort of slewed round and went into the water – pulling me in after him!'

Diane, Philip and Vera were doubled up with laughter by this time.

'It's not funny!' Ron protested. 'At least,' he giggled, 'it wasn't at the time.' Then he, Mick and Barry joined in with the laughter.

'You could have picked a less auspicious time for an unscheduled swimming gala!' Diane managed to say. At that moment the washing machine bleeped and, between them,

Diane and Vera transferred the clothes to the tumble-drier.

'You'll have to wear these Billy's Farm t-shirts with your suit trousers,' Diane informed them as she consulted her watch. 'It's going to be touch and go whether your undies and trousers will be finished before the Prince gets here at twelve.' All eyes watched anxiously as the assorted garments bounced around in the drier.

At five minutes to twelve the receiving line of six people – and one goat – was in place in front of the garden, three of them feeling rather uncomfortable in slightly damp underpants. Mick was suffering the most as his suit trousers had shrunk even further.

Billy stood motionless with his cart behind him. His coat shone – the canal water had done it good! His eyes looked directly ahead – no evil, no menace, just pride.

Other volunteers and members of the 'Billy's Farm4Kids' club were stationed at various points around the farm, ready and eager to demonstrate to their Royal visitor the variety of activities available at Billy's Farm.

'I feel as if I'm lining up for England before an international,' Ron said.

'I don't think they'll play the National Anthem,' Barry answered, raising his eyebrows.

At twelve o'clock exactly the motorcade drew up outside the cottage, leaving a cloud of dust in its wake. As the lead car came to a halt a man jumped out of the front passenger seat.

'Good morning!' he called.

'Good morning!' they replied in unison. He opened the rear door and Diane stepped forward.

'Good morning, Your Royal Highness, and welcome to Billy's Farm.'

The Prince's motorcade sped back down the track in a cloud of dust and everyone breathed a sigh of relief. It was over! What an occasion! Everything had gone perfectly – and Vera's biscuits were appreciated by all! As they watched the last car disappear round the bend Mick turned to Philip.

'Phil, could I possibly borrow your overalls and get these trousers off. They're so bloody tight, they're killing me!'

'Of course!' Philip laughed.

A few minutes later they were all sitting round the kitchen recounting the high spots of an amazing day. Philip took a bottle of champagne from the fridge. 'You're privileged, you know. We don't get the best bubbly out for every Tom, Dick and Harry,' he said.

'Did you know,' Barry raised his eyebrows, 'that those were the names given to the escape tunnels that the prisoners were digging out of Stalag Luft III?'

'Was that the one they based *The Great Escape* on?' Mick asked.

'Yes.'

'Well,' said Ron, laughing, 'this place has certainly been a great escape for me. I sometimes wondered if I'd ever get over losing my Daphne. But this place – and particularly the garden with those lovely roses and my special Billy – it's like a sort of memorial to her. I've enjoyed every minute I've spent here.'

'What a lovely thing to say!' Diane said. 'Thank you, Ron.'

'No. Thank you,' Ron replied.

'I suppose it's been something of an escape for me too,' Barry said. 'I'll admit that although I'd been looking forward to retirement for an awfully long time, when it came … well, I was lonely – lonely and bored. I'd intended to start birdwatching but, somehow, I couldn't find the enthusiasm for it. Then I met you boys, and then there was Billy, and then this place. You can't be lonely here – and now there's Vera.' He leaned over and held her hand.

'If you're talking about escaping,' Mick joined in the conversation. 'I escaped from that old harridan of a wife and I'm pleased I did because if I'd still been married I doubt I'd have been in The Navigation that day. I tell you, I'm really glad you two blokes came in. I've now got two mates I can rely on – and this place has given my life some purpose. I think I can understand now why Siobhan got frustrated when I never did any jobs around the house. Working with you fellows has taught me to start jobs – and finish them! I've even started doing some work on my own boat.'

'Well, gentlemen,' Philip said. 'We never realised how much this place meant to you all. And we thank you too for the years of hard work you've all put in – yes, and Vera, too – to make Billy's Farm what it is today. We certainly could never have done it without you.'

It's been a great escape for us too,' Diane added. 'An escape from the rat race of running a business in London!'

'So,' said Mick, 'we're privileged, are we? You don't open the good stuff for any Tom, Dick or Harry, you said?'

'That's right,' Philip agreed.

'But you do open it,' said Barry, a big grin breaking out across his face, 'for this particular Ron, Mick and Barry.'

'Oh, very good!' said Philip as they all burst out laughing.

'I've been waiting for the opportunity to say that for years!' Barry laughed and raised his eyebrows even higher.

'Can I say something?' Vera asked as the laughter subsided.

'Of course, Vera. The floor's yours. Go ahead,' said Diane.

'I know you shouldn't speak ill of the dead and don't get me wrong. Rodgers was a good enough man. But he wasn't very good at appreciating other people or what they did for him. We sort of rubbed along together, as you might say, but he wasn't a great one for showing love. I miss him, of course, but now I've got my Barry...' She smiled sweetly at him and he smiled back. 'Well, things are different. Let's put it that way. So I've escaped too. I've escaped from my past. We all have in our own different ways.' An emotional tear rolled down her cheek. Barry tapped her hand in a gesture of support – and love. There was silence for a few moments while Philip gently eased the cork out of the bottle of champagne with a gentle pop and went round filling their glasses.

'Just half a glass for me, please,' said Barry.

'Thanks,' said Mick. 'I'll have the rest of his.'

Diane looked around and smiled at the assembled group. Her dream had become a reality.

'Has anybody realised where all this started?' Ron suddenly asked. 'We've all escaped from something, but do you know what the common denominator is? The one thing that's brought us all together? The one thing that's brought us all to this farm? The one thing that's done us all so much good?' They all looked at Ron. He raised his glass. 'To Billy!' he said. They all raised their glasses together.

'To Billy!' they repeated in chorus.

❋

The chapter titles

All the titles to the chapters in *Three Men and a Goat* are either the first lines or the titles of songs in Mick's vast repertoire. They are:

'Getting to Know You' – from *The King and I* (Rodgers & Hammerstein), 1951. Mick has a taste for musicals.

'Home Cookin'' – by Livingston & Evans (1951) and recorded by Bing Crosby in 1951. One he remembers from his childhood.

'Friends and Neighbours' – by Lockyer & Scott (1954) and recorded by Billy Cotton and his Band. Mick used to listen to *The Billy Cotton Band Show* on Sunday lunchtimes on the old Light Programme.

'Young and Foolish' – by Hague & Howitt (1954) and recorded by many singers including Ronnie Hilton. Another one from his younger days.

'Oes Gafr Eto' – this is the first line of 'Cyfr'r Geifr' ('Counting the Goats), a Welsh folksong that Mick learned during his brief membership of a male voice choir. He asked a Welshman in the choir what it meant, only to be told that the man did not speak Welsh, but thought it meant 'Where's the goat?' Mick left the choir when he discovered that baritones rarely have the tune – and the conductor discovered he could not sing in tune!

A more accurate translation is 'Is there another goat?'. But, as we all know, there is only one Billy!

'The Lonely Goat(herd)' – from *The Sound of Music* (Rodgers & Hammerstein), 1965. A bit of a cheat here! The song is more about the goatherd than the goat, but Mick doesn't know any other songs about goats.

'I'll Be There' – by Holland, Dozier & Holland (1966) and recorded by the Four Tops. The full title is 'Reach Out I'll Be There', but Mick would not let a small matter like that get in the way of his singing.

'Fings Ain't Wot They Used T'Be' – by Norman & Bart (1959), the title song from yet another musical.

'With A Little Help From My Friends' – by Lennon & McCartney (1967), recorded by the Beatles and covered by Joe Cocker and the Grease Band. Mick saw the Beatles live in the early sixties.

'Goin' Home' – by Dvorak/Fisher/the Bible, uses words set to music in an American folk song and used by Dvorak in his 9th Symphony, 'From the New World'. Another one Mick picked up from the male voice choir.

'We All Stand Together' – by Paul McCartney (1984), and recorded by Paul McCartney and the Frog Chorus. A bit modern for Mick, but McCartney was a Beatle, wasn't he?

'Come On Over To My Place' – by Mann & Weil (1965) and recorded by the Drifters. Another one from his teenage years.

'Welcome To My World' – by Winkler & Hathcock (1962) and recorded by many artists including Jim Reeves. Mick was not that fond of Country & Western music, but he quite liked this one.

'School Days' – by Chuck Berry (1957) and recorded by him, one of Mick's heroes.

'A Wonderful Day Like Today' – from *The Roar of the Greasepaint, the Smell of the Crowd* (Bricusse/ Newley), 1964. Musicals again.

Also by Rupert Ashby

'Izzie'

A Child of the Cut

I n the years before the Second World War Isobel Horne –
'Izzie' – is a boatgirl with a burning ambition to learn how
to read. She is encouraged by her mother, but a family
tragedy almost drives them
off the canal. Then along
comes George Andrews to
save the situation. War is
declared, and George's call-
up again puts them in
danger of having to leave
the cut. But then Jean joins
the crew, and events turn
Izzie's world upside-down
and drive the story on to
its dramatic conclusion,
when her ability to read
becomes more important
than she could ever have
imagined.

Half Cut Theatre

Rupert Ashby is the nom de plume of Derek Harris. Under his other soubriquet of Half Cut Theatre, he has been performing canal-themed one-man shows in and around his home city of Peterborough since 2003. His repertoire consists of:

Up the Cut

An amusing and informative history of the canals of England and Wales, illustrated with songs, some involving audience participation.

Folk of the Cut

Similar in style to Up the Cut and looks at the people involved with our canal system from the early engineers to restoration by the volunteers of today.

Characters on the Cut

Told from the viewpoint of an observer at 'The Pub on the Cut', the audience is introduced to a variety of characters, past and present, who have been drawn to the canals of this country, including an 'Idle Woman' and a 'Gongoozler'.

A Cruise on the Cut

A slide presentation looking at the architecture and engineering of the British canal system.

Want to know more, or book a show? Visit his website at www.halfcuttheatre.com

- As to the origin of the name – Half Cut Theatre – the word 'canal' was rarely, if ever, used by the boating families back in the commercial days. The waterway was always referred to as 'the cut'. Add to this the fact that your author is rather partial to the odd pint of real ale, and it all seems rather obvious!